A Donkeyman's Journey

Part One

The Latvian Exile

David Evardson

ISBN: 9781790617791

ALSO BY THIS AUTHOR

The Fenwold Riddle
The Fenwold Inheritance
Gelding For Beginners
The Crooked Link
A Donkeyman's Journey – Part Two :
The Loyal Englishman

A Fitter's Life (Compiler & Editor)
The Life & Times of a Grimsby Marine Engine Fitter
By John Evardson

www.DaveEvardson.com

CHAPTERS

AUTHOR'S NOTE / ACKNOWLEDGMENTS

A donkeyman was responsible for all things mechanical aboard the early steam smacks and trawlers. This novel is based on the lives of my great-grandparents, Kahrl and Juhla Evardson, using a few known facts and family memories, supplemented by guesswork and pure invention. Some real historical figures play their parts alongside family members, but other active characters are fictitious.

Thanks to: Grimsby historian George Black (RIP), Aunts Brenda & Pat, Uncles Ken & Walt (RIP), my father John Evardson (RIP), Gertrude (Pat) McCall, cousins Julie, Gwennie, Sandra and Jeffrey, Aigars Evardsons, Diana, Jo, Maureen & Jacky Williams, Jackie Collins & Grimsby Writers, Liz & Stuart Conolly (presentations & engineering references), Ivy Smith, Bruce Cardwell (South Shields references), Jennie Cartwright (Lincs Inspire), Elizabete Rutens (early research), Kevin Smith (Evardson Tribal Pages) and Ruta Suce (Latvian references).

Also: Ancestry.co.uk; Curly's Corner Shop Blog; Latvia and Latvians (Latvian Welfare Fund, Central Board Daugavas Vanagi 1978); O.S. Map of South Shields 1895 (Alan Godfrey Maps); South Shields Through Time (Michael J Hallowell); South-Shields.MyBy.co.uk; Tukums Tourist Information Centre; Google.com; Wikipedia.org.

CHAPTER ONE
1878 : I – FROM KAIVE TO RIGA

The city of Riga slept.

A chilly mist rolled in from the Daugava River, sweeping the docks and probing the adjoining passageways with inquisitive fingers. In town along the main streets a few gas lamps flickered, poorly illuminating the empty thoroughfares. But down along the back lanes darkness ruled, where creeping shadows combined to smother walls and cobbles with their dismal hues. Wise men didn't stir abroad on nights such as this. Husbands snored beside their wives at home, while sailors clung to whores in dockside taverns. Only wraiths and wayward spirits roamed these dark alleys, as if to prepare a gloomy stage for dreadful doings.

Footsteps approached. Their jaunty tread announced the figure of Herr Gerald Stein, a man of ample frame. And of ample means too, judging from his fine woollen cloak, his fancy feathered hat, expensive leather shoes and white kid gloves. Without breaking step, he briefly touched his breast and smiled. For there, beneath his cloak, was concealed his bulging purse, the product of a night's rewarding gambling. He relished the thought of tipping out its contents onto the walnut desk in his study, and checking the extent of his good fortune – for a gentleman would never count his winnings while seated at the card table. His mansion being just around the next corner, he slid a hand into his waistcoat pocket and extracted the front door key.

Then he stopped.

Did the night play tricks with his hearing? No, surely it was only a rat, on a scavenging outing from the docks. Or a mangy dog, snuffling among the household rubbish for a discarded titbit. And yet … he could have sworn those were human footsteps he'd heard. He turned around and peered into the gloom.

"Hoy! Is someone there? What . . ?"

A slashing blade stifled his cry, brutally thrust and twisted to slice through jugular and windpipe. His startled eyes had time enough only to glimpse the crimson flood that now drenched his clothing, before he slid to the ground, limp and lifeless.

His attacker knelt and soon located the purse. A second man approached. The slayer looked up at him.

"He cried out! He might have been heard! We'd best be quick!"

Then seeing the torrent of blood, his accomplice gasped, "My God, man! You've done for him!"

"I had to silence him. Here, take the money. I'll head for the docks. We'll meet tomorrow. And don't forget our bargain."

The two turned on their heels and made off in opposite directions towards their respective lairs.

The killer's fears were soon confirmed. The victim's cry had not gone unheard. An oil lamp flickered from the upstairs window of a house close by, a casement swung open, and a sleepy head leaned cautiously out to view the macabre scene below.

Cries of 'Police!' and 'Murder!' soon echoed up and down the shadowy lanes, followed by running footsteps, angry shouts, a scuffle, and the jangle of coins spilling onto the pavement. At the site of the assault, folk in night attire leaned over the body, shaking their heads and solemnly crossing themselves.

As a shy autumn dawn scattered rust-red sunbeams among the chilly streets and passageways, the news flew abroad that a murder had occurred, with a suspect already in custody, refusing either to admit or deny responsibility for the crime.

Over the ensuing weeks the wretch maintained his silence, despite the best interrogative efforts of the Chief of Police.

Even at his trial he offered no plea. The City Prosecutor declared the prisoner's guilt to be beyond doubt, on the grounds of his having been apprehended running from the scene in possession of the victim's purse. That the murder weapon had not been found was an unfortunate detail, but it may have been discarded down a drain, or else carried away by some creature of the night.

Without hesitation the jury of respectable citizens agreed with the Prosecutor and declared the accused guilty of the murder of one of their brethren.

Even when convicted, still he uttered not a word, but remained mute right up until the morning when Death walked again – this time in the old town square. Now Riga's citizens gathered to hiss and jeer as the condemned man approached the block, where he knelt, hands tied behind his back. An agonising hush preceded the *swish* of the blade, followed by a sickening *thud* as his head hit the bottom of the basket. Immediately a satisfied cheer rose up from the throng, glad to see justice done, their city's streets made safe again.

But there was one man in the crowd whose cheer was feigned and hollow, because he knew the executed man was innocent of murder.

And for that he had good reason.

* * *

"Hurry up, Kahrl! We'll be late for supper!"

The elder youth bent forward, hands on knees, to catch his breath. "Is that so, little brother? Then why have you made me chase you all this way through the village?"

The youngster frowned. "To bring you to the old oak, that's why! If you're going to leave tomorrow, you know you have to touch it for luck!"

That was the legend. Kaive's ancient oak tree, as the oldest in Latvia, was widely believed to possess supernatural powers. Though in Kahrl's sceptical opinion, touching its ancient bark for good fortune before a long journey was nothing but a concoction, brewed by generations of crafty innkeepers, who profited from the flow of gullible émigrés. Over the years the fable had spread far beyond the confines of the village and even the province of Kurland. Still, in spite of his scepticism, he was prepared to indulge his younger sibling's innocent conviction that the myth was true, in part out of brotherly affection, but mostly for the sake of a peaceful life.

So he approached the lump of gnarled wood with feigned reverence, and dutifully pressed his palm to its hardened surface, now almost smooth from decades of contact by other departing Latvians.

"There, Fritz! Satisfied? Am I now safe to make the long and arduous journey all the way to Riga? After all, so much can go wrong in the space of two hours, can't it?"

The lad pouted. "Well, you never know. Your train might be derailed, or someone might forget to shift the points and make it crash into another engine, or, or … anything!"

Kahrl tousled the boy's hair and laughed. "It's just as well I touched the tree then, isn't it? Come on, supper will be getting cold. I'll race you!"

Their mother stood on the porch with arms folded as they approached the cabin. Kahrl's keenness for manual labour had made him lean and muscular, so that he could easily outrun his brother, who being eight years his junior still had some growing to do. But just before stepping onto the porch Kahrl feigned a stumble, letting Fritz overtake him at the last moment.

"I beat you! I beat you!" the youngster yelled, while Kahrl and his mother exchanged knowing smiles.

"Come on in, you two," she said. "We're having a treat tonight, but if you're not quick it'll swim back into the lake!"

"Hurrah, it's fish! I love fish!" Fritz yelled, already at the sink and working the pump to rinse his hands.

"That's right," she said. "Now wash up and come and sit down, all of you."

In this she included her husband, Johann, already tapping out his pipe on the edge of the hearth while resting his wooden leg on a stool. With winter approaching, the fire had smouldered for most of the day, spreading a gentle warmth throughout the cabin. But now he frowned at the chilly blast from the open door, shifting his weight to his good leg to give the embers a gentle prod with the poker. Then he reached over and added a few chunks of wood from the log basket, causing cheerful fingers of flame to brighten up the little room.

As his wife placed the serving dishes on the table, she sighed and said, "I was just thinking ..."

"Too much thinking is bad for the brain, Luiza," he joked.

"*I was thinking*," she insisted, "that it may be a long time before we're all together again like this."

Kahrl protested. "Oh, come on, Mama. I'm only going to Riga, not half way across the world. Besides, I'll be coming back to see you whenever I can."

His father shook his head. "That's easy to say, lad. But you'll be working six days a week, and your Sundays will be precious. You'll not want to spend them travelling back and forth to see us. You're bound to make friends, and you should be with them. Then there's the cost. I don't mind covering the price of your ticket tomorrow, but I couldn't manage it every week, and your wages as an apprentice will barely cover your food and lodgings. Your mother's right. We should relish this evening and keep it in our memories."

When all were seated he said the grace, which was followed by soft 'amens' from his wife and their younger son.

Luiza pursed her lips. "I see we're still going through this silly agnostic phase, Kahrl."

He helped himself to bread. "I don't mean to be disrespectful, Mama, but I have to be true to my conscience."

She sliced and shared out the fish. "The reason, so far as I can see, is in all those books you read. Ever since that new bookshop opened up in Tukums it's been spreading all sorts of dangerous ideas among you young folk. If you want to be brainwashed, why can't you be satisfied with the Bible?"

He suppressed a smile, amused by the irony of her suggestion.

His father cut in. "Now, Luiza, don't be too hard on the boy. It's natural for young people to question the given truth about things. He's almost a man now. Let him make up his own mind. When he's had a few hard knocks and knows something of life, he'll find the path that's right for him. Fritz, don't eat so fast, for goodness' sake."

"Sorry, Papa. This fish is so good. What bait did you use?"

His father's eyes widened. "My own concoction of squashed worms, mixed with bits of rancid pork and mouldy cheese, the smellier the better!"

Luiza pushed her plate away. "Johann, must you? It's disgusting!"

"Sorry, dear. I'll change the subject. Come on, finish your meal."

He looked at Kahrl. "There are many things I should have said to you, son, but soon it'll be too late." He held up his fork, and Kahrl prepared himself for a lecture.

"I want you to work hard, listen to your betters, improve and prosper." He touched his wooden stump. "You know I lost this in sixty-nine at Sedan fighting for our Prussian landlords against the French." His eyes glazed over for a second. "The French fought well enough, poor devils, but their generals hadn't a clue."

"Johann, you're rambling," his wife cut in.

"Eh? Oh, sorry. Anyway, I was decorated and pensioned off, and was thankful for the continued tenancy of our smallholding here.

"My old captain was a resourceful fellow. After the war, when Russia was expanding her navy, he turned to managing his family's engineering business in the shipyards at Ventspils and Riga. When I wrote to him I felt sure he wouldn't refuse you an apprenticeship. At your age you're a bit late in starting, but he knows I've needed you to help with the farm while your brother put some flesh on his bones. And you've done a good job in looking after the steam engine that drives the sawmill. That's why Captain Heuer is willing to shorten your apprenticeship."

Kahrl chased a potato around his plate with his knife. "Father, you know I'm worried about leaving you short-handed."

"We've discussed this before. You deserve this chance to follow your own path in life. Since the railway's come it's clear you're besotted with engineering. And it's a good choice of a trade. It's where the future lies. This smallholding and mill are ours for as long as your mother and I can pay the rent, and my soldier's pension will cover that. You've helped me get in our supply of firewood for the winter, and the vegetables and livestock almost take care of themselves."

Kahrl noticed a little twist appear on his mother's lips.

"As for felling trees, chopping wood and transporting the timber to the railhead at Tukums, we can afford to pay a man to help with the heavy work. We'll hardly know you're gone."

Kahrl fought to stop the stinging tears that welled up behind his eyes. He made a mental note, once he'd settled in his new lodgings, to check regularly that they were managing without him. His mother had already made him promise to write home, and he wouldn't let her down.

"Don't expect Captain Heuer do show you any special favours though. With the Ventspils yard taking up most of his time, you might not even get to meet him. You're to seek out his foreman. But don't try pulling strings just because your old man fought alongside the firm's owner. Your workmates won't thank you for that. And it'll embarrass me if I get wind of it. Keep your nose clean and don't get into any trouble. And remember, if you disgrace yourself, you also disgrace your family. Understand?"

"Yes, Papa."

"Well, enough said about that. You've always been a good son. I'm proud of you now, and I look forward to being prouder still. Finally, by all means have a drink with the friends you'll make, but don't overdo it. Always put something aside for a rainy day. And, speaking of drink …"

He took hold of the flagon of watered beer that stood at the centre of the table, and ensured everyone's cup was filled. Then, raising his own tankard, and signalling his wife and younger son to do likewise, he proposed the toast.

"To Kahrl. To a bright future!"

They responded in chorus. Then he looked at Kahrl and said, "Well, go on. Why the long face? This is supposed to be a happy occasion. You can drink to your own future, can't you?"

He raised his cup and glanced at each family member in turn saying, "To all of our futures! And to Latvia!"

* * *

Next day being market day in the regional capital of Tukums, after an early breakfast Kahrl said his final goodbyes to his family. With mixed feelings he grabbed his pack and set off by prior arrangement as passenger in a wagon belonging to their neighbour, who had some surplus vegetables to sell in town.

Since the cart didn't possess a seat wide enough for two adults, it was from among the sacks of produce in the rear that he viewed the village of his birth as it receded into the distance. Only now did it occur to him that he might not see Kaive again for a very long time.

One or two early rising villagers shouted their good wishes as he waved an arm and smiled, responding with his own words of thanks and farewell.

"Paldies! Atvadas!"

Once outside the village, the world was still quiet, save for the chafing of the birds, the steady beat of the gelding's hooves on the hardened sandy road, and the creaking of the wheels as the little vehicle rattled its way past hamlet, forest and farmland. He exchanged few words with the driver, who was in any case only half awake, the horse having made this journey a hundred times before.

Though fond of his home region, he was far too excited to get emotional. What mattered was the truth, proven by science, mathematics and logic. These had been the substance of his voracious reading, at least half the contents of his sack comprising books. Already fluent in Latvian, Russian and, to a lesser degree, German, he also carried an English tutor, which he imagined might prove useful some day. To pass the time he took it out now and flipped through its pages, thinking how strange a tongue it seemed to be. His eyes soon glazed over …

He awoke with a jolt when the wagon wheels exchanged level ground for cobbles, and his eyes blinked to take in the pretty town of Tukums. On the left he passed the Lutheran church where his family worshipped most Sundays. Then came the market place, where the cart drew up and the driver turned towards him.

"Give us a hand unloading my stuff, would you Kahrl, and setting up my trestle?"

He jumped down. "Yes, of course. It's the least I can do."

After helping, he took his pack and exchanged pleasantries with his neighbour. Then he walked further along the main street, past the magnificent town hall, shop fronts and fine houses, and down the hill to the end of the road. Here the buildings petered out, giving way to open ground and the approach to the station, where the train was scheduled to leave for Riga in about an hour's time.

After buying his ticket he wondered whether to go back into town and browse inside the bookshop. But he didn't want to make himself late. Besides, there would be a treasure store of books to pore over when he reached the capital.

He settled on a bench on the platform where he opened his pack, and smiled. His mother had provided him with a fresh loaf and plenty of cheese for his journey. The bread's aroma quickened his appetite. After all, nearly two hours had passed since he had last eaten.

"Late breakfast?"

He hadn't noticed the smart young man who now addressed him from an adjacent bench.

"No. Second breakfast. Want some?"

"That's kind of you, but I've just had a pastry and tea at the cake shop in town. Are you going to Riga?"

Kahrl nodded. "You too?"

"Yes." The young man offered his hand. "Rudolf Krutzberg. Pleased to meet you."

From his name, he must be of German descent. He looked about Kahrl's own age, though in contrast quite dapper in a pressed dark suit and shiny shoes. His hair was short and topped by a smart hat with a curved brim and narrow silken hatband, as well as a flashy blue cravat. All of this clashed with Kahrl's simple jacket and moleskin trousers, working boots and big peasant peaked mob cap, from under which his long curls protruded.

"I'm Kahrl Evardson," he replied. "I'm pleased to make your acquaintance."

"That's an unusual name. Is it Swedish?"

"It could be, but to be honest I don't know its origin. My father's parents were freed serfs, and he thinks their landlords must have chosen a family name for them."

"We've come a long way in such a short time. And a good thing too. The days of serfdom belong in the history books. Don't you agree?"

This fellow intrigued Kahrl. Clearly born into money, here he was extolling principles that must have clashed with his privileged upbringing. He wondered if this dandy made a habit of baiting every bumpkin he met while on his way to join his society family in Riga. He couldn't resist a bit of probing.

"I'm not sure about that. As far as I can see we country folk are as tied to our present landlords as our grandparents were. The only difference is that they were called serfs, while we are tenants."

Rudolf moved over to sit beside him.

"You don't mind, do you?" He didn't wait for an answer. "You're right, up to a point, of course. You don't change how people live just by calling them something different. But you do have some advantages over your forebears. For example, how many of them would have been able to travel to Riga of their own accord?"

"Not many, I suppose. Unless at their master's bidding. But you have to admit there's still a huge gap between the ruling classes and peasants like me."

Rudolf didn't flinch. "Quite right. Quite right. My point exactly. But what's to be done about it?"

Kahrl looked him in the face. "Done? Why, nothing, except that we peasants have to work to better ourselves. We have to make the best of whatever talents have been given to us, don't we?"

Vigorous nods from Krutzberg. "Yes, of course, I believe that too. But some are given more than talents. An unfair advantage in life over the majority."

"Those born into wealthy families, you mean? But that's just the luck of the draw," Kahrl countered. "Latvia is part of the great Russian Empire, and we value the security that brings. But we also have our German landlords who, in the main, are very fair, encouraging education and providing stability. And we native Latvians can move up in society if we apply ourselves. If I can prosper through my own hard work and some good fortune, that will satisfy me."

"Kahrl, I think you have something of the philosopher about you."

"I don't know about that. I do like to read about other people's ideas. But my mother would say such stuff is for fools and dreamers."

"Perhaps the world could stand a few more dreamers. Have you heard of a man called Karl Marx?"

"No, I don't think so. Is he a friend of yours?"

Rudolf laughed. "Ha! If only he were! What discussions we could have if he happened to be a passenger on our train! No, he's a German economist and intellectual. He maintains that those who control capital are going to ruin the world, and that economies should be run by representatives of the workers. After all, they are the real creators of wealth by the use of their hands and brains. Something like that, anyway. It's an interesting concept, don't you think?"

Now Kahrl was sure this fellow was pulling his leg. It would be interesting to see how much of Krutzberg's outpourings were truly held beliefs. And when the assembled train approached from the sidings, and he took out his lower class ticket from his jacket pocket, he realised that he was about to discover the true extent of this wealthy young man's liking for equality.

The magnificent engine screeched to a halt and a few people stepped aboard while the pressure valves issued a burst of excess vapour with a loud *hiss!* Though he'd seen locomotive engines several times since the line from Tukums to the capital had opened earlier in the year, he was still mesmerised by the sheer majesty and perfection of these awesome machines. He understood the basic principles of steam power, initially learned from books, then more recently from close experience, operating and maintaining the little engine that drove his father's sawmill. But it was the application of that power to transport by land and sea that fascinated him the most. He greatly admired the men who operated and maintained such mighty ships and trains, and he felt privileged that he was going to become one of them. Eventually, anyway.

He stepped forwards and slung his pack over his shoulder while he glanced towards the lower class compartments near the front of the train, closest to the smoke and steam. Then he turned to shake hands with Rudolf and thank him for his interesting observations, expecting him to make for the first class carriages at the rear.

But instead Krutzberg stood up and amazed Kahrl by gesturing towards the front coaches.

"Aren't you coming?" he asked. "Oh, I see. You thought … Actually, I've never seen the point of wasting money on a first class ticket. And I love the smell of steamy boiler smoke. Besides, I find I meet far more interesting people closer to the engine."

* * *

Earlier when Kahrl had contemplated this journey, he imagined he would pass the time by admiring the scenery and reading one of his books. But it was soon clear that his new acquaintance had other ideas.

"You spoke earlier about acquiring skills of some sort, Kahrl. Is that the purpose of your trip to the capital today?"

As he spoke Rudolf winced and shuffled his bottom on the plain wooden seat. Kahrl suspected this outing was something of an experiment for this rich city boy. He looked fidgety whenever the flimsy carriage jolted and rattled over the points, as if the experience of cattle class travel were new to him after all. But Kahrl wasn't one to prejudge.

"Yes, I'm due to report to the shipyards this afternoon to start my engineering apprenticeship. How about you? What brought you to a boring outpost like Tukums?"

"It's only boring to you because you've lived here all your life, or so I'm guessing."

"You haven't answered my question."

"I'm studying history at the university. This isn't part of the curriculum, but I had a few days free and wanted to travel in the countryside and get a feeling for the small towns and villages. And the … people."

"You were going to say 'peasantry', weren't you? Are you uncomfortable with the word?"

"I suppose I am. It smacks of the old days of serfdom, and makes me ashamed of my own class."

"That's strange. I don't feel at all uneasy when someone refers to me as a peasant. It only means that I live and work in the countryside. I can even take some pride in the fact."

"Hmm, that may be. But you'll find that not everyone who calls you a peasant means it as a compliment."

"So, what is it that you find so fascinating about us? Is it the way we dress?"

"No. It's … the feeling of being of the countryside. That's what fascinates me. Especially as the advance of industry is likely to sweep away much of this before too long."

"That's funny. My father made the same prophesy only last night. Do you truly believe it?"

"Certainly I do. Just think. Only a year ago there was no railway here. And the rate of invention keeps accelerating. We can't even imagine what wonders await us in the next half century."

"But that's good, surely? New inventions improve everyone's lives, don't they?"

"They should. But as a historian, I'm not just interested in what's to be gained. I'm more concerned about what will be lost."

"Oh, I see. You mean, things like cholera, typhoid, open sewers, dawn to dusk labouring in the fields, mothers dying in childbirth …"

Rudolf shook his head. "No, not just those things. I …" Then his face cracked into a grin. "You devil, you're mocking me!" Then he added, "I think we should lighten our conversation for the rest of the journey."

Eventually the train slowed and rattled past a series of magnificent villas behind the beaches and sand dunes of the coastal district known collectively as Jurmala. This was where wealthy Russian and German families passed their summer vacations, and bathed in the pleasant waters of the Gulf of Riga. Little suburban stations now came thick and fast, indicating the train's proximity to the capital.

"We'll soon be there," Kahrl said, clutching his sack.

"You say you have to report for work this afternoon? Why don't I treat you to lunch? There's plenty of time," Rudolf suggested.

"That's kind of you, but I want to have a good look at the docks before I report. You know, reconnoitre. Get my bearings."

"Very sensible. Some other time then."

Saying this, Krutzberg put his hand inside his jacket and pulled out a card. "This is where I live."

At this point the train crossed the iron railway bridge spanning the Daugava River, towards Riga proper. Kahrl's heart pounded with excitement at the sight of the huge city before him, vibrant with the movement of road and river traffic. And people. Thousands of people, it seemed, going about their daily business. How did they manage to keep from bumping into one another? Well, he would soon find out.

"Kahrl? Kahrl! My card."

He looked at Rudolf, smiled and took the item out of politeness. Then he suggested, "Is there perhaps a tavern where we could meet for a few drinks?"

"Yes, yes indeed!" Rudolf pulled back the card, took out a crayon and scribbled an address on the blank side. "I realise it's difficult for you to fix a time before you know for certain when you'll be free. But you can leave a message behind the bar here when it's convenient for you. Ask for the barmaid called Karolina."

"Thanks. Oh, by the way. Just out of interest, what business is your family in?"

"Shipping, mainly timber. We export it. Mostly to England, for their coal mines. You know, pit props."

The carriage was now in a bustle as all of its occupants prepared to get out at the terminus. On the platform the two young men shook hands again and Kahrl asked, "Which way is the dockyard?"

"Follow the track back to the bridge, staying this side of the river, and then turn to your right. Keep going along the bank past some railway sidings until you come to a dock with a sign saying 'Riga Breaking Yard'. That's where you want to be."

"Breaking yard? Are you sure that's it?"

"They do repairs and maintenance too. They've serviced some of my family's steamers. I don't get involved much in the business, but no doubt that's what you'll be working on."

"Ah, that's a relief. Well, thanks, Rudolf. I enjoyed our chat." Then, tapping the card, he said, "I'll be in touch."

CHAPTER TWO
1878 : II – INAUSPICIOUS BEGINNINGS

"Hey, you, boy! What the hell d'you think you're up to? I'm sick of you beggars snooping round my dock to see what they can pinch. Now bugger off, or you'll feel the sting of my cane across your arse!"

The speaker had a deep, raucous voice and must be one of the biggest men Kahrl had ever seen. Swarthy, bald and bareheaded, barrel-chested with dirty overalls and Cossack boots, his snarling expression reminded Kahrl of yesterday's catfish. Because of his size, this giant's age was hard to assess, but Kahrl imagined he must be his senior by about ten years. His immediate inclination was to turn and run as fast as he could.

But he had every right to be here. So he stood his ground, gripping his sack to his body with one arm, while raising the other in a token attempt to protect himself, should the giant's cane come smashing down from its present position a full metre above his head.

He gulped and forced some words to form in his dry throat, expelling them as best he could on his faltering breath.

"Please, mister, I'm not a beggar. If this is Herr Heuer's shipyard, I'm expected."

On mentioning the name of his father's old army captain, Kahrl was relieved to see the man bring his stick to a less threatening position by his side, though his expression and manner remained fierce and belligerent.

"What's your name, then?" he snarled.

"It's Evardson, sir. Kahrl Evardson. I …" He took an envelope from his inside jacket pocket. "I have a letter of introduction from my father."

The fellow snatched and ripped open the envelope, unfolded the letter, glanced at it, and cast both items to the ground. Kahrl stooped to retrieve them.

"Leave them there! I know all I need to know about you!"

Kahrl hesitated, and a gentle breeze caught up the little scraps of paper and whirled them over the wharf and into the adjacent dock. He followed their progress with saddened eyes, wondering if he would ever again see his father's immaculate script.

"Now," said the big man, "You'd better learn who *I* am. I'm in charge here and, from today, I'm the most important person in your life. You'll address me as 'sir' at all times, and I'll address you how the hell I like. You look to me a bit like a rabbit. Yes, a puny, scared peasant rabbit. That'll be your new name as long as you're in my charge. Is that understood?"

Kahrl nodded.

"You'll do as I say and you'll do it well, or else I'll have your guts for garters. I see what you're up to. You've come here early to worm your way into my good books. Well, you're not in my good books. In fact, you've inconvenienced me, coming snooping round here an hour before you're expected. I ought to punish you for that, but I'll let it go. Only this once, mind. Any questions, Rabbit?"

"Please, sir, could I …?"

"Could you what?"

"Could I please see my contract? My indentures? Don't I have to sign something?"

The big man grunted and hesitated, as if his brain were trying to recall something important.

"Oh, yes," he growled, and looked Kahrl up and down with a sneer. "Apparently you're twenty. It's hard to believe it though, looking at you. So you're too old for a normal apprenticeship. Your training will consist of doing every task I give you to do. Sometimes you'll be allowed to watch the fitters while they work on a job, but we can't afford freeloaders here. So make sure you learn fast."

Kahrl shuffled his feet.

"Something else troubling you, Rabbit?"

"Well, sir, I was just wondering. If there aren't any formal indentures, how will anybody know I'm qualified?"

The foreman sneered. "Oh, I'm sure your father's influential friends will provide you with some sort of paperwork when it's deemed you've learned enough."

So, that was the issue. The reason for this man's antagonism towards him was what his father had warned him about. Simple jealousy that he'd wangled this apprenticeship through a friendship forged with Captain Heuer on the battlefields of Europe. Well, he'd show them that he could pull his weight, and justify his presence here by his own hard work and diligence, not through any family connections. Nor would he flinch from any task they might care to set him.

"Please, sir, there are some other things …"

"What?"

"About my pay, board and lodgings?"

"Oh. Yes. Well, for your board and lodgings we've made a special arrangement. You see this dock?"

He could hardly have missed it. It looked huge, more than ten metres wide by at least a hundred in length. At the moment it was occupied by the sorry carcase of a rusty old iron river barge. There were large wooden lock gates at the far end, while just beyond the landward edge stood piles of roughly sawn timbers of varying shapes and sizes. He was suddenly struck with the notion that he was to fashion some kind of bed out of them. But the truth of the matter wasn't quite as bad as that, though equally bizarre.

"Usually there'll be a vessel of some sort in there. Most times it'll be something like this, a useless old wreck that's come to be stripped down and broken up for scrap. Or, if you're lucky, it'll be a sea-going wood steamer brought in for maintenance or repair. Either way, that's your sleeping quarters taken care of. And since you'll be getting 'em for free, so to speak, you can act as watchman at the same time. Don't worry, you'll soon learn to sleep with one eye open. Oh, and don't go bringing any lady friends back to your lodgings, such as they may be. Not that even the alehouse tarts would venture down here for their amusement." His pursuant laugh was spawned in the gutter.

Kahrl wanted to refute his unkind implication, but he daren't do or say anything that might anger this man, other than to clarify the practical issue of his sleeping arrangements.

"I see, sir. But, what if there's no vessel in the dock?"

"Then you can sleep in the shed next to the main workshop. The watchman duties still apply though. There's some bedding in there. You might like to get it cleaned. The last bloke who slept in it wasn't too keen on bathing much, as I remember.

"As for food, wages and washing, that's simple. Heuer's agent comes here at noon every Saturday to give me the next week's schedule, and to deliver the men's wages. You'll be given a weekly allowance of five roubles to cover the cost of your eatables. You can buy them at the central market in town. But you'll need to haggle if you want to avoid starving half the week. Still, it'll be a lesson for you in economics. You might have a bit left over for a drink or two. But if you're ever drunk on the job you'll be out on your arse. Understood?"

Kahrl nodded.

"There's a public bath house not far from the market. Anyone'll tell you where. Saturday afternoons are reserved for men and boys. You can finish work early at four o'clock, so you've no excuse for not keeping yourself clean. And if you drop the soap, mind how you pick it up. They get some funny blokes in there sometimes. Know what I mean? Oh, and by the way, can you swim?"

Kahrl gulped again. He wondered if the question related to part of his duties, and stared down with distaste at the murky waters of the dock.

"No, sir. At least, not very well. There's a lake near our cabin where I used to go …"

"All right. I didn't ask for your life story."

"Why do you ask, sir? Is it important?"

For once the ogre smiled, but not in a pleasant way. He nodded towards the dock.

"It is if you fall in there. If you do, don't expect me to jump in and fish you out! The best you can hope for is that someone will chuck one of those things in after you."

He nodded towards a couple of cork life preservers that hung from posts on either side of the dock. Kahrl understood that this information was to constitute his safety training.

"Thank you, sir," he mumbled. "I'll be careful."

He found it hard to take in everything that the ogre had said. The life ahead of him sounded like something on a par with Hell. When he recalled the comforts of his family's cabin in the woods, he wondered if he'd done the right thing, and whether the life of a simple peasant wouldn't have suited him better after all.

But he couldn't give up the race at the first hurdle, and throw Captain Heuer's kindness back in his face. If only for his family's honour, he had no choice but to make the best of whatever was to come.

* * *

His mind was in turmoil. What in the world had he let himself in for?

He lay on the bunk in the old barge's cabin, having gathered together a few ragged blankets to cover him.

Reflecting on the events of the day, he couldn't deny that it had been an adventure, to say the least. From the pleasure of making a friend on his rail journey from Tukums, to the unbridled antagonism of this man who was to be his master for who knew how many years, no wonder his emotions were in a whirl. Apart from his insistence that he be addressed as 'sir', he didn't even know his foreman's real name. He would have asked one of the fitters, but he hadn't yet met them, as they'd been working on the barge, so low in the dock that you had to stand right on the edge to see much of it.

The ogre had had him working until dusk, cleaning and sweeping around the fitting shop and shed (which apparently doubled as the foreman's office) and tidying the assorted piles of heavy timber. Though his father had given him some money for food as well as his train ticket, after the afternoon's work and his journey he had been too tired to walk back into the city to buy provisions. He was thankful that his mother had stuffed the bread and cheese into his knapsack. The dry remnants had provided him with a meagre supper before turning in. With nothing left for breakfast he planned to visit the market before work early the next day, to buy something hot to eat and stock up with basic provisions.

Now he stared out of the grubby cabin windows at the grey stone sides of the dock, illuminated only by weak moonlight, while bits of congealed green seaweed clung to the ropes, chains and ladders that hung from the grimy walls.

A sudden movement on one of the ropes caught his attention. He screwed up his eyes to see better in the poor light, then recoiled when he realised what it was.

A rat.

They must have been there all day, hiding in drains, cracks and crevices, daring to come out into the open only after human activity had ceased outside. Now they could scurry about at will, on the lookout for anything edible.

He had never been afraid of rats. Wary, yes, because of their association with filth and disease, but never fearful. As wild creatures, he even sympathised with their need to eat and determination to survive.

He reasoned that the rats were outside, and shouldn't be able to get into the cabin where he slept, or intended to sleep if he could just relax. Though the barge was old and in the process of being dismantled, the cabin had been left intact and still attached to the floating hull. The door and windows were securely shut. He'd made sure of that on first entering.

So he was safe. Now it was imperative that he get some physical and mental rest, if he was to face whatever tomorrow was going to bring. He thought about Rudolf, and their lively discussions. He would contact him very soon. Tomorrow was another day. His eyelids grew heavy, and soon he was asleep.

Dreaming of rats.

* * *

He woke with a jolt at first light.

This wasn't some weird act of will. It had always been his habit to rise with the dawn, regardless of the time of year, ever since he had been old enough to help on his family's smallholding. A necessity too, if farm animals were to be watered, fed and in some cases milked at the start of their day. Human time meant nothing to a pig, a hen or a milk cow. Each had its own inner clock, which mustn't be ignored if they were to thrive and be productive. He wondered if he would ever lose this habit, as he became less of a countryman and more of a city dweller. That was if he were to survive long enough here to make the transition.

Yawning he pulled on his clothes and peered out of the cabin windows, making a quick visual sweep of the dock walls. No sign of rodents. He grabbed his sack, went out and secured the cabin door behind him, and stepped across the short gap onto the stone steps that led up to the top of the dock.

At ground level he took in a few deep breaths of the fresh morning air and shivered while he took a rabbit skin jerkin from his sack. Removing his jacket and pulling on the jerkin he soon felt the benefit, and with his jacket worn on top with his mob cap to keep his head warm, he was ready for the kilometre or so walk to Riga's central market.

He wondered if he might be too early for any of the traders to have set up, but he needn't have worried.

His first stop was at a stall patronised by market workers and early-rising labourers, selling hot bread rolls and a thick chicken broth, followed by piping hot tea, all for just ten kopecks. This would serve him as an inexpensive breakfast. But he would need more fuel for his body later in the morning, then something for lunch and supper too.

Bread and cheese were essential staples, so he bought a small loaf and a chunk of smoked hunter's cheese. The cheapest cooked meats on sale were pieces of fried pork and chicken, so he selected enough of both to see him through the day. All this came to twenty-two kopecks, but he fumbled for change, until the busy stallholder huffed and rounded it down to twenty.

Fish was plentiful, but not cheap. Besides, most of what was on display was raw, and he didn't yet know if the dockyard had proper cooking facilities. There was some very appetising smoked haddock, but on asking the price he realised he would have to wait until he could afford a piece as a treat.

Then he discovered the fruit section. Much of the produce on show he had never seen before, being imported from warmer climes. There were bananas, figs, oranges, pineapples and even mangos. But, colourful and tempting as these exotic fruits appeared, all were priced well beyond an apprentice's budget. Instead he chose some seasonal fruits, an apple, a pear and some plums, all for just five kopecks.

Finally he found a stall selling rustic cloth and blankets. Though not cheap, he bought a clean, new woollen blanket, which he stuffed in his knapsack.

Thus well provisioned for the day ahead, he turned to make his way back towards the river. But then he realised that he had made no allowance for drinks. Tea was the obvious choice. He could share it with his workmates to gain their goodwill. So he turned back and found a stall selling bags of leaves for infusing with hot water. These were on the expensive side at ten kopecks a pack, but ought to last for several days, and so be worth the outlay.

On his way back to the dockyard, still having plenty of time, he decided to make a detour through the old town area. Here he found many beautiful civic buildings, churches and fine houses, some having ground floors serving as shops. The front window of one of these displayed stationery, which reminded him that he must take the trouble to write home to his family. There was a problem though, as he didn't yet have a return address. He couldn't very well quote 'Heuer's Breaking Yard, Riga'. Nor would he care to have his parents' letters intercepted by his unpredictable foreman.

Now the prospect of suffering the ogre's jibes and rough handling for a whole day dragged his spirits down again. He forgot about his fine surroundings and the letter writing, and with a heavy heart he plodded back towards the dockyard.

On arrival he saw two men in overalls, not much older than him, standing by the main fitting shop door, each smoking a pipe. He approached them and removed his cap.

"Good morning. I'm the new apprentice, Kahrl Evardson. I'm pleased to meet you." He offered his hand.

They looked at one another and burst out laughing.

"There's no need for such formality, young Kahrl," one of them said. "Lighten up a bit. We're not going to bite you."

Kahrl smiled with relief. "I'm sorry. But I met the foreman yesterday while you were working on the barge. He wasn't very friendly."

"Don't mind him," said the other fitter. "He's a bully, especially with the apprentices. By the way, I'm Gustav and he's Klaus. People think from our names that we're Germans, but we're native Latvians, and proud of it."

"Me too. I'm from Kaive, near Tukums."

"I've heard of it," said Gustav. "Isn't it the place with the famous old oak tree?"

He nodded. "I'm a bit worried about what I can do to get on the foreman's good side. He seems to harbour a grudge against me for some reason."

He recalled his father's insistence that he shouldn't divulge the arrangement with his old captain. So he only said, "He won't tell me his name and says I should just address him as 'sir'. I don't know what I've done to annoy him."

The two men exchanged serious glances.

"It's like this here," said Klaus. "First, as for getting on the foreman's good side, forget it. He doesn't have one. Second, you couldn't have known this, but the yard has been losing money for a while now."

Gustav took over. "We used to make a decent profit servicing Krutzberg's timber boats, but for some reason that work has tailed off. Word has it they're getting their maintenance done by an English firm where their boats land, on Tyneside." He pointed towards the dock. "All that's left are these measly demolition jobs, and they only earn us a lousy commission on the scrap value. So the firm had to let our old watchman and labourer go, and look for other savings wherever they could. Any new machine tools we get are rejects from the Ventspils yard. Then a couple of weeks ago, on top of that, we learned from the agent that you were coming to join us."

He looked embarrassed, so Klaus helped him out. "To put it bluntly, the yard's not earning enough to justify an apprentice. The foreman thinks you'll slow us down and lose us customers. And if that happened, the gaffer might decide to cut his losses and give us all our marching orders."

Kahrl's expression had grown more rigid as Klaus had explained the situation.

"But that makes no sense!" he protested. "It's true, I've had no formal engineering training. But I've learned what I could from books and know enough to keep our wood mill in good shape. I may not be very big, but I'm not a young kid. I can cut and shift heavy timber as well as doing all kinds of farm jobs. Don't you see that I can be more than just an extra pair of hands? And they're only paying me a pittance! I promise you I'll learn fast, then I'll soon be an asset, not a liability!"

He stood glowering, his jaw thrust forward. Then he took a deep breath and let it out, to expel some of the anger he was feeling.

"Has anyone asked why Krutzberg moved his fit-outs to England?"

"Probably cheaper," Klaus offered.

"And how do you two feel about my being a drag on the business?"

Gustav answered, "Before we met you we feared there might be something in that. From what I see and hear now though, I think you'll make a good worker. But it's the foreman, not us, that you're going to have to convince, if you want a quiet life. Unluckily for you, he's a stubborn sod and unlikely to change his attitude. You may as well try and learn to live with it. Toughen up and stand your ground, but don't antagonise him. He's a rough sort.

"As to his shyness about his name, it's because his brother was executed for murder not long ago. People still talk about it and he wants to avoid any association with the crime. Though there are those who suspect he was involved."

"Really?" Kahrl gasped.

"It can't be proven," Klaus said. "It's probably just gossip. But be careful. Don't do anything to make him lose his temper."

"I'll try not to. What's his real name, then?"

"It's Stefan Karpov. He's Russian, as if you hadn't guessed. I get along with most Russians in Latvia, but a few of them think they're better than we are, just because we're part of their glorious Empire. Well, he's one of those, though I reckon most of his compatriots would choose to disown him."

Gustav added, "Remember, we didn't tell you any of this, so don't call him by his real name. It's best to stick with 'sir'."

Klaus asked, "Got anything good in your pack?"

"Just my day's provisions. And I bought some tea." He pulled out the packet. "Would you like some? Where can I boil up some water?"

"Good lad," Gustav said. "We usually bring beer, but tea will make a change. There's a boiler in the fitting shop. It makes the steam for the little engine that drives all our machinery. We'll show you how to fire it up, though, from what you've told us, I'd guess you already know what to do. But that'll be your first job every morning. Sorry we've no teapot, but you can make it in the mugs. Fill them from the little tap underneath the boiler. Come on, I'll show you."

As they went into the workshop Klaus said, "You can't go on working in those clothes, Kahrl. You'll ruin them. I'm about your size. Another short-arse, eh? I'll lend you my spare overalls until you can buy yourself a couple of pairs from the chandlers. Make sure you get the good quality thick ones. If you wear them over your long underwear in the winter, you'll be snug enough. Of course, it's always warm in the fitting shop once the boiler's going."

Kahrl's spirits were like a bouncing spring, from high to low and back to high again almost in the blink of an eye. He was relieved that these two fitters seemed like normal, decent men, which he found almost unbelievable after yesterday's experience.

He made three cups of strong, black tea, which they stood and sipped in the cool riverside air.

"Can you explain something to me?" he asked.

"What's that?" said Klaus.

"Well, you've told me that most of the work at the moment is dismantling vessels, but I don't understand how you accommodate the bigger boats for repairs and maintenance. How do you get them into the dock, when the water's so low?"

Gustav smiled and said, "As a country boy I'm guessing you've never seen how lock gates operate?"

He shook his head.

"Come on then, and we'll explain."

They took Kahrl to the far end of the dock, where it met a broad channel leading up-river to the open water of the Daugava, with the much larger timber boat terminus nearly a kilometre beyond.

"This is a graving dock," he said. "Imagine it's empty, with no vessel, no water, and the gates closed. If we want to bring in a big timber transporter for routine servicing, we open the bottom paddles in the gates at high tide, letting the water in gradually until the level's the same as on the outside. That means the water pressure is equalised, making it easy to open the main gates and let the big boat in. Then we close the gates fully to maintain the level inside the dock even when the river level drops at low tide. When we've finished, we wait for the next high tide and open the gates again to float the boat out into the river."

Now Klaus took over. "Then if we want to do dry dock work, such as cleaning a vessel's bottom of barnacles, or repairing a plate, or simple dismantling, we bring the boat in as Gustav just explained. But then we wait for low tide and let the dock water out through the paddles, until it reaches the depth we need to carry out our work. In the case of this barge, we've more or less finished the above deck demolition, except for the cabin. We'll be letting some more water out later today, so we can start cutting up the metal hull and finish the job."

"Will I be able to operate the gates?"

"Don't get too excited," Gustav warned. "It's a tricky operation, and you can do a lot of damage if you open them at the wrong time. You'll have to be trained and supervised until you know how to do it."

"It's not engineering though, is it?"

"No, it's not, boy. But I can promise you this. Some day when you're qualified you'll thank your lucky stars you served your apprenticeship here, in this tiny scrap yard of Riga, instead of the huge yards at Ventspils. And shall I tell you why?"

He nodded.

"I've nothing against the Ventspils yard. Apprentices there get a good training, with the most modern equipment and facilities. But it's such a big operation that they have to specialise. They have a man whose only job is to open and close the lock gates. None of the apprentices there will ever learn how to do that. But here, in this shitty little knacker's yard, you have to do much more than engineering. And I promise you, when you've served your time with us, you'll be capable of doing any job in any shipyard anywhere in the world, and also on any ship you'd like to mention."

Kahrl nodded as Klaus spoke, realising after all that he was privileged to be here. He couldn't wait to start learning.

When he turned his face towards the city, he noticed that a clock on one of the old town buildings was visible from where he stood, and he was amazed at how quickly the time had passed.

"I'll go and rinse the cups under the boiler, shall I?" he asked.

"I can see we've a well brought up young lad here, Klaus," said Gustav. "We'll have to mind our manners. Yes, go on, son. It's a good sign that you're the tidy type. If you apply the same principles to your workplace, you won't go far wrong."

Kahrl collected up the cups, but before returning to the fitting shop observed, "Isn't the foreman a bit late? It's well past starting time."

"Huh!" said Gustav. "That's nothing unusual. We'd get the sack if we adopted his standard of time keeping. It's one rule for us, and another for him. Anyway, why do you complain? Can't you wait to see your friend again?"

"I wouldn't say that. But what should I do until he gets here?"

"Well, for a start, you can come and help me open the paddles to let some water out," said Gustav. "Then come down into the dock and watch us do some cutting and dismantling. If you're attentive we might let you help us later. That's unless Karpov has something else up his sleeve for you."

Once more filled with dread at the prospect of the foreman's eventual arrival, Kahrl first tidied away the mugs and then followed Gustav towards the lock gates.

From here they had a good view of the river beyond, and it was obvious that the tide was lower now. So when Gustav worked the windlass that opened the bottom paddles, he wasn't surprised to see the excess water in the dock gushing out into the river. While this was happening, Klaus adjusted the ropes securing the floating vessel. After a few minutes virtually all of the water had flowed out of the dock, leaving only the odd puddle here and there.

"Wow!" Kahrl said, peering down into the dock. "I didn't realise how deep it was!"

"About ten and a half metres," the fitter said. "Deep enough to accommodate the draught of an unloaded timber transporter. That's if we ever see one in here again. Well, shall I go first?"

Gustav picked up his tool bag and preceded Kahrl and Klaus down the stone steps. With each step, Kahrl felt the growing sensation of descending into a giant grave. At the final footfall he looked up and was almost overwhelmed by the depth of the enormous pit, which seemed so much deeper than when viewed from the top. Lowering his gaze to take in the sides of the dock, he noticed several lengths of heavy rope suspended from iron rings set into the walls, and three narrow ledges at one metre intervals from the bottom.

"What are the ropes and ledges for, Gustav?"

"The ropes are for securing floating vessels. The ledges give support for assembling cradles out of timber props for dry dock work, for bigger boats with a keel. You'll have noticed the timber stacks at the end of the dock. That's another job the fitters at Ventspils don't get to do. They have carpenters to build the timber frameworks for them."

Kahrl looked at the two fitters, forced a cheeky grin and said, "Well then. I think it's about time I got my hands dirty."

CHAPTER THREE
1878 : III – FORGING FRIENDSHIPS

"Rabbiiiiiiiiiit!"

The foreman's gravelled baritone cry boomed across the dockyard, making the hairs on the back of Kahrl's neck stand on end. The moment he had dreaded since finishing work the previous evening had at last arrived. He must now face the ogre, the man who he suspected would be a twisting thorn in his side until the day he could call himself a qualified engineer.

He had been working alongside Gustav and Klaus, watching and learning how to free and tap out the rivets and welded joints that held together the barge's heavy metal plating. They had also shown him how to use the giant shears and metal saws to cut and tear through the plates. As far as Kahrl could make out, boat breaking involved attacking the metal with all kinds of sharp or heavy objects with as much strength as a man could muster.

Hearing Karpov's summons, Gustav put down his saw and turned to Kahrl. "You'd better go and see what that bastard wants. Don't worry, he doesn't often get violent. He just likes yelling a lot."

Kahrl hoped he was right. Leaving the two fitters to carry on with their work, he made his way back up the stone steps. At the top he paused to take a deep breath in preparation for the dreaded interview. Then, nervous but determined, he straightened his back and strode into the workshop cabin, where he noticed that the ogre had something in his hand.

"What's this here?" the foreman demanded.

"It's a packet of tea, sir. I bought it on the market this morning, for all of us to use."

Karpov leaned towards him, so close that Kahrl was sure he detected liquor on his breath. It smelt like vodka. From his glazed look and general demeanour, Kahrl could swear the man was drunk.

"Make me some, then, Rabbit."

He took the pack, spooned some of the tea leaves into a cup and added water from the boiler. Then he passed the cup to Karpov.

The ogre took the hot cup without a word, only raising it and taking a mouthful with a loud *slurp*.

"Hmm," he muttered, and for a moment it seemed he might be considering a word of thanks.

It never came.

"First job today, boy. I've just been to the latrine and it needs emptying."

"Latrine, sir?"

"Yes, latrine. Don't tell me you don't know what a latrine is. Do you want me to spell it out?"

"No, sir."

He hadn't expected this to be a part of his job. If he'd needed to consider the matter, he would have guessed that gangs of night soil men collected all human waste in the early hours. That was the system in Tukums anyway. At home in Kaive, there was enough land for each tenant family to have their own arrangement.

But he daren't argue the point.

"Where should I empty it, sir?" he asked flatly.

"I don't bloody know!" Karpov yelled, then gesticulated with his arms. "There's a place along the bank somewhere. Ask one of those two lazy buggers!" Then he sat down in the cabin and picked up a newspaper.

Kahrl turned away and walked back to the dock, where he shouted down to the fitters, "Can you tell me where the latrine has to be emptied?"

Klaus made the long climb up to speak to him.

"We should have mentioned it, Kahrl. To be fair, it's a job that always falls to the junior apprentice. We've all had to do it in our time. We're too far out of town for the night soil collectors. Besides, being right next to the river, it's not as though there's far to go to dispose of …"

All that Kahrl could think was, 'I'll have to do this every day until I leave this place.'

He steeled himself. "Where do I empty it?"

"There's a little sluice about fifty metres along the bank. Tip it down there. It goes straight into a deep channel and gets taken out into the Baltic by the tides and river currents. Look, here's a tip. Check the bucket level every time you use the latrine, and when it's half full, empty it. That way nothing will slop out of the sides when you pick it up. Always take a piece of rag to put round the handle, and wash your hands with soap and hot water after you've replaced the empty bucket."

Kahrl turned away, mentally preparing himself for this unsavoury duty, and swearing that he would never divulge this part of his job to his family or friends.

Having completed the task without mishap, he reported back to the cabin for further instructions. What would his next job be, he wondered? To empty the dock one bucket at a time into the Daugava River?

But as he approached the cabin door, he heard the sound of long, sonorous exhalations of breath, accompanied by deep growling noises. When he opened the door a crack, for once he allowed himself a grin.

Karpov was snoring.

* * *

Kahrl spent the rest of the day helping Klaus and Gustav with the barge's demolition (including its wheelhouse). The ogre had shut himself away in the cabin, and it was Gustav's opinion that he must have a bottle of vodka in there with him. He emerged late in the afternoon, when he walked to the edge of the dock to check on their progress, scratched his left buttock, and then left the yard.

Because of the demolition work, Kahrl realised he would have to sleep in the foreman's cabin that night. Karpov had left quite a mess on the table and floor, so he first folded up his newspaper, then cleared away the scraps of food, apple peel and empty bottles, before having a good look around.

As well as the table and a chair, a grimy mattress lay in one corner, and a cupboard stood in the other, containing various items of crockery and utensils. Attached to the wall he found a cabinet containing a selection of surgical spirits and dressings. With all the heavy work he'd seen Klaus and Gustav doing that day, with such potentially dangerous tools, there must be occasional cuts and bruises.

He planned to eat early because he wanted to go out into the city and find Rudolf's suggested meeting place. He didn't expect his new friend to be there, but wanted to leave a note for him to rendezvous the following Sunday.

Before setting out he made his bed as best he could, turning over the existing mattress, which he would replace when he could save enough money. Then he laid sheets of Karpov's newspaper over it and spread his new woollen blanket on top. He bundled up the soiled bedding and found an old sack to put it in. Concealing his knapsack at the back of the corner cupboard, he grabbed the sack of bedding, locked the cabin door and set out for the city.

Dusk was falling. There was a moon, but the sky was very cloudy and a light mist was on the river. As he walked away from the dock it crossed his mind that it would be dark when he returned. But he was confident he could find his way back.

The tavern he was looking for was called the Black Pig, and on seeking its location from a group of well dressed people in the old town, his impression was that it wasn't a place that any of them would patronise. However one of them told him it was somewhere near the railway station. So he turned his face in that direction.

Asking again soon brought him to the door of the inn. He put his hand in his jacket pocket and checked his funds. His earlier purchases had made quite a hole in the kitty his father had given him. He did some quick arithmetic and worked out that he had just enough to see him through until he drew his wages on Saturday. That was barring any other expenses that might arise before then.

He walked inside, went up to the bar and ordered a mug of beer. He handed over a coin to the barmaid, and took a mouthful of the refreshing drink.

"You wouldn't be Karolina, would you, miss?" he asked her as she handed him his change.

"No, sweetheart. She's serving at the other end of the bar, just around the corner. Shall I tell her you want to talk to her? What name is it?"

"It's Kahrl, but she won't know me. I'm a friend of Rudolf Krutzberg."

A couple of minutes later a handsome young woman with short blond hair stood in front of him.

"Hello, dear," she said. "I'm Karolina. Did you say you were Rudolf's friend?"

"Yes, that's right. He said we could meet here, and that I could leave a message with you. Would that be all right?"

"Of course it would. What shall I tell him?"

"Tell him that I'll be looking out for him on Sunday after lunch, would you please?"

"Surely. He comes in two or three times a week with his college friends. Most of them are only slumming, but

Rudolf likes to sit and chat with the other customers. What did you say your name was?"

"It's Kahrl Evardson."

"All right then, Kahrl. Consider it done. Anything else I can do for you?"

"I need a postal address for receiving letters from my parents. Could I use this place?"

She smiled. "I don't see why not. But you look as if you come from a respectable family. It's going to sound a bit strange asking them to address their letters to the Black Pig. Better just give them the number and the street."

"Thanks. Is there a laundry around here?"

"There is, but they'll have closed by now. Have you much washing? Is that it in your sack?"

He nodded.

"You don't want to bother with a laundry. I'll do it for you. When do you want it by? Tomorrow night suit you?"

"Are you sure you can get it dry by then?"

"We've an overhead drier in the kitchen, and there's always a fire in the grate this time of year. Your stuff will be clean and dry, if a bit smoky."

"That's kind of you," he said. "How much …?"

"Wait until I've done it. Pass it over." She took the sack and lifted it up and down. "You can pay when you collect it. It'll be less than the price of a beer. Oh, excuse me. There's a customer. See you tomorrow night."

"Tomorrow night," he confirmed. "Thank you, Karolina."

He stood at the bar and sipped his drink, happy in the knowledge that there were, after all, some kind people in this place. He looked around. Although his present clothing was crumpled and dusty, he was a tad more presentable than most of the tavern's other clientele. But after two days of travelling and working in the same garments, and with only one change of clothing in his knapsack, he would soon need to find a regular laundry service. He couldn't rely on sympathetic barmaids. Perhaps eventually he could afford some proper lodgings, but he'd have to wait and see whether his weekly allowance would run to that.

He exchanged small talk with some of the locals, but didn't buy a second drink. He must watch his budget. He downed the last dregs of his beer, said his farewells, and stepped out into the street.

The evening city was bustling. Fine carriages flashed by conveying even finer people to the theatre or opera. Gentlemen wearing white gloves, evening suits and smart hats strolled in pairs to their clubs, while young society swains in tub carts sat beside their beautiful young ladies, so close together as to verge on the indecent. But nobody objected, suggesting that standards of behaviour in that respect must be a far cry from those back in Tukums.

He walked on through the old town, where behind curtained windows groups of diners supped and chatted in expensive looking restaurants.

Further on, towards the river, the streets grew emptier and not so well lit as in the main town. Before too long the city noise subsided, and his surroundings took on a gloomy, unsettling air. The quietness was interrupted once or twice by disturbing sounds, doors banging and people shouting in the distance, all of which made him quicken his steps until he reached the river and turned right towards the dockyard.

As he had expected earlier, there was little in the way of artificial light, and the moon was all but obscured by a grey, cloudy sky. The mist on the river had thickened and occasional foggy gusts blew onto the land and obscured his view. To check his bearings he stopped, and in that moment he had the distinct impression that he was being followed.

He decided to make for the dock and the refuge of the cabin as fast as his legs could carry him. At first all he heard were his own rapid footsteps and heavy breathing, but then he thought he heard panting, like someone gasping for air. Whoever could it be? What did they want of him? Well, he wasn't about to stop and find out. He quickened his pace, until for the final hundred metres he actually sprinted towards the cabin door.

He fumbled in his pocket for the key. He forced it into the lock and let himself in, re-locking the door from the inside, then stripped to his underwear and dived beneath the woollen blanket.

He was safe.

But the panting resumed from just outside. Even worse, it was now accompanied by the frightening sound of someone, or something, clawing at the external woodwork. Whatever it was must be desperate to get inside. For what purpose he didn't want to contemplate. Could it be the rats again? If the crazed scratching continued much longer the flimsy door would give way and he'd be defenceless against any attack. He must be prepared to defend himself, but with what? He got out of bed and felt around in the darkness on the adjacent table top, until he found what he was after. He gripped Karpov's cane and stood, foursquare before the door, ready for the onslaught he expected to burst through at any moment.

Then the scratching stopped. It was replaced by a pathetic whimpering, a heartfelt plea for help which couldn't have been produced by either human or rodent.

He lowered the cane but kept it ready by his right side. At the same time he turned the key with his left hand and reached for the latch. Cautiously he widened the gap, peering through to see whatever it was that craved his attention.

It was a big, black, ugly dockyard mutt with matted fur and old fighting scars on its face. And it was injured.

His first instinct was to reach down and comfort the poor creature. But he hesitated, for fear that it might bite him. From its size he didn't doubt that it could defend itself under normal circumstances. Also it may have collected some foul disease from snuffling in the filthy drains and gutters. So, keeping his distance, he uttered some comforting sounds while he figured how best to handle the situation.

He needed some light. He stood up and looked behind him. He remembered earlier seeing an oil lamp on the table. Screwing up his eyes he now made out its shape, but how was he to light it?

He reached under his bedding to retrieve a sheet of the foreman's newspaper. With this he fashioned a taper, and spoke some more soothing words while he squeezed past the dog and made for the fitting shop. Sufficient embers still glowed in the boiler furnace to ignite the taper. Cupping a hand around the flame he returned to the cabin and lit the lamp, providing light enough for him to tend to the injured animal.

He wrapped some rags around his hands and coaxed the pathetic creature to shuffle inside the hut. Here he knelt to examine his patient, a young adult bitch. She couldn't have whelped for some time, if ever, for her teats were hardly developed. No doubt she was able to fend off advances from other dockyard strays. Gently he felt her back and sides, and she didn't wince at all. It was a different matter though when he touched her feet, her left rear pad in particular, for the bitch issued a shrill *yelp!* when he put pressure on it.

"Now, now," he whispered, "I'm sorry. I won't hurt you again."

He soon saw what was wrong. She must have stepped on something sharp, like a shard of glass, for there was about a centimetre and a half of broken skin, and when he took his hand away he saw the dark stain of blood on the protective rag.

There wasn't much he could do straight away to soothe her pain. But he might be able to help speed up the healing, or at least prevent the wound from developing into something worse.

He took one of the cups and filled it with warm water from the boiler. While she rolled her eyes towards his face, the animal allowed him to give the affected paw a good soaking. He would wash the cup in boiling water in the morning (and remember to serve up Karpov's tea in it).

Taking a length of dressing soaked in spirit from the first aid cabinet, he applied it to the wound to clean it. Then he wrapped another length around the foot and tied it with a knot on the top. It was good that the injury hadn't been to a front paw. She'd find it easier to keep a damaged back foot off the ground by walking on three legs, which she must do for several days at least.

He found a bowl in the cupboard, half filled it with cold water from the boiler feed tank and set it down next to her. She didn't drink now, but might get thirsty during the night. She also refused his offer of some cheese, so he put it back in his pack to try again in the morning.

Then he cleared up, extinguished the lamp and turned in, by which time his patient was dozing comfortably.

As he also gave way to a sudden fatigue, he relished the creeping warmth and weight of the new blanket and thought, 'Four new friends in two days. Things can't be all that bad.'

* * *

He awoke with the dawn, recalling that he had an additional task this morning, before heading to the market for his breakfast and shopping.

The bitch also stirred, and raised herself on to her front paws to lap some water from the bowl.

"Good morning, Dog," he said as she tilted her head and looked back at him. If she was in any pain, she couldn't have noticed yet, but it was hard to tell in this confined space. He must get her outside.

He opened the door and whistled her to follow him. Just as he had hoped, she naturally transferred her weight to her good back foot and skipped outside on three legs. And the dressing appeared to have held through the night. Each day that it stayed in place gave the wound a better chance to heal. Ideally it would need changing in a few days, but he doubted the opportunity would arise.

He reached for his sack and took out the cheese that she'd refused the night before and dropped it on the ground in front of her. As she snapped it up he saw that her teeth were well developed. When bared they made a formidable looking weapon. This was an animal you wouldn't pick a fight with. But she needed more sustenance. As he would soon replenish his food store anyway, he took all the edible remains, comprising bits of chicken skin and pork fat, stale bread and some more cheese, and scattered them in front of her. Within a few seconds they were gone.

After slurping up the rest of the water, she turned her back on him and trotted awkwardly to the end of the dock. Here she stopped, looked back at him, and then set off towards the town.

Kahrl stood in his undergarments with hands on hips, and said out loud, although there was nobody to hear him, "Well, Dog, thank you for your company. I hope you enjoyed your breakfast."

His routine was falling into place. Now there was full daylight he found some matches at the back of the cupboard. He would tidy up the cabin, fuel the boiler furnace from the wood and coal store in the corner of the fitting shop, take care of his ablutions and then make for the market to buy his morning meal and daily rations.

He would save his least favourite task until after work. Emptying the latrine bucket, he decided, was not something he could face before breakfast. Doing it last thing, he would then have one final good wash to rid himself of the day's filth before going into the city.

* * *

On his way back from town, Kahrl took a detour to the timber quay to find the chandler's shop that Klaus had spoken of.

Here was another dock, though much larger than the one further along the bank at the breakers' yard. A big boat was moored at the quayside and on approaching the dock area he gasped at the size of it. For although during the last two days he had watched various vessels making their way up and down the river, those had been far enough offshore to appear little more than children's toys. This one was close up and real and, in his experience, easily the largest boat he had ever seen at close quarters.

Even at this hour several men were busy hoisting huge bundles of timber onto the deck and stowing them. He wondered if they included any of the few planks that he and his father had recently carted to the rail yard in Tukums. From what he knew it was probable that this cargo was destined for the coal pits that fuelled the great industrial powerhouse of England.

He could have stood for hours watching the various comings and goings, but he mustn't be late for work, so he turned away and sought out the shop that Klaus had mentioned, and bought a new set of overalls. He would buy a second pair out of his first week's pay.

On leaving, he noticed a freestanding wooden booth with a hoarding outside announcing, 'Passenger Tickets Available Here.' The notice included a sketch of the very ship that lay in the dock, or one very much like it. And underneath in smaller letters was a brief description of the facilities, which included 'all meals, private amenities and cabin maid service'.

He tried to imagine what 'private amenities' might comprise, and couldn't help comparing them with his daily ritual of emptying the latrine bucket at the dockyard.

It struck him as odd that a huge boat such as this one, built to serve the onward march of industry, should also cater for independent travellers. He knew that packet ships sailed from another quay not far from here, offering cheap passage to the thousands of emigrants wanting basic transport to the labour-seeking industrial nations of the west. Those migrants were poor folk just like him. Some of his neighbours in Kaive had seen their sons make that journey to a new and hopefully more prosperous life. But he knew nothing of the special people who occupied private cabins on board these huge timber freighters.

And so he made himself a silent promise.

'One day, I'm going to be one of those people.'

CHAPTER FOUR
1878 : IV – BEST LAID PLANS

Saturday saw some brightening of Kahrl's spirits. For mid-day brought the weekly visit to the dockyard of Captain Heuer's agent, Herr Muller. The ferret-faced little man drove in on a tub cart with a squeaky wheel, wearing a smart black suit and carrying a shiny black briefcase, from which he produced a cash bag and a ledger.

With the briefest of formalities he marched into the little cabin that was now Kahrl's home and bedroom from dusk until dawn, seating himself at the table. From there, he summoned them in order of seniority and counted out their wages, getting them to sign for them in his ledger.

Last and least in the pay parade, Kahrl received the meagre sum of five roubles as expected. But even though the amount was small, still he felt a surge of pride while signing his name. For this was his very first wage, and he felt he had earned every kopeck of it.

While signing, he couldn't avoid noticing the amounts paid out to the two fitters and the foreman. He wasn't in any way taken aback to have his relative worth to the firm so starkly confirmed. But eying those figures filled him with determination to better himself and eventually see similar sums appear against his own name.

What did surprise him was that, while Klaus and Gustav had signed their names normally, the foreman had used the symbols 'XX' of an illiterate. No wonder the ogre had so brusquely dismissed his father's letter of introduction at the start of the week. He had simply lacked the ability to read it.

Rejuvenated by his Saturday afternoon bath, Sunday found Kahrl enjoying his first free day since arriving on the train from Tukums.

He spent the morning exploring further Riga's old town area, its ancient buildings and colourful park, which followed the course of the moat that years ago had encircled the island of ancient houses, churches and civic buildings. He wore his second suit consisting of pressed jacket and trousers, which were identical to the clothes he'd arrived in. So, although he still looked like a peasant, at least he felt presentable again.

He had decided to minimise the need for laundry expenses by keeping this suit for best, only for wearing into town on Sundays. He would make use of his first one at other times as required, for example, if he should venture out on an evening. In the mornings, there was no shame in visiting the market in his overalls, as did many of the other early-rising workmen. That way, he could get as much wear as possible out of his first suit before having to take it in for cleaning and pressing. After all, his allowance was small, and his father's advice had been to set something aside for emergencies if he could.

However, as the day was a Sunday, and a cool one at that, he had decided to dine, have a drink and wait for Rudolf in the relative comfort of the bar at the Black Pig.

Karolina served him a hot plate of pork, potatoes and cabbage alongside a mug of beer.

"No laundry today, Kahrl?"

"No, Karolina, but I'll have some tomorrow night, if that's all right. Though I do feel I'm imposing on your kindness. I should use the normal public wash house."

"Not at all, dear. I can use the few extra kopecks, and I'm sure you'll be needing to save your cash."

Her pity was almost embarrassing. He hoped nobody had overheard their conversation. He forced a smile and tucked into his meal.

As he downed the last dregs of his beer, Rudolf arrived as expected and greeted him warmly.

"Hello, my friend! It's so good to see you again! Can I buy you a drink?"

"That's kind of you, Rudolf, but I've just had one and, to tell you the truth, I'm not used to too much of it. I'll wait for a while, if you don't mind."

"I quite understand. There's nothing worse than developing a habit for the drink. All good things in moderation, I agree." He paused for a second, then added, "But I am actually quite thirsty, so I'll just order one for myself."

Having done so, he sat down opposite Kahrl.

"Now then, tell me all about your week. How's the apprenticeship going?"

"Very well, thank you, Rudolf. I'm working with two first class fitters. They've shown me how to work the lock gates, and fill and empty the dock, depending on what type of work we have to do …"

He went on to describe in detail how the lock worked, and how he'd helped to cut up and demolish the old barge, but soon realised how boring this must all sound to his classically educated friend.

But Rudolf smiled politely and said, "It's good that you're learning all these things so soon. I realise you're on the first rung of a long ladder, but I'm certain that you'll fulfil your dream of becoming a master tradesman."

In the company of this sophisticated young socialite, Kahrl felt that that day lay aeons into the future. He tried to turn the conversation in another direction.

"And what about you, Rudolf? What will you do when you've graduated from the university?"

His friend sagged a little and stared at his beer. "My father wants me to go into the firm with him. But I'm not sure it's the life I want, running a shipping line. It's such a complicated business, what with insurance, and finance, lawyers and joint stock companies. I'd feel uncomfortable having all those people working for me. And besides, it would make me an out and out capitalist."

"Sometimes we have to do what we're born to do. Do you have any brothers?"

"To step into the role instead of me? No, unfortunately. That's what makes things so damned difficult. I love my parents, and of course I don't want to disappoint them."

"Do they know how you feel about this?"

Rudolf sighed. "I've tried bringing up the subject, but I can't seem to get around to laying my cards on the table, so to speak."

"What would you like to do instead? Where does your real interest lie?"

"Oh, that's easy. Politics. Trouble is, as far as my family's concerned, they'd be the wrong kind."

"You mean, your interest in social reform?"

"You're recalling our conversation on the train. Yes, I do feel passionately about such things. I believe a great change is about to wash over Europe, and it'll turn everything upside down."

"I hope it doesn't come before I've finished my apprenticeship, or it'll all have been for nothing."

Rudolf laughed. "Not at all. Whoever's in charge, society will always need engineers. Just you keep your head down and see it through."

"I intend to. But, if you were interested in political change, wouldn't you be at an advantage if you were at the helm of a successful business? I mean, just think how you could use your power to assist and promote the reform process."

Rudolf's jaw dropped as he took in Kahrl's remark. "Do you know, that's one of the wisest notions that's ever been put to me?"

"I was just following a logical line, Rudolf. It's really no business of mine."

"As long as I count you as a friend, my life is your business, Kahrl. And vice versa. I'm so bowled over by what you've just said that I wish there was something I could do to help you in your own chosen career."

Although at first inclined to set aside Rudolf's offer, he realised he shouldn't turn down such a well intentioned opportunity. After all, nothing ventured . . .

* * *

The two friends spent the next hour swapping memories of their respective childhoods, so different in obvious ways, but similar in terms of the importance of family. By the time they parted, they had agreed to make this Sunday afternoon meeting a regular event for them both to look forward to. They could also report progress in their respective careers.

Also before leaving they had agreed upon a bold but simple plan, the aim of which was to ensure the continuation of Captain Heuer's engineering facility in Riga.

"Right, that's settled then," said Rudolf. "Tomorrow morning I'll go to my father's office and find out why we've gone over to using an English firm for our routine fit-outs."

"You're sure you won't get into trouble, poking your nose in all of a sudden?"

"On the contrary, I'm sure that Father will welcome my taking an interest in the family business."

"When do you think you'll be able to report back?"

"We both visit the Black Pig on odd occasions during the week, so no doubt we'll bump into each other. But as you'll need feedback before next weekend, let's fix a meeting for Wednesday evening."

"Good idea. Then, depending on what you find, I'll decide what I'm going to say to Herr Muller. It's not going to be easy. A bit awkward in fact, given my humble status."

"Oh, I don't know," Rudolf mused. "You're the new boy, wet behind the ears. You'll probably get away with asking a few cheeky questions."

"I hope so."

He daren't admit, even to Rudolf, just how much he dreaded the prospect of carrying out his part of the plan. He felt nauseous anticipating it. He would need, next Saturday, with the benefit of Rudolf's findings, to privately engage Captain Heuer's ferret-faced agent in a conversation concerning the firm's methods of working. The most opportune time would be when he and Herr Muller were alone together in the office, after the other men had received their weekly pay, and wandered off into separate corners of the works to check their money.

He expected a rude rebuff to his cheeky overture, but knew he had at least to try, for the sake of all their futures.

After Rudolf had left, the barmaid came over to clear the table, and he decided to ask her a question that had been on his mind for the past few days.

"Karolina, just out of idle curiosity, how much would I have to pay for full bed and board at the Black Pig?"

"That would cost you five roubles a week, young man. When would you like to move in?"

He shook his head. "Not until I'm earning a bit more, I'm afraid," he answered gloomily.

Laying out his entire weekly allowance would leave nothing for his lunches, clothing, laundry, drinks and the rest. So, for the time being at least, he would have to be content with the current arrangement of sleeping either on board whatever boat should occupy the dock, or in the cramped and scruffy little workshop cabin.

Thinking of his domestic situation brought his family to mind, and the fact that he had still to fulfil his promise to write to them. So, on his way back to the dockyard, he went into the stationer's shop and bought a pen, a bottle of ink, some writing paper, envelopes and blotting paper. At fifteen kopecks this little haul wasn't cheap but should, he reckoned, see him through several months of letter writing.

Clutching the brown paper parcel containing his purchases, he hurried back to his hut, where he set them on the table and, making the most of the remaining daylight, began composing his letter.

* * *

Marijas iela 16, Riga

29th October 1878

Dearest Mother, Father and Brother Fritz,

I trust that you are all in excellent health and that all is well with the smallholding and timber cutting.

I am pleased to tell you that I arrived safely in Riga and established myself in my new employment and conveniently situated lodgings, in whose comfortable surroundings I now write to you.

The work is very interesting though sometimes strenuous, but this is good because it will help me to develop a more healthy physique. Also to this end I am eating very well and enjoying all the varied food that a city such as Riga provides in abundance.

I have already made some respectable friends, but promise not to allow my social life to detract from my primary goal, which is to become a qualified engineer.

I have not yet had the pleasure of meeting Captain Heuer, as the major part of his business keeps him in Ventspils. However should the opportunity arise I shall certainly thank him for his generosity in granting me this rare opportunity.

Although I would very much like to be with you all at Christmas, this will not be possible as the trains will not be running. Also we are too busy at work for me to be allowed any extended leave. I shall try my best to come and see you as soon as I can get away in the New Year.

I shall of course keep you informed of my progress.

Your loving and devoted son and brother,

Kahrl Johann

* * *

The mood in the dockyard during the following week was, to say the least, subdued. The only contracts were for the demolition of four small fishing craft, all with wooden hulls. They were to be dismantled over the next two weeks, two at a time. The ultimate scrap values would be minimal, and the commission would come nowhere near to covering the demolition team's wages.

On a positive note, Kahrl had been allowed to operate the lock gates, as the size and weight of each boat would withstand any damage that might result from an error on his part. Fortunately (or, more accurately, because of his determination no to blot his copybook) his handling of the task had passed without mishap.

Gustav and Klaus had also given him further tuition in the use of some of the machine tools in the fitting shop, if only on pieces of scrap metal.

Karpov's attitude to Kahrl had not altered however. He was still morose and obnoxious towards him. Kahrl had learned to keep out of his way, except for the few occasions when the ogre found another unpleasant task for him to perform. At these times he would do his best to comply, and avoid giving the foreman an excuse to chastise him. Otherwise he stayed close to Klaus and Gustav, always firing questions at them and eager to learn.

In some ways this week's contract, though far from financially rewarding for the firm, proved satisfying for the demolition team. Having begun with two more or less complete vessels, the breaking progressed well until Friday afternoon saw a virtually empty dock with neat piles of sorted scrap awaiting collection along the landward side. It only remained for the salvage merchants to examine and weigh the materials before removing them with their carts.

As the week drew to a close Kahrl became ever more nervous about his planned Saturday noon conversation with Herr Muller. But his apprehension was balanced with excitement, as the outcome of the interview could well improve matters for the whole team.

As before, the agent arrived in a tub cart, one of whose wheels still squeaked annoyingly. At last the appointed moment arrived, the foreman and two fitters had received their pay, and it was Kahrl's turn to go into the hut with the agent to collect his own wage.

"Good morning, sir," he said with a nervous smile.

Herr Muller, clearly unused to such pleasantries from junior members of the workforce, merely sniffed and returned a barely polite, "Morning."

He then counted out five rouble coins, which Kahrl checked and pocketed. Following this, the agent turned the ledger round to invite him to sign for his money, and handed him the pen.

This was the point where Kahrl had decided to say his piece, figuring that he would have Herr Muller's full attention until the writing implement was returned.

So, before signing, Kahrl held up the pen and began, "I feel I'm learning a lot here, sir. I wonder if I could ask you, on your next meeting with Herr Heuer, to express my sincere thanks for the opportunity he's given me."

Muller's brow developed a deep furrow, while his eyes followed the nib of the pen, which Kahrl waved around in the air as he spoke.

"Er, yes, yes. If I see him, I will." And his gaze shifted to the ledger page, as if to force the pen nib to follow and complete the transaction without further delay.

But instead Kahrl continued, "It's a shame that we've stopped doing fit-outs for Krutzberg's boats. Have you ever considered, instead of making them bring their ships hcrc to our dock, sending our fitters to do the work while they're loading, on their own wharf? It would mean they could put to sea a day earlier, or possibly more."

The man's expression froze. It was clear that he didn't know what to say, so that only one clipped word emerged from his tight mouth.

"What?"

Kahrl wasn't about to miss the opportunity presented by the agent's hesitation.

"Yes, sir. I have an acquaintance who has some knowledge of Krutzberg's operations. He says the reason they're now fitting out in England is because of the time and effort involved in bringing their unloaded ships from their timber wharf to our yard for maintenance. So it seems to me that we should take the work to Krutzberg's wharf, and do the fit-outs while they're unloading."

Muller found his voice. "It seems to you …? Do you really have the gall to offer an apprentice's opinion on matters that are far beyond you?"

"I'm sorry, sir. I was only …"

"You were only taking a great liberty, young man. I fear our foreman is failing in his duty to keep you in check."

He paused. "Besides, if we send the fitters to his wharf, what on Earth do we do with this dock?"

Kahrl forged ahead. "Exactly what we're doing with it now. Demolition. Only set on two labourers to do it. It doesn't merit the skills of master tradesmen. It's a waste. With just the two labourers wages to pay, you might even make a profit on this side of the business too."

With this, he decided he'd said enough.

Herr Muller took a deep breath, and pushed the ledger a little further towards Kahrl. He signed it. The agent stood up and closed the book with an abrupt *snap!* Then he snatched the pen from Kahrl's hand and pocketed it swiftly.

Without another word, Muller walked to his waiting tub cart, climbed aboard, cracked his little whip and drove away without looking back.

Kahrl's heart pounded. The agent's reaction had been close to what he'd expected. At that moment, he'd be turning Kahrl's suggestion over in his mind. It should at least give him food for thought. And an approach from Rudolf's people coincidentally proposing something similar could well deliver the result that they were both hoping for.

He turned and exited the cabin – and walked straight into the barrelled chest of Stefan Karpov.

Kahrl's face drained as he realised the ogre had been standing close by and must have heard most, if not all, of his audacious proposal.

The foreman grabbed his arm, squeezing it tightly as he commenced a tirade that made Kahrl quake with fear.

"What the hell do you think you're up to, Rabbit? Are you trying to sabotage our living, you young bastard? I can't believe what I've just heard! And who are you, an ignorant peasant, to think you've learned enough in two weeks to advise your betters how to run their business? That man was right. I've been letting you off too lightly!"

"But, sir," Kahrl pleaded, "I was only …"

"You were only selling us all down the river! Can't you see what he'll do now? Oh, yes, he'll take your advice about setting on two labourers instead of us. Then do you know what he'll do? He'll sack the bloody lot of us! Come here, you flaming idiot, while I whip some sense into you!"

Saying this he grabbed his cane, raised it as far as he could above his head, and brought it down with force across Kahrl's left shoulder.

The apprentice crumpled to the ground, his right hand clasping the shoulder, above which a thin red line of open flesh on his neck already threatened to open and ooze with blood. Fortunately the top of his overall had taken most of the force below this point, but the severity of the blow was enough to prevent him from rising.

Karpov raised his arm again to deliver another thrashing, but was prevented by Klaus and Gustav, who had run across on hearing his threats.

"That's enough, man!" Klaus yelled, pulling on the foreman's raised arm. "You'll bloody kill him!"

Restrained by Klaus, the big Russian slackened his stance, and shrugged off the fitter's grasp.

Gustav was already pressing a cloth to Kahrl's wounded neck, while the now deflated Karpov walked away muttering, "He's done for us. He's bloody well done for us."

* * *

Karpov's assault didn't deter Kahrl from dining as intended at the Black Pig the following lunchtime. As soon as he arrived in the bar, it was clear that Karolina noticed a change.

"That's an attractive cravat you're wearing, Kahrl," she observed. "Is it cold out?"

"Just a bit. My Mum packed it in my knapsack when I left home. I don't want to catch a chill."

"It's nice and snug in here though. Aren't you going to take it off?"

"No, I think I'll keep it on. I'll have a beer and whatever you're cooking today please."

"All right, sweetheart. It's a juicy mutton shank, and to go with it we have some boiled turnip and roast potatoes with some tasty gravy. Will that be all right?"

"Very nice," he responded, trying hard to sound enthusiastic, though in truth he had little appetite.

Although the initial pain had been considerable, it had soon diminished to a dull soreness, accompanied by a slight nausea. However the shock of the attack had immobilised him for a couple of hours afterwards. Klaus had insisted he lay on his mattress for the afternoon, and keep as warm as he could. Karpov had slunk off muttering that the injured apprentice could 'do what he bloody well liked'. Examination of the wound by the two fitters suggested a doctor wouldn't be necessary, which was a relief to Kahrl, as he had no idea whether he could afford that kind of expense.

He'd been unable to face any food on Saturday evening, so he'd woken that morning feeling very weak, but still with little inclination to eat. He did manage to drink a cup of hot tea, after which he felt more like chewing on some bread and cheese. He must try and keep his strength up. And it was most important that he keep his regular Sunday appointment with Rudolf.

When his meal arrived he picked at it with his utensils, and was still playing with it when his friend walked in, bearing a broad grin.

When he saw Kahrl however, his expression turned to one of concern.

"My dear friend," he said, "Whatever is the matter?"

Kahrl looked up and managed a weak smile.

"A bit of an accident," he replied casually, pulling down the red cravat to partially reveal the prominent slash of broken skin underneath it.

Rudolf looked horrified.

"My God! That's a whiplash! Who the hell did that to you?"

"I'd rather not go into that, if you don't mind," Kahrl mumbled.

"But it's a serious injury, man!" his friend insisted. "Whoever did it needs a taste of his own medicine. I'll be happy to do the honours. Come on, tell me."

"I appreciate your concern, Rudolf. But I don't want to make things worse. I don't believe that one violent act can be cancelled out by another. I want to put it behind me. There are more important issues at stake here. It would be wrong to allow this to divert our attention from our plan to save the dockyard."

Then he added, "I wish you'd sit down. You're making me nervous."

Rudolf took the chair opposite and leaned forwards. "It's to do with our plan, isn't it?"

Kahrl met his gaze with a vacant stare.

Rudolf sighed. "All right. We'll set it aside. But if I ever discover who did this to you, please don't blame me if I can't match your Christian sense of forgiveness."

Kahrl replied, "Don't misunderstand me, Rudolf. I'm not a Christian, except by upbringing. And I don't forgive him. But I truly believe that all violence is futile, even if it has right on its side."

Rudolf shook his head. "You're an extraordinary fellow, Kahrl. And you can take that as a compliment. Very well, let's not allow this to distract us from our immediate objective. But, is there anything I can do to help you meanwhile? Do you want me to arrange a medical examination? I'd be happy to pay for it."

Kahrl was shaking his head before his friend had finished speaking. "No, no, thank you all the same. The wound will soon heal, and the rest is only bruising. It's not too painful. I think my body has had a shock, which a couple of good nights' sleep will cure, I'm certain."

Rudolf pulled his chair closer to the table. Still with a tinge of concern in his voice, he asked quietly, "Well then. How did things go?"

Kahrl sniffed. "Things went very well, in my opinion." He paused.

Rudolf's impatience was written on his face. "So, you managed to put our idea to your employer's agent?"

"Yes. As we planned, at yesterday's pay parade." He paused again.

"And …?"

"And, as I expected, he told me I was crazy and stormed off."

Rudolf laughed, and then frowned.

"And your interpretation of his storming off is that things went very well?"

"I think so, yes. You see, the seed has been planted. All it needs now is a little sun and rain. I'm hoping you've come here this afternoon to announce a favourable weather forecast."

Rudolf smiled again. "Nicely put," he said.

"And?" Kahrl asked. Now it was his turn to be impatient.

Rudolf's smile broadened. "Let's not play mind games, my friend. I think I know who will win, and it isn't me. Let me tell you what's happening with my people."

"Go on, then."

"I put the proposal to my father and the General Manager in the main boardroom. The idea of bringing your fitters to our wharf to carry out each routine mechanical inspection, without interrupting loading, was met with unanimous approval. I have to admit that I took credit for the idea, mainly to get into my father's good books. I hope you don't mind?"

"If you'd said it was Heuer's apprentice's idea, they'd have laughed you out of the room."

"Quite. And there was an added bonus. The General Manager remembered that, as well as the cost of the fit-out in England, we also have to pay at least a day's wharfage while the work's being done. So that's another saving.

"But wait until you hear this. He reckoned that shaving off at least two days from every turnaround should enable each boat to make twenty-five per cent more trips between here and England every year. It's like expanding the fleet by a quarter without a single rouble in capital outlay!"

Kahrl gasped. "By Heavens, I'd never even considered that! So what happens now?"

"First thing Monday morning, our Development Director has to approach Herr Heuer's agent, to formally propose a continuing contract, subject to both sides agreeing mutual terms. Our only stipulation would be that the basic cost of each fit-out mustn't exceed what it was before we moved our business to England."

"That's brilliant!" Kahrl gasped. "I don't know anything about the pricing, but I do know our firm needs this contract badly. And you mustn't waste any time if you're to brief your Development Director about the details. When will you be seeing him?"

"Don't worry. He already has all the information he needs to put our company's formal proposal on the table."

Kahrl screwed up his face. "Are you saying what I think you're saying? Who is this Development Director?"

Rudolf sat up and grinned.

"You're looking at him," he said.

* * *

Lying awake that night on his scruffy mattress, Kahrl thought about Rudolf's rapid transformation from university student to director in his father's shipping firm. He contrasted this with his own status in life. A simple peasant, whose greatest ambition was to become a mere mechanic. And the fruition of even that unimpressive dream still seemed but a remote possibility.

Was he jealous of his friend's advancement? He didn't believe so. He certainly didn't envy Rudolf's involvement in the cut and thrust of business management. Much of that made Kahrl yawn just to think of it. Perhaps, though, it would be nice never having to worry about money, or where his next meal was coming from.

His greatest fear was that his perceived insolence could easily lead to his dismissal. That would be unbearable, given the sacrifice his parents were making to allow him to come to Riga, while they eked out an uncertain living in Kaive. To return so soon and admit failure would disappoint them terribly and shame him to an extreme degree.

Worse still, what if this crazy plan was indeed to backfire as Karpov had predicted? Who could truly know what was in Captain Heuer's mind? Perhaps it had always been his intention to run down this uninspiring dock until it became no longer viable. It would be a lot simpler to shut it down and concentrate on the more profitable yard in Ventspils. This might be just the chance that Heuer was waiting for.

But there was one other thing that was forcing his spirits down just now. It had to do with Klaus and Gustav. So far they'd been kind to him, even though they hadn't in their hearts truly welcomed his inclusion in their little team, because of his additional cost to the already faltering business. He couldn't blame them for that, nor if they'd been less tolerant of him for that reason.

But they hadn't. They'd been good to him, tried their best to teach him what they knew, and consoled him over Karpov's barbaric treatment. But, notwithstanding their concern following the foreman's attack with the whip, he was sure he'd detected an alteration in their behaviour towards him.

After persuading him to lie down in the cabin for the rest of the day, he'd been able to see them occasionally through the open doorway during the course of the afternoon, in close conversation interspersed with frequent nods in his direction. He knew they despised Karpov, but that didn't mean that they disagreed with what he'd said.

The risk he had taken hung over him now like a black cloud. Perhaps the fitters believed that he really had betrayed them, and that his impudent interference could only bring about the outcome that he now feared above all other things.

CHAPTER FIVE
1878 : V – A CRUCIAL DECISION

From Monday morning life in the dockyard shuffled along under a bleak routine that mirrored the weather, which brought grey skies and an annoying, steady drizzle all along the Baltic coastline.

As a general rule, rain wasn't a reason to stop work, and Kahrl soon realised the benefit of a leather cloak and hat, various examples of which his three co-workers possessed. Unfortunately he didn't.

Sadly for him, as might otherwise have been the case prior to his apparently calamitous outburst, neither Gustav nor Klaus showed any concern about his discomfort. Previously they would have suggested some makeshift covering to keep him dry, but now they ignored him as they got on with bringing the third and fourth of the dilapidated fishing boats into the dock for dismantling.

He huddled for shelter just inside the cabin door, expecting any moment to receive a rebuke from Karpov. But it was clear that the foreman had also chosen to ignore him, and in fact the ogre acted as if he were simply not there.

This state of affairs couldn't continue. How could he do his job if his colleagues gave him the cold shoulder? If the scheme he and Rudolf had cooked up didn't produce results, it looked as if he might have to seek alternative employment, or run home with his tail between his legs. An ignominious waste of his first big chance in life.

His low spirits had even driven him to consider foregoing his usual morning shopping trip into town, but he had soon banished that thought as a foolish spite against himself. He must continue to eat regularly, or risk physical breakdown on top of mental turmoil.

When the others stopped for their mid-day meal breaks, Kahrl did the same, though he still had little appetite. Seated on the chair in the little cabin, he chewed on some cheese and bread, and stared vacantly through the open doorway.

Now that work had ceased and all was quiet, he listened idly to the sounds that, for most of the day, went unnoticed. The twitter of birdsong from a copse a little way along the riverbank, the screech of gulls following a fishing boat in the river, and the barking of dogs competing for scraps of food that some dock worker had discarded.

From further away came the feint noise and bustle of the main docks and quayside, and even the whistling and chuffing of trains as they made their way across the railway bridge away up river. He also fancied he heard the distant hoof beats of some equine, and tried to imagine what style of carriage it might be pulling. He soon acknowledged the futility of this game however, because he could never know the nature of the combination, as the vehicle would of course be heading for some remote destination.

Except that it wasn't. The hoof beats were growing louder, meaning the cart must be coming nearer. Not only that, but he was convinced he recognised the approaching vehicle from the rhythm of the horse's hooves and the familiar squeaking of a complaining wheel.

Herr Muller? On a Monday?

Stepping outside the cabin he watched the others' gawping surprise at the agent's approach, and Karpov was already heading towards the tub cart as it drew up next to the hut. He grabbed the horse's halter as Muller stepped down, as usual clutching his black briefcase.

"What brings you here today?" the foreman demanded. "More fishing smacks for breaking?"

Herr Muller hardly acknowledged Karpov, except to say, "No, it's him I've come to talk to."

He pointed at Kahrl.

The foreman looked aghast as the agent pushed past him, took hold of Kahrl by the arm, pulled him into the cabin and closed the door.

Kahrl's heart beat so fast that he feared it was about to burst. Was this how the firm usually conducted a dismissal? Would he find himself on his way back to Tukums on tomorrow morning's train? He gulped, and prepared for the worst.

The agent released his grip, sat down, and took some papers out of his case. He didn't beat about the bush.

"I don't know what connections you have with Krutzberg's line, young man," he spat out, "but I've had a proposal from them this morning that virtually replicates the ideas you put to me here on Saturday."

Kahrl couldn't tell from his tone whether this was good or bad. So he just said, "Oh?"

"Yes. Well, if they've somehow influenced you to ensure they derive the maximum advantage for themselves from this proposal, I'd be inclined to make an example of you."

Kahrl had to respond. "Sir, I can promise you that's not the case. I do have an acquaintance who has some influence in their organisation, and when I learned that this yard was in danger of closing, I asked him to see if there was any way of preventing that. I admit it was a selfish act on my part, because I desperately wanted to continue my apprenticeship here."

"Hmm," Muller sniffed. "If that's the honest truth, I'll let your impudence go. I can't deny that this offer throws a welcome lifeline in our direction."

Kahrl allowed himself a smile of relief.

"Does that mean …?"

"I've already telegraphed Herr Heuer with the details of the proposed contract, together with my recommendation to accept."

Kahrl couldn't hide his elation. "Oh, sir, thank you! Can we tell the others?"

The agent allowed himself a little smirk. "I don't see why not, though I expect …"

Then he paused, and surprised Kahrl by reaching over to him and pulling down his collar.

"What's this?" he demanded. "Who did this to you?"

Kahrl could only issue an incomprehensible grunt.

"Never mind. I think I know."

Then he stood up and opened the door abruptly. Karpov almost fell over the threshold.

"Eavesdropping as usual, I see," Muller sneered. "Did you do this to this boy?"

Karpov was defiant. "He deserved a thrashing. He put ideas to you that could have closed us down for good!"

"Really? Well, I've no doubt that by now you'll have discovered that that wasn't his intention. What have you got to say about that?"

For once the bully's mouth remained shut, though the look he directed at Kahrl spoke volumes.

The agent resumed, "You were right in one respect. Even before seeing this evidence of your savage brutality, I had decided that this new arrangement could dispense with an engineering foreman. The team we'll recruit for the demolition work will include a general foreman-clerk who'll need to be literate. So I've brought your final week's wages."

As he said this, he drew the familiar cash bag from his case, and counted out some money on the desk. Then he took out his ledger, opened it and handed Karpov his pen.

"Sign."

Grim-faced, the foreman scratched his 'XX' against the only entry on that page.

"I won't insist on your working the week out. As far as I'm concerned, you might as well pack your gear and go now. And if you're thinking of making trouble, I'll have to consider reporting you to the police for common assault. Make up your mind."

Kahrl thought that Herr Muller must be very brave. He stood there, looking like a ferret on hind legs, sternly peering up at this great bear of a man, who without doubt could have slain the little fellow with just one blow. Kahrl envisaged the cogs of Karpov's overtaxed brain grinding through the likely outcomes of whatever action, violent or passive, he was considering carrying out next. In the end he must have realised there were too many witnesses for him to get away with flattening the agent, or Kahrl, or both of them. Though there was no doubt in Kahrl's mind that he could have done it with ease.

Eventually the ogre scooped up and pocketed the money, and turned to leave. After taking a dozen steps though, he halted, looked back towards Kahrl, and made a statement that the young apprentice would never forget.

"You're riding high now, Evardson. But I promise you, one day I'll bring you down to my level, you see if I don't. So keep looking over your shoulder, Rabbit. You'll never know just how close I am behind you."

And he walked away.

* * *

For the rest of the day Gustav and Klaus went out of their way to be pleasant. Not that they'd shown any direct antagonism towards Kahrl during that short period of uncertainty.

But he understood their reservations. The changes to come might have excluded the need for qualified fitters.

Karpov had put that idea in their minds. They must have been going through torment, but Kahrl was certain they realised now that he wouldn't have knowingly put their jobs at risk. However nothing more was said about the matter and, as far as Kahrl was concerned, that was for the best.

Instead they talked at length about how the contract would affect them, and what would be needed to support their new method of working.

"We ought to have a selection of tools and stuff with us, but we can't keep a permanent engineers' store on Krutzberg's wharf," Klaus said.

Gustav nodded. "But there's a limit to what we can take in our tool bags, and you can bet your life we'll need something we didn't pack."

Klaus laughed. "And it's a long walk back to our store here. We could do with some transport, like a cart."

"Good idea. And a strong horse to pull it. We might need to bring heavy components back to the fitting shop for machining, or replacement parts we fabricate here back to the ship. But Heuer won't want to employ a drayman."

Their eyes swivelled round to rest their gaze on Kahrl's face.

"That suits me. I'm used to looking after animals. I don't mind taking care of the horse as long as I still get mechanical experience as well. We'll need facilities though."

"There's more than enough room here for a stable," Klaus said. "And a shelter for the cart. It shouldn't be a problem."

Kahrl added, "Don't forget there's the cost of feed to consider. With no grazing, a working animal will need oats as well as hay. I'll get some prices."

"Good lad," Gustav said.

Then Klaus coughed, giving Gustav a sideways glance, as if they'd prepared something they wanted to say.

"You know, Kahrl, what that bastard said to you before he left … You don't want to take it to heart. He was probably in his cups again. He'll have more important things to think about …"

"Yes," Gustav added. "Like finding someone stupid enough to set him on."

* * *

Sleep didn't come easily for Kahrl that night.

Neither of the hulks in the dock possessed sleeping quarters, so he had had to make do with the hut again. At least with the original filthy bedding now freshly laundered, he wouldn't catch anything unpleasant from it. Lack of funds meant he must still sleep on the soiled mattress, but he always covered it with newspaper and took care that only one side of his sheet came into contact with it.

The events of the past few days raced around in his head. The risk he had taken in putting his proposal to the agent, Karpov's violent reaction and Herr Muller's final decision – all of these combined to sharpen his senses and rule out any hope of relaxation.

On top of this, the fine details of the new working arrangements fired up his brain like a miniature steam engine. There were so many plans to make, and so many things to acquire. Surely Herr Muller knew there would be a certain capital outlay from the start. Kahrl had made a list, with the help of the two fitters, of tools and fitting shop equipment that needed replacing, if the fitting team were to deliver a first class service. Then there was the expense of the horse and cart, and their associated running costs. It was as if the responsibility for the project's success fell upon him personally, a prospect that he found almost overwhelming.

Potential pitfalls and challenges occupied his overworked brain until well into the early hours, when at last his insomnia gave way to a shallow, uneasy slumber.

But even this wasn't to last.

It was the flickering light that first disturbed him. Having slept so badly he cursed what at first he took to be the intruding dawn. But then he noticed through the cabin window that the light reflecting on the low clouds was shimmering and changing colour. The fleeting notion that he might be witnessing the northern lights (which he had read about, but never seen) was soon dispelled by the loud *crackles* and *smacks* of burning timber. He quickly donned his overalls and boots and went outside, where he peered down into the dock.

Both of the fishing boats were well ablaze.

His first instinct was to look for a way to try and dowse the flames. But there was no fire-fighting equipment to hand. Or at least, if there were any pressure pump and hose anywhere in the dockyard, they had never been pointed out to him.

He looked towards the city, and wondered if the authorities there operated a fire watch system. But with no sign of help approaching, he deemed that unlikely. In any case, the minimal risk of a dockyard blaze spreading to the city probably made it not worth bothering with.

So all he could do was stand at the side of the dock and watch the two little boats burn. What an ignominious end for the derelict craft, which would wipe out their salvage value, small as it must be. And, as the commission on nothing would also amount to nothing, the outcome for the firm this week would be a big fat zero to set against the workers' wages. Even worse, he imagined the yard would have to compensate the owners for their loss.

He shrugged. These things were really none of his concern. Yet he *was* concerned. Why should that be?

Perhaps because, even though he'd been here for little more than two weeks, he already felt an affinity with the outfit and his co-workers. Taken alongside Herr Heuer's favour in offering him the job, it seemed he had already developed a strong sense of loyalty.

But how had the fire started? Because of the excitement surrounding the new contract, little work had been done on the boats that day. Besides, Klaus and Gustav always complied with the rule never to carry their pipes, tobacco or matches when working with timber. Apart from that, he knew that anything capable of igniting a fire, such as oil lamps or furnaces, were either removed or disabled before any work was carried out.

Given his restless night, he was certain he couldn't have slept through an electrical storm. So that ruled out a spark from a lightning bolt. Truth was, there was no way in which this could have happened without human intervention.

He was by now also puzzled about the depth of the water. That evening when they'd packed in work the fitters had left the smacks resting on cradles in a dry dock. But in the meantime someone had let four metres of water in. The tide was on the ebb when he'd turned in, and a glance towards the river now told him it was well below the level of the water in the dock.

Now standing right on the edge, he mused as to why anyone would want to try and float the vessels.

Almost as soon as the question entered his head, he felt an almighty shove from behind, which sent him hurtling through the air. Instinctively filling his lungs with as much of it as he could inhale, he fell headlong into the murky water, meeting the surface with some force, and creating an almighty *splash!*

Back home in Kaive his father had given him a swimming lesson in the nearby lake, but that had been in water shallow enough for his feet to touch the bottom. Could he swim well enough now to save himself from drowning in deep water? He didn't know.

But he was about to find out. He recalled his father's instructions, and pushed back as hard as he could with his hands, while making a frog legged shape with his lower limbs, and shoving back to displace water with his feet.

It seemed to be working, but he was still well below the surface and wondering if he could hold his breath for long enough. He was also unsure of where he should be heading. He ruled out making for the nearby stone steps, because that was the side where he'd gone in. For all he knew, his assailant might still be there, ready to make sure he didn't come out alive. His best chance would be to make for the opposite side, around the prow of the nearest burning hulk, and towards one of the ropes that hung from the dock wall. He struck out and passed the closest vessel as planned. By now he felt as if his lungs were about explode. And he was no nearer to the surface. His heavy footwear and clothing were dragging him down. He managed to push off his boots, but he was far too weak by now to get rid of his overalls. In fact he was almost ready to relieve the enormous pressure on his lungs and give in to drowning.

But then there came a commotion behind him. Perhaps his attacker was throwing things at him to keep him. But no. Whatever was causing the turmoil was moving towards him. He felt a firm grip on the collar of his overall and realised that he was being pulled upwards. With this assistance, a few more desperate strokes brought him to the concrete wall, where he grabbed a suspended rope. With a couple of pulls he broke surface, desperately gasping for air, and thankful now for the flickering light from the still burning fishing boats. There he hung, limp and exhausted, filling his lungs not just with air, but also taking in quite a bit of smoke, which made him cough uncontrollably.

Across his mind flashed the memory of an incident back home, when he and his father had helped some neighbours contain a forest fire. As his father had shown him then, he now pulled his soggy kerchief from out of his wringing wet overalls pocket and tied it around his head and over his nose to help filter out the worst of the smoke. Then he saw something in the water that made him smile.

How could he mistake her black coat and the glint in her eyes? After all, had he not recently spent a whole night in her company, tending to her injured foot?

The bitch paddled just below him, looking close to exhaustion after her tremendous effort. Where she had come from, he had no idea. He supposed she'd been hanging around the dockyard, out of sight until she found an opportunity to repay his recent kindness. Whether she had been trained to help drowning sailors, or merely made use of her natural skills, he could never know.

But one thing was certain. If he didn't get her out of this dock soon she might well lose her own life, a cruelly ironic reward for her act of bravery. He drew on all his resources and pulled himself hand over hand by the rope to the topside of the dock and climbed out. Then, keeping low, he hurried to the lock gates at the far end. Checking the water on the other side, he confirmed that it was near enough low tide, so he worked the windlass to open the paddles and bring down the level in the dock.

He hurried back to check the dog's condition, and saw that she remained afloat, though struggling now to tread water. After a few minutes, the depth had fallen enough to expose the first ledge, so he returned to the gates to close the paddles.

From the end of the dock he saw that she'd had sense enough to heave herself up onto the ledge, where she now lay, exhausted but with her eyes turned upwards towards him as he approached, and slowly wagging her tail.

He could think of nothing else to say but, "Good girl."

Now that she was safe, he picked up a heavy spar from the timber pile, and called out in the smoky darkness.

"Whoever you are, come out and let me see you! Otherwise I'll send the dog after you!" He doubted that he could deliver on that threat, but he waved the heavy shaft of wood in the air to show that he meant business.

There was no response, and it seemed his attacker had melted back into the night, perhaps believing his grizzly attempt on Kahrl's life to have been successful.

He looked at the spar in his hand and realised it wasn't much of a weapon. Had his attacker decided to hang around, perhaps it wouldn't have been a good idea to challenge him to a fight. Especially dripping wet with no boots on. And even if Kahrl had been able to gain the upper hand, how would he reconcile knocking his opponent on the head, considering his declared moral stance on the futility of violence? He had to admit that, all in all, he was relieved that the assailant had decided to leave.

He looked down again towards the ledge where, still soaked and fatigued, the bitch now forced herself to sit up. He encouraged her to stand and walk along the ledge. She responded, then shook herself semi-dry. Kahrl noticed that the bandage was no longer in place, which didn't surprise him.

He walked around the landward end of the dock, where the timber piles were stacked, and from there to the place where he had been shoved in. All the time he beckoned her to follow along the ledge until it gave way to the stone steps leading up from the dock bottom. Here she had the sense to transfer from the ledge and up the steps towards him, her tail now wagging vigorously.

At the top she shook herself almost dry, and he stooped and gave her a cuddle saying, "Are you going to let me have another look at that cut, girl?" He gently grabbed the woolly fur on her neck and led her towards the cabin. There she allowed him to examine her wound, which he judged to be healing up well. The bandage must have come off only recently, probably during her heroic rescue. So he cleaned up the foot and tied on a fresh dressing, and then offered her some scraps of food and a drink, which she declined. But she seemed to want to stay with him. He was glad of her company too.

He figured that his assailant was unlikely to return so soon to the scene of his crime. Even so, as additional precautions he locked and bolted the cabin door and lay the wooden spar in a handy position beside his bed. Then he discarded his sodden clothes, dried himself as best he could, lay down between the sheets, and closed his eyes.

As he drifted off his mind revisited the dramatic events of the last hour.

Only one person in Riga knew, or thought he knew, anything about his swimming abilities, and that was Stefan Karpov. But because on that first day the foreman had cut him short when asking if he could swim, Kahrl hadn't been allowed to expand on his answer. So, if the Russian wanted to kill him, he would have chosen drowning as the best bet.

There was little doubt that falling into an empty dock would have killed him outright, but it would also attract police attention as a potential murder, whereas a drowning was more likely to be written off as an accident. Tenuous reasoning, perhaps, but it would explain why the dock had been partly filled before the attempt on his life.

But Kahrl had survived and, in anybody's book, the bid to drown him amounted to attempted murder, which he guessed must rank as a serious crime. It might even count as a capital offence. There was already one convicted murderer in the Karpov family, and even based on Kahrl's sketchy testimony, a jury might well be inclined to convict him out of hand.

But that wouldn't amount to proper justice, because Kahrl couldn't be one hundred per cent certain that Karpov was the guilty party. After all, he hadn't actually seen his attacker, either before or after his involuntary swim. Apart from that, he didn't want to be responsible for anybody's death, not even Karpov's.

And he drew little satisfaction from knowing that the bullying foreman's life was, for the time being at least, entirely in his hands.

CHAPTER SIX
1878 : VI – A FRESH START

Loud banging on the door woke him with a jolt. Urgent shouting forced him out of bed, and for a second he wondered why he had no clothes on.

Then he recalled the night's events, and reached instinctively for his makeshift club. But Gustav's voice soon brought him to his senses.

"Kahrl! What the hell's happened? Are you all right?"

The dog sat up and issued a low *growl*, but he calmed her by stroking her head. Then wrapping a blanket around him, he slid back the bolt and opened the door, to see the fitter's anxious face staring back at him.

"Thank God you're unhurt, lad. Don't you know what's happened? Both the boats have been burned to a cinder! Didn't you hear or see anything?"

"Yes, I did," Kahrl mumbled, stepping outside. "Is there any tea on the go?"

Just then Klaus walked up and glared at him saying, "I think we'd all like to have some. But we'll need to wait. Unfortunately someone forgot to fire up the boiler."

"I'm sorry, Klaus," Kahrl yawned. "It's been quite a night. I didn't get much sleep."

"Never mind. I've just done it. It's not as if we've much to do today, apart from clear up the mess. I'll go and assess the damage."

Gustav asked again, "So, what happened?"

Kahrl sat on the chair with head in hands. "It was hard getting to sleep last night, what with everything that's happened over the last few days."

"Tell me about it. My wife's complaining I'm keeping her awake with my thrashing about."

"Yes, so, when I finally did get to sleep, it was only to be awoken not long after by the sound of the boats burning. I got up and went to have a look, but there was nothing I could do, except just watch them burn. I stayed around to make sure none of the sparks flew up and set fire to the cabin. Then, when the worst was over, I turned in to catch some sleep. Next thing I knew, you were banging on the door."

At this point the bitch came out to see what was going on.

"Hello," said Gustav. "What's this then?"

"Just someone who looks after me."

Gustav gave him a puzzled look, then shrugged. "Locking yourself in with a guard dog sounds sensible enough to me."

Kahrl nodded. "You get a bit twitchy, sleeping alone so far from the town. And I've taken to locking and bolting the door at night as an extra precaution."

"I don't suppose you noticed anyone skulking around, who might have started the fire?"

Kahrl hesitated. Omitting some of the truth was one thing, but he didn't want to tell a direct lie to his workmates. On the other hand, neither did he want to start a process that could lead to Karpov's execution, however beneficial that might be to Kahrl's own safety.

"No," he replied, satisfied that that was the literal truth.

Then Klaus returned and asked something that caused Gustav's jaw to drop.

"Did you know someone's let three metres of water into the dock?"

Kahrl answered calmly, "Yes, I noticed that too. I couldn't figure it out. But this is starting to feel like an interrogation. You don't think *I* started the fire, do you?"

"No, of course we don't," Gustav assured him. "But we're going to have to report all of this to Herr Muller. He'll want answers to these questions. He might even want to notify the authorities."

"I doubt that," Klaus said. "Without a solid suspect, Riga's police won't want to know."

"But there is a solid suspect," Gustav argued. "Our old friend Karpov."

"Who hasn't," Klaus argued, "been seen near the dockyard since Muller gave him the boot yesterday. That's right, isn't it, Kahrl?"

He gulped and answered, "I certainly haven't seen him."

"I'd lay you five hundred to one, though, that our sod of an ex-foreman is responsible for this," Gustav insisted.

"Me too, but it's still only supposition," Klaus said. "Besides, apart from some sort of twisted revenge on the firm that, let's face it, won't be an enormous financial inconvenience, where's his motive?"

At this, Gustav put his hand on Kahrl's shoulder, saying, "It's here, my friend. The motive was murder."

"Explain please," said Klaus, as Kahrl's face drained of colour.

"Ever since this lad joined the firm, that piece of scum has treated him like dirt, given him all the shitty jobs, cajoled, insulted and even whipped him. We both saw it. But it took this young man to work out a solution to turn the dock around. As a result Karpov not only lost his job. He was also thoroughly humiliated. What further motive do you need?"

Klaus frowned. "I understand all that. I just don't see why you think it was an attempt to kill him. After all, the cabin wasn't burned down, was it?"

"No, because Kahrl's instructions as watchman were to sleep in whichever vessel lay in the dock. And Kahrl is someone who usually obeys orders from his superiors."

"I see," Klaus drawled. "You mean, you think Karpov expected Kahrl to be sleeping in one of those boats?" Then the implication hit him. "My God, the bloody bastard!"

Gustav turned to Kahrl again. "Now think, lad. Are you sure you didn't see Karpov hanging around before the fire?"

Kahrl shook his head. But it shocked him to realise that Gustav's analysis was entirely credible. And so was his further conjecture.

"Floating the boats would make it harder to save yourself, because you'd have to swim for it. Can you swim?"

What a question. He couldn't answer it truthfully, because his four-legged saviour hadn't given him time to find out. But he couldn't tell them that. Again he would have to deflect their questioning.

"I don't know. I'm a country boy, remember?"

Gustav sighed. "Karpov must have assumed you couldn't. So, what do we know? Some nameless person came into the yard last night, let in enough water to float the boats and then set them alight. There was nothing you could do and you didn't see the perpetrator. Is that about it?"

Kahrl nodded.

Klaus said, "Well, anyway, it's lucky you chose to sleep in here instead."

Kahrl shrugged. "Neither of the boats' cabins seemed as comfortable. I'm sorry."

"Don't be sorry, lad," Gustav insisted. "Nobody's blaming you. You can sleep where you like. It's a bloody mean arrangement in any case if you ask me. You should be paid enough to cover decent board and lodging, instead of having to find a new bed every few days, like this poor bloody dog!"

Kahrl murmured, "I don't mind, honestly. I realise the firm couldn't afford to pay me much. I'm lucky to have this apprenticeship."

"If you ask me," Klaus said, "I think you're too bloody good for this firm. A young chap as loyal and able as you deserves a lot better."

Gustav said, "Well, things are going to change from now on. If Muller doesn't figure out something fair for you when he comes here on Saturday, I'll want to know why."

"That goes for me too," Klaus added. "It's through your contacts that we've been able to get this new deal with Krutzberg's. You're in a strong bargaining position if you want better pay and conditions. So don't be shy when the agent comes."

"All right, I won't. Thanks for the advice."

"But who is this friend you have inside Krutzberg's organisation?" Gustav prodded. "Can't you tell us?"

Kahrl was put on the spot by this question. He didn't want to divulge his relationship with Rudolf. He couldn't say why. Perhaps it was that he didn't want to declare all of his cards while negotiations were still in play. But mostly, he just didn't want to spoil things.

"I'm sorry. You know I trust and respect both of you. Call it superstition, but I'm afraid if I tell you the name of my contact, everything will unravel and come to nothing."

"That's all right," Gustav reassured him. "We're only being nosey buggers. It doesn't matter that much. As long as the contract is sealed, we're all going to be more secure from now on. By the way, do you have that list of stuff we'll need for the new contract?"

Kahrl opened the cupboard in the corner of the cabin, took out his sack and extracted some papers, which he handed over.

Slipping the costings inside his coat and fastening his top button against the cold, Gustav set off in the direction of the city.

"Where are you going?" Klaus asked. "You haven't had your tea."

"I'll have it later. Muller should know about this without any delay. And while I'm at his office I may as well explain to him what we need to buy if we're going to save this yard."

*　*　*

"By God, just look at this!"

Klaus stood with hands on hips on the edge of the dock, surveying the damage and mess in the aftermath of the fire.

"There's nothing worse than a fire on a floating vessel, Kahrl. If we're going to do this job properly, first we have to rake in as much of the loose debris as we can and get it out of the dock."

Kahrl wore the fitter's spare overalls, while his own lay across the boiler top to dry. He'd told Klaus that he'd foolishly rinsed them out (which was close enough to the truth), forgetting that he lacked a spare pair.

"Wouldn't it make the job easier if we waited for the next low tide and let the water out?"

"No, lad. If we do that we run the risk of clogging up the paddles. And with three metres of water we'd need divers to clear any obstruction, which all costs money. It's best to pull out the loose stuff first before we open the paddles."

As they worked Kahrl reviewed his motives for concealing the whole truth about last night's events from his workmates.

On reflection, he saw that Gustav's theory about the arsonist's intention was far more plausible than his own. Karpov had set fire to the boats believing that Kahrl was asleep on board one of them. Assuming he couldn't swim, the foreman had let water into the dock to impede any attempt to escape the fire. He would then have waited in the shadows to see the job through, only to observe Kahrl emerge from the workshop cabin and stand, an easy target, on the edge of the dock. Having shoved him in, the assailant would have departed, soon after which the dog arrived to dive in and pull Kahrl to the surface. If the bitch hadn't been there, he would probably have drowned. The fact that Gustav didn't know about his being pushed in or the ensuing rescue was almost immaterial. Either way, the implication was clear.

Kahrl had been the victim of an attempted murder. And the obvious suspect was Karpov.

Even if he didn't know already, Karpov would soon learn that his attempt on Kahrl's life had failed. Would he let his hatred rest, or would he try again?

On the other hand, what if the attacker hadn't been Karpov? A deranged tramp, perhaps, or simply a compulsive arsonist? Apparently there were crazy people at large who had a compulsion for starting fires. With all he'd gone through lately, Kahrl realised that he might not be thinking rationally. But there must be some chance that the big Russian wasn't to blame. And he couldn't bear the responsibility of sending an innocent man to the block. Not even one as detestable as Karpov.

Then again, he was right at the start of what he hoped would prove to be a promising career. He didn't want anything to ruin his chances of completing his apprenticeship. Wasn't it therefore sensible to report the incident to the police, and let them sort out the truth?

But if he did, he would have to come clean about having been pushed in. If he'd mentioned it before, there was no doubt that the fitters would have insisted on involving the law. And Karpov would have been convicted on a supposition, which in Kahrl's eyes would be unjust. No, he couldn't allow that to happen. He realised few men would agree with him, but he held to the sincere belief that it was better for a guilty man to live, than for the wrong man to die. He detested the various instruments and processes of execution, favouring life imprisonment to judicial killing, which was to him barely more respectable than lynching by the mob.

Holding to such principles, he realised he would in future have to watch his back and avoid contact with his old foreman. Meanwhile, he wasn't looking forward to more nights sleeping in that cabin, with or without his canine companion to protect him.

It was hard work raking the floating debris around to the stone steps and carrying bundles of it up to the top. At first he and Klaus took turns at raking or carrying, but it soon became obvious that Kahrl had a knack with the long-handled rake, so Klaus let him specialise in that part of the job.

By eleven o'clock they had amassed a sizeable pile of charred timber, so they started shifting it in a barrow to a space beyond the fitting shop, which over the years had accommodated occasional bonfires.

While they were doing this Gustav returned from Herr Muller's office, so they left off work for a tea break.

Klaus pulled a wad of tobacco from his pouch and stuffed it into his pipe. "Well, Gustav? What's the news from High Command?"

Lighting his own pipe Gustav replied, "Generally good, I'm pleased to report. Muller had a quick look at our list of requirements while I was there, and there was nothing he took exception to. But he wants a chance to review it before he gives it its final approval."

"That's fair enough, I suppose," said Klaus.

Kahrl handed them their tea and asked quietly, "And what of the … other matter?"

Gustav drew on his pipe and exhaled a great cloud of aromatic tobacco smoke. "He was shaken by the news of the fire and the danger you were in, but not too concerned about the financial loss."

Kahrl looked at him over the rim of his mug. "Did you tell him what you thought about it?"

"He's an intelligent man. I told him the facts. I reckoned it best to let him draw his own conclusions."

He paused to draw on his pipe again, but Kahrl could hardly stand the silence.

"And they were . . ?"

"He only said he'd need more time to consider those as well. But he did ask me if Karpov had been seen hanging around. I told him 'no'. Anyway, how's the clean-up going on? You don't seem to have shifted much."

Klaus grinned. "You cheeky sod. While you've been living it up in the city we poor buggers have been breaking our backs raking and shifting. Haven't we, Kahrl?"

Kahrl tried to smile and nodded, feeling that Gustav might be hiding something from them. And he was right.

"Oh, I nearly forgot." He looked at Kahrl. "Herr Muller asked me to give you this. Hold your hand out then."

He tipped three shiny roubles into the apprentice's palm.

"He wants you to find proper lodgings for the rest of the week. He says he was never really happy about your night watch duties and sleeping arrangements. He's already engaged a proper night watchman who'll be arriving as we leave this evening. And he'll discuss your pay and conditions with you further when he comes on Saturday morning.

"And one more thing. He asked me to thank you for adding the final item to our list of requirements."

"What final thing was that?" Klaus asked as Kahrl's cheeks reddened.

"Something about grease for Herr Muller's tub cart wheel."

* * *

Saturday came, and Herr Muller's cart arrived at noon as usual, both of its wheels now silent. He stepped down with slightly more of a spring in his step than Kahrl remembered from earlier visits.

He wasted no time.

"I want to speak to you all together in the cabin. Kahrl, can you make some space for us all?"

But since moving to his temporary lodgings with its comfortable bed and hot meals, he had already cleared away the rough bedding from the cabin floor. The others followed him inside, where the agent took the chair, while the three workers stood to hear what he had to say.

"I'll give you your pay before I leave. First, about the fires. As nobody was seen in the vicinity, we can only assume that they were either accidental – which, I confess, I find hard to accept – or an act of jealous sabotage. I think we all have our suspicions as to the perpetrator's identity but, without positive proof, I think we should draw a line under the incident and move on. The loss to the company is minimal, only a token compensation to the vessel owners, with which they are quite happy.

"So, now that that's out of the way, I can give you all the news I know you've been waiting for. I can tell you that the contract was signed yesterday for Heuer's to service all of Krutzberg's timber transport vessels on their own wharf."

The four of them shook hands and clapped each other on the back, even Herr Muller managing to crack his usually blank face to accommodate a broad grin.

He continued, "As a token of appreciation for your individual and collective loyalty, Herr Heuer has agreed to the following weekly increases to your wages. Starting from today, each of the fitters will receive an additional two roubles."

Klaus and Gustav exchanged grins.

"Kahrl, you will receive an additional two roubles and fifty kopecks. This should enable you to establish permanent board and lodgings in a respectable part of town. Your pay is to be reviewed every six months, when increments will be awarded reflecting improvements in your competence, aimed at bringing your wage into line with the qualified fitters within no less than five years, given your current age. However further employment after that point cannot be guaranteed.

"Understand that this will require serious application on your behalf, young man. You will be expected to enhance your training with suitable evening classes at the Free Maritime College. Armed with your diplomas and craftsman's certificate from here, you should be able to find work as a fitter with any reputable firm, whether in Riga or further afield."

"Thank you, sir. I'm very grateful," Kahrl assured him. "My ultimate wish is to become a chief engineer on a steamer, and I realise that will require a lot of studying and hard work. I won't let you down, I promise."

"As to the list of requirements, which Gustav delivered to me on Wednesday, these are all acceptable, and I will arrange letters of credit so that you as a team can make the appropriate purchases. This is all subject, of course, to my final approval before any contracts of sale are entered into. Herr Heuer has approved a maximum budget for these, which mustn't be exceeded."

Again, all three members of the fitting team exchanged grins of satisfaction.

"From your estimates, I assess that there is room for items which may have been overlooked. Do any of you have any further requirements not already listed?"

The two fitters shook their heads.

"Please, sir," Kahrl said, "could we arrange some improvements to the latrine? It's degrading to have to dispose of the contents manually. As it's a downward gradient to the sluice, a simple pipeline could be installed …"

"I don't want to hear the gory details, Kahrl. I'll arrange for a pipefitting contractor to come and size up the job. It can't be too complicated. I'm sure there'll be enough money in the budget to cover the cost."

The meeting concluded, all three received and signed for their increased pay, and watched the agent climb back into his cart, gather the reins and instruct the horse to walk on.

When he was out of sight they stood in a ring, spontaneously joined hands and did a nondescript dance, the only accompaniment being the music of their *whoops* and laughter which, if truth be known, Herr Muller would probably have heard even above the sound of his horse's hooves as he drove back towards the city.

When the dancing stopped, the three men exchanged congratulations again, while one overriding prospect ran through Kahrl's excited mind.

His tentative lodging arrangements since Tuesday could now be made permanent. From that moment, he no longer had to sleep in a scruffy cabin on a soiled mattress, or in a filthy bunk on a condemned barge or fishing boat, keeping one eye open in case of further attempts on his life or the unwanted company of rats.

Now he was rich. Now he could afford the luxury of full bed and board at the Black Pig tavern.

* * *

"So, Kahrl, how are you settling into your new home? Does it suit you?"

"If you could have seen my former lodgings, Rudolf, you'd understand why I think I've moved into a palace. I have a room of my own, with a heavy door that keeps out the wind. The room also has a papered ceiling with a tiled roof above, with proper guttering so the rain can never seep inside. The walls are covered with decorous paper with pictures in frames hanging here and there. My bed has a clean, soft mattress, with crisp, laundered sheets, blankets and a downy pillow, so that, oh, how I slept last night!

"And I have my own earthenware washing bowl and a mirror, and a desk for writing my letters home, with a chair, and even a little table in the corner where I can have a snack if I feel like it. And yet, even with all these luxuries, I still have space enough to dance a jig if the mood takes me!"

Rudolf smiled. "And no doubt you'll be eating better, now that you can come down here for a wholesome breakfast every morning as well as a hot evening meal. No more early trips to the market, eh?"

"Oh, I don't know about that," Kahrl replied. "I've become quite used to wandering about the market of a morning. I was beginning to get to know some of the traders. It's become a necessary part of my education. I even found a stall selling second-hand books! Anyway, I'll still need to buy something for my lunchbox every day."

"I'm pleased your circumstances have improved. It would have been sad if your memories of Riga had been only of poorly rewarded toil and disappointment."

"I don't mind the toil and, having seen the city from the level of the sewer rats, my improved status only increases my appreciation of this marvellous place. I intend to get to know it much better, from the perspective, if not of a gentleman, then of a loyal citizen."

His friend slapped the pub table. "Well said! In fact, we'll do it together. To be honest, having been born and grown up here, I probably take for granted much of what the city has to offer. You've seen the old town, and no doubt with your practical eye you've already come to admire the architectural styles and beauty of many of its buildings. But with a proper guide I'm certain you'll appreciate it so much more."

"I'll look forward to that," Kahrl said. "But there's a more pressing matter I have to ask you about."

"Ask away, Kahrl. If I can help you, you know I will."

"Well, no doubt Herr Muller will pass on the information in due course, but my workmates and I are keen to know when the first of your company's ships will require our services."

"Ah, yes. That's a very good question. We do have a boat that's just about to leave Tyneside, but she will have had her last fit-out at the English yard. So she should only need a superficial inspection when she puts in here in a few days. That should be some time on Tuesday, depending on the tide. But that's not the only route we operate, remember. There'll be other boats coming in from different points of the globe requiring full fit-outs over the next couple of weeks. The first of those is scheduled to dock on Thursday."

"Hmm. That doesn't give us much time to prepare. We'd hoped to have had a portable store up and running for the first job. But that might not be possible. Not by Tuesday anyway. Tomorrow I have to go shopping for a draught horse and cart."

"It seems you're going to be busy. I hope you'll leave a few hours for some enjoyment."

"Of course," Kahrl laughed. "As long as whatever you have in mind entails nothing I couldn't write home and tell my mother about!"

* * *

Kaive

4ᵗʰ November 1878

Dear Kahrl Johann,

Thank you for your very welcome letter. Your father and I are so relieved to hear that you have found good lodgings and settled into you work. I am sure your colleagues will count themselves lucky to have such a conscientious, hardworking young man in their midst.

We have taken on a young itinerant worker. He is Latvian, from the Vitebsk region, where life is more difficult for those who were born into serfdom, even though it has, God be praised, finally been abolished there. He seems a good boy, about your age, but tall and quite strong. He will help your father and Fritz with the felling and cutting, so that we may earn a little extra money.

Signs point to a mild winter, and we pray that this will be the case. However we have a plentiful store of wood for our fire.

We hope you will listen to your superiors, and make a success of your life. A visit at Easter would be wonderful. But if pressure of work makes it impossible, please don't fret. You must do nothing to inconvenience your employer.

Make sure you always wear your long underwear during the winter months, and eat heartily whenever you have the opportunity.

Fritz sends his love, as do your father and I.

Your loving Mama, Papa and Brother.

* * *

His mother's letter was waiting for him when he arrived in his room after work on Monday.

The day had been the busiest he'd known since starting work at Heuer's dockyard only a matter of weeks ago. Herr Muller, all credit to him, had been waiting for the crew when they arrived first thing that morning. Kahrl had fired up the little boiler in the fitting shop, so that over tea they set about discussing the day's hectic schedule.

The agent confirmed Rudolf's forecast that the first of Krutzberg's boats needing a rudimentary engine check should be docking around noon the following day.

"I want you to visit a couple of dealers to obtain quotes for a good horse and a sturdy cart. I've already arranged for a carpenter to send a team to erect a stable block with a storage loft and shelter for the cart. I've also ordered some hay, corn and stable utensils, but you'll need to keep the food under cover and away from the rats until the stable's erected. In case we can't organise the horse and wagon today, get hold of a good handcart as well. We can always use that as a reserve should the need arise."

He then opened his case and took out some papers, which he handed to Gustav.

"These are letters of credit to cover your purchases. All bills should come to my office for payment."

He then looked at each of the three workers in turn.

"Are you all up to this?" he asked.

They all nodded.

"Good. If you've any time remaining today, you'll need to sort out your tool bags and equipment for tomorrow's job. What you can't carry can go on the handcart, or wagon, as applicable. And I want you all in freshly laundered overalls tomorrow. I don't want to hear that Herr Heuer's fitters are a scruffy lot.

"And one more thing. What you get up to on this dock I leave to you. But on the client's premises there'll be no smoking on the job, no wasting time chatting to the other dockworkers, and no spitting or swearing. Got that?"

Nobody argued.

"Does the night watchman I engaged appear to be suitable?"

"Yes, sir," Klaus replied. "He's a big strapping lad. I don't think he'll stand for any bother."

"Good. In due course I'll be employing two labourers for the breaking work. They'll report to you two, Klaus and Gustav, but I'll be here every Saturday lunchtime to give them their weekly schedule. Any questions?"

The two fitters had nothing to say, but Kahrl still had something important on his mind.

"Please, Herr Muller, sir, the latrines?"

"Oh yes. A pipefitter will be here later this morning to install a privy with a waste pipe to the sluice down-river."

The agent then snapped his briefcase shut, and stepped into his tub cart. "I think that's everything. I look forward to a successful and profitable future for us all."

So saying, Muller turned his rig around and trotted off towards the town.

* * *

As Kahrl tucked in to his fish supper in the bar of the Black Pig on Wednesday evening, Karolina asked if the meal was to his liking.

"Yes, thanks," he replied. "Fish has always been my favourite food. We rarely get it in Kaive, except when my father can coax a catfish from our neighbour's lake. He hauled out an enormous one the day before I left home."

Just stating this simple fact made him feel homesick, and he let flow the words he had only meant to be thinking.

"I do miss my people."

He blushed and followed up with a quick apology.

"You've no need to be ashamed of that," Karolina said. "Believe me, most young men who leave home don't give their family a second thought. Most of them can't wait to sow their oats and drink the taverns dry."

He blushed again. These weren't issues he was used to discussing, let alone with a woman not much older than himself.

"Did you leave a girl back home?" she asked.

"No. There was one some time ago, who I believed might have married me, when my circumstances allowed it. But she went off with a soldier. I heard no more from her, so I hope and suppose she remains contented with him."

"Oh, that's bad luck," she said. "Well, don't you worry. If you keep on bettering yourself as you've been doing, you'll have the pick of the young lasses, just you wait and see."

He nodded at his plate and said, "I'd best finish my fish before it gets cold."

As he did so, he told himself that he mustn't weaken and give way to flirtatious distractions. His work was the most important thing to him now.

* * *

After reading a book for an hour or so he retired early. He now had a nightshirt, which was more comfortable than sleeping in his long underwear. Once snug under the covers, he pulled the top sheet and blankets tight under his chin, relishing the luxury, and thinking how preferable this was to the wretched pits that he'd recently occupied.

As usual he found it hard to sleep, because his mind kept going over the programme of events for the following day. This would see the first full fit-out under the new contract, and everything had to be in place. The new cart was already loaded with spare tools, components, nuts, bolts and washers, in fact just about anything and everything that might be needed for servicing a marine steam engine. One of his first tasks in the morning would be to harness the draught horse to the cart and drive it the kilometre or so along the quayside to Krutzberg's wharf, where the big timber carrier was expected to dock around noon.

'Tap, tap.'

He was startled by a gentle knocking on his bedroom door, and shuffling on the landing outside. His mouth became dry and his heart began to pound. He was too jittery to light the lamp, and didn't want to start a fire. So, as quietly as possible, he crept out of bed in the darkness and went to the door.

"Who is it?" he whispered.

'Tap, tap.'

Gingerly he unlocked the door, and opened it a crack. This was enough for his visitor to slide inside the room and move towards his bed.

Bare feet padded gently past him and across the rug.

A familiar scent assailed his nostrils, and very soon, as his eyes became accustomed to the darkness, he made out the shape of his uninvited guest, who sat upon the floor beside his bed, with a front paw outstretched.

He took it in his hand and knelt beside her.

"So, you've found me again. How on Earth did you get in?" he whispered. He assumed the bitch must have slid in by the tavern's front door just as the last customers were leaving. Either that, or else she'd come in through the kitchen, where the cook often left the back door ajar to expel excess cooking smoke and steam.

"You can't stay here, you know. Not after tonight anyway. I'm sure the landlord won't allow a scruffy young streetwalker like you to lodge in his classy hotel. You can sleep on the floor here tonight, but in the morning you're going to have to leave."

Having thus laid down the law, he got back into bed feeling satisfied that he had put the mongrel firmly in her place.

CHAPTER SEVEN
1878 : VII – A TASTE OF POLITICS

"What concoction of canine breeding is that supposed to represent, Kahrl?"

Rudolf had just walked into the bar and ordered a drink, before turning to face his friend, who sat at his usual table about to enjoy some fruit to follow his Sunday lunch.

"Ah," said Kahrl. "You've noticed the dog."

"How could I not? It's hardly a lap dog, is it? Where on Earth did you get it? And, what's more to the point, why?"

Kahrl hesitated, and then said, "It's sort of adopted me."

Rudolf sat opposite him with his beer.

"Explain please."

"While I was staying at my hovel on the dock, it arrived at my door one night with an injured paw, so I administered some basic first aid. It disappeared the following morning, but ..."

"I know," said Rudolf, holding up his hand. "It waited for you to move into more acceptable accommodation before deciding to take up residence."

Kahrl suppressed a laugh. "That's not far from the truth. It sneaked upstairs and into my room a week ago and, as I didn't want to cause a commotion by kicking it out so late at night, I let it stay until the following morning."

"And then you kicked it out?" Rudolf mocked.

"Actually, yes. But it sort of … came back."

"Obviously. And what do you propose to do with it?"

"What can I do? It helped me out …"

"Helped you out?" Rudolf's eyebrows almost made contact with the ceiling. "What on Earth do you mean?"

Although he counted Rudolf as his closest friend and confidant, he had vowed never to share with anyone the story of Karpov's supposed attempt on his life at the dock. To do so could cause all sorts of problems and spoil what had, at last, turned out to be a positive change in his fortunes.

"Let's just say I had a problem, and like a friend, she was there when I needed her."

"Hmm. Intriguing," Rudolf said. "All right, you can have your little secrets, but that surely makes things even, doesn't it? You helped her, and then she helped you. Debt paid. Goodbye. No?"

"Not exactly. In the first place, she doesn't seem to want to go. And in the second place … I'll admit it. I've sort of taken to her."

Rudolf sat back in his chair. "Oh, no, not true love! I can't bear it! I think I'm going to puke!"

Kahrl took his joke stoically. "I wouldn't say that, but just you watch this. Make a sudden move towards me."

"What, like this?" Rudolf rose from his chair and reached across the table to grab a hold of Kahrl's collar.

The bitch emitted a low, threatening growl, which lasted only for a few seconds, during which time she fixed her gaze on the offending hand. Then, seeing that the aggressor hadn't let go, she raised herself with her back arched, and shifted her warning up to another level, a deep-throated, demonic *snarl*. This attracted the attention of most of the tavern's clientele, but none more so than Rudolf, who blanched and released his grip, sitting back in his seat like a chastised schoolboy.

"Was that the final warning?" he asked nervously.

"I think so, but I can't be certain, because nobody I've tried it on has got past that stage before backing down. It's probably just as well. We'd better shake hands, just to show her we're friends."

Rudolf accepted his offer without hesitation.

"She'll let you stroke her now," Kahrl said.

"Do you mind if I do that a bit later, when she's forgotten about this little episode?"

"All right, but from what I know of her she has a long memory."

"Hmm. And what does your landlord think to this new tenant?"

"At first I didn't expect him to tolerate a dog as a boarder. But once he'd witnessed a demonstration of her talents, he said he reckoned she'd be a useful deterrent to potential troublemakers."

"I've never seen any troublemakers in here," Rudolf countered.

"Well," Kahrl grinned. "Now you know why."

"I can see this is going nowhere," his friend said. "But you haven't answered my original question. What breed is she exactly?"

"None, exactly. She's a dockyard mongrel, though I reckon her forebears must include some robust breeds."

"Robust? I suppose that's one description. But you have to admit – and I'm assuming she won't be insulted if I make an honest observation – she is rather on the ugly side."

"Hmm. I suppose she's not the most attractive of hounds," Kahrl conceded. "She bears several scars that I can only assume are the trophies of scraps with other dogs. But in a way that's an advantage, because nobody's likely to want to try and entice her away from me."

"I wouldn't fancy having her stretched across my hearthrug. Does it cost you much to feed her?"

"Hardly anything. It seems the market traders already know her. She does her rounds each morning to sweep up the off cuts of gristle, stale bread and cheese ends that they toss her way. And she's no stranger at the fish quay. She picks up odd bits of discarded guts and small fry there. So far, I haven't had to lay out a single kopeck on her. Anyway, our relationship is pretty flexible. She sleeps next to my bed most nights but likes to stay out sometimes. I don't worry about her because I know she can take care of herself. She comes and goes pretty much as she pleases."

"What do you call her?"

"Just 'Dog'. If she has another name, I've not yet discovered it. Not one that she'll raise an eyebrow to anyway."

"And have you taught her any other tricks?"

"Tricks? She's not a performing circus animal, you know."

"I'm sorry. I just thought that, if she's as intelligent as you've made her out to be …"

"My dear Rudolf, a dog's ability to understand a human's instructions and then to carry them out blindly is hardly a measure of intelligence."

"Oh? And how would you propose to gauge a dog's intellect then?"

"By its ability to understand a human's instructions, but then, after weighing them up, and assessing them as frivolous, to ignore them. That's what she's good at. Knowing when to say 'no'."

Rudolf opened his mouth to say something, but soon closed it again and shook his head. He drank a mouthful of beer, and then, nodding at what lay in front of his friend on a platter in the centre of the table, he asked, "Well, are you going to eat that?"

"Eh? Oh, this. Yes, of course. Would you like some?"

"That's very kind of you. Yes please, I'd love a piece. You do know what it is, don't you?"

"Yes. The first morning I went to the market I saw some of these, but of course I couldn't afford to buy one. So I promised myself that, when I did have the funds, I'd buy a whole one to myself. This is it. It's called a mango. And I don't mind sharing it with you. Have you had one before?"

"Yes, but like you, as a treat. My father considers exotic fruit an unnecessary luxury, when there are so many perfectly good home grown varieties available at far less cost."

"Your father's right," Kahrl admitted. "But I couldn't resist just this one taste of decadence. I hope it's worth it."

"It will be, I can assure you," Rudolf said, his eyes now fixed firmly on the exotic fruit. "That's if you ever get around to peeling the damned thing."

"I'm just going to," Kahrl assured him, then hesitated.

"How …? What's the best way to …?"

"Hand it over." Rudolf produced a sharp knife and picked up the multicoloured fruit, skilfully rolling it around in his hand. "It's a good example. You have to remember there's a large, hard seed pod in the middle …"

"This is probably the only mango I'm ever going to eat, Rudolf. I don't need a lesson in its composition. Just cut it, will you please?"

"All right," he laughed. Then he made a few deft slashes through the skin and into the bright yellow flesh, resulting in eight juicy crescents lying on the platter in the middle of the table.

"Go on then," he said to Kahrl. "Have your first taste of mango. Best to hold it in your hands. You don't eat the skin, so tear the flesh away with your teeth. It'll be messy, but I promise you it'll be worth it."

Kahrl picked up a slice and, turning the skin away from him, sunk his teeth into the soft pulp, and bit off as much as he thought his mouth could hold.

A tantalising bitter-sweetness spread over his tongue and palate, the like of which he had never experienced. He was about to chew, but decided against it, hoping to savour the exotic flavour for as long as it lasted. But the pulp was so soft and slippery that it slid towards the back of his tongue and throat, forcing him to chew what little remained in his mouth, while allowing the juicy nectar to wash over his teeth and gums. Finally he swallowed the last morsel of flesh, leaving the exquisite taste to slowly dissipate until only its memory remained to sooth his senses, leaving him with a deep feeling of satisfaction and well-being.

"Not bad, eh?" Rudolf asked.

"Not bad? Are you sure this stuff is really legal? I think I've just enjoyed the most wonderful sensation that it's possible for the human mind and body to experience. Well, you've had it before. Don't you agree?"

Rudolf smiled. "I agree it comes a fairly close second to … would you mind?"

"Be my guest," Kahrl said, and watched him eat the second slice. Together they consumed the entire fruit, and then licked the remaining juices from their sticky fingers before wiping them clean on Kahrl's dinner napkin.

"How's the job going?" Rudolf enquired.

"It's been a hectic week. Having a mobile store on the wharf works well. I'm watching and learning as much as I can from Klaus and Gustav, and if there's something they need I only have to nip down the gangway, or walk-ashore as the sailors call it, to the cart and grab it for them. Of course, at first one of them has to show me whatever it is, because I don't know all the names. But I'm learning fast.

"I'm pleased to say I found a good horse. A big strong gelding, though docile and showing no sign of physical defects. He's lucky, because he gets to stand around a lot, and the sailors and dockworkers spoil him, giving him bits of carrot and such. I'll have to watch that he doesn't get fat! But what's the impression from your side? Are you getting any reports back from the captains?"

"From what I hear, they're loving the arrangement. As they and their crews are paid by the crossing, being able to cram in more voyages by reducing the turnaround times means they can earn more money, so nobody's complaining."

"But it means you have to drum up more business, doesn't it?"

"That's not a problem. Because of our reduced costs per voyage we can afford to compete on price and win more contracts from the English agents. Many of them have offices here in Riga, you know. It's no skin off their noses which firm provides the transport for their pit props, masts and spars. So they naturally choose the cheapest seaworthy vessels. That's the positive side of capitalism at work."

"But doesn't your reformist philosophy discredit capitalism?"

"Not the aspect of it that assures the lowest price and the best quality for the final consumer, through honest competition. It's the bending of the rules to obtain an unfair advantage or profit that I'm against, such as profiteering, and unfair returns on invested capital, often at the expense of workers' pay and welfare."

Kahrl judged that he was close enough now to Rudolf to risk a cheeky enquiry. "How does your father's firm stand in that respect? Do you think your crews receive fair wages?"

Rudolf's expression suggested he took the question seriously. "I don't deny we could improve the lot of some of our more menial workers. But it's going to take time to change the culture of those in charge."

"You mean, your father?"

"He can be quite stubborn. He sees labour as a commodity that has to react to the economic laws of supply and demand, just like a supplier of materials."

"Have you told him you disagree with him?"

"It's very difficult. I'm in a delicate position, especially now."

"Because you've been thrust into this new position of Development Director. I understand that. You don't want to rock the boat, so to speak. But eventually, as an insider, you can bring about change. Outside, you're powerless."

"Exactly. I knew you'd understand my position. You've probably gathered that this job I've been given is little more than a sinecure, a sort of learning post, similar to an apprenticeship in a way. It's going to take some time before I'm influential enough to redress any imbalances in a way that doesn't harm the business. And my father wants me to finish my degree before he'll let me take a real part in running things."

"And you believe that's possible? That you can make a difference?"

"Yes, I do. But, as I say, it's going to take patience and time."

"From what you've told me before, your fellow intellectuals don't sound as if they possess a lot of patience. What happens if your hand is forced?"

"I can only hope and pray that that doesn't happen. My inclination would be to bend with the wind, but men like my father would see things differently. Please don't misunderstand me. My father is a good man, but his beliefs and working methods are fixed. He and his contemporaries would strongly resist what they saw as the theft of what they had acquired through their own efforts."

"In which case, there might be only one course of action for the reformers."

"Yes, I know."

* * *

Marijas iela 16, Riga

18ᵗʰ November 1878

Dearest Mother, Father and Brother Fritz,

Thank you for your letter. I cannot express how important it is for me to receive news that everything is going well for you all in Kaive.

I hope you are all in good health. I have taken Mama's advice to eat heartily, and my new lodgings provide me with a hot meal every weekday evening, and for lunch on Sundays. Last week I even had a mango! (It's an exquisite fruit from the tropics).

I have been able to move to better accommodation because of the generosity of Captain Heuer, who has recently raised our wages. This is because of a lucrative new contract with the successful Krutzberg line, which operates from a wharf not far from our dock.

But, enough of the boring details of my work. Suffice it to know that the future looks promising if I continue to learn and work hard, which of course I intend to do.

Tell Fritz that I now have a pet dog! She is an adult mongrel who seems to have taken a liking to me. My landlord has agreed to my keeping her, and I must say that she is proving good company.

I have also befriended a young student named Rudolf, who is about my age. We both like to read and have many intelligent discussions, and so far have managed not to come to blows!

I was pleased to hear that you have taken on a young man to perform the tasks I used to do. I am sure he will be a great help to you.

I will close now, because Rudolf will be coming soon to take me to a lecture that is to be given tonight by one of the professors from the university.

Your loving and devoted son and brother,

Kahrl Johann

* * *

When Kahrl walked downstairs from his room into the bar, Rudolf was already waiting for him.

"Excuse me if I'm late," Kahrl said. "I had to finish a letter to my family. I want to take it to the post office during my lunch break tomorrow."

"That's all right. I'm early anyway. My father and I had a bit of an exchange at dinner, and I stormed out."

"I'm sorry to hear that, Rudolf. Has something gone wrong at work?"

"No, no, it's nothing like that. I hardly go there anyway. You'll remember, he considers my education more important."

Kahrl unravelled the scarf he held in his hands. "What's the weather like outside?"

"Cold. I think the wind's coming from the Urals. Full of Russian spite."

"Not raining though?" Rudolf shook his head. "I think I'll put on my cap anyway. You don't think they'll laugh at it, do you?"

"No. The majority will be socialist students who style themselves on the peasantry. Don't be surprised if some of them are also sporting Latvian peasant mob caps, even though they're mostly from the German landlord class."

Kahrl held the outer door open for him. "Like you, you mean?"

Rudolf laughed. "I suppose so. My grandfather made his money from buying up land and renting it to the newly freed serfs. That was before he invested in shipping. We're what the nobility refer to as *nouveau riche*. Some of the higher born students still look down on families like mine."

"Where is this talk taking place?" Kahrl asked. "In the new town area?"

"No. We'll need to take a cab to the suburbs. We often meet in quieter districts, so as not to attract too much unwelcome attention."

"From the police, you mean?"

"For some reason the powers that be don't like us plotting their downfall, so they send plain clothed agents to keep an eye on us. But by changing our venues, we're able to keep one step ahead of them. Ah, here's a free cab."

He raised an arm and whistled for the rig to stop, and they climbed aboard, Rudolf handing a slip of paper to the driver.

"Best not call out our destination for all and sundry to hear," he whispered to Kahrl.

As they drove south-eastward of the city Kahrl noticed how the standard of architecture soon lost its charm, until some of the areas they passed through could only be described as shantytowns.

"Surprised?" Rudolf asked him. "Don't be. This is what cities look like all over Europe. The industrial revolution needs drones to keep it supplied with manual labour. It offers lousy wages, with equally lousy housing, but also the promise of a better life, to the hundreds of thousands of peasants and country folk who are sick of breaking their backs tilling the land. Unfortunately they don't realise that they'll still be breaking their backs in order to keep their landlords and employers in the manner to which they've become accustomed."

Kahrl coughed. "You sound bitter. Is this the subject you and your father quarrelled over this evening?"

"Partly," Rudolf admitted. "But when I'm talking to him, I find it hard to express my thoughts, and end up sounding foolish and naive. I suppose it's because I look up to him, which I have done, ever since I can remember. It's not easy to face someone you love and respect, and throw everything they've taught you back in their face. So you skirt around the subject, partly out of fear of chastisement, but mostly because you don't want to hurt their feelings. But that's what happens anyway, so that I end up storming out in frustration."

"That's a shame." Kahrl recalled the relationship he'd had with his own father. Compared to that of Rudolf and his parent, it had been perfect, except for those long periods, when he was much younger, when his father had been away fighting other people's wars. But he wasn't about to eulogise about his simple peasant upbringing, lest his friend be further upset by the contrast between them.

Having passed the scruffy townships of the labouring classes, they drove through a kilometre of open land, before approaching an old mansion, built perhaps a hundred and fifty years earlier in the Gothic style. Lights flickered only in a couple of downstairs rooms as the cab pulled up outside the front door. Rudolf handed the driver some money and the two friends stepped down onto the gravel drive.

"Shall I wait, sir?" the driver asked.

"Yes, please," Rudolf said, handing him another coin.

Kahrl fiddled in his coat pocket, saying, "Shall I?"

But Rudolf waved away his suggestion, saying, "My invitation, my treat."

The driver accepted the money with thanks, cracked his whip and drove the cab around to the rear of the property.

Rudolf knocked on the door, and was greeted by a young man who held a book in his hand.

"Your names please, gentlemen?"

Rudolf gave them and the young man ticked them off in his book.

"You're only the third party to arrive. If you'd like to go through to the drawing room on your left, you'll find coffee on the sideboard. I'm afraid we have no servants, if you wouldn't mind helping yourselves."

They thanked him and walked through, Kahrl whispering, "I suppose having servants would have looked a bit odd, given the nature of the meeting."

Rudolf sniggered and made straight for the coffee table. "Black or ... oh, there's no cream. Black will have to do."

Kahrl looked around the room and noticed that all the furniture had been pushed to the edges, and rows of wooden chairs set out in ranks, facing a table and chair at the front.

"Black will be fine," he said, hesitating to admit that he'd never tasted coffee before. His parents had never considered investing in the paraphernalia associated with crushing and percolating the little black beans. Such things were counted as luxuries in Kaive. And since he'd come to

Riga, he'd seen no reason to divert from his usual choices of beverage, either tea or beer.

He took the cup and saucer from Rudolf, nodding his thanks.

"Shall we sit down?" he asked.

Kahrl shook his head. "It's expected at this sort of gathering to wander about and mingle, chatting to the other guests."

"Oh," Kahrl said. In that case, I'll have to put the saucer back on the table."

Rudolf screwed up his brow. "Whatever for?"

"So I'll have a hand free to scratch my nose."

"Why, is it itching?"

"Well, no, but if I keep thinking about it, it will."

Rudolf sniffed. "A gentleman doesn't scratch an itch except in private."

"Really? Why's that?"

"Because … because he'd have to put down his saucer, which he wouldn't be able to do, as he'd be mingling and chatting with the other guests."

"That's why I wanted to leave my saucer on the table. I promise I won't spill any coffee from my cup."

Rudolf sighed again, with a little more force this time.

"Look, your coffee's only warm now. Just drink it and leave both the cup and the saucer on the table."

Kahrl smiled. "Good idea."

He slurped down the coffee, while his friend coughed to mask the noise.

"Sorry," Kahrl said. "It was warmer than I'd expected."

Then he set down his crockery as suggested. "That's better. Now I've got both hands free, I can scratch away to my heart's content."

"I hope you'll try not to though," Rudolf implored. "Come on, let's talk to those two students over there. I recognise one of them from my history lectures."

Rudolf did most of the talking, while Kahrl wondered if the bitter taste left by the coffee would ever wear off. He tried to nod, shake hands, and make the right responses, all in the right places. And he came to understand how difficult it must be to live the life of a young gentleman. It seemed you had forever to consider details of etiquette, little mannerisms, and conversational rules of which he had little or no knowledge. The overarching objective, he deduced, was not to offend, and not to stand out, except by showing off your cleverness by uttering the occasional not very funny quip.

The room soon filled up, and Rudolf introduced him to several of the other attendees, whose names he immediately forgot. One thing he noticed though was that they all seemed to have German surnames, and it occurred to him that he might well be the only native Latvian in the room.

He was relieved when someone clapped his hands and invited everyone to take a seat. A nondescript fellow sat on the chair at the front, and the man who had spoken introduced him as Professor Wilhelm Junge.

All eyes and ears were now on the evening's speaker.

"Good evening, gentlemen," he began.

"I want to talk about a mighty force that presently slumbers all over Europe. From the countryside to the industrial cities, from the coal mines to the timber yards, from the iron works to the vineyards, the common worker toils, waiting for what he sees as his birthright. The right to a living wage, the right to proper housing, to sanitation, and to education.

"Yes, I say to you, these things are a right, to those who give their labour to enrich the fortunate few who happen to be born into lives of comparative luxury."

He continued in this vein, extolling the virtues of the common man, and decrying the excesses of the idle rich.

Kahrl acknowledged that there was something in what he was saying, although somehow it was very extreme. For example, the few controllers of capital he knew appeared to be good men – Captain Heuer, Herr Muller, and his landlord at the Black Pig. On the other hand, he could think of examples of men from his own class who didn't deserve all those things that Professor Junge had mentioned – Stefan Karpov for one.

But overall, he credited Professor Junge as being a very good speaker, no doubt possessing intelligent foresight about the great political upheavals that were likely to shake the whole of Europe and, perhaps, the world.

At the end of the lecture, everyone applauded, some quite vigorously, and the man who had introduced Professor Junge asked if there were any questions from the floor.

There were a few, mostly from young students who wanted to say how much they agreed with Professor

Junge's interpretation of the present social difficulties facing the working classes. Then there was a brief silence.

Kahrl raised his hand.

Rudolf looked at him aghast, and tugged at his sleeve. But he wouldn't be deterred. There was something he wanted to say, and he might never have another chance to express his point of view to such an influential gathering. So, although he was nervous, he nevertheless stood up when the great man acknowledged him.

"Sir, gentlemen," he began shakily, "My name is Kahrl Evardson, and I'm a Latvian."

He detected a few mocking sniggers, but decided to ignore them.

"Only weeks ago, I was a peasant working in the fields and forests of Kurland. I came to Riga to take up an engineering apprenticeship, and was fortunate to strike up a relationship with my good friend, Rudolf Krutzberg, who is seated next to me.

"During this period, I have had the pleasure of meeting and working alongside quite a few people, not just of my own class. And although, no, *because* I am young, and inexperienced, I watch, I read, and listen, and learn. And I think I have learned this.

"There appear to me to be good and bad men everywhere, regardless of creed or political persuasion. The capitalist system is by no means perfect. But if it is to be swept away, how do we know that whatever replaces it will be free of imperfections? I don't ask this question to justify capitalist excesses. I ask because it's something that honestly worries me.

"I'm not qualified to question Professor Junge's analysis. But if, as he predicts, a universal purge of economic and political hierarchies is about to sweep through Europe, isn't that going to require the expenditure of tremendous energies on the part of the reformers? Not to mention the awful consequences of potential conflict, displacement and human sacrifice. So here's my point. Wouldn't it be better if all that energy were directed towards transforming capitalism into a kinder, less divisive system? Why can't there be curbs on profiteering, regulation of cartels that fix prices, and a minimum living wage for all workers? Not an overthrow of capitalism as an economic system, but organised changes that would benefit everybody, and not just the few?"

He sat down, and then stood up again. "Sorry, thank you." Then he sat down again.

Every head in the room was turned in his direction. So, of course, he blushed, looked downwards and fiddled with his cap, which he had just removed from his pocket, in case he needed to make a quick getaway.

But then a very strange thing happened.

Herr Junge began to applaud. His lone clapping sounded weird, though it wasn't to last for long. For soon, most of the other people in the room had joined in the applause, and those closest to him were even tapping him admiringly on the shoulder. Also by now, Rudolf was smiling broadly and shaking his right hand, so that Kahrl had to replace his cap in his pocket with his left.

Kahrl realised the applause was just a sycophantic reaction to the Professor's gesture. When it subsided, the speaker addressed his remarks directly to him.

"Young man," he said, "I congratulate you on your clear and forthright argument. It shows that you have given these matters a degree of consideration. But my advice to you is this. Attend to your engineering studies, at which I am certain you will excel, and leave the complexities of political and economic theory to those who devote their intellect to such matters."

There followed a ripple of laughter from among the Professor's devotees, after which the meeting broke up.

Kahrl turned to his friend. "Did I say something out of turn, Rudolf? I fear the Professor wasn't as much impressed with what I said, as with how I said it."

Rudolf curled his lip. "Pay no heed, Kahrl. He and his kind are fixed in their views. They want revolution, and will always shout down, in their own condescending way, those who don't go along with their ideas. Whenever they ridicule you, it's because they see your arguments as threatening. Just know that I approve wholeheartedly with everything you said."

At this point an audience member of advanced years, who had been seated not far away, approached them and introduced himself.

"Kris Janis Plieksan, gentlemen. I'm a Latvian like you, Mr Evardson. And probably like your father, I'm a peasant farmer. But I read widely, and like to follow these so-called lectures. I suspect they're a subtle vehicle for recruiting potential revolutionaries.

"Don't get me wrong. I'm a reformist. But my priority is to promote the nationality of the Latvian people, not bloody revolution. It galls me when I see one of our German landlords' idle sons make condescending noises towards any Latvian who has something important to say. I hope Junge's insult tonight won't deter you from speaking your mind in the future."

Kahrl thanked him, in his nervous mood neglecting to formally introduce Rudolf. But then, the fact that his friend might appear to be one of those German landlords' idle sons might not have gone down well with Mr Plieksan, he imagined.

After muttering a few polite 'goodnights' the two friends sidled out of the room and went outside to find their cab.

SIX YEARS LATER

CHAPTER EIGHT
1884 : I – A FATEFUL OUTING

A large mirror hung at the foot of the stairs on the wall of the short passage leading to the public bar of the Black Pig. Coming down from his apartment Kahrl always found it a great temptation to someone who prided himself in his appearance, at least, when not on his way to or from work. After all, there wasn't much improvement to be made to a master fitter's overalls when his workplace was a greasy engine room. But when the daily toil was ended, he liked to look smart for social occasions.

It being rather late in the year, he had selected a smart tweed suit with a stylish cloak, brogues and protective galoshes, with a green cravat, topped off with a narrow-brimmed hat with matching green silk band. He cringed when he recalled the rustic clothes of that scruffy young apprentice of six years past. The only concession he now made to his peasant origins was his preference to keep his hair long enough to cover his collar.

Checking in the mirror, he brushed away a couple of dog hairs before acknowledging the rumble behind him, which signalled the downward approach of his trusty companion.

"Oh, so you've decided to come with me, have you, mutt?" he remarked. "Are you sure you're up to the walk, old girl?"

Now advanced in years, the bitch had lost much of her former agility, but she still chose to accompany Kahrl on most of his excursions. And, as long as she wanted to, he was inclined to let her amble along, usually some distance behind him. That had always been her way.

He pushed open the door and entered the bar, where Rudolf waited, drinking and chatting to the landlord's wife. The dog pushed past him and slunk under a table.

They exchanged greetings, and Rudolf reached to drain his beer mug.

"Please don't hurry on my account," Kahrl insisted. "In fact, I think I'll join you in a small one."

He smiled at Karolina and placed a coin on the counter, while she poured him a half litre of beer.

"How are your lovely wife Teresa and children, Rudolf?"

"All well, I'm pleased to say. You know, Kahrl, it was the best thing I ever did, getting married. Having a young family of your own gives you a different perspective on life."

"It must be a big responsibility though."

"That's the marvellous thing about it. It's such a pleasant responsibility, a privilege rather than a duty. And watching the children grow is a great joy – almost a miracle taking place before your eyes."

"Are you trying to make me feel envious?"

"Well, what's stopping you? You're a master tradesman now, and financially sound. Salubrious as your present accommodation may be, I'm sure you don't want to spend the rest of your life living in a hotel."

Karolina was cleaning glasses not far away from them. Kahrl smiled at her, saying, "Here's the reason I've never married. I'm afraid I was beaten into second place by my landlord, the lucky husband who won the hand of this beautiful lady."

"Always the charmer!" Karolina said. "I'm surprised some gullible young lass hasn't fallen for your flattery before now."

Rudolf winked. "I'm inclined to think that several have. But this slippery fish has always managed to avoid the matrimonial net!"

Kahrl studied his beer. "That's rubbish. It's just that the right girl hasn't yet come along."

"Well," his friend said, "don't leave it too long. You're twenty-six and that's pretty long in the tooth in the marriage stakes."

Kahrl changed the subject. "Another drink? I'm sure we've plenty of time to get to the warehouse before the fun begins."

He referred to the huge store that abutted the market area, just a few minutes' walk from the Black Pig.

Rudolf gave him a sideways smile. "Fun? I must say, I've never looked on these socio-political lectures as a source of amusement."

"Ah, but isn't this one supposed to be different? This young fellow's reckoned to be something of an entertainer, isn't he?"

Rudolf stifled a yawn. "He writes and reads poetry, if that's what you mean. No, that's not fair. He also researches ethnic Latvian music and folk songs. He'll probably give us a recital. I gather he has a little group of musicians and other performers with him. All university students, of course."

"Well, that could be fun, couldn't it? Are they any good?"

"I've heard no direct reports, but as their research and recitals are part of their curriculum, if they've applied themselves to their studies as they should, I suppose they must be all right."

"If they're students, then they can't be much over twenty, can they? I wonder what their parents think to their performing to the masses."

"Speaking of parents," Rudolf said, "we both met the boy's father some years ago, at your very first lecture outing, if my memory serves me well. You remember, the one where you got up to ask a question and almost caused a riot."

"A riot? Go on, you're pulling my leg. I do recall the one you're referring to though. God, when I think how I must have embarrassed you! I had a lot more cheek in those days! I soon learned to keep my mouth shut in front of an audience after that."

"More's the pity. You used to speak spontaneously when you first came to Riga. Now you're like the rest of us, always guarded and careful to rehearse your words before you allow them out for an airing. It's a sad reflection on the times we live in."

Kahrl nodded and glanced around the bar, checking that there was nobody present here he didn't know. "You're right. There are too many eyes and ears looking and listening for dissenters from Mother Russia's great scheme. There's talk they want to make Russian our official language, rather than German. The Romanovs won't be happy until the Baltic States are all subsumed into their Greater Russia."

"Nobody can say what the Romanovs want. My guess is they're scared to death of all these pressures for reform. I'm sure their occasional spear waving and sabre rattling is just a demonstration of their strength of will. I think they'll crumble under pressure when it comes to the crunch."

"I'd rather not be around when that happens," Kahrl said. "I'm a pacifist, as you know. All right then, I'm a coward. I admit it. I'd sooner run than fight."

Rudolf shook his head. "Nobody really knows whether they're a coward or a hero until they're put to the test."

"You sound like my father. Finished your beer? All right, let's go."

They left the tavern and walked towards the market, the dog following several paces behind.

"Isn't it a bit strange holding one of these sessions openly in the city?" Kahrl asked.

"This one's different, being promoted as a cultural event. I gather the organisers want to attract some of the Latvian workers as well as the intellectuals. The store owner has donated the warehouse space."

"That's good of him. I hope he's cleared his goods away though."

"What do you mean?"

"It'll be easy for members of the criminal class to slide in among the workers. What's usually stored there?"

"Fruit and vegetables mainly. I saw the porters this afternoon as I walked near the market, moving all the crates up against the walls."

"There could be some fun after all then. More seriously though, it could easily turn political."

"What makes you say that?"

"You said yourself we met the boy's father seven years ago. I remember clearly what he said then."

"Yes, so do I. He didn't appear to have any sympathy for hot-headed revolutionaries though. Quite the reverse, in fact."

"True, but he didn't care much for our German landlords either. He came over as a proud nationalist. The kind who'd be willing to fight to establish an autonomous Latvian state."

"This is all heavy stuff, Kahrl. I think we'd best just look and listen tonight. No arguing. And no agreeing either. Remain non-committal if it gets radical. Remember, you never know who you're talking to, or who's listening."

Kahrl lowered his voice. "You think the secret police will be there tonight then, do you?"

"I'm certain of it."

* * *

The two friends were by now old hands at picking out the plain clothed policemen who attended these meetings. In fact, it had become a sort of game for them. But there were a few uniformed officers in attendance too, standing close to the doors and clearly on the lookout for any trouble that might break out at such a large gathering.

Soon the audience was assembled. Everyone stood, as bringing in so many chairs would have been out of the question. Though most would not have heard them before, when the performers took to their makeshift stage the crowd allowed them the benefit of the doubt by applauding politely.

The young poet's name was Janis Plieksan, though he liked to call himself Rainis. He and his little troop turned out to be very entertaining.

They began with some sets of traditional tunes, played skilfully on a multi-strung *kokle*, as well as a reed whistle or *stabule*, and an ornate but musically annoying rattle known as a *trejdeksnis*. Fortunately the fellow who played the latter used it sparingly. In between each set of tunes the long-haired Rainis would recite a piece of poetry, either from Latvia's literary tradition, such as it was, or one of his own compositions. But none of these could be said to be more than innocently patriotic in a wholesome, pastoral sort of way.

Rainis and his friends next sang several Latvian folk songs, accompanied by the same instruments. These were performed very competently, and were received by the large audience with much enthusiasm.

The songs themselves were innocuous enough, concerning mildly flirtatious meetings between milkmaids and woodsmen, some containing clear sexual symbolism which might have offended a female or juvenile ear, but skirting around the taboo subjects of Latvian nationality and foreign oppression.

As the evening progressed however, the subject matter of the poems and songs became less subtle and more stirringly patriotic, so that openly anti-Russian and anti-German phrases, together with blatant lampooning and chastising of both the occupying races, brought the evening's entertainment to a close with a crescendo of frenzied applause.

Kahrl could easily imagine that many of the ethnic Latvians in attendance would take home memories of the gentle folk songs and beautiful music, together with the culminating message that Latvia deserved to exist as an independent state, free to seek her own destiny. They would thereafter connect those two strands, ever more to associate the idealistic concept of a rural idyll (which, in truth, had probably never existed) with the blurred vision of their country as a sovereign nation.

As the crowd moved out through the large warehouse doors, and the performers packed away their books and instruments, there came the sudden cry of "Stop! Thief!"

Finding himself cut off from Rudolf in the melee and not far from the place where the call had originated, Kahrl noticed a constable in pursuit of a large man carrying a box – presumably containing fruit. He told himself to mind his own business, but his instinct was to follow in case he might be of some assistance. From the eager panting behind him, it was obvious that the bitch was of a like mind.

The thief and the policeman disappeared around a corner, and when Kahrl and his dog followed they almost bumped into the two men, struggling for ownership of the box. Almost straight away the heavy article fell to the ground, so that the contest was now between the thief and the policeman, the first of whom, to Kahrl's consternation, produced a long-bladed knife.

Kahrl stood back, for he knew nothing would be achieved from putting himself in danger. But the bitch, her nature being such, threw herself at the pair and then with a loud *yelp!* immediately fell away, apparently injured. Kahrl noticed a splash of blood on her fur, but she was too close to the grappling men for him to help her, until the policeman too fell to the ground, clutching his side.

Now the assailant made off, only glancing back once, before disappearing into the blackness of the night.

Kahrl had to a make a heartbreaking choice now. He stepped past the dog and went first to the policeman to check his injury, only to find the knife still protruding from the poor fellow's side. He grabbed the handle, wondering whether or not the blade should be removed, when he heard an angry voice behind him.

It was then that the awful shock hit him like a steam hammer. The anger was being directed at him! He glanced in the direction of his accusers, as more angry people gathered behind them.

"Hey, you there! Stop! Hold that man!"

"He's just stabbed that policeman!"

* * *

Appalled at the accusation levelled against him, his first reaction was to try and explain the situation. Surely they would understand. They must see he wasn't the type to carry out such a heinous assault. They only had to look at the way he was dressed to realise he was a gentleman!

Then it occurred to him that most of these people were poor working men, as he had been several years before, to whom the cut of someone's clothing was no guarantee of their honesty, nor of their ability to commit an act of violence.

In an instant his perspective shifted to view the scene from where they stood, seeing what they saw – a man holding the handle of a knife, whose blade had penetrated several inches into the side of an officer of the law.

There could be only one conclusion, and so just one course of action he could take.

He let go of the dagger, lowered the body gently to the ground, took to his heels and ran.

He ran as fast as he had ever run in his life, past the fine houses just beyond the market and far out towards the shanties, before circling back into the city, where he slowed his pace, partly to avoid unwanted attention, but mostly because he was exhausted. He kept to the dark, back streets, avoiding the occasional lamplight and melting into the shadows, until at last his escape route brought him to the back door of the Black Pig.

The sweat from his exertion, having cooled and condensed, now ran down his back in icy rivulets, making him shiver, even as he sneaked through the still warm kitchen, where he tried to ignore the stares of the scullery maids.

From here he took the back stairs to the upper floor and made for his apartments. He glanced to either side of him as he unlocked his door, entered his room, and locked himself in again before collapsing onto his bed.

He lay stunned, his mind racing in all the wrong directions, for a full fifteen minutes, before voicing the inevitable conclusion to his mental turmoil.

"I can't stay here."

There were, apart from his good friend Rudolf, several other devotees of the lectures who would recognise him if described as a wanted felon. Some would be only too eager to name him, as he had by now earned a reputation as argumentative, on the few occasions when he could be bothered to air an opinion.

It would be just a matter of time before there came a knock on his door, and he'd be taken into custody. With witnesses to assert his guilt, there could be only one possible outcome.

So he gathered a few belongings into his old knapsack, together with his secret store of ready cash.

Without further ado he left his lodgings of six years, wondering if he would ever see them again. He retraced his steps and exited the building via the kitchen, once again taking the back streets towards a temporary hiding place he hoped would never occur to the authorities.

* * *

If he had approached the old breakers' dock at this time under any other circumstances, he would no doubt have felt a surge of nostalgia, in view of the many memories of his five years' apprenticeship spent between here and Krutzberg's wharf.

The past year had seen him working as foreman fitter for a marine maintenance firm, where he had been earning good money, sending regular sums home to his parents, even opening a savings account at the bank, and still having sufficient left over to indulge himself and enjoy an active social life.

All of that was now just a dream. Because of what had happened this evening, he would be forced to leave Riga, a city he had come to love and feel a part of, and flee to … to who knew where?

He wondered if Pieter, the watchman, would be on duty, but then remembered hearing that Captain Heuer had retired due to ill health, and that his successors in managing the dockyards had decided that this little outpost no longer justified its continued operation. Had the watchman been here, it wouldn't have presented any problem, for they had become quite friendly over shift changes, freely sharing several confidences. Kahrl was certain he could have told Pieter his version of the evening's events without fear of suspicion or repetition.

But tonight all was quiet, dark and abandoned. The good-natured gelding he had purchased, looked after with affection, and which had served the company well over the years, had long been removed from his stable. Kahrl hoped his new masters would be as kind to the big fellow as he had always tried to be.

The stable was still intact however, and although draughty, for comfort and cleanliness its loft was preferable to the dingy old foreman's cabin. In any case when he tried the door of the latter it was locked, and he wasn't inclined to add breaking and entering to a charge of attempted murder, or possibly even outright murder.

The unfortunate policeman had shown no signs of life as Kahrl had lowered him to the ground before fleeing the scene. He hoped the poor fellow might have been taken to a hospital and revived.

He climbed up the rickety steps to the storage loft, choosing the cleanest remnants of straw he could find, and fashioned himself a bed of sorts. Using his knapsack for a pillow, he lay down and found his thoughts turning to the bitch.

She had taken a slash from the robber's knife before falling to the ground. He was sure of that. But as to the severity of her wound, he had no idea. He recalled their first meetings, and how she seemed to have sought him out. Why, he never really knew. Perhaps it had been the machinations of Fate, just like tonight's incident. In those days he had barely tolerated her, with her erratic comings and goings, but after a while he'd become attached to the mongrel. If he lost her now above all other friends, even Rudolf, he didn't think he could bear it.

Feeling alone and ashamed, he gave way to a fit of silent sobbing, and then, mercifully, to sleep.

In his dreams he revisited over and over again that terrible episode, starting with his innocent pursuit of the fruit thief, and culminated in his fleeing the horrific scene. Each part of the dreadful drama was re-enacted in slow motion, so that he saw again in detail the deeds, clothing and faces of all of the players – the unfortunate policeman, the thief and the two men who had first accused him so vehemently. Their twisted faces danced before him now.

He awoke abruptly, sharply aware of a crucial realisation.

If those two witnesses had been so close, they must surely have seen everything that happened. The robber fighting with the law officer, the flash of the blade as it punctured his midriff, the intervention of the dog, and only then Kahrl's going to the aid of the fallen policeman.

They must have known he wasn't the culprit. They must have made up their minds to falsely accuse him.

And no wonder. For after repeatedly calling the events to mind, he felt certain he remembered the facial features of one of those false accusers.

He had lost a bit of weight since Kahrl had last seen him, but the more he considered it, the more certain he was of the man's identity.

It was Stefan Karpov.

* * *

The following morning he splashed his face with the trickle of stale cold water from the little tap underneath the boiler, and decided to forego breakfast, this being an easy decision, because he had failed to bring along any food. He cursed himself for not including some scraps when he had hurriedly packed his knapsack, but there was nothing now to be done about the stupid omission.

There might be some old, dry tea leaves in the cabin, but still he couldn't bring himself to break in. Besides, he would need matches and dry wood to fire the boiler, and he wasn't even sure it was mechanically sound any more. So his parched mouth and rumbling belly would both have to wait.

What was more important was getting out of Riga before the authorities caught up with him. He would need help in this, and for that there was only one person he could turn to.

By way of altering his appearance he stuffed his hat and fine jacket into his knapsack, and also removed his galoshes. Better to let the dockside mud spoil his fancy brogues. The night's fitful slumber had crumpled his shirt and trousers enough for him to pass for an itinerant beggar.

Thus clumsily disguised as a tramp, he made his way towards Krutzberg's wharf, where a timber boat was moored up, about half its cargo loaded and stevedores rushing about intent on completing the job. He didn't recognise it as any he had worked on alongside Gustav and Klaus. It looked no more than a couple of years old – evidence of how well the firm must be doing, since Rudolf had been vigorously pursuing new contracts to deliver more and more timber to British and other European ports. The ship's name was painted on its hull, the Dama Katrina.

As his friend was now playing a much bigger part in the operations of his father's business, Kahrl knew he was to be seen every day down here on the company's quay, checking with the cargo foreman that loading or unloading was proceeding to schedule, and that all other work to prepare the ship for its outward journey was going to plan.

Kahrl hid behind some crates on the quayside awaiting collection by their owners, and with every transport that arrived anywhere nearby, he fretted in case his cover be removed, thereby exposing him to the general gaze.

To add to the likelihood of discovery, today it looked as if Rudolf had been delayed, because it was almost noon before Kahrl saw him alight from his usual cab.

When his friend walked close to the crates on his way to speak to the stevedores, despite feeling weak now from his hunger, Kahrl managed to issue a shrill whistle.

Rudolf stopped and looked around, whereupon Kahrl moved out, still crouching but within his friend's range of sight.

"Go away, you ruffian!" Rudolf exclaimed.

"It's me, Rudolf! It's Kahrl!"

His friend stopped and looked around. "My God, man, whatever's happened to you? Where have you been all night?"

Still keeping to the ground Kahrl said, "I need your help. Is there somewhere we can talk in private?"

His friend looked towards the vessel.

"Follow me." He preceded Kahrl up the gangplank. If anyone had watched Rudolf's progress, from the gait and posture of the creature that followed him, they might have been forgiven for believing he had acquired a pet chimpanzee.

But the dock workers were too busy to pay them any heed, and once on board, the two made for one of the cabins, of which the Dama Katrina possessed four, for the transport of private passengers.

Once inside Kahrl said, "Before you say anything, have you any food on you? I've had nothing since we left the Black Pig together last night and I'm ravenous."

Rupert felt in his jacket pocket, and handed the contents to Kahrl, meagre as they were. "There are a couple of biscuits here. I grabbed them at breakfast because I knew I was due for a busy morning."

"Why's that?" Kahrl asked, already munching.

"Because I've been at police headquarters until now, making a statement."

Kahrl sat forward. "Why? Did you see anything?"

"No. I told them I was some way behind you, but they were keen to collect as much evidence as possible. What in Hell happened, Kahrl?"

He acquainted his friend with his full and frank version of the terrible events. When he'd finished, he asked, "The policeman … is he …?"

Rudolf shook his head. "Dead, I'm afraid. You're now officially wanted for murder."

Kahrl hung his head as the enormity of that statement hit home. Then he looked up at his friend, asking, "While you were at the police station, did you see either of the two supposed eye witnesses?"

He shook his head. "Everyone was interviewed separately."

"Well, I recognised one of them. Do you remember that Russian foreman I told you about, the one who took an immediate dislike to me when I first started my apprenticeship?"

"Stefan something, wasn't it?"

"Stefan Karpov. I only caught a glimpse, but I'd swear he was one of them."

Rudolf hesitated. "In that case, why don't you come and put your version to the Prosecutor?"

Kahrl recoiled. "What? And hand my head to them on a platter? Would you take the risk that they wouldn't rather close the book on the case with an execution, sooner than see justice done?"

"You could be right. A quick result would put a feather in their caps. But what are you going to do, Kahrl?"

"I don't know. Maybe you could make enquiries as to Karpov's whereabouts. Though I doubt you'll convince him to change his story, as that would just be an admission that he'd perjured himself in the first place. Also he has a history of violence, and I wouldn't want you to put yourself in any danger.

"We may have to accept that there's not much to be done. Anyway, I've already decided – accepted, even – that my life in Riga is finished. I'll leave letters for my landlord, employer and parents, explaining everything, if you'll see they get them."

"Of course I will. But, where will you go?"

"I haven't quite worked that out yet. Ventspils, maybe?"

"But you're known there, aren't you?"

"The company's headquarters are situated there, but I never went to the town and nobody from there ever visited our little outpost. Mind you, if I bumped in to Heuer he might recognise me."

"How so, if you've never met him?"

"My mother always said I was the double of my father when he was a young soldier. And Heuer was my father's captain. They virtually won the Franco-Prussian war between them. No, I'll have to think of some other town. Trouble is, I don't know anywhere else."

"You know ships though?"

"Yes. A good engineer needs to know his way around any sea-going vessel. A post at sea would be ideal. I'd hardly need to come ashore in Riga. Wait, though. You're not telling me you have a vacancy on one of your boats?"

Rudolf nodded. "I checked earlier. There's one on this ship, actually."

"Brilliant! So, would you consider me for the job?"

"Of course. You're more than qualified for it. You'd better stay here in this cabin for the time being. I'll ask the Chief Engineer to show you your quarters when he comes aboard."

"Oh. That rules out one suitable vacancy. I don't suppose it's for Second Engineer either?"

Rudolf shook his head. "Sorry."

"Greaser?"

"Not as lowly as that. Can you do welding?"

"Of course I can do bloody welding!"

"Well, that's all right then. The vacancy is for a welder, to look after the ship's pipework. Bit of a cushy number, actually. But I'm afraid it doesn't pay awfully well."

Kahrl shrugged, smiled and offered his hand.

"Good enough pay for a fugitive murderer, I'm sure."

They shook hands on the deal and Rudolf looked embarrassed to do so. Then he said, "You, know, you ought to think about changing your name. If I register you under your real one the port authorities might put two and two together. You don't need to alter it much, just so it doesn't jump off the page for some ambitious young clerk to recall seeing it on a police poster."

"That makes sense. Well, since coming to Riga I speak more German than I do Latvian, so I may as well become a German, until I can clear my name."

He reached inside his knapsack and hauled out his jacket, removing a piece of paper from an inside pocket.

"What's that?"

"My birth certificate. I always keep it with me. See?" He handed it to his friend, who screwed up his eyes to decipher the faded writing.

"Carl Ewertsohn," he read out. "Is that you? I didn't realised you'd already changed your name."

"I haven't. The cleric at the Lutheran church in Tukums only spoke German, and my father, bless him, had no writing skills then, so that when he said my name the cleric merely wrote down what he believed he'd heard. That was it. What do you reckon? Will it do?"

"It'll have to. At least it'll look different enough on paper, and that's the most important thing. If you're ever challenged in connection with last night's trouble, you can pass it off as an unfortunate coincidence. Just try to refrain from speaking Latvian, and you should be all right. After all, it's a Latvian they're after. Not a German."

"*Jawohl, Herr Krutzberg,*" Kahrl replied half joking, but he felt bad agreeing so readily to forsake his national tongue.

"Perhaps I should make some changes to my appearance too. I could grow a bushy moustache and have my hair cropped."

Despite the implied irony of this suggestion, his friend said, "Good idea. There'll be a barber on board, essentially for the gentlemen passengers, but the crew make use of his services too. He can cut your locks off for you. As for the moustache, you'll have to grow that yourself. I'd better go now. I'll drop by again before you sail."

"Thanks. Just one more thing. Do you know what happened to the dog?"

"From what you've told me, she must have instinctively put herself between you and danger. And, in so doing, she made the ultimate sacrifice, I'm afraid."

He leaned forward and touched his arm, saying, "I know you loved that dog, Kahrl. I'll see that her remains are properly disposed of. And don't worry. I'm sure these elaborate precautions will prove to be only temporary."

When Rudolf left him, Kahrl glanced gloomily around at his surroundings. The cabin had been made up, with a luxurious feather bed with clean sheets and blankets, an inset dressing table complete with vanity mirror, water jug and bowl, as well as a little wicker basket containing samples of soaps and shampoos.

In his present unkempt state he knew he mustn't defile the cleanliness of this neat little berth. So he lay his jacket and some of his clothes on the floor, made a pillow out of his knapsack, and tried to get some rest.

Drowsily he recalled, as a young apprentice, standing in front of the little kiosk that advertised tickets to occupy one of these sumptuous cabins. At the time he had promised himself that he would, one day, do that very thing.

And now Fate had decreed that his dream come true, if only for a few hours, though sadly in these unforeseeable and tragic circumstances.

CHAPTER NINE
1884 : II – A NEW MAN

Kahrl woke abruptly to repetitive knocking on the cabin door. He checked his timepiece. It was mid-afternoon.

His immediate fear was that it might be the police. Recalling his vow to act and speak only in German he called out, "*Gott in Himmel! Wer ist da?*"

The reply came in Latvian, and though he then understood that it was the Chief Engineer who had come to find him, nevertheless he must keep to his plan and feign ignorance of his own language.

So he called out in the Teutonic tongue, "*Ich verstehe Sich nicht!* I don't understand you! Can you speak in German please?"

"Very well," came the reply. "I'm the Chief Engineer."

Kahrl opened the door, as his visitor continued, "If you'll gather your things, I'll take you to your quarters. You'll be sharing a crew's cabin with a couple of Latvian fellows, both trimmers, or stokers, if you like. It doesn't matter, as they're either raking out the coal so that the ship doesn't turn over, or chucking it in the firebox to keep the engines going."

The fellow, who Kahrl judged was getting on in years, seemed to possess a wry sense of humour, and showed no sign of animosity. He might as well go along in the same informal vein.

"I hope they bathe before turning in after their shifts. I don't fancy sharing a cabin mired in coal dust."

The Chief's response was a little less cordial. "There's a crew's sea water shower on the aft storage deck. All male crew members are expected to maintain good personal hygiene."

Kahrl cast a final glance around the cabin to check he hadn't left anything. Unlikely, considering his basic belongings. He followed the Chief into the companionway and through a warren of bulkheads and corridors.

"Did you say 'all male crew members', sir? Does that mean there are some female crew aboard?"

"There will be when we sail tomorrow. But don't you go getting any ideas, young fellow. The cabin maids are good girls from good families. We carry two to tend to our passengers' needs."

"I'm sure they're quite respectable, sir. If I happen to meet either of them, I assure you I shall regard and treat them as ladies."

"Good. Mind that you do then. Not that it's likely, as they have their own cabins alongside the passengers'. And that part of the ship's out of bounds to the rest of the crew. Here are your quarters."

The cabin he would be sharing looked not much bigger than the shed he had occupied as an apprentice in the breakers' yard, and about half the size of the one he'd just vacated, and that was meant to accommodate just one person. But there were three separate bunks in here that looked and felt comfortable enough. Under present circumstances he couldn't really ask for much more. In any case, it would only be for a few days at a time. With luck he'd find something more comfortable for the couple of days in dock in England. As for their return to Riga, he couldn't risk going ashore there, but if the coalmen were Latvians with families he should at least have the cabin to himself for the layover.

He wondered what England would be like. After his recent troubles the prospect of exploring that great country was the only bright star on the horizon. As part of his general reading he had kept up his study of the language, and even taken to striking up conversations with British visitors to the Black Pig. In the main they had been sailors, but in spite of their reputation for rowdiness he had found, once you got them on their own, that they enjoyed chatting about their families, wives and sweethearts at home – just like any other European he'd met.

He had by now accepted his predicament and, regardless of last night's low point, he now felt more positive, and even began to consider how he was going to approach his new job.

He imagined he would be working with the engineering team, dismantling, cleaning, replacing and fixing worn and broken pipes in the engine room and other parts of the ship. Tomorrow, unless the Chief had already planned a standard induction tour of the ship, he would ask if he could explore and familiarise himself with the layout of the vessel.

But the thing that was now foremost in his mind was food. From the rumblings in his gut, the two biscuits

Rudolf had fished out of his pocket three hours ago were hardly enough to prepare him for his new job. But where would he find something to eat at this time of day?

He needed to locate the galley. He wondered where, on a ship carrying passengers as well as crew, would be the most logical place to put the kitchen facilities? Somewhere between the two distinct groups of people, he reasoned. Somewhere close, then, to the passenger cabin where he'd rested before the Chief Engineer had come along and interrupted his nap.

He set off to retrace his tracks and, more by luck than logistics or clarity of memory, eventually found himself back in the passengers' quarters. From here he set out for all points of the compass, hoping to locate the galley, but without success. He opened in vain countless doors in his futile search until, pushing against another, and expecting to find just one more empty cabin, instead he was greeted by the alarmed expression of a pretty young girl in the process of unpacking a travel bag.

"I'm so sorry, miss," he began automatically in Latvian, then checked himself, only lucky that she, too, had expressed her rebuke at the same time, her indignant words overriding his own. She spoke a standard of German so natural that it could only have been the language of her childhood.

"What on Earth are you doing in here?" she demanded. "This is a private cabin! Go away, before I call for the Chief Steward!"

He stuttered. "I … apologise. I didn't mean to alarm you. I've just joined the ship as a welder, and I'm trying to get my bearings."

"Oh," she said in a less aggressive tone. "Very well. I'll overlook your intrusion. But I'd thank you to leave me to get on with my unpacking, if you don't mind."

"Of course, miss," he stammered. "I … I'll leave you now."

He closed the door, sighing and cursing himself for doing something so foolish. And he hadn't even started the job yet! Had she been anything but kind, she would surely have reported him.

He returned his attention to relieving his hunger, and very soon found the door for which he'd been searching. He pushed it open gently and went in. He found most of the food stores locked, which made a lot of sense, as a precaution against both men and vermin.

But there was a large tin with a tight lid, labelled 'Bread', and on opening it he was rewarded with half a loaf. A similar container yielded up a lump of hard cheese, and he imagined these would curb his hunger until morning, when the rest of the crew arrived in time for the mid-day sailing. He reasoned, or hoped, that they would all need feeding, and that he might then enjoy something more substantial.

He filled a jug with some water from a tap at the metal sink, before leaving the galley with his booty and returning to the tiny cabin that he'd be calling his home for the foreseeable future.

After consuming half of the food and water he realised that the light would be fading in a couple of hours, and the gas mantles wouldn't function while the ship's engines were idle.

On his brief return to the Black Pig he had included his writing implements among the belongings he'd stuffed into his knapsack. If he was going to write those letters he'd spoken of to Rudolf, he would have to do it before darkness fell.

So he knelt at one of the lower bunks, which served as a passable desk, and composed hurried notes to those who needed to know about his situation.

Afterwards, he climbed onto the bunk and allowed his heavy eyelids to close. But before yielding to sleep, he was conscious of an image that danced before him without any bidding. Even with all the troubles that now hung over him, he found himself entranced by the facial features of the lovely young girl into whose cabin he had stumbled.

He didn't know how, but he must try his utmost to see and speak to her again soon.

* * *

Marijas iela 16, Riga

18th October 1885

Dearest Mother, Father and Brother Fritz,

It is with a heavy heart that I have to write to you of an unfortunate incident that occurred to me last night.

I had been attending a concert with my friend Rudolf, when I went to the assistance of a policeman who was in pursuit of a thief. Sadly the thief stabbed the policeman and I stopped to help the poor fellow as the robber ran off.

Unluckily for me, I caught hold of the knife with which the criminal had committed this terrible assault, and two of the closest witnesses accused me of being the perpetrator.

Faced with such damning evidence, I had no choice but to flee, and to leave Riga where I would be unlikely to receive lenient treatment for my alleged crime.

For all our sakes I dare not divulge my current whereabouts. The address at the head of this letter will no longer be applicable, as I have been forced to abandon my lodgings. I am safe and well, in good company, and even in honest and gainful employment, in which I hope to improve and prosper.

None of this present strife is of my own doing, but is simply the result of an unfortunate misunderstanding. I am devastated that I have let you down. This was never my intention, and one day I hope to right this terrible wrong and clear my name.

Until then I must continue this present subterfuge, but I shall keep you informed, if only in general terms, of my progress.

I have some savings in the bank in Riga, but I am not presently in a position to access them. I shall enquire of my friends who have knowledge of such matters as to how I might best have them transferred back into my control. So please do not concern yourselves about my ability to sustain my mind and body, as thankfully poverty plays no part in my present predicament.

In the unlikely event that the police should come to you enquiring of my whereabouts, you can honestly tell them that you know nothing, and you have my permission to show them this letter as proof of that fact.

Please forgive my burdening you with my troubles. I hope you will keep me in your thoughts, as I continue to hold you in mine.

I remain,

Your loving son and brother,

Kahrl Johann

* * *

Even though his sleep had been restless, it had also been long. The churning of recent events had given rise to turbulent dreams, after which he had settled into an extended period of physical and mental rest. Even his hunger hadn't woken him during the night, so that when he opened his eyes at about seven o'clock, his first desire was for food.

While still drowsy he stumbled out of his bunk and made for the companionway outside the cabin. He recalled having seen a door bearing a sign saying 'Crew Washroom and Toilets', where he used the facilities and washed as best he could at a sink with a cold water tap. Refreshed, he returned to his cabin and fell upon the mouldy remains of the bread and cheese.

These important practicalities completed, his thoughts should have turned once more to his desperate situation. But all he could do had been done, and there was nothing more to be achieved by further fretting.

Instead his mind wandered and once again brought the young girl's face to his inner eye. Because his recent ordeal had so stirred his emotions, he wasn't sure if their chance meeting was the reason for his change of mood this morning. He only knew that, in contrast to the downward drag of his present bad misfortune, there was now also a warm and comforting glow that suggested something more positive just within his reach.

When encountering the girl, he had supposed her to be a passenger. But on reflection he realised that couldn't be the case. Passengers would only be allowed aboard on the day of departure. No, she must be one of the cabin maids, a co-worker. The Chief Engineer had warned him about avoiding fraternisation, which he accepted as a sensible rule while at sea. Then again, if she didn't object …

But no. If, as he believed, she was a respectable girl, why should she risk her good name in accepting overtures from a man who could be ten years her senior? For the moment he must bide his time. But he was already certain in his heart that he adored her.

He did his best to focus on what lay ahead. This was his first day at work and his professional pride insisted he make some kind of an impression. First he ought to report to the engine room.

Just as he was about to leave the cabin and find somebody to ask for directions, he heard voices in the companionway and the door burst open, revealing two large fellows carrying kit bags. He wasn't surprised to see the two stokers, but from the looks on their faces they weren't expecting to see him.

"Who the Hell are you?" one of them demanded, in Latvian. Kahrl was thinking this idea to feign no knowledge of the language was going to be tedious, to say the least. But he had already made it plain to the Chief that he only spoke German.

So he shrugged and said, in that language, "Excuse me, I don't understand."

"What are you doing here?" said the other big man, in adequate German.

"I'm the new welder. The Chief Engineer told me to bunk up in here with you two." He held out his hand. "Carl Ewertsohn."

Their faces registered neither pleasure nor disappointment, but rather something more like resignation. But after a short pause the Latvian who had just spoken accepted his greeting and said, "I'm Andris, and he's Ingus. We're brothers." He backhanded his sibling gently in the stomach, then pointed to their new cabin mate.

Ingus also grudgingly shook Kahrl's hand.

Kahrl was about to apologise, but why should he? He assumed the ship had managed without a welder for some time, providing these two with a little more comfort than was usual in a three berth cabin. He guessed they weren't happy about sharing again, but it wasn't his fault.

Still, he felt awkward. So he forced himself to concentrate on practicalities.

"I was sent for at short notice, so I had no opportunity to buy overalls. I don't suppose either of you could lend me a pair until we dock in …"

"South Shields," Andris supplied. It's our destination on Tyneside. Do you know England?"

"I've never been there, but I know a bit of the language."

Andris laughed. "Well, if you've learned English from a book, forget it. You'll never understand them where we're heading."

Kahrl frowned. "How long will we take to get there?"

"In a hurry, are you?" asked Ingus, handing him a clean boiler suit from his kit bag.

"Thanks. No, I'm in no rush. I just wondered …"

"Four or five days, depending on the tides and the weather," Andris offered. Then he turned to his brother and said, "Have you forgotten the sailor's first rule? When it comes to your crewmates, don't be so bloody nosey!"

This made Kahrl smile. "It's all right. I'm not offended. And thank you again for this." He put the overalls on over his dishevelled suit, rolling up the sleeves and bending to turn up the ill fitting legs. He was conscious that the brothers were curious about the clothes he was wearing, but if Andris had been serious about that first rule, he felt no compulsion to satisfy their natural curiosity.

"I'm afraid it's all favours I'm asking, but could you show me the way to the engine room?"

"Hang on," Andris said, taking a coin from his pocket and turning to Ingus. "Flip for first shift? Picture or number?"

"Picture!" Ingus shouted, while his brother flipped, caught and turned the coin.

"It's a five. Your shift. I'll relieve you at six."

"Come on, then, Carl," Ingus said, and led him through the warren down into the nether regions of the ship. He wasn't sure why, but nevertheless took it as a good sign that the big fellow had addressed him by his given name.

When he'd shown him the bulkhead leading to the engine room, the stoker left him, saying, "The Chief will be in there. He starts early on sailing days. I'm going up to give a hand with the coal loading."

He stepped over the lip of the bulkhead and closed the metal door behind him. Beyond he heard the rumble, roar and hiss of the steam engines firing up. Peering into the gloom he made out the figures of three men. He recognised the Chief, who was conferring with a man he assumed must be the shore fitter, because they appeared to be working through their handover checklist. The third was another stoker who, mired with sweat and grime, must have been shovelling the fuel into the furnace for the past hour. He hoped the fitter didn't, by some cruel trick of Fate, turn out to be either Gustav or Klaus. A chance face-to-face with either of them now could prove disastrous. But then he remembered that they had both transferred to Ventspils when the old firm had closed down. He approached the two men and coughed.

The Chief looked up. "Oh, it's you, Ewertsohn. There's no welding work just yet. I assume you can handle a shovel?"

He frowned. "Yes, sir, but …"

"Good. We all muck in here. I expect you to do the same. Go and help the trimmer in the coal hold. Loading is behind schedule because of a starboard list. It'll need to be corrected before we leave port. You can take a turn at stoking the furnace later. You'll find her a hungry beast. I want a full head of steam so we can put to sea at noon. Every hour we lose costs money. Always remember that as your basic mantra, and you won't go far wrong."

Without giving him a chance to comment, the Chief went back to his checklist.

So he mumbled, "Yes, Chief," and went off to find Ingus near the coal chute.

'Oh, well,' he thought. 'At least it'll give me a chance to get to know my cabin mate.'

* * *

Trimming and stoking turned out to be the two most exhausting jobs he had ever done. Though he was used to servicing steam engines of any size, which meant drawing on tremendous resources of knowledge and skill, he had never known a task that called on such reserves of physical strength and agility. Shovelling great spades full of coal and redistributing it from starboard to port of the enormous coal hold had left him with aching muscles that he never knew he possessed, in his arms, neck, back and legs. Helping to stoke the enormous furnace that heated the big pressurised boilers was almost as strenuous, and his borrowed overall was soon covered in a film of fine black coal dust.

Though he and Ingus worked like automatons, it occurred to him what the term 'welder' really meant aboard this ship. A general dogsbody.

He was so relieved when the big man told him they'd done enough, and they could both take a meal break now that the last of the coal had been loaded. He'd been thinking he might have to make an excuse, just to take a rest. So they put aside their shovels, dusted themselves off as well as they could, and then made their way to the dining area next to the galley, where a few crewmen were already eating, seated on benches alongside tables edged with lengths of wood. He knew this was to stop mugs and plates sliding off, once the ship was on the high seas, pitching and rolling. Through a hatch Kahrl glimpsed the frantic activity going on in the galley, to the loud accompaniment of rattling pans, slamming oven doors and a continuous stream of shouting and swearing.

When they approached, a young galley boy almost threw two platters laden with hot food onto the counter. Collecting utensils from a tray beside the hatch, they took these over to the nearest table and sat down. The meal of pork, potatoes, cabbage and gravy would have been more than enough for Kahrl under any circumstances, but today there would be no leavings.

"You've some stamina for a little fellow," Ingus observed with a mouth half full of cabbage.

"I don't mind a bit of honest toil," he replied. "I can't deny you're not easy to keep up with though."

"Don't try to, my friend. I've had years of practice. I like my food, though, and all that hard work sharpens your appetite."

Kahrl could only agree with him. He felt as if he could eat a horse, and followed Ingus' lead in shovelling down the simple but delicious food just as they had shovelled coal into the furnace.

"Do we pay for this?" he asked in between mouthfuls.

"Didn't they give you a contract? Food and lodging all found. So make the most of it, matey!"

Just then he heard his name being called out. He looked around and saw Rudolf standing in the doorway. Making an apology to the big stoker, he got up and walked over to his friend, who handed him a small suitcase.

"I took the liberty of going to your room and cramming some more clothes and things in here. I thought you could use a couple of sets of overalls as well. You'll also find a pipe and some tobacco in there. Do you want me to take your letters?"

"Yes please." He took the case and set it down on the floor. "They're are in my inside jacket pocket. Hold on." He shrugged out of the top half of his borrowed overalls, and pulled out the letters, which he handed to Rudolf before manoeuvring back into his boiler suit top. One or two of the crew looked at him, but they must have been strict observers of 'rule number one', because they went straight back to their meals without comment.

"Thanks for doing this for me, Rudolf. I don't know how I'll ever repay you."

"It's nothing. I know you'd do the same for me if our positions were reversed." He lowered his voice. "I've put a few roubles in the case as well, so you're not short of cash when you get to England."

Humbled and grateful, he lowered his voice and said, "Thanks. Are there any developments? You know …"

"No. They're still scouring the city for a long-haired Latvian agitator. They haven't turned their attention to the docks yet. You should be all right here."

"Thanks. Will you come aboard next time we dock, in a couple of weeks?"

"Of course. Take care of yourself."

"You too." They shook hands and Rudolf took his leave, while Kahrl turned and went back to finish his meal.

* * *

He laboured alongside the two brothers intermittently over the next couple of days, and found that in between times he was able to enjoy a fair amount of leisure.

Nobody bothered him much. The Chief's rule about helping out when needed seemed to him a sensible one, especially at sea, where every man depended on the cooperation of his comrades for his own health and safety. It seemed the perfect model for any well run community.

He found he got on pretty well with Ingus and Andris. In spite of their initial annoyance they were good cabin mates, always ready with a joke and interested in where he'd come from, but never invasive if he chose to keep certain issues to himself. They were also tidy, and always cleaned up any mess they made. But this must be a general rule at sea, where sloppiness wasn't tolerated in any shape or form. He found these were ways that suited him.

He was by no means new to dirty work. A fitter saw plenty of that, and it was often remarked that ships' engine rooms were only clean because most of the dirt went out on the fitters. But he didn't like *being* dirty, so he availed himself daily of the after deck sea water shower. It was cold, but invigorating. And there was a free on-board laundry, which meant that you could start every shift in clean overalls.

Feeling refreshed and having again dined well of an evening, he would read in the cabin or take a turn on the deck. Like the sea water shower, out of sight to the stern end of the cargo deck, where the piles of timber were stacked, the small area of deck available to the crew while at sea was aft of amidships, sectioned off from the passengers' exercise deck with a little metal railing.

It was on the third night of the trip, when they were navigating the Oresund channel to the east of Denmark, and while he admired the lights of Copenhagen to port, that he noticed her on the other side of the barrier, admiring the same view.

He was glad he'd taken the trouble to clean himself up and change into something more presentable than his boiler suit. The pipe and tobacco that Rudolf had brought helped lend him an air of nonchalance, though he hoped it didn't make him appear too common.

He realised that he mustn't approach her. Given the speed at which his heart was beating, he wasn't sure that he'd have the nerve anyway. It must be the case that the cabin maids took their evening exercise alongside the passengers – a sensible arrangement, since they must be ready to attend to their needs at all times.

He stood as close as he dared to the demarcation rails without appearing too eager, with two hands on the upper rail, and his right foot resting on the lower one, holding his pipe in such a way as to appear like a passenger who had strayed to the wrong end of the ship.

"You're not going to jump, are you, sir?"

'My God,' he thought. 'She's actually speaking to me!'

He turned his head, removed his foot from the rail and looked at her, while trying to suppress a nervous facial twitch. Then he lifted his hat, and smiled. It was now or never.

"No, miss. I was just admiring the city of Copenhagen. It's quite lovely in the evening, don't you agree?"

Coyly she looked down, shuffling her feet, perhaps fearing that she shouldn't have addressed this person. But he had the curious feeling that she didn't want their conversation to end .

He now had a chance to admire her long flounced dress, decently buttoned up to her neck and only just revealing the points of her pretty little shoes. She also wore a bonnet against the cool night air. She looked a picture.

"I didn't know it was Copenhagen, sir," she said. "I'm afraid I'm not very well versed in geography."

He wanted to say that he owned some books on the subject, which he would be only too pleased to lend her. But that would be going too far. Besides, he remembered that it wasn't true either, because he'd left most of his collection back in his lodgings at the Black Pig.

"Did you really think I was going to go overboard?" he laughed.

She raised her face towards him. 'Oh, joy, what beautiful eyes!' he thought. He hoped the shadow above his lip, the beginnings of the moustache he was trying to grow, didn't look too much like a dirty smudge.

"I … I wasn't certain."

Now for the big question. She would either respond, or run.

"My name is Carl Ewertsohn", he said, flourishing his hat, but not too much. "May I know whom I am addressing?"

She hesitated, and seemed to be thinking very hard what she should do next. She could so easily make an excuse and turn away from him now.

"It's Juhla, sir … Juhla Rachoan."

"That's a very pretty name," he said predictably, though believing every word. But dare he risk breaking this fragile exchange, with an observation that might be construed as being as flirtatious as it was intended to be?

He took a deep breath.

"And, if I might be allowed to say so, a name well befitting of its very pretty owner."

Another interminable pause. It was hard to tell in the fading light, but he thought the look on her face had turned to one of astonishment. Whether that was good or bad, he had no idea. He had better take remedial action.

"I'm so sorry if I've spoken out of turn. I can assure you that was never my intention. I'll leave you to finish your stroll. Good night, Miss Rachoan. Juhla."

He turned to leave the deck, hearing the rustle of her dress as she also moved away. But then came the sound he had wanted to hear. For once he was glad of his somewhat clumsy surname. Her response was feint, but he fancied it went beyond the realms of polite rectitude.

"Goodnight, Mister . . . Carl," she said.

CHAPTER TEN
1884 : III – FINDING LOVE

Juhla.

He couldn't stop repeating her name in his head. It slid so easily across his tongue, as if that organ had been fashioned just to produce that sound. The myriad words that had passed that way before had been mere rehearsals for this moment.

Juhla and Carl. Carl and Juhla.

The linking of the two names was a natural progression, as far as he was concerned. This was the conjoined result of Fate's machinations. A combination that had always existed, lying dormant, awaiting the day and the hour of their inevitable meeting. The rest, the certain unity, would follow. He truly believed that. So strong was his attraction to Juhla Rachoan.

And there was in his mind no likelihood that her reciprocal feelings would fail to materialise. The two had arrived on the Earth for this very purpose. Any other consequence of their first meeting was unthinkable. It was an irrefutable outcome. Fate intended them to be together.

And because of his strong belief that she would from henceforth be an essential part of his life, and since she knew him from the beginning as 'Carl', he resolved from that moment to fully adopt, even in his mind, the name that appeared on his birth certificate. No longer would he think of himself as 'Kahrl'. He was a new man now, with an altered identity. He would reserve his boyhood name for writing to his parents.

Of course, he had to accept that it was possible, even probable, that as yet, she was unaware of the significance of their brief exchange. How could she? After all, she knew nothing about him. He wasn't even sure if she realised that the dapper gentleman she had spoken with on the deck this evening and the unkempt lout who had barged into her cabin the day before sailing were one and the same person. Perhaps it would be best, in future conversations, not to refer to that earlier meeting. Not until they came to know one another better. Obviously he must tell her some time. For there could be no secrets between life partners, as he was already convinced that they were.

Still lying awake in the early hours, and trying hard not to fidget and upset the beauty sleep of his coal hole companions, he now reflected on her surname, Rachoan.

Of German origin, apparently. But not of the nobility or entrepreneurial class, unless her service as cabin maid were part of some peculiar plan to educate her. That seemed unlikely. But no doubt all would be revealed in time.

Putting that aside, his very final thought, before at last falling asleep, was that, in the course of the past five days he had experienced both the lowest and highest points of his time thus far on Earth.

* * *

As he had done every morning for the last few days, following a hearty breakfast in the crew's canteen, he reported to the engine room, expecting to be dispatched again to help the stokers feed the hungry furnace or trim the reducing stocks of coal. But this was not to be.

He was surprised to find the Second Engineer on duty, whereas so far it had been the gruff Chief who had given him his daily orders. He reckoned he'd worked out how they must organise their shifts – twelve hours on and twelve off. But now his simple theory had been confounded.

"No Chief this morning, sir?" he quipped, clipping his tongue for fear the Second Engineer would tell him to mind his own business.

But the Second must be a tad more forthcoming than his superior, and soon provided an explanation for the altered arrangements.

"I gather you're new to sailing outside coastal waters, son?" he said.

"Aye, sir."

"Well, you must have natural sea legs, or you'd have noticed we turned around the top of Denmark just before breakfast. We're out of the Baltic mill pond and into some proper sea. Didn't you feel the altered motion?"

"Not particularly," Carl assured him. Or perhaps his mind was sufficiently preoccupied to dampen the effect of the sea change.

"Huh! Well, I must admit you look all right. You should think yourself lucky. Seasickness may seem a joke when you see others suffering, but you have to experience it yourself to appreciate how bloody awful it can make you feel. Anyway, I'm afraid the Chief is one of those who never got over their first taste of it. Though he's been at sea this past thirty years, it still puts him on his back. Fortunately I'm like you. The rolling around doesn't bother me any more. So I've been taking it easy so far this trip, but I'll be seeing more of the engine room for the next two days."

"Sounds like a fair system," Carl said. This fellow seemed far easier to get along with than the taciturn Chief. But again, the impression might just have been due to Carl's general euphoria.

"I had a brief chat with young Rudolf Krutzberg before we sailed. He confided that you were a close friend and you'd had a run of bad luck. I don't pry into people's business, so I don't want to know anything about that. It was what else he told me that stuck in my mind."

At once Carl's throat dried up, and he felt the colour drain from his cheeks. Surely Rudolf wouldn't have divulged particulars of his recent troubles.

"You've signed on as a welder, but according to Rudolf, you're capable of much more. It occurred to me what a waste it is for you to spend the journey with a shovel in your hand."

He withdrew some papers from the breast pocket of his boiler suit.

"Here are the schematics of the Dama Katrina's pipework and ducting. I'm not one to wait for a problem to happen before taking action. I'm of the new school that believes in preventive maintenance. So I want you to go around the ship and familiarise yourself with the layout, then devise a plan to visually check the integrity of the pipework. Give me a written report at the end of your shift. You'll find me either here, or in the galley. You're authorised to remove any internal panels for your inspections, except in the passenger areas. Any work needed there will have to take place in between trips, unless there's an actual leak. And don't worry about the Chief. I'll explain to him what I've asked you to do."

Carl grinned and took the papers. "Thank you, sir," he said, and went away feeling glad to be making better use of his abilities.

* * *

He did what the Second Engineer had directed him to do. Many, he knew, would consider the work uninteresting. But it knocked the socks off shovelling coal.

Also, though rudimentary, for once it required using the skills of his trade, so in that way it was more satisfying. Not that he looked down at all on those who performed the most menial jobs on board. Every function had its value, and in some ways keeping the boilers fuelled to drive the propeller must be among the most vital tasks on the ship.

He worked diligently all that day, even whistling some of the folk tunes he remembered from the recent recital given by Rainis and his friends. But he broke off, recalling how, soon after hearing those tunes, his whole world had been turned upside down. He carried on working in silence, reflecting on the darker side of his recent history, but after a while he fell naturally into whistling again.

At the end of the shift he delivered his day's report to the Second, who seemed satisfied with it. Eagerly then, Carl went first to the galley, where he ate sparingly, for he was far too excited to have much of an appetite. Then after a refreshing shower he spent some time flitting between the washroom and his berth, making himself presentable for his delectable cabin maid.

This was all much to the amusement of the two stokers.

"I think our little friend has another rendezvous tonight," Andris cajoled. For the life of him Carl couldn't see how he knew anything about his earlier liaison.

"Only with the stars," he parried. "Don't you know I'm interested in astronomy? I'm dressing in my warmest clothes against the autumn night air."

"Well," Ingus pitched in, "it seems funny to me that your warmest clothes happen also to be your courting clothes!"

"Have you two nothing better to do than creep around spying on me?" he retaliated. "Because I can see no other way that you could know anything about my business! Besides, whom am I supposed to be meeting on the all male crew deck?"

They both cracked up laughing then. Carl pursed his lips, unable to see the joke.

"Ah, little fellow!" Andris said cheerily. "I'm afraid you gave yourself away last night while you were sleeping!"

Carl was astonished. He was certain he'd never talked in his sleep before. But how could he be so sure? For the past six years he'd slept in a brick-walled bedroom with only his trusty hound gently snoring on the floor beside him. He could hardly refute Andris' observation on the grounds that his dog had never complained!

"Juhla!" Ingus mocked. "Juhla, I love you!" And they both dissolved into fits again.

There was nothing Carl could say if he wanted to retain their goodwill – such as it was.

But Andris made a good fist of a reconciliation by saying, just before he left them, "Good luck, young friend. Honestly, I mean it. I hope things go well for you."

He forced a smile at the door and then turned to go.

But then he heard Ingus' voice shouting after him, "But we want to hear all the juicy details when you get back!"

* * *

He made his way to the recreation deck and took up his usual position next to the little railings. As the Second Engineer had said earlier, there was a marked difference in the sea condition. Now that they were crossing the North Sea proper, there was something of a swell on, producing waves big enough to rock and roll the ship about indiscriminately.

He had intended to adopt his nonchalant pose, as on the previous evening, with one foot on the lower rail and both hands on the top one. But on attempting this, he soon found the position untenable, for the motion of the ship on the churning water pulled him, first in one direction, then in another, until he thought his shoulders risked dislocation from the strain. So instead he stepped backwards, leaning against the iron wall of the stairwell behind him, his feet planted in a fixed position, and his trunk swaying from side to side to compensate as best it could for the vessel's haphazard gyrations.

Looking seaward, there wasn't much in view of any note. They had by now swung far enough away from the Danish coast to remove any evidence of that country's existence. The light mist that hovered over the surface of the sea, making the whole scene look and feel quite eerie, also hampered visibility. However, in spite of the undulating motion, he felt no inward signs of seasickness, and for that he counted himself fortunate.

He had earlier decided to complete his devil-may-care stance by lighting a pipe, but somehow he felt his arms and legs had enough to occupy them in keeping him upright. So he merely stood, and swayed, and waited.

And waited.

He must have waited for at least an hour and a half, but she didn't appear. He even plucked up the courage to call out her name a couple of times, in case she stood out of sight some way away from the little dividing railing, afraid of venturing too far because of the ship's motion. But by then a fresh breeze had sprung up and the noise of it muffled his feeble calls.

It was then that he began to feel badly done to, even annoyed. Ignoring the fact that they hadn't actually agreed to meet again, he felt let down, and made to feel foolish.

Worse, he would have to come up with a face-saving lie when interrogated by the stokers.

Humiliated and deflated, he decided to let the experience serve as a lesson, and never more to take the beguiling charms of a pretty young girl so seriously. After five more minutes he gave it up and returned to his cabin.

Once there he put on a brave face for his mates, so that when they asked him, "Well, how did it go?" he replied blankly, "Very well, thanks."

Then he undressed and tried to sleep, hoping he wouldn't wake either of them in the early hours by cursing womankind in general, and one fickle cabin maid in particular.

* * *

His only course of action was to throw himself into his work for the next couple of days at sea before docking at South Shields. Needless to say he didn't waste any more time getting his best clothes soaked by standing in the sea spray on the recreation deck, based on the slim chance that Juhla should deign to put in an appearance.

They docked in the middle of the afternoon of the fifth day, and under normal circumstances he should have been excited to be arriving in a new place. And even more thrilling, a new country.

He had read much about England and it had always interested him. After all, it was the world leader in both industrial and military terms. In view of its economic and innovative superiority, he imagined that Englishmen would be arrogant and puffed up. But when Ingus and Andris introduced him to the dockland alehouses, it soon became clear that the people (the working classes, at least) seemed as varied in their manners and attitudes as did the citizens of Latvia.

They had all drawn advances against their pay, to see them through the next two days, the balance of which would be settled when they returned to Riga, and usefully this had been provided in the equivalent British currency. Their advances amounted to eighteen English pence apiece, comprising a bright silvery coin called a shilling plus a smaller one known as sixpence (or colloquially as a tanner, or a sprat, or even a kick). Twenty shillings comprised an English sovereign – although few of these were on view in the public houses they visited.

Rubbing his advance coins together in his pocket as they walked down the gangway, he asked his companions, "What are we going to spend our money on?"

"We're going to try and get you cheered up, for a start," Andris said. "I'm sick of seeing your miserable face every time I look at you. I'm guessing this isn't the first time you've been given the cold shoulder by a girl, and nor will it be the last. We've all had some of that. Isn't that right, Ingus?"

"You've got to learn to take the rough with the smooth," his brother sermonised.

If they only knew.

But he knew that in one respect they were right, even if they had no knowledge of the far greater misfortune that had recently visited him. There was nothing to be gained from moping and feeling sorry for himself. Life had to go on.

"Yes, but what will eighteen pence buy us?" he said as they walked along the quayside towards the little town.

"It'll buy us beer, eatables and a doss house bed for two days – and nights!" Ingus leered, slapping him heartily on the back as he said it.

"I've never been a great drinker," he confided.

"Well, now's the time for you to learn. Mind you, you'll find English ale's nothing like Latvian beer. You've got to give it a chance to grow on you. But if you don't like it, there's always Jamaican rum. I never met a sailor who didn't like that!"

The prospect of drinking lessons with these two didn't exactly fill him with joy. But they were just being kind, in probably the only way they knew. How could he throw their good natures back in their faces?

Setting aside the gory details, suffice it to say that he ended up in his bunk on the ship that night having learned his lesson well. His two mentors had suggested they visit as many pubs as possible and consume a pint of ale in each. The plan worked well until, in the fifth alehouse they'd patronised, he disgraced himself by being sick over the bar room floor. Though he expected this to result in his ejection, instead the mishap only evoked hilarity among the clientele. A skivvy was sent in bearing sawdust, shovel and mop bucket, the mess was soon cleared up and the drinking continued as before.

Not for Carl, though. What little sense he still had was enough for him to admit that he'd had enough. He tipped the skivvy a penny for her trouble, bade farewell to his companions and staggered back to the ship.

Just before negotiating the gangway he happened to look up and noticed a face peering out through one of the passenger cabin portholes. He thought nothing of it and intended making his way to his quarters. At some point – he wasn't sure where, because his befuddled mind was in no condition to take note of such details – a young woman approached him and stuffed something into his jacket pocket. She glanced at his drunken face and then turned away, returning to wherever she'd come from.

Next thing he knew, he had reached his berth, where he slipped out of his now dishevelled best suit, fell into his bunk, and was at last able to close his eyes. But each time he did, the cabin and the whole world beyond it seemed to whirl around him, invoking an intense desire to be sick again. He so desperately wanted to go to sleep, but couldn't fend off this dreadful nausea. Finally he forced his legs out of the bunk, dropped to the floor and dragged himself to the toilet, where he relieved his stomach of its poisonous contents. Only then was he able to return to his bunk, allow his eyelids to fall and drift into a mercifully comforting slumber.

* * *

He awoke with the dawn. Since leaving the farm seven years earlier he had grown out of the habit because, he assumed, it no longer fitted in with his lifestyle. But this morning, for whatever reason, his body's internal clock must have reverted to type. He didn't know why. Perhaps it had something to do with the hammer pounding on his skull from the inside.

One glance confirmed that his two friends must have found the beds they were hoping for, whether doss house or whore house, somewhere in the town.

He staggered to the washroom and splashed his face with cold water, then returned to pick up his suit from the floor where he'd dropped it before turning in. He straightened out the trousers and jacket as best he could, then carefully hung them up inside the little cabinet at the end of the bunks.

It was then that he remembered the woman who had approached him on his way to the cabin, and felt inside his jacket pocket. He withdrew the little piece of folded paper and pressed it out against the cabin wall.

It read, "Please come to cabin maid quarters. Juhla very sick."

CHAPTER ELEVEN
1884 : IV – A WAY FORWARD

He cursed himself, and vowed never again to exceed his capacity for drink. He dressed quickly, glad that by now he knew his way around the ship well enough to find the servants' quarters without wasting any more time.

Still clutching the note he stopped at the cabin door. It was opened just a crack, so that he could see peering out a slice of the face that had watched him stumble aboard the previous evening. He knocked and she beckoned him in. Then he held out the note and mumbled, "Juhla?"

The maid nodded towards the bunk in which his darling lay, and when he stood rooted to the spot she offered him a chair beside the sick bed, saying in Latvian, "Thank goodness you've come," not so much as a complaint but rather a genuine expression of relief.

No time for language games now. He sensed that matters were far too urgent for such trivialities. He looked at his poor Juhla lying ashen in the bunk beside him.

In his native tongue he asked her colleague, "What's wrong with her?"

"She has a high fever. She was complaining of muscle pains and headaches yesterday. She's delirious now and makes no sense when she tries to speak. But yesterday she told me she'd recently visited an area in Riga affected by typhoid."

The poor girl – she can't have been much more than seventeen – wrung her hands with worry. He didn't want to be harsh with her but she must have detected his serious concern when he demanded, "Why on Earth didn't you send for a doctor?"

She looked at her patient. "She wouldn't let me. She thinks that, if the Chief Steward finds out, she'll be put off the ship and abandoned in a foreign hospital. She said she didn't think she could bear that."

He had to agree that her fears might be well grounded.

"When did the symptoms first appear?"

"A few days ago, just as we entered the North Sea. We both believed she was just seasick at first. Then she became rapidly worse. She made me promise not to tell anyone she was ill. I've been doing all of the cabin work and trying to tend to her. But now ..."

His heart went out to the young lass. What she must have gone through didn't bear thinking of. He hoped she took it as a brotherly gesture when he placed his hand on her arm to comfort her. The hope was answered when she melted into his arms and clung to him, sobbing on his shoulder.

Gently he pushed her away, handing her a kerchief from his pocket. She dried her eyes and blew her nose saying, "Thank you, sir. Juhla said she believed you to be kind."

His shame almost overwhelmed him.

There he had been, on that evening when she failed to turn up on the recreation deck when, in truth, they had made no spoken compact to meet. And he, forswearing his feelings and cursing all womankind, and all because of his stupid pride and selfish disappointment. And while he wallowed in his own self-pity, she lay here suffering in her sick bed.

But he would make amends, if it wasn't too late. He addressed her companion.

"What's your name, dear?"

"It's Ruta, sir."

"She must see a doctor, Ruta," he insisted.

"But …" she began.

He had to stop her. "I'm an engineer. All I know is machinery. I'm helpless in even imagining what I may do for her. She has to have expert medical attention."

He approached Juhla's perspiring form, frustrated that every word he had just spoken was true. At first he felt useless, but then he told himself that, as a master of his trade, he had one thing in common with those who practised the sciences. He knew the importance of logical thought.

He felt her forehead. "She has a fever. We must try and cool it. Can you soak some clean rags in cold water, and keep mopping her brow with them?" It sounded simple and pathetic, but the girl nodded.

"Good. I assume the Chief Steward isn't on board?" Ruta shook her head. "In that case I'm going ashore to find a doctor. I'll bring him to the ship. And if he does have to remove her to a hospital, I promise I'll stay with her."

Even then, he wondered how he might hold to such an assurance without losing his job, yet he resolved with all his heart to do so.

He left that cabin and didn't look back. In a secret pocket in his jacket he kept the money that Rudolf had loaned him – twenty roubles. He hadn't intended to use it, but to rely on his wages, meagre as they were, together with the small amount of cash from his room at the Black Pig. But if he must break that promise today, he swore he would repay his friend to the last kopeck as soon as ever he was able.

He ran down the gangway, dodging the coal loaders to cross the wharf and timber yard, having no idea where he was going. In his haste he almost knocked a man over, tripped and landed on his behind upon the hard concrete.

Half dazed, he accepted the uniformed arm of the man he had collided with. As he got to his feet he was shocked to see that he had bowled into a constable of the law, who now stooped to regain his helmet from the ground.

"In a hurry, young man?" the burly policeman enquired.

As they dusted themselves down Carl blushed and said, searching for the correct words of English, "I'm sorry, officer. I have to find a doctor. I'm from that boat over there, and someone on board is very ill."

"Oh, I see. Well, Doctor Strong is the Port Physician. If you can still run you'll reach his house within ten minutes. Now, listen. Go up this street here. You know, where the dockside pubs are?"

Carl knew them only too well.

"At the end you'll come out opposite a big graveyard, you'll see St Hilda's church on the far corner. But go right onto Railway Street – follow the disused tramlines – under a railway bridge and then left onto Claypath Lane. Follow this under a second railway bridge to the end, and then go left again. You'll see the Doctor's house facing you where two streets meet.

Carl concentrated and repeated, "Church, right, bridge, left, bridge, left, then straight ahead."

"That's it. Now, get on, lad."

Carl was off like a shot, shouting, "Thank you, sir!" back over his shoulder while he ran. Clearing the dock area he heard the constable yell, "And don't go knocking any more policemen down!"

He paid little heed to the morning traffic or details of the town's fine buildings that sped by as he ran. All of his powers and faculties were focussed on just this one objective until, as the constable had promised, in a matter of minutes his goal was in view.

It was a solid mansion of two storeys, with a front storm porch bearing a brass plate announcing, 'Dr James Strong, M.D.'

He rang the bell and was greeted by a maid in a black skirt and blouse with a white apron. She looked him up and down.

"Yes?"

"I must see the Doctor, please, miss," he said, fighting for breath.

"Are you ill?" she asked. He was relieved that her accent wasn't as strong as those he'd tried to decipher in the pubs he'd visited the night before. He fumbled for the appropriate words to get his urgent message across.

"No. It's not for me. One of the cabin maids on our ship has … Please, may I speak to the Doctor?"

She tossed her head, as if inconvenienced, and retreated inside, closing the door, while Carl stood in the street, still regaining his breath and wringing his hands with worry.

After a while she returned and opened the door wider saying, "He might be able to fit you in. Sit in the waiting room please."

There were a couple of people ahead of him, and although he later recalled the room being cold but quite ornate, he was far too concerned about Juhla to take in his surroundings. He did notice that the other patients looked at him oddly, he guessed because of his foreign clothing. When his turn came, the maid nodded him into the consulting room.

He found the physician more affable than his maid.

"Now, young man, what can I do for you?"

"I am Latvian, arrived yesterday on a steamer from Riga. One of the crew, a passenger cabin maid, has a high fever. I wonder if you could come and examine her."

He looked surprised. "On your boat, you mean? I don't know …"

"Please, sir. I have money." He showed him Rudolf's roubles. "I will pay you for your trouble. This is two weeks' wages for a master tradesman in Riga."

Still he looked doubtful.

Then Carl said something that made the Doctor almost jump out of his plush leather chair.

"She says she has been in contact with some typhoid patients."

"In that case," he said, "I must see her without delay."

Already he was donning a cloak and top hat, looking, Carl thought, as if he were on his way to the opera. He called out to his maid, "Hattie, go and hail us a cab."

He collected his bag and beckoned Carl to follow him. A cab was soon to hand and they climbed aboard. Doctor Strong urged the driver to use his whip if necessary, and turned to Carl with a statement that sent shock waves through his body.

"You realise, of course, that if this does turn out to be typhoid, our Public Health Authority may well insist the ship be quarantined?"

If that were the case, then Carl would definitely lose his job. But it was more for Juhla's sake than for fear of this consequence that he uttered a silent prayer to whatever higher power might be listening.

Arriving on the quay Doctor Strong paid the cab and sent it away, then urged Carl to lead him to the patient. Once inside her cabin, the Doctor approached Juhla and unfastened his bag. Then he turned to Carl and asked, "Are you this young woman's husband, sir?"

"No," he said, shocked at the suggestion.

"In that case, I think it would be appropriate for you to wait outside."

"Yes, sir," he mumbled, backing into the companionway. Juhla's colleague then closed the cabin door, leaving him alone.

During the long ten minutes of the examination Carl went through all kinds of agony, worrying about what was going to become of this girl who seemed to have placed so much trust in him, on the basis of one short and trivial conversation. Did he have the right to imagine that this meant she cared for him in some small way? If so, was Fate once again going to intervene and spoil something he'd dared to hope might bring a little light into his tragic life?

At last the door opened and the Doctor came out, snapping his bag shut.

"How is she?"

"She'll be all right. There's no rash and she says she had no other symptoms up to a few days ago. I'm glad to say it isn't typhoid. She's caught a very heavy cold on top of a bad bout of seasickness."

He must have noticed the unbridled relief in Carl's expression, for he added, "Don't worry. If she's kept snug, warm and well fed she'll soon recover. Make sure she gets plenty of hot drinks. Tea's best, if you have it. You did right in fetching me out. It's always best to make certain in these cases."

Carl grabbed his hand and shook it vigorously. "Thank you so much, sir. How much do I owe you?"

The Doctor seemed to weigh him up with his look, as if to estimate how much he could afford. More than that, unless it was Carl's wild imagination, fired by the mutability of his recent emotions, Strong seemed to evaluate this dishevelled young seaman in that glance, in a way that was quite unnerving.

"Give me one of those Latvian roubles. I'm something of a coin collector and, as I've provided you with nothing but my time and some common sense advice, I'll be satisfied with that. And I'll find my own way off the boat. I won't take a cab back. It's not a bad day and I have no other patients, so I think I'll walk. Goodbye, young man."

Carl watched him leave.

Then he turned his glance to where that sweet girl lay, and it was impossible for him to describe how it felt to know that she was out of danger. For a moment she opened her eyes, as if knowing he was staring at her, and gave him an almost imperceptible smile, while her voice murmured weakly, "Thank you, Carl."

He then addressed her companion. "I'll go now, Ruta. But please let me know if there's anything further I can do."

"I will," she said. "Thank you for coming."

* * *

On the return journey to Riga he continued with his survey of the ship's pipework, making his report each morning, first to the Second Engineer and, during the latter and less rocky part of the trip, to the Chief. The Second must have convinced him that this was a better use of his time and skills than developing calluses on his hands from handling a coal shovel.

He received daily reports from Juhla's companion, by way of notes pushed under his cabin door, concerning her state of health. To avoid their ribbing, in the presence of his cabin mates he gave the air of patience and neutrality. But in reality he could hardly wait until she was well enough to meet him once more on the recreation deck.

It was the day before they were due to dock that a note arrived with the simple message, 'Meet J this evening'.

As had been the case more than a week earlier, before Juhla's health had taken its downward turn, Carl ran the gauntlet of the mocking stokers in preparing for the rendezvous. Spruced up and nervous as a schoolboy, he hurried up to the appointed spot and found her already there on the other side of the little railing.

He doffed his hat saying, "Good evening, Juhla. I'm guessing you're in better health today." Such was the opening sentence that he had rehearsed over and over again, which was just as well, as his heart beat so fast that its palpitations threatened to interfere with his concentration.

"Thank you, Carl. Yes, I feel much better today, though I still have a bit of a sniffle."

"In that case," he suggested in all sincerity, "you shouldn't stay out too long in the cool air. I hope you're well wrapped up against the elements."

She stepped towards him so that he could see a stout scarf around her neck and a bonnet tied tightly upon her head. She also wore a thick cloak about her shoulders.

"See," she said, "I'm quite snug and warm."

Having suggested a short exchange, he now realised that, if he had something important to say, he shouldn't beat about the bush. And the most crucial fact that he needed to express was that he would be unable to leave the ship while it lay alongside the wharf in Riga.

But she pre-empted his planned disclosure with an alternative suggestion that made him reconsider.

"Carl, I want you to come and meet my mother in Majori, in the Jurmala district. I know she would want to thank you for your kindness. It's only a short train ride. Will you come?"

He weighed up the potential risks. After collecting his balance of pay at the port office, instead of returning to the ship, they could share a cab to the station and take one of the frequent trains along the coast to the salubrious suburb where she and her mother lived. His new moustache was now quite well developed, and the visit during his lunch break to the ship's barber to have his long hair shorn contributed much to his new look. On such a direct route, the chance that they should bump into anyone who might identify him as the fugitive Latvian should be slight. Also by keeping to German he should be able to rebuff any such accusation, claiming any perceived resemblance to be coincidental. Aside from all that, his heart urged him to follow where Fate now beckoned.

"I think I should enjoy that very much," he replied. "Though I must protest, I neither deserve nor expect any thanks for doing what any gentleman would have done in such circumstances."

"You are indeed a gentleman," she said. "And if I may be so bold, I must say that I approve of your shortened hair. It lends you more dignity."

Because he had no idea how to respond to her remark, and in fairness to her current delicate health, he decided to bring their conversation to a swift conclusion. But again she beat him to it.

"I'm told we should dock in the late evening tomorrow. By the time we've attended to our disembarking passengers, we shall have missed the last train. So I suggest we stay on board until the following morning, when we may draw our pay and go to the station."

"I agree. And I think we should make a rule, to protect your good reputation. Whenever we're on board ship, we should only meet here with this railing between us. That way, we won't really be contravening the regulations, and nobody should challenge our friendship." He didn't mention that this would also help him resist temptation.

Though the peak of her bonnet partly concealed much of her face, he was sure he detected a cheeky little smile play about her lips.

"That sounds very sensible," she said. "Shall we meet by the walk-ashore after breakfast the day after tomorrow?"

She stepped forward again and held out her hand. He wanted badly to lean over the rail and kiss it, but noticed that she held it positioned for a handshake, which he duly undertook, feeling a little foolish.

"Yes, let's do that," he said. "Goodnight then."

"Goodnight, Carl," she replied.

* * *

As he lay in his bunk, wishing for sleep to come and reduce the conscious time that must elapse before their next meeting, all Carl could see was her face, all that he could hear was her voice. How would he manage to get through the following day, without seeing her at all?

And she was beginning to appear to be something of a conundrum. From what he'd seen and heard of her so far, he would have marked her as genteel working class. And yet her mother, and Juhla herself, he assumed, lived in the fashionable resort of Majori, the summer home of wealthy Germans and Russians. Her surname, Rachoan, was also difficult to place. He assumed it was German, but he hadn't come across it before. Well, no doubt all would be clarified sooner or later. He certainly looked forward to viewing her mother's villa from the inside.

But the fact that there were so many interesting things to discover about Juhla only sharpened his desire to know her better. Thankfully, sleep soon rescued him from this whirlwind of unanswered questions.

* * *

Carl fought hard to quell his nervousness as he set out with Juhla from the quay towards the port office, where a few other crew members were already queuing to collect their settlings. The plan hatched with Rudolf barely two weeks beforehand required him to remain concealed. And yet here he was, willing to risk everything because of his adoration for the lovely creature who walked by his side.

But the pride he felt in having her accompany him more than countered his fear of being recognised. He looked at her and smiled, hitching his knapsack into a more comfortable position as he struggled with her bags. He had never understood why a lady's possessions required twice as much baggage as a gentleman's. She had tried to insist that he allow her to carry at least one of her cases, but of course he was far to eager to impress to allow that.

Having drawn the balance of their pay (in Juhla's case, all of it, as neither of the cabin maids would dream of venturing ashore in a foreign port), he had expected to be forced to set out on foot to find a cab. But the canny cabbies of Riga must have had a nose for crews landing with money in their pockets, so there was no shortage of transport waiting adjacent to the pay office.

The cab they selected brought them to the station within ten minutes, and to his relief they attracted no undue attention during the ride. On arrival, he helped her down, paid the driver and took up their bags again.

"Would you mind getting the tickets, Juhla?" he asked. "I've rather got my hands full."

When she returned he was pleased to see that she had chosen two of the least expensive seats, taking this as a sign that she shared his tendency to be careful with money.

They walked onto the platform and found a bench with space for them both. Placing the luggage on the ground, he fumbled inside his jacket pocket for a coin, which he handed to her."

"What's that for, Carl?" she asked.

"For the tickets, of course."

She pursed her lips. "Now look, I want to get this straight from the outset. I may not earn very much, but it's enough to pay my way. I don't expect you to fork out for everything, just because you're my … companion."

He hadn't ever heard a girl of such tender years speak so forthrightly. He was also intrigued by that little pause. What had she been about to say? My escort? My young man, perhaps? The possibilities excited him.

When the train arrived, they found bench seats in the crowded front carriage, where they were forced to sit close together. The pressure and warmth of her body against his side, even though through several layers of clothing, was something he hadn't anticipated, and he realised it would be indecent to allow such contact to continue. He therefore muttered an apology while straining to pull himself a little distance away from her. Coughing politely, to her credit she did the same, so that they each suffered much of the journey in fixed positions of awkward discomfort.

On approaching their destination however, Juhla became excited at the sight of her neighbourhood. Carl had to admit that he always found the vision of those magnificent villas quite compelling, as examples of a majestic style of architecture in colourful carved wood and stone. In their excitement they couldn't help but wriggle in their seats for better views out of the carriage windows, so that they came again accidentally into physical contact. This time, though, they both saw the latent humour in the situation, reacting with embarrassed giggles.

The train drew to a halt and they stepped down onto the platform. The painted sign at the little station office told him that the name of this particular halt on the line that ran through Jurmala was called Majori. Taking in the glorious sight of the opulent district, he had to ask the question that had been bothering him for the past few days.

"However did you come into contact with typhoid in such a neighbourhood as this?"

"I should have explained. I was visiting an aunt a few weeks ago. She lives in the shanties outside the city. That horrible disease had visited a neighbouring household. I'm afraid standards of sanitation are not very good there."

Now he was even more confused. What kind of family had close branches in districts exhibiting such contrasting conditions?

But when he looked at her, it was to see the dawn of realisation awakening in her startled eyes.

"We don't own any of these fine houses, Carl! We inhabit rooms in one of them. I apologise for not telling you sooner, but the truth is that my Mama is in service to a Russian family. They visit rarely now, but because the relationship goes back to the time of my great-grandparents, we are retained during their absence. It's a most agreeable arrangement for Mama and me."

"Juhla, you don't have to explain your family's circumstances to me. But now at least there won't be any misunderstanding when I meet your mother. So thank you for telling me. But I don't want you to think this makes any difference my feelings for you."

There he went again, putting his foot in his mouth. Having probably embarrassed the poor girl, he began a clumsy apology. But she put a finger to his lips to stop him.

"No, Carl. Don't say you're sorry. I want to believe you mean what you say. Don't you understand how important that is to a girl?" And then she kissed him gently on the cheek, taking his hand and leading him towards a particularly attractive mansion.

He paused to take in its formidable appearance. The house comprised a large main timber-clad structure with annexes to its right, the smaller a low conservatory, and the larger providing additional accommodation, but set back from the main building. To the central frontage of the main structure was a two storey appendage some four or five metres in width, comprising an elegant veranda to the lower floor, housing the front door, above which was a substantial covered balcony, topped off with its own symmetrical pitched roof. The architect had excelled himself here by installing an inverted horseshoe-shaped central support to this upper element. This, the only curved feature of the frontage, stood at least three metres high, in attractive contrast to the straight lines of the walls, doors and windows. The whole was protected by wooden shingles and painted a subtle cream.

Generous planting, especially to the rear, with indigenous pine saplings would, for a future generation, provide the illusion of a peasant house in the woods. A fairytale cottage, but on a far grander scale.

Juhla must have understood how much he was enthralled by the beauty of the villa, for even though she must be missing her mother, and impatient to arrive home, she let him linger until he'd fully taken in the building's majesty.

Presently he smiled at her and said, "Shall we go in?"

Still holding his hand, she led him around to the rear of the house, until they came to a door in the recessed two storey annexe. It was at this point that he realised she couldn't have forewarned her mother of her intention to bring a guest home with her. She let go his hand to open the door, while he stood on the threshold, removed his hat, and screwed it up in his sweaty hands, like the peasant that he knew he was and would always be.

"Mama!" she shouted. "It's Juhla! I've brought a friend to see you!"

* * *

Carl sat in their little scullery, acutely embarrassed, in a comfortable armchair before a welcoming log fire, a kettle set to boil on the trivet, while Juhla explained to her mother how he had saved her life, though ignoring the fact that it had never been in any danger.

He deduced that the two women occupied the lower storey of the annexe to this huge house. He wasn't surprised that their domestic language was German. Nor was he at all curious as to how these descendants of the race that had once ruled his country had been brought down to such reduced circumstances. All families had their histories, and there must always be casualties, or so he supposed.

But at least they were not starving poor. Because of a long-standing arrangement, which by now would be accepted on both sides as a matter of honour, the wealthy Russian owners of this house would forever provide domestic work for Juhla's mother and in time, he supposed, for the girl herself on her mother's passing.

Except that Juhla might already have made a move to secure her independence from the situation. Although at present a mere cabin maid, with her forthright manner he felt she possessed the determination to break away from convention and find her own place in the world, if that was what she wanted.

After the telling and re-telling of his selfless act of chivalry, over several cups of tea, his now empty stomach began to protest (inaudibly, he hoped). Whether or not she had heard his gastric rumblings, Juhla's mother suddenly stood up and clasped her hands to her face.

"Goodness! I'm quite forgetting my manners. You've had a long journey, sir, and must be hungry. Let me prepare a meal for you. Though we're used to simple fare here, I hope you'll find our food wholesome and satisfying."

He didn't protest, partly because he didn't want to hurt her feelings by refusing her hospitality, but also because the fresh air had given him a keen appetite. But why she imagined the simple journey from Riga should have been a trial for him, but not for her daughter, he found quite amusing.

"Juhla, you can sleep with me tonight and this young man can have your room. Now, why don't you two young people go for a walk while I'm preparing lunch?"

He glanced at Juhla, and it was obvious from her look that she found her mother's remark as blatant an attempt at matchmaking as he. In a way it was a relief because, whatever Fate had in store for them, it was good that his presence over the next couple of days wasn't going to be met with any resentment.

Juhla handed him his jacket and, donning her cloak and bonnet, said, "Come, then, Carl. I'll show you some more nice houses, and we can have a stroll on the beach."

Once outside she took his arm, snuggling into his shoulder. For his part, he was determined to take no liberties, but couldn't help but be touched by such simple acts of affection.

And as they strolled past the fine mansions of Majori, it occurred to him that, after all the doubts and fears of the past two weeks, he really did feel as strongly about her today as he had on that first meeting. And now, unlikely as it had seemed from the outset, it would appear that this lovely girl on his arm had similar feelings for him.

"Would you like to see the beach?" she asked.

"Why not?" he replied, and she steered him from the road, between two of the neighbouring villas, through a thin line of silver birch trees growing in the dunes, and finally onto a beach so long that, looking to the left and right, he could see neither end of it. And at this time of year, they had it pretty much to themselves.

Now content to view this beautiful part of the Gulf of Riga in silence, for his part he thought it the perfect time and place to share with her the reason for his serving on board their ship as a lowly welder. Taking all into consideration, and though his heart was in his mouth, it seemed obvious to him that, if he were to wait another year, there would never be a more suitable opportunity to say to her what he had to say.

So he stopped and turned to face her, while she looked up at him expectantly.

"Juhla, I think you know that I'm very fond of you. And I would like to think that you care just a little for me. But, before our acquaintance should develop into a closer friendship, because of my position, I feel I owe you this opportunity to reject my attentions."

She raised a finger to his lips.

"Don't be silly, Carl. You don't have to apologise for only being a welder. I've heard people say you're very good at your job, and you're bound to earn promotion before too long. And even if that means you looking for employment on another ship, I won't mind."

He was about to correct her misunderstanding when her mother called to them from beyond the birch wood.

"Juhla! Carl! Lunch is ready! Hurry now!"

And so the opportunity to disclose the dreadful truth was lost.

CHAPTER TWELVE
1884-85 – AN IMPOSSIBLE CHOICE

Late the following afternoon they stepped from their cab as it pulled up on the busy wharf, close to the foot of the gangplank, where Juhla insisted on taking down and carrying her own bags.

Though he found her serious tone amusing, he tried not to show it. "We are at our workplace now, Carl. We must conduct ourselves as independent employees. I shall see you this evening at our usual meeting place."

They exchanged smiles and he watched her walk up onto the ship, while he paid the cabby from the shared kitty purse that she had insisted he keep for them. This was to be replenished, when needed, in equal shares in order to fund their joint excursions during their leisure time ashore. That had been her firm stipulation, and his arguments to the contrary had been obstinately brushed aside.

As he slung his knapsack over his shoulder, a familiar voice hailed him, and the hearing of it brought on a feeling of overwhelming guilt.

"Carl! Wherever have you been?"

He realised at once that Rudolf's accusing tone was well justified. It made him feel like a naughty schoolboy caught coming out of the tuck shop when he should be at his lessons.

His friend drew closer and, glancing about him to check for eavesdroppers, he hissed, "Didn't we agree you were to stay on board the ship when in Riga? Whatever were you thinking of, man? I've been twice to see you and found you missing! I've been worried sick! I ask again – where have you been?"

Carl's tone was contrite. Andris and Ingus wouldn't be expected for several hours yet. "Come up to my cabin if you've time, and I'll explain everything," he muttered, wondering if he could justify his absence, when he should have remembered his friend's promise to come and see him. And it wasn't as if Rudolf's visits were for anyone else's benefit but Carl's. His infatuation with Juhla had blinded him to his obligations towards his foremost friend and benefactor. He owed Rudolf an apology at the very least – and an explanation too. Once inside the cabin he closed the door behind them.

"Rudolf," he began, "I am so sorry that I allowed our planned meeting to slip my mind. That was unforgivable of me. But something wonderful has happened. Something I could never have dreamed possible. I don't know if you saw me arrive, but if so you'll have noticed a young lady with me. Her name is Juhla Rachoan, and I can confess to you now that she is the woman with whom I plan to spend the rest of my life."

Rudolf's dark expression lightened gradually as he listened. Carl explained that the journey to Juhla's mother's lodgings in Majori had been safe and uneventful (with respect to his fugitive status). When he assured his friend again that he had found true love at last, Rudolf's face broke into a smile.

"How can I be anything but happy for you? I was beginning to fear you were destined to become a crotchety old bachelor. Of course this puts a different perspective on things. But from now on you must alert me to any deviation from your usual habits. I assume you've explained everything to your young lady, and that you'll be spending your shore leave at Majori for the foreseeable future?"

Though he hadn't yet had a suitable chance to tell Juhla the full story, he intended to do so if and when the opportunity should arise.

So he nodded. "Juhla is very close to her mother, and she's a good woman – we get on very well. I feel safe staying with them. But in future, if ever I need to change my plans, I shall leave a note for you at the port office."

"A good idea. And I shall do the same. So remember always to check. Otherwise I shall come to see you during the last few hours before you are due to depart, except in the case of early morning sailings, when I shall rendezvous with you on the preceding evening."

Carl nodded his understanding of the arrangement.

"Did you deliver my letters?" he asked.

"To your employer and landlord, yes, by hand. Both were read in my presence, and each of them expressed his regret for what happened. Neither of them believes that you could have murdered anybody. I was told to assure you that a job and good lodgings will remain available to you whenever you consider it safe to return."

Carl sniffed away the stinging behind the eyes. "I'm grateful to them for that, though I fear that day will never come. I have to start thinking about alternative plans for my . . . I mean, for our future. What about the letter to my parents?"

"I couldn't deliver it in person, I'm afraid. I placed it in the trusted hands of a carter whom I've known for some years, and who travels regularly to Tukums. He promised to make a detour to Kaive on his next trip and give it to your people."

He felt glum at this talk of his parents, but fortunately Rudolf was quick to change the subject.

"I made enquiries about Karpov as you asked. His job as foreman at Heuer's appears to have been the last in his legitimate career. After his dismissal nobody in their right mind would consider employing him. He's established himself as some sort of criminal overlord in the shanties, where he's well known as the worst kind of thief – one who steals from the poor as well as the rich. Being a violent man, as you know only too well, I could find nobody who would agree to approach him, not even when offered money. But he has been heard in the poorer taverns repeating his original account of the killing, and confirming you as the assailant. The only comfort is that he still describes you as a long-haired Latvian peasant."

It must have been obvious that this news didn't cheer him, for Rudolf changed tack once again.

"But you spoke of the future. What path have you been considering?"

"Nothing definite as yet. And if no obvious course presents itself, I suppose it wouldn't be the end of the world to leave things as they are for the time being."

Rudolf gave a little smirk. "I can think of someone who'll probably find that hard to accept."

"I know. The arrival of Juhla in my life will bring its own challenges. But as I feel now, the idea of a future without her would be hard to contemplate. Of course I realise she'll be expecting marriage and children, and that's what I want as well. It's just a question of when."

"Sooner rather than later, if you want my advice, old chum," Rudolf said. "Courting within the confines of a working ship is all right as a temporary arrangement, I suppose. But you'll soon reach the stage where, without wanting to sound indelicate, the suppression of your natural desires will be tested to the straining point."

Carl blushed at his friend's directness, but at the same time he knew he was right. He and Juhla had effectively exchanged their declarations of love. Under normal circumstances, marriage should follow within no more than a couple of years.

"You're an experienced married man, Rudolf. Of course I trust and respect your advice on these issues. I shall give the matter some serious thought."

* * *

The next morning found him in low spirits. He told himself that this was a natural reaction to the prospect of matrimony, or rather to the cold practicalities of achieving that objective.

But he had enjoyed these last two days in Juhla's company, and before speaking to Rudolf he had been almost walking on air. Not that he attached any blame for his change of humour to his friend. But Rudolf's common sense reaction to Carl's good news had made him consider Juhla's likely expectations, as well as his own prospects.

But with a working day ahead, he was forced to set aside such worries and focus on his duties.

On reporting to the Chief Engineer, he was cheered when he congratulated him on the preventive maintenance work he'd undertaken on the previous trip.

"On this voyage though, I'd like you to stay in the engine room, and get a bit of experience of the way things work down here."

He didn't dare divulge that he had nearly seven years' experience of servicing, fitting out, repairing and rebuilding marine steam engines just like this one, with two of those years served as a master tradesman. But still, he was more than pleased with the Chief's suggestion.

"Watch what I do, and if there's anything you don't understand, just ask."

"Do you want me to help the greaser with the lubrication in between times, Chief?"

"If you like."

Carl was in his element. The sight of the huge piston rods and connecting rods performing like great plodding workhorses had always enthralled him, and now he was to get the chance to stay and watch the engines operate during an actual sea voyage.

He was careful to make mental notes of the things that his training hadn't taught him, such as the Chief's reaction when the engine room telegraph signalled an instruction from the Captain or Second Officer from the bridge deck above.

At last he felt he was learning something.

He fell into an easy routine of looking after the ship's pipework and helping around the engine room during the days, and meeting Juhla for their platonic trysts in the early evenings. On docking at South Shields he would accompany her on walks into the town and around the local parks, which they found charming enough. Although they would both spend the nights in port on board ship, they never broke their rule of self-imposed restraint. The end of each trip would see them collecting their pay and taking a cab to the station, from where they would make their regular pilgrimage to Majori and her mother, who made it increasingly clear that she expected news of their wedding plans before many more months should elapse.

The pressure was on Carl, but marriage was out of the question as long as he remained a lowly welder. Though he went over and over the simple mathematics in his mind, he could see no way of stretching his meagre wage to support, feed and house himself, a wife and one or two children.

Perhaps he should have asked Rudolf if he might perform some other task on board the ship that paid better wages. But his friend had done so much already on his behalf that he could never bring himself to broach the subject. For all he knew, Rudolf might well have been funding his pay out of his own pocket. At the very least, the money was adding to the ship's expenses, thereby reducing the profit from each voyage, so somebody was feeling the financial effect of his presence on board. That the company should bear an even greater burden was too much to ask. He recalled Juhla's earlier suggestion that he obtain work elsewhere, but he felt it was too late for him now to explain why he had no employment prospects in Riga. To break the news to her now, after all this time, that he was a fugitive from the law, would only confirm what she must already suspect.

That the man she had attached herself to was of no substance, an aimless time waster.

* * *

In the spring of the following year, during the outward leg of one of their voyages, they reached that point on the route where the ship entered the more choppy waters of the North Sea. Following their usual pattern, because of the Chief's struggle with seasickness, he and the Second Engineer swapped watches.

By now Carl was spending most of his time in the engine room, looking and learning while helping the greaser keep the machinery lubricated. It was clear that the Chief saw his job as welder as something of a sinecure, imposed on the engineering team by the ship's owners. He didn't think the Chief resented this in any way, or at least he never gave that impression. After all, he wasn't paying Carl's wages. To his credit he never probed for an explanation, but Carl had the feeling that the Chief liked to keep an eye on him. Or perhaps he saw him as an extra pair of hands, best kept within reach to help when needed, rather than being left to their own devices. The Second was acquainted with the Chief's arrangement, and seemed content to have Carl in attendance.

Both Chief and Second were inclined to have their meals brought down to them in the engine room, so as to avoid leaving the engines unattended while they ate. Such was the case today, and it was late one afternoon that Carl turned from some oiling to see the Second doubled over and clutching his stomach.

"What's wrong, sir?"

"That bloody pork! I knew it tasted funny. I think it's food poisoning. Send the greaser for the ship's doctor. I'm sorry, son, but I'm going to have to lie down."

With that the poor fellow collapsed on the engine room floor, to all appearances unconscious.

When the medic arrived, he confirmed the Second's self-diagnosis and arranged for him to be moved to the sick bay. On leaving, almost as an afterthought, he said, "Better get the Chief down here to take over."

Carl was surprised he seemed not to know about the Chief Engineer's seasickness, or perhaps he was embarrassed about it and kept it quiet. Doctors could do little to cure the complaint in any case. Besides, what he had suggested was clearly the correct procedure given what had happened. So Carl asked the greaser to go and see what condition the Chief was in.

On his return he made a charade of someone spewing up their guts, which was a clear enough answer as far as Carl was concerned.

During all this drama the Captain had rung down a couple of instructions for speed variations, and Carl had responded accordingly. But he knew he shouldn't be taking such responsibility. For one thing, if a mishap should occur, the ship's insurers would undoubtedly refuse to meet any claim for damages. He had to get word to the bridge.

For the third time, therefore, he sent the beleaguered greaser to inform whoever was at the helm that the ship was without any qualified person in charge of the engines.

Very soon a serious looking fellow appeared in the engine room doorway.

"Who are you?" he bellowed.

"Carl Ewertsohn, welder, sir," he replied.

"And what are you doing?" he yelled above the engine noise.

"At the moment, sir, it looks as though I'm operating the engines."

"Are you qualified to do so?"

"Not as a welder, sir – but I have a master fitter's qualification, my time served working for Herr Heuer, of Ventspils. I also have a diploma in marine engineering from the Free Maritime College in Riga."

"Hmm. Impressive. I'm the Second Officer. Just been rousted from my bunk and appraised of the situation. I'll need to get you to sign some insurance documents later. In the meantime, you'll adopt the temporary position of third engineer. So carry on until someone can relieve you."

"Aye, sir. Thank you, sir."

Carl was elated. This could be his ticket to a better job with improved wages. If he could only convince them that the post of third engineer was a necessity, then it might be possible to make the sums add up and contemplate asking for Juhla's hand in marriage.

On their meeting that evening, though he said nothing to her of his hopes of promotion, he was naturally much more cheerful than he had been in a long time, so that she rewarded him with happy smiles and girlish laughter.

Later as he lay in his bunk he dared to see brighter times ahead, and the prospect of marriage adequately funded was no longer the spectre of misery that he had lately imagined.

* * *

But his sudden promotion was to be brief. The following day saw the Second Engineer back on watch, admitting to be still a little sore in the stomach, but otherwise more or less recovered.

The first thing he did when Carl arrived in the engine room was to thank him for stepping into the breach.

"No thanks needed, sir. It was a real pleasure, believe me," he said with a grin.

The Second made no further comment, so Carl decided to broach the subject that had been on his mind overnight.

While he examined and tapped the pressure gauges, Carl coughed and said, "Don't you think it might be advisable to retain someone in the rank of third engineer as a permanent arrangement, sir? I mean, to provide relief for you and the Chief when required? It would make life easier whenever he's indisposed, I think."

His face cracked into a half smile.

"I don't blame you for asking, son. Our little arrangement to allow the Chief some respite in rough waters is known to the owners, and as long as it doesn't interfere with the ship's progress, and doesn't cost them anything, they've always been willing to turn a blind eye. What you're suggesting would certainly involve further outlay. And in any case, under normal circumstances, it shouldn't be an ongoing requirement. So I'm afraid we've no alternative other than to stick with the status quo.

"But I've spoken to the Captain, and he will arrange for a three roubles bonus in your pay at the end of this trip. But his appreciation can go no further than that."

Carl knew his disappointment must show in his face.

"Besides," he continued, "even if such a vacancy arose, you'd have to produce your indentures. And something tells me you wouldn't want to do that, would you?"

Carl fell silent. Like the Chief, the Second must have wondered why a qualified fitter would accept a job as a welder. He had no reason to believe that Rudolf would have revealed his circumstances to anyone aboard, from the Captain downwards. So the Second must have put two and two together, and worked out that he was in some sort of trouble.

It was true that showing his indentures would also reveal his true identity, for they had been drawn up in his Latvian name – the one that appeared on the police wanted list. He supposed he was lucky that neither the Chief nor the Second had asked him outright about his predicament. That old first rule applying again, he assumed.

He turned to do some polishing and spoke no more on the matter. But he was crestfallen, for two reasons.

First, though the Second's canny insinuation left him feeling in no danger of being exposed, it was discomforting to realise that he was looked on as someone having something to hide, which was absolutely the case.

And the second reason for his depressed mood was the realisation of a fact that would forever thwart his ambitions. He would never be able to apply for a job as fitter or engineer working out of the port of Riga.

* * *

Later on that voyage, one evening after dinner, he and Juhla kept their usual rendezvous on the recreation deck. Having nothing better to talk about, they spoke of their most recent visit to Majori, and Carl mentioned again his appreciation of the variety and standard of architecture of the beautiful villas there.

But not for the first time, he found it difficult to turn the conversation around to matters of the heart. It was plain that she, too, had somehow lost the nerve or ability to express any words of a romantic nature.

Perhaps they were both tired from their work on board, or maybe they had fallen into a routine of complacent acceptance that their relationship was going nowhere. Whatever the reason, it had seemed out of the question even to skirt around the issues of courtship and matrimony.

After their brief and chaste conversation, they parted, as usual, amicably enough, she leaning across the railing to place a sisterly kiss upon his cheek.

Later on in his bunk, the prospect of marriage seemed as remote as it had ever been – for several reasons.

First, there was the difference between their ages. He was now a man of twenty-seven, whereas she was a mere girl of seventeen. When they had first declared their feelings for one another, he had been happy to react to her almost childlike behaviour with equivalent dalliance. But as they grew older, would she find him too austere and serious as her husband? Moreover, would she come over to him as annoyingly immature and juvenile? Would he do better to wed – if that was what he wanted – with a more mature woman at least a few years closer to his age?

Second, what had he to offer? The wage he earned as a welder was just about adequate for a single man. But it wouldn't support a wife and children. The cost of rent, food and clothing for three persons or more under anything but the poorest circumstances would far exceed his current wages. And, as his recent conversation with the Second had established, any hopes he might have had for promotion were as chaff blowing in the wind.

And third, there was the spectre of legal retribution hanging over him, even though unfounded. It was bad enough having to duck and dodge the attentions of the authorities with only his own inconvenience and discomfort to consider. To have to do the same while being responsible for a growing family would only multiply their collective misery.

In his mind he went over some of the things he had said to Rudolf just a few months earlier, about his undying love for Juhla, and how he couldn't imagine a future without her. In his heart he still believed them to be true. But when he seriously considered the practicalities, it seemed clear that any chance of a successful marriage looked very, very slim.

* * *

Embarking on their following trip, beginning with an evening sailing, something occurred that tipped the balance and caused him at last to reconsider his position.

Finding the usual childish mocking of his cabin mates too tedious even to honour with a rebuttal, he made an excuse and went up to the recreation deck a full half hour earlier than usual. He stood alone on the starboard side, watching as the ropes were let go and the anchor stowed aboard, following which the ship slid slowly down-river to join the deep central channel, the bow pointing towards the mouth of the Daugava and the open Baltic Sea beyond.

As she straightened course he glanced across the water, where he was able to gain a fairly clear view of the bank to the north of Krutzberg's quay. This being an area he knew well, he let his eye trace the shore until his gaze fell upon Heuer's old dock and the now dilapidated buildings of the breakers' yard – the fitting shop, cabin and stable block.

Though some distance away, through the clear evening air he had the illusion that he was almost able to touch the shore, and detected some motion around the old stable area. And the more he looked, the more certain he became that some person was trespassing on his former workplace.

Not that it really mattered. That area had long been unused and unloved. If some vagrant had selected the hayloft for his night's rest, well then, good luck to him.

But as the ship drew closer, and he screwed up his eyes for an even better sighting, the size, the shape and, more than anything, the swagger of this fellow's gait appeared familiar to him. And whether it was a matter of seeing what he wanted to see, or even seeing what he feared to see, he was left with no doubt in his mind as to the identity of that person.

He revisited the sighting over and over again throughout the evening, even during his meeting with Juhla, so that she complained that he was paying her no attention, and later still, as he lay in his bunk, incapable of sleep.

He tried to rationalise what he had seen. Karpov's presence around the docks should have come as no surprise. But it had shocked him to see the fiend literally retracing his own steps. How long would it be before the ogre confronted him, either in the street, or near the station? This sighting of his nemesis only brought home ever more clearly the likelihood of his own exposure and inevitable arrest.

And wasn't he deluding himself, if he imagined he could escape the law by confining himself to this ship and clandestine little jaunts ashore with Juhla? Apart from the fact that the police must be actively seeking him, what if one of the crew should report that there was a man on board the Dama Katrina with a name sounding a lot like that of the wanted killer?

He thought again of Juhla, having to endure the poorest conditions, perhaps with one or two ailing infants at her breast, her inadequate husband providing only the most basic of sustenance and shelter. And should he be apprehended, and imprisoned, or even worse, how would his little family survive then? Finding no answers to these desperate questions, his heart grew heavier.

The truth was simple, and awful. For her sake, he must abandon her now, while the consequences of that cruel act, though considerable, should at least be bearable. For his own part, he would have to try and withstand the awful pain of their parting as best he could.

And that was how he came to make the most terrible decision of his life.

* * *

He was resolute in what he must do. However cruel and shameful his denial of all that was dear to him, it was clear that any alternative course of action would result in even greater strife and misery for Juhla.

He loved her too much to put her through that. Perhaps causing her this momentary pain would allow her to forget and even despise him. Let that be the case then, for expunging her affections for him would enable her to recover and get on with her life. She was blessed with her beauty. In time she would no doubt meet some fine young gentleman with the means to provide her with the security and happiness that she deserved.

All that remained was to decide how best to perform the act of betrayal.

He had considered explaining the situation to his darling, relating to her all of the difficulties that for the past months had so tormented his churning mind. But that would just prolong the agony for her. She would try to counter his disclosures with the very same proposals that he had already considered, only to have these dashed by some other compelling argument to the contrary. No, that way would be too painful to contemplate.

Perhaps he could leave her a note. But his twisted logic reasoned that it might stand forever as a symbolic barrier to her forming any new relationship. He didn't want that either.

No. The best course for them both would be for him to disappear from her life without explanation. He would then merely become a cad, a disappointment, a man she once believed she knew and loved, but who turned out to be nothing but a disappointing idler who only trifled with her affections. Ultimately she would hate him, and that would be the kindest outcome of all.

He made no mention nor gave any hint of his intentions to anyone. As far as Andris and Ingus were concerned, he was still the besotted, love stricken fool who had shared their berth these past few months. All in all, apart from their childish mocking, they had been kind towards him and he would be sorry to leave them. But the loss of their friendship would be just another casualty of his desperate plan.

And then, of course, there was Rudolf. A man never had such a friend. When Carl considered his kind acts, his thoughtfulness and advice, not to mention the money he had loaned him, he could almost have wept at the prospect of disappointing him to such an extent. He had considered writing him a note, and asking the Chief or Second to pass it on to him. But that was bound to raise questions as to why Carl himself couldn't wait and speak to him personally on their return to Riga. Though he didn't know much about maritime law, he supposed that jumping ship was a criminal offence. Certainly it was a serious breach of contract, and any suspicion that such a thing was on his mind could cause all sorts of trouble. He must therefore leave his friend to review his opinion of him without any explanation, and if as a result he should come to despise Carl, then let that be a necessary compounding of his self-inflicted punishment.

When the opportunity arose he removed the contents of the small case that Rudolf had given him, and stuffed them into his kit bag along with his spare clothes.

It was a cool April evening when the Dama Katrina docked at South Shields, and the soft mist of a sea fret lay across the dockyards. While he knew Juhla would be engaged with tending to her paying passengers as they prepared to disembark, he took his bag and joined some of his shipmates as they lined up to collect their advances of English coin.

Then he stepped down the gangway and onto the quay, hitched his sack over his shoulder, adjusted his hat, and walked off into the mist.

CHAPTER THIRTEEN
1886 – THE ABYSS

When you've lost everything – money, possessions, friends, hope, self-respect – you do at least have one consolation.

You have nothing left to lose.

Your responsibilities are limited to providing your own food and shelter, with nobody else's needs or feelings to consider. Your initial remorse, akin to a heightened sense of self-indulgent nostalgia, gradually declines to a core of numb recollections, which are easy enough to set aside, with the occasional help of a little rum. A case of one poisoned spirit taking the place of another.

After jumping ship in the Tyneside port of South Shields during the spring of eighteen eighty-six, Carl clung to the anonymity of the shady taprooms of the dockside pubs. Buying the cheapest of food and making his drinks last for hours helped to eke out what little change he had. But the need of sustenance and the solace of alcohol meant his advance of eighteen copper pennies had little chance to burn a hole in his pocket. By the end of his third day ashore he returned to his cheap doss house with just his two overnight lodging pennies chafing against one another.

He must find some work.

His crippled mind and poorly nourished body were incapable of carrying out the duties of an engineer, or even of a welder. To present himself as a skilled tradesman in his present state would see him laughed out of any of the port's machine shops. But he was just about able to use a brush and shovel, so next morning he scoured the dockland foundries and engineers' stores, looking for work as a general skivvy.

This produced a few pence on the first day, enough to buy a little food and pay his doss housekeeper. Anything left over went on rum. Thus he sustained his feeble body just enough to carry on performing the most menial tasks.

Eventually he must have worked as a drone in almost every engineering establishment on those docks, tidying up after the machinists and metal workers, mostly in silence, so as not to risk disclosing his origins or motives. This was his punishment – drudgery, humiliation, and isolation.

He felt like a rat in some scientific experiment, running around an unrelenting wheel in exchange for a minimum of food and water. How long would the rat survive this pointless cycle of work and reward? Would it become absorbed into the compelling rhythm of repetitive activity, or realise at last the futility of its moronic behaviour, fail to cooperate further, and find some quiet corner in which to curl up and perish?

This latter course had never appealed, either because it would have represented the rejection of his parents' investment in him, or because he was simply afraid to die. So he remained upon that treadmill for what he supposed must be weeks, which so easily turned into months. He couldn't be sure, because with the aid of his daily dose of rum he soon lost all track of time, even the tally of St Hilda's church bells announcing each passing Sunday. The little money he was earning was just enough to sustain him physically for the menial tasks that he performed, and to keep him reasonably clean and shod. And yes, to satisfy his thirst for the golden liquor that brought him his only relief.

One morning he ventured out from his doss house, as by now was usual, with nothing in his pocket, to find that all activity on the docks appeared to have ceased. It wasn't a Sunday. That had been just a couple of days earlier. Even then, there was usually some activity, because the tides never stopped. Besides, he'd learned to set a couple of pence aside, as each week progressed, to see him through the Sabbath. Today he was penniless, and almost convinced himself that the world must have ended.

Then a young ragamuffin ran past him and shouted something that at one time would have filled him with a sense of warmth and goodwill. Today, however, the familiar words left him chilled and deflated.

"Merry Christmas, sir!"

What was he going to do for food this Christmas Day? For once in the year, all trade was suspended, even the ship owners acknowledging the birthday of Jesus of Nazareth, the friend of the poor. If He had met Carl that day, no doubt He would have offered him sustenance. But those who worshipped Him were at home now, feasting with their families.

He dragged his weary body to the market area, and found a few scraps of fruit and vegetables not swept away from the day before. But there wasn't enough to sustain him. And then from behind a stall he noticed the glint of amber in a discarded bottle. Some trader must have celebrated early, but neglected to take his remnants home. Perhaps he feared a nagging wife.

The bottle was a good quarter full. He took hold of it and dragged it around with him, taking a sip here, and another there, keeping him company all day, until the time came when he needed to lay down his head.

Having not even the tuppence he needed for his doss house pit, he was faced with the prospect of sleeping rough. Fortunately, though the weather was cold, there was neither snow nor rain. He found a sheltered corner in the market place, where he gathered together some old newspapers, screwed them up to form some sort of bed, and a piece of ragged sacking, which he spread over himself, hoping to retain his body heat.

His mind fogged by liquor, he lay awake for a while, waiting for merciful sleep to come. Through the mist of his semi-consciousness a single thought screamed at him.

He couldn't go on living his life like this.

He must do something about money. All this time he had carried around with him the remaining nineteen of Rudolf's loaned twenty Latvian roubles, and although he had always realised their value, he had never considered that they could be of any use to him in this foreign place. There also lurked a forlorn notion that he might repay his friend some day. In any event, if he had passed one of them across the bar of any of the dockland pubs here, he would surely have felt the landlord's hand on his collar.

But his position was desperate. He needed to convert Rudolf's money into sterling. Though his mechanical training had been thorough, his knowledge of banking, in particular international finance, was at best limited. He needed help. But from where?

Instantly his befuddled brain threw up a face and a name. Trying hard to hold on to these, he drifted off to sleep.

* * *

Early next morning he set off with an empty stomach, an aching head and not a single English farthing in his pockets. With gritted teeth he retraced the steps he had taken a lifetime ago, on that awful day when he had feared Juhla to be seriously ill.

As he had done then, he now rang the bell and the same dour maid, wearing what seemed to be an identical black skirt, blouse and white apron, answered the door. Removing his hat, he felt sure he detected a glint of recognition in her eye.

"May I see Doctor Strong, please?" he asked as clearly as he could, in spite of the hammering that was going on inside his head.

Her reticence suggested that, faced by an unshaven man in filthy clothes, she was searching for an excuse to turn him away. Eventually though, she opened the door fully and nodded him into the hall.

"Wait here," she said, and went off towards the consulting room.

Soon she returned and beckoned him into that office. He must be the first visitor of the day, and cautiously he entered to find Doctor Strong in his waistcoat, standing next to a sink, with shirt sleeves rolled up, and drying his hands on a towel.

"Oh, it's you," he said, smiling. "You're up with the lark."

Carl had no idea of the time. He no longer owned a timepiece of his own, and tended to rely on his peasant body clock. His eye drifted towards the large wall clock in the surgery. He wondered if a quarter to eight might be a little early for a consultation.

He was about to apologise, but Doctor Strong held up his hands.

"Never mind, young man. You're here now. How's my patient?"

It took Carl a few seconds to think to whom he could be referring. Then he twigged, and mumbled, "She's very well, thank you, sir." He should have choked on his words, for it was impossible for him even to imagine poor Juhla's present physical or mental state.

"Oh, good. Does someone else on your ship need my attention, then?"

He tried to clear the thought of Juhla's suffering from his mind. He must concentrate on the situation in hand. He fought to put into words what he had planned to say.

"No, sir. I wondered if you wanted some more Latvian roubles … for your collection."

He reached inside his jacket and extracted the small bag containing the coins.

A profound silence fell on that room, disturbed only by the ticking of the wall clock. Then he heard a hissing in his head, which caused him to inhale deeply to clear his brain. But the hissing became louder, while the Doctor and his maid looked on, their faces immobile, expressionless, as if time were standing still. Then the world about him dissolved into darkness, his legs buckled, and he felt himself falling …

* * *

He came round on the consulting room couch with a blanket draped across him, the Doctor and his maid standing beside him. The maid wafted a small opened bottle under his nose, the sharp tang of whose contents must, he supposed, have restored his consciousness.

"I'm sorry," he drooled, but could think of nothing more to say.

"When did you last have a meal?" the Doctor asked.

"Some scraps of cabbage," he replied. "Yesterday lunchtime."

"And you've been drinking, haven't you?"

"A bit," he conceded.

"More than a bit, I'd guess," the Doctor said. Then he whispered something to his maid, who left the room.

Doctor Strong performed a few simple tests on him, and asked if he believed he could walk without stumbling. He nodded and let himself be helped off the couch. The

Doctor led him out through the hall and into another room, where a table was laid with a single place setting, and a plate of fried eggs, bacon and sausage.

"I want you to eat that," he said. "And drink plenty of tea with it." He indicated a large tea pot that sat in the centre of the table.

The offer was irresistible. Though still a bit groggy, he was very hungry, so he tucked in with relish.

"Now listen to me," Strong said as Carl attacked the meal. "If I hadn't met you some time ago and gained a favourable impression of you then, you wouldn't have been allowed into my consulting room this morning. I might even be sending for a policeman, given the amount of foreign money you're carrying. But I have a feeling you're no ordinary wastrel or alcoholic. Do you want to explain what's happened to you?"

Carl chewed on a crunchy piece of bacon.

"I jumped ship, several months ago," he admitted. "I spent my advance, and those roubles are all I have. A friend gave them to me. I'm sorry to put you to this trouble, sir."

"So far you've been no trouble. But I hope this episode will serve to demonstrate the consequences of substituting liquor for good, wholesome food. Do you understand what I'm saying?"

He nodded, and poured himself some tea.

"I believe you came about that money honestly, so I'll do what I can to help you. If you'll trust me I'll take it to my bank and ask the manager to change it at a fair rate into sterling. Do you mind my asking what you need this money for?"

"To fall back on when I can't earn enough to feed myself. Just a few pence a day."

"What sort of work are you doing?"

"Cleaning."

He paused. Then he said, "You're capable of better, I think."

"Used to be."

He gulped some more tea.

"Let me put a proposal to you. I'll get this money changed, on condition that you allow me to hold it for you. I want you to come and have breakfast with me every Sunday morning for the immediate future, and tell me how much you need to supplement your income. That way, it should last you longer, and not tempt you to go on a bender. Would you agree to that?"

"I … yes. But what about your family, sir?"

"I'm a bachelor. I can please myself. Now, I have to attend to some other patients today, but if you'll return here on Sunday, say, around eight-thirty, we'll talk some more and I'll tell you how much these roubles are worth."

"Thank you, sir. But, please tell me. Why are you helping me like this?"

"For one thing, I have a professional interest in the new science of psychology, and I won't deny that I find you an interesting subject for extended examination. Aside from that I can't sit back and watch a healthy, intelligent young man throw his life away. Between now and Sunday I want you to think about what sort of a future you want. Oh, just a moment."

He dipped into his waistcoat pocket and handed over some coins.

"This should keep you going until the weekend. Make sure you spend it wisely. You can repay me when you're back in funds."

* * *

That meeting affected him greatly. Doctor Strong had looked through Carl's adopted shroud of worthlessness, and seen something of value. For so long Carl had told himself that he was nothing, of no account. But the Doctor made him realise that he was fooling himself. He still had his knowledge, and with a little practice might retrieve his mechanical skills, and return to some serious engineering work.

He was puzzled though as to why the Doctor was so keen to befriend him in this way. The claim that he would make an interesting case for his medical research could only provide part of the answer. He also seemed concerned about Carl's reduced circumstances on a human level. It was strange. Since leaving home he had met all sorts of folk – some good, some not so good. But he had to accept that there had been a limited number of occasions when certain people had for some reason taken a shine to him.

His family back in Kaive hardly counted in this, because the love of a parent or sibling came naturally – or such was his limited experience.

Then there had been Rudolf of course, who had almost adopted him as his 'little peasant friend'. Carl had never resented his patronising way, because he had proven such a good companion, and all of their dealings had resulted in Carl's advancement or protection. It had been Rudolf who had introduced him to Riga's free nautical colleges, where he had undertaken extra studies to achieve a diploma in marine engineering to augment his tradesman fitter's certificate.

Even Herr Muller, his old employer's agent, though at first rather brusque and dismissive, once he accepted Carl's ideas, had altered his opinion and been more than fair in rewarding him as he progressed through his apprenticeship.

Next had come Juhla. It pained Carl to think of her now, but still he couldn't help revisiting that sweet feeling of disbelief when he had first realised that she cared for him.

And now, this professional man, this Doctor of Medicine, for some reason had chosen to offer him a hand of friendship.

Did these people see some quality in him that he wasn't aware of?

Whether or not this was the case, he decided that, if he still had the strength and potential, he would do whatever he could to make amends for the disappointment he had brought upon those who loved him. And in the following few days before he was due to join the physician for Sunday breakfast, he would take time – in between his otherwise soul destroying jobs – to think how he might begin his climb out of this abyss and back into the realms of sanity.

* * *

Doctor Strong had loaned Carl sufficient money to ensure he needn't go hungry before their next meeting. During that time he learned the truth in the adage that what nourishes the body also feeds the mind. With three square meals inside him, as he lay in his bunk that night, he found he was able to concentrate in a way that had eluded him for the better part of a year.

His first firm realisation was that, however mean and pathetic had been his choice of work, he had at least during that horrible period worked and cleaned out just about every warehouse, fitting shop, coppersmith's forge and shipwright's premises on that dock. He knew every fitter, mate and foreman who walked its wharves and worked on its vessels, from old rusty tubs to the brightest new steam trawlers. The range of potential work was immense, and all he had to do was convince someone that he was a capable engineer – and give him a chance to prove as much.

He put these ideas to Doctor Strong at his breakfast table on the following Sunday.

"That's very good, Carl," he said. "You're beginning to think positively. I'm convinced that positive thinking can bring about a change in one's mental state."

"But it takes intervention, sir. If I hadn't come to see you, I believe I should have been in the same state."

"And how would you describe the state of mind you were in?"

"I felt worthless, depressed. But it was self-inflicted. A stronger man would never have debased himself as I did. I even recall a moment when I almost felt less than human, and derived a perverse satisfaction from being so."

"That's very interesting," he said. "We must talk more about this some time. But tell me, what do you propose to do now?"

"If you'll let me have some of my money, I want to buy some new boots, overalls and basic tools. How much did your banker let you have for my roubles?"

"The best rate he could give me was ten roubles to the pound. So your nineteen roubles yielded one pound and eighteen shillings. Will that be enough to put you back on your feet and give you time to find a decent job?"

"Doctor, you wouldn't believe how little I've been existing on for the past nine months. This will be more than enough. I'll need five shillings of it to kit myself out."

There was a rare skip in his step as he left the Doctor's house and made his way back towards his lodgings. The next morning would see him in the chandler's shop to make his purchases. Then, proud in his smart new working gear, he would visit each fitting shop in turn until he found one that needed a master marine steam engine fitter.

* * *

By Monday afternoon he had a proper job. The firm that took him on had just secured the contract to service the big new migrant packet ships that brought Jews and other émigrés from oppression and poverty in Russia and the Baltic states.

There had always been room for the Jewish community in Latvia. For several decades there had been large areas where they could live undisturbed. Now it appeared that governments were becoming less tolerant towards them and restricting their ability to make progress in life. It made him feel ashamed that his countrymen should discriminate against people because of their religion, but felt that the greater part of this oppression wasn't coming from ethnic Latvians.

Those of sufficient means with any sense were now moving their families across the world to new lands. Many who landed here and at other North Sea ports would travel (many by canal barge, for that mode of transport was much cheaper than rail) across the country to Liverpool and Birkenhead to join the huge liners to new York and beyond. A few though would stay in England and work in the mills and other factories that were crying out for workers to operate their machines.

The job he'd found wasn't a secure position, because the firm didn't have sufficient contracts to provide work every day. These migrant ships were very much like the timber transporter he'd sailed on out of Riga, except that these happened to sail from the port of Konigsberg in Prussia.

So in between fit-outs for his main employer, he was free to offer his services as a jobbing fitter at other machine shops on the dock, which were engaged chiefly with maintaining the engines of the smaller converted steam tugs and few purpose-built trawlers that were lately being commissioned.

This variety made his work all the more interesting, plus of course he was earning good money at last, so that he was able to abandon his doss house bunk for more comfortable lodgings in the pleasant district of Westoe, a short walk from the dock.

He now felt confident enough to do something he'd wanted to do for a while now. Before his recovery he had been too scruffy to dare an approach to the Corporation wharf where the Dama Katrina berthed. The dock police would have taken one look at him and sent him away with a flea in his ear.

But now he resembled a respectable human being again. So he made sure to pass the wharf every day on his way from one job to another, until one day he found the Katrina moored at her usual berth.

He returned mid-evening, when most of the crew would be in the alehouses, pulled up his collar – for he mustn't be recognised – and made straight for the part of the ship that housed the cabin maids' quarters.

Turning the corner into the corridor leading to Juhla's cabin, he noticed a young man in civilian clothes coming out of the female crew's toilets beyond. Carl ducked back behind the corner, crooking his neck to see where he was going, and was amazed to see him enter what had been her cabin. He then heard muffled speech and laughter coming from within. Well, whatever was going on, it was none of his business, but it was now even more imperative that he complete his mission. He stepped forwards and tapped on the cabin door.

It opened a crack and a painted female face appeared, and smiled seductively.

"Oh, you're a new one. But you'll have to come back later, dearie. I'm busy at the moment."

"I'm sorry, miss. I wonder if you know a cabin maid called Juhla Rachoan?"

She grinned. "Well, if you've a date with Juhla, you're about a year too late. She doesn't sail with this line any more." She added, "But if you're not fussy, come back and see me at nine this evening."

Embarrassed, he said, "Thank you, but it was Juhla that I really wanted to see. I'm sorry to have disturbed you."

He crept off the ship, keeping to the shadows, and walked away from the wharf and back to his lodgings.

He kept up his Sunday breakfast meetings with Doctor Strong, who still took an interest in his progress. But apart from that first five shillings, he didn't need to ask him for any further advances from Rudolf's money.

"What do you want me to do with this money then, Carl?" the Doctor asked some weeks later.

"Could your banker hold it for me in a savings account, sir? Now that I'm earning decent wages, I should be able to make regular additions to it."

"I'll talk to him," he said. "I Imagine you'll need to go in and fill in some forms."

* * *

"Sit down, please, Mr …"

"Evardson … " he responded automatically, but then bit his tongue. He hadn't given any thought as to which variant of his name he should use for banking purposes. But it would be unlikely that the Riga police would have cause to contact a bank in a minor English seaport.

"My given name is Carl." He spelt it out. "It translates to Charles in English, I believe. Could I sign for withdrawals in that name?"

The bank manager looked over his spectacles at him, but his expressionless face indicated neither approval nor disapproval.

"It's up to you what name goes on the account, Mr Evardson. If you have a passport or birth certificate for verification?"

He panicked for a second. He had both. His birth certificate, issued by a cleric of the Lutheran church in Tukums, gave his name in German – Carl Ewertsohn. His passport, however, bore the Latvian version, so he took it from his jacket pocket and handed it to the banker.

He examined it for what seemed to be a very long time. Then he spoke.

"It gives your name as Kahrl, with a 'K' and an aitch."

"There are alternative spellings, sir." He managed a weak smile. "I'm afraid the political history of my country is rather complex …"

The bank manager coughed, made a note and handed the document back to him.

"I've put you down as Charles Evardson. Is that right?"

"Yes, please."

There was a paper to sign, and that was that.

He now had an English sounding name, and a safe place to keep his money.

The bank manager got half up out of his seat, as if poised to conclude the brief interview. But Carl hadn't quite finished.

"Could I ask your advice about something before I leave?"

The manager resumed his seat. "Of course."

"I have a deposit account in Riga, but I was forced to leave in a hurry, and had no time to withdraw my savings. I wonder, is there any way in which I could somehow move that money into my account with your bank, without having to return to Riga myself?"

"I'm sure there are ways and means, Mr Evardson. It would require a written instruction from you to your bank in Latvia authorising them to release the funds in the form of a draft. However, rather than entrust that note to the international post, it would be wise to have it couriered via London – the process could involve considerable costs and commissions.

"Would you like me to start preparing the paperwork?"

"No, not just yet, thank you. I'll have to give it some further thought."

TWO YEARS LATER

CHAPTER FOURTEEN
1888 – A PLAN FOR REDEMPTION

"For Christ's sake, Charley, can't you give her a few more knots? If those Grimsby buggers beat us to the grounds we won't get a look-in!"

With an eye on the pressure gauge Carl removed his cap and used it to wipe the sweat from off his brow, taking care to hold his stance as the smack ploughed through another massive wave.

Poking his head up through the hatch he yelled back against the howl of the storm towards the wheelhouse. "I've already told you, skipper. You're getting all this rust bucket can give you. It might help if you had her bottom scraped once in a while. Besides, you know as well as I do, there's enough fish for everyone."

"Aye, there should be," the skipper growled. "But those bastards 'll ram you soon as let you get your snout in the trough. Last time out I could swear they were lining up to cut through our trawl!"

"Oh, yes," Carl sneered. "And risk a fine and a fouled prop for the pleasure? You're bloody paranoid, do you know that?"

"You mark my words, Charley. It'll come to that one day. Just because they've got the biggest fleets, the Hull and Grimsby crowd think they own the soddin' Dogger Bank.

Not that they're averse to screwin' each other as well, mind you. It's like a bloody free-for-all out here sometimes!"

Carl couldn't help but smile. Cliff Gosling was in his element. He loved the thrill of the chase, living on the edge of danger. And his claim that the big ports resented the smaller ones taking 'their' fish only added to the excitement. He behaved as if he were a David waging war against Goliaths.

More like a little boy pinching apples, Carl reckoned. Mind you, all this scrumping was proving to be a very rewarding game.

And Carl had to admit he was a willing accomplice in this unrelenting battle for a share of the sea's bounties. It was a huge improvement from the life of a dockyard sewer rat that he'd known only a couple of years before. Under Doctor Strong's guidance he had somehow managed to turn his life around and reclaim his pride, first as a shore fitter and then as a sea-going engineer. The fact that he'd somehow earned the nickname of 'Charley' didn't bother him. In fact, it made him feel like one of a very special clan.

Cliff owned a couple of smacks and had approached Carl in the pub one evening some twelve months past. The vacancy was for a donkeyman. On a small boat that meant engineer and Jack-of-all-trades. The deal included a generous share of the profits from each trip. Cliff had a nose for where the fish were, and as a result he and his crew of four enjoyed a series of good landings, resulting in Carl's bank passbook showing a very healthy balance.

But the crew knew that Cliff expected them to put in the maximum effort in return for their share of the rewards. He had no time for slackers and wouldn't spare a cuff round the ear for any idling deck apprentice.

Now he turned his head to throw a command to the starboard deck. "Steve, take the wheel a minute. I'm burstin'."

The mate put down the section of net that he'd been checking alongside the two deckhands and stepped into the wheelhouse. He saw the half empty whisky bottle by the wheel and turned to raise an eyebrow at Carl while the skipper stumbled aft to do what he had to do. Carl kept a straight face and went back to the engine. Cliff's drinking didn't bother him. He knew he'd stop when they got among the fish and shot the trawl.

Four hours later saw them at the grounds, and there were just a couple of other smacks in the vicinity. The wind had settled a bit but the sea was still choppy. Though it was mid-afternoon the sky was so full of cloud that you'd think it was nearer dusk.

"Hope you don't mind working in the rain, lads," Cliff jibbed. By now they all had their oilskins on.

"What? You mean we've got a choice then, skipper?" joked one of the deckies.

"Less of your chelp, you cheeky young sod, or else you'll find yourself back in the workhouse. Now get those bloody nets paid out."

While they did this Carl kept the revs low, keeping the tub steady, to avoid fouling the nets on the propeller, but giving enough forward motion to stretch them out ready for a good tow.

They struck a shoal within fifteen minutes and soon they were all giving a hand to haul the heavy catch inboard, then with a pulley hoisting the bagful of silver darlings until it was high enough for the mate to untie the knot and empty the contents onto the deck for stowing in the fish pound.

"Not bad," the skipper conceded. "Another couple of hauls like this and we'll be heading for the Coronation. Let's get 'em cleared away for another go."

* * *

"Another pint of ale, Charley?"

With its proximity both to the St Hilda coal pit and South Shields' commercial docks, the public bar of the Coronation Inn was all of a mid-evening bustle. Pitmen and fishermen vied raucously for the reputations of hardest drinkers, keenest dart throwers, and most fantastic storytellers on Tyneside.

But although there was rivalry here, there was also respect.

Respect for deckhands missing fingers through frostbite or an unforgiving winch wire. Respect for older miners who coughed up spots of the deadly dust that coated their lungs.

The greatest respect, though, was for the absentees. The shipmates washed away in screaming gales. The unlucky miners gassed or crushed in rock falls or underground explosions. Every man here was a thankful survivor, who worked and played hard, forever to argue the claim for his respective trade as the most dangerous job in the world.

"Go on, then, Cliff. I'll have to make it the last for tonight, though." He lay down a domino on the slate tabletop. "A double five and a single equals fifteen. Three fives, and five threes, so that scores eight. I'll just mark that up. You're eleven behind."

The skipper scowled. "We did say we were playing for a farthing a point, didn't we? Anyway, I can't understand you. It's not as if you're married. And you're not the kind of man to go whoring. What's there to stay sober for? Why the vow of abstinence?"

"Hardly abstinence, skipper. But I've told you before. I know what it's like to be drunker than you could ever imagine, and I don't want to know that feeling again. Not ever. I don't mind a couple of pints to be sociable, but I know my limit. Besides, one of us has to keep a clear head for the fish market in the morning. You know how those merchants like to try and screw us."

"You're bloody right there, Charley. They seem to have a different method of counting from the rest of Creation."

"I know. Remember Grayson last week, putting eleven tickets out when he'd only bid for ten boxes? They must think we're idiots. Mind, we should get a good price tomorrow. From what I see and hear there's only two other smacks landed today."

"I think I'll take a leaf out of your book, Charley, and make this next one my last for tonight." He caught the maid's eye. "Two more pints over her please, Bella!"

"Mind you, if this were Grimsby, we'd be getting far higher prices. A two and a three scores one."

"How do you know that?"

"Easy. Two plus three equals five, so one five scores one. You should know, you taught me this bloody game! I'm beginning to see why, an' all."

"No, Cliff. I mean about Grimsby fish prices."

"Oh." The skipper placed a finger against the side of his nose. "I've got my spies, you know. Besides, the Grimsby lads have something that none of the other North Sea ports have."

"And what's that?"

"A daily direct rail connection to London. That means they can land their fish in the afternoon, sell it on the Grimsby market first thing next morning, see it on its way to London by nine o'clock, and have it on the tables of the posh West End restaurants that very same evening. How fresh is that?"

"And the rich diners will pay a premium for fish that's so fresh?"

"They certainly will. Of course the merchants and the M.S. and L. Railway take more than their fair slice of that. But the smack owners and crews benefit too. It 'ud be nice to dip a finger in that little honey pot."

"You'd have to get in quick though, wouldn't you, Cliff?"

"How do you mean?"

"Well, once the word got round, everyone would want to land their fish at Grimsby. Then there'd be too much supply and the price would come down again, wouldn't it?"

"Good point. Which is why the Grimsby fishing barons make it virtually impossible for outsiders to get their noses in the trough."

"They can't stop smacks from other ports landing their catches at Grimsby though, Cliff, can they? Double two and a single makes six, scoring two."

"No. But they can charge what they like for dock dues, wharfage, landing fees and auctioneers' commissions. By the time all that lot's taken off your settlings, you might as well have landed your fish at your home port."

"So, you're snookered? By the way, fancy a game of billiards later?"

"No, Charley, you're too good for my pocket. Let's stick to the fives and threes. I'm knocking, by the way."

"Can't go, eh? Well, I've only two dominoes left, which just fit, a four and a one scoring one. That means I beat you by thirteen, but as that's unlucky let's call it twelve. At a farthing a point that means you owe me three pence."

The skipper fumbled in his pocket as the drinks arrived. He counted out three pennies.

"I'll get this," Carl offered. "There you are, Bella. Keep the change."

"Oh, you're always so generous, Charley," she said as the skipper scowled. "Oh, by the way, someone was in here earlier today asking after you."

Carl sat bolt upright.

"Asking after me? What did he look like?"

"Skinny bloke, very smart, dressed in the German fashion, you know, nice suit with a pointy hat. Left his card on the bar. I think he scribbled something on the back. Hold on, I'll get it for you."

She returned with the card, on the face of which was printed: 'Herr G. Muller, Investigator'. On the reverse someone had scribbled 'Station Hotel, Room 5'.

Although Muller was quite a common German name, Carl wondered. Could it be … ?

* * *

Part of him was intrigued, part of him unnerved by the forthcoming reunion, if indeed that was the correct way to describe the impending meeting. It might prove to be more of a confrontation. Either way, the prospect was unsettling. In spite of his disastrous initiation to life in England, with Doctor Strong's support over the past year and a half he felt he was at last making a life for himself, through gainful application of his engineering skills. Now just when his fortunes seemed to be bowling along on an even keel, along comes this name from the past to create a potential crosswind.

The main concern he had, if indeed this was the Herr Muller he knew, was the gentleman's most likely motive for seeking him out. Perhaps he'd been sent by the Riga police to persuade Carl to return to Latvia and face their dubious brand of justice. If that were the case, their choice of agent would seem inappropriate, to say the least. Were it to come to a test of force, Carl believed that even he would be capable of overpowering such a slightly framed fellow.

Aside from that (though the theory hadn't been tested, for he'd not seen Herr Muller since receiving his master's certificate some five years previously), Carl thought he could count Captain Heuer's manager among his few allies, rather than someone who wished him ill.

All things considered, he felt that a meeting with Herr Muller could do no harm, and that there was always the remote possibility that he might even learn something to his advantage.

Carl's lodgings for the past year had been in Taylor Street. Not, perhaps, the most salubrious part of the town, but respectable working class nevertheless and a short walk from the port area.

The landlady was a kind, middle-aged widow called Madge Albright. Like most of the South Shields landladies who took in paying guests, she was used to the odd hours kept by her sea-going lodgers. And if there was a tide at four-thirty in the morning, you'd be awoken at three with a hearty breakfast plus sandwiches of fried herring roes to keep you going as you steamed towards the grounds.

Today being settling day, he had risen early enough to attend the morning's fish market, and together with Cliff had witnessed the sale of their catch for a good price. On receiving his poundage, he had deposited a large portion of it at his bank in town and made his way straight to the Station Hotel. There he had asked at the reception desk if he might speak with Herr Muller who, he was now informed, was on his way down to meet him.

If Carl had been expecting anything but the most cordial of greetings, he could now feel relieved, because Herr Muller approached him, wearing his usual shiny black suit, and carrying his trademark shiny black attaché case, with one hand outstretched, his familiar ferret-like face beaming with an affable smile.

"My dear fellow! I can't tell you how happy I am to find you here safe and well. That is, I hope you are in good health. I had feared it might be more difficult to establish your whereabouts."

Carl returned his smile. "I am well, Herr Muller, thank you. It's good to see you too, looking as fit as ever. But I can't imagine what brings you all this way to see me."

"You shall hear of that very soon. Would you take some morning tea with me? Or, I do believe they have coffee here, if you prefer that?"

"Thank you," Carl said. "Coffee would make a pleasant change."

Herr Muller ordered the drinks and led Carl over to a private corner.

As they sat down, Carl said, "You found me easily, then?"

"I spent a few days enquiring at various taverns. It was apparent that you had become quite well known in the town – with some notoriety as an expert at a game known as dominoes, I believe – and I was soon directed to your regular haunts, where I scattered my cards liberally."

"Ah, yes." Carl took out the card his old employer had left for him at the Coronation. (He had always regarded Captain Heuer's agent as such, since he never actually met the great man himself.)

"It says here that you are now a policeman of some kind, sir."

"Not quite. You must know that Heuer's breaking business finished a few years ago. It was a sensible move, because it only just covered its expenses, and the land and dock were in demand to cater for the ever expanding packet ship trade. It seems everyone wants to leave for the Wild West!"

Carl's expression was fixed as Muller continued.

"Captain Heuer had received several offers for that prime position, and I wasn't surprised when he gave in to common commercial sense and put it up for auction. This meant, of course, that part of my job became redundant, and retaining me just to oversee what was by then a very straightforward working arrangement with Krutzberg's – in no small way due to your own endeavours – I felt rather wasted my talents.

"Because of my length of service, Captain Heuer awarded me a modest pension. However, being an active man and still, I believe, having many good years left in me, I decided to embark upon an entirely different profession."

Carl offered, "From what it says on your card, you seem to have made an exciting choice."

"Ah, that's what everyone thinks. But if the truth be known, and I were to describe to you the minutiae of detailed checks and clerical procedures involved in most of my commissions, you would consider my chosen career one of the most tedious on Earth."

"Really? If it wouldn't be breaking any confidences, what does the larger part of your work entail, Herr Muller?"

"The assignments break down into two distinct types. The first is commercial in nature. It concerns resolving disputes between contracting parties, as to whether movements of funds between their accounts accurately reflects the terms and conditions of their usually complex legal contracts."

"Why don't they just consult an accountant or lawyer?"

"I can perform the required investigations at one quarter of the cost that those gentlemen would charge."

Carl nodded. "And the other part?"

"More delicate. It concerns investigations regarding infidelities by wives, husbands or sometimes fiancées. It can be very tricky work, involving keen observation and interpretation of the various parties' comings and goings. And unless the observed behaviour is so outrageous as to be absolutely conclusive – which, I am pleased to say, is seldom the case – then whatever evidence can be amassed may only be the result of precise observation and recording of peripheral events, which impinge upon a time frame and location when and where the alleged indiscretions may be deduced to have occurred."

"I see," Carl said, though in truth he didn't quite. "Would it be right to assume that the purpose of your visit to me here doesn't involve either of these two types of investigation?"

"You always were a very perceptive young man. That's why this commission is such a pleasure for me. A double pleasure, in fact. First, because of its novelty. And second, because it involves meeting you again and finding you well."

"That's a very kind thought, Herr Muller. Would it be within your remit to let me know who has sent you to find me?"

"Of course. That person is none other than Herr Rudolf Krutzberg, the friend with whom you cleverly conspired to save Heuer's marine maintenance business in Riga. At the time you chose not to divulge the identity of your co-conspirator, but the gentleman appraised me of the details when he approached me to seek you out."

Carl was enlivened to hear Muller speak Rudolf's name. "How is Rudolf, Herr Muller, and how are his wife and children?"

Muller smiled. "I am pleased to report that they are very well indeed. But your friend has been worried about your circumstances, though from what I can see he has no cause for concern. So, my report pertaining to his first instruction will be positive, and one that I shall enjoy making."

"There are other elements to your quest, then?"

"Just one. And, for my part, a simple task. I have to hand you a letter from Herr Krutzberg. I am sure that, if he had had knowledge of an address, he would have posted it to you in the usual way. In this respect, you see, I act as a postman. The difference being that I am prepared to convey back to Herr Krutzberg any response you may have, although of course you are at liberty to reply in the form of your own letter, which you may either trust to the international postal services, or give to me, thereby saving yourself the trouble and cost of procuring a stamp."

Muller now opened his shiny black attaché case and extracted an envelope.

Carl took it and said, "If you don't mind, Herr Muller, I think I would like to read this at my lodgings. I will meet you here tomorrow at this time and let you have my response.

* * *

Laipu iela 5, Riga

10ᵗʰ December 1888

My Dearest Friend Kahrl,

You will by now have heard from Herr Muller that I am desirous of knowing your present circumstances. I do so miss your companionship, our discussions and arguments as to how best to right the world's wrongs.

I appreciate that you suffered a calamitous setback four years ago following the events at the central market.

When you resolved to assume an alternative identity and take the position of welder, you seemed to accept that change stoically, and I would gladly have continued to support you in your new situation. I was happy for you when you struck up a friendship with the cabin maid Juhla Rachoan, and hoped that this might bring you some happiness and renewed purpose in life.

Your sudden disappearance came as a great shock to us all, and at first we feared that you might have suffered some calamity during your shore leave in South Shields. However, as Miss Rachoan had expected to meet you on board, we felt it more likely that you had, for your own reasons, chosen to break ties with your family and friends.

Because I know you to be among the most selfless of men, I am certain your motive was never to hurt those who loved you. Whatever your reasons, be assured that we are ready to forgive and understand your actions.

Now, I come to the most important part of my letter.

New information has come to light concerning the events of that night at the central market. An eyewitness has come forward with a statement which, if true, entirely exonerates you. As a result the police are willing to review the case. Once your name is cleared, this means that you may safely return to Riga in your former capacity.

Even if you were reconciled with your present circumstances, I would ask that you at least return a line or two to tell me about your new life.

From a selfish point of view, the happiest outcome would be if you could be persuaded to return to Latvia, if only for a brief visit.

I remain,

Your most devoted friend,

Rudolf

P.S. You will be pleased to hear that, three years ago, my wife presented me with another son, whom we have named Johann (your middle name).

$$* * *$$

Carl read through Rudolf's letter several times.

He found each subsequent reading of it more moving than the last, to the extent that he eventually put it to one side and allowed himself some quiet tears.

After composing himself, he tried to analyse his old friend's words as dispassionately as he could. After a while though, he found this impossible, and decided that he needed some help to interpret its salient messages. Only then could he decide upon an appropriate course of action.

Since being rescued from the streets by his benefactor, Doctor Strong, three Christmases ago, the physician had remained Carl's closest confidant and advisor. During their consultations (Doctor Strong referred to their talks as *analysis*) Carl had described in intimate detail most of the important events of his life. It was therefore befitting that he share the contents of the letter with the Doctor. As his morning surgery would by now have ended, Kahrl decided to waste no time.

He walked along the route that he had sprinted four years earlier, on the occasion of Juhla's illness, giving him time to take notice of the town's layout, with its fine houses, new horse-drawn tramway and railway bridges. All around there was the vigour and clamour of commerce and industry, the pulsing lifeblood that drove the unstoppable march of progress. What his father had predicted, on the night before he had left Kaive ten years ago, was coming true before his eyes. And he was glad to be a part of it. This was his home now. He belonged here.

But the letter had reminded him of the people he had left behind. The leaving had been painful, however much he had reasoned its inevitability. He had been forced to make a choice, and hoped he had opted for the least heartbreaking for all concerned, Juhla in particular. But he knew now that you couldn't measure heartbreak on a scale. A heart was either broken, or it wasn't. Now, from a distance, abstracted, the pain he knew he must have inflicted struck back at him like a giant steam hammer.

By the time he knocked upon Doctor Strong's door, his spirits were as low as they had been in a very long time.

The maid opened the door and greeted him with a smile. "Oh, good morning, Mr Evardson," she said. "I'll just see if the Doctor is free, if you'd like to wait in the drawing room."

It was strange, this relationship with Doctor Strong. For some reason he had been taken under the man's wing for protection and mental healing. Of course he had read about the treatises of the new revolutionary psychologists, and understood that their theories interested his English benefactor. And he believed that their consultations had been helpful. But he could never know whether time alone might have produced similar results.

"My dear fellow, how nice to see you! An unscheduled visit, but nevertheless a welcome one. You'll take lunch with me, I hope?"

Carl shook the physician's extended hand. "That's very kind, Doctor Strong. I will accept because otherwise I will be taking up your time and preventing you from eating."

"Is everything all right?"

Carl reached into his inside pocket and took out the letter. "Before I answer that question, I'd like you to read this, sir."

"Come through to the dining room. I'll look at it over a drink."

A few minutes later he set the letter on the table and poured himself another glass of wine.

"You were right in coming to me with this, Carl. I can understand if it's opened up some old wounds. But first, let me ask you, what do you consider to be the most important element of this letter?"

There was no hesitation. "The opportunity to clear my name, of course."

The Doctor nodded, saying, "And therefore …?"

"Then I could return to Riga, marry Juhla and …"

"Find happiness? But aren't you happy now? You're making a good living doing what you always wanted to do."

"That's true, but I'm still in love with her. When I think about the way I deserted her, I can hardly bear it."

"Love or absolution, Carl?"

"Sorry?"

"If you went back, would it be to regain Juhla's love, or to assuage your perceived guilt?"

"Must I separate the two objectives?"

"Perhaps. Or at least acknowledge them. Assuming Juhla forgives you and takes you back, thereby relieving you of your guilt, are you sure you won't later resent having abandoned your life here in England?"

Carl thought carefully before he answered. "You don't pull any punches, Doctor. I assure you that I would never do that. I will always love her, and I will always feel guilty for what I put her through, regardless of the outcome."

The Doctor smiled. "Well then, what are you waiting for?"

"You may need to read the letter again. I find Rudolf's paragraph about the new witness somewhat conditional. He doesn't say I'm off the hook, only that the police might be willing to review the case, if the new testimony proves credible. What would you do in my position?"

The physician looked ponderous. "I can't say. I have no idea how the Latvian police operate. Only you can assess the risk that they will arrest you on sight if you return. I must say, your friend Rudolf's overall tone seems very positive."

"I look upon Rudolf as a brother, and I would trust him to the same degree. He has been a dear friend to me, as I must have told you many times before. But he has his family, his respectability, and his money. His right to these has never been questioned. However much he would want to, how could he really put himself in my place?"

The Doctor shook his head. "Perhaps, by applying subterfuge, you could go back unannounced – let us say, indirectly – and thereby avoid the police. Perhaps in this way, if you were careful, you could assess the situation first hand. Find this witness and hear their testimony. If your friend proves to be mistaken, perhaps you could make your exit in a similar fashion. At least then you will have done all that was in your power to try and regain your life in Riga, safe in the knowledge that you could, if all else failed, return here and continue as before."

Carl hesitated. This was a side of the good Doctor that he hadn't seen before. Had he heard him correctly? Was he really suggesting that Carl undertake such an elaborate approach to what should be a simple trip abroad? Then he remembered that this was the man whom, at this moment, he trusted above all others.

"How do you suggest I go about it?"

"Well, to begin with, avoid travelling to Riga on one of Krutzberg's timber boats. You could bump into someone who recognised you. I assume you possess a passport?"

Carl nodded. "Of course. I seldom get asked for it though. I usually show my seaman's pass."

"But you'll be travelling as a passenger this time. Do you have your passport with you?"

He took it from his jacket pocket and handed it over.

"This identifies you as Kahrl Evardson. You won't want to go advertising that surname. You need to find a Russian Imperial Consul who'll issue you with a replacement document in your German name. You've mentioned before that your birth certificate was issued in German. Tell the Consulate officials that you've lost your passport. They should be able to issue you with a replacement based on your birth certificate. It should only cost you a few roubles."

Carl frowned. "I don't think there's a Russian Consulate in South Shields."

"Neither do I. Let me think. You know, your best bet might be to buy a passage on one of the packet ships returning to Konigsberg in Prussia. There's bound to be a Russian Consulate there. The ships carry coal from here, but I'm sure they'll accommodate a returning migrant. If challenged when you disembark at the port, show your original passport. It's unlikely a Prussian port will be interested in Latvian police matters."

"Yes, that should work," Carl said. "From Konigsberg I can either make my way by coastal barge or overland through Lithuania to Ventspils, and then by rail to Riga."

The prospect of the journey also fired him with the idea of making some self-indulgent diversions en route.

The Doctor smiled at him. "You sound as if you're up for this, Carl."

"Yes, sir. I think I am."

CHAPTER FIFTEEN
1888-89 : I – RETURN TO RIGA

23 Taylor Street, South Shields

20ᵗʰ December 1888

My Dearest Friend Rudolf,

It was a joy and a surprise to receive your letter via the hand of Herr Muller. For reasons that you will understand as you read on, I should rather place my reply in the hands of that good man, than to entrust it to the postal services of England, Latvia and points in between.

I could not begin in the space of a few pages to describe my despair in having to turn my back upon my past. However it warms my heart to hear that I am forgiven by those I hurt the most.

You display great perception in deducing that I found myself mentally in a very dark place after leaving my ship. Following an abysmal year spent literally in the gutter, I was fortunate to meet a kind physician by the name of Doctor Strong who, through his interest in the new science of psychology, helped me embark upon the long process of healing my mind. From that point I was able to begin re-building my self-esteem, until now I am earning good wages as a fishing smack engineer.

To hear that the charges against me may be dropped of course fills me with great anticipation, but I must take care to ensure my paperwork is in order for my safe passage to Riga.

You are clearly too much of a gentleman to mention the financial debt that I owe you. Coming to Riga would enable me to relieve my conscience and repay the twenty roubles that you so generously loaned me when I was in trouble.

I note from your letter heading that you now occupy one of the lovely houses inside the old city. I cannot say for sure when I shall be able to return to Riga, but if one night in the near future your servants should hear four knocks repeated on your front door, please tell them not to be alarmed, but to offer sanctuary to your old companion.

I remain,

Your true and grateful friend,

Kahrl

* * *

It took Carl a few days to prepare for the journey. Apart from packing a bag, he had to obtain enough Russian currency for food and shelter along the way. Doctor Strong had suggested he would achieve a better rate of exchange if he swapped his sovereigns for roubles in Ventspils. But as it would be several days before he reached that port, it had also been necessary to order some Russian currency from his bank in South Shields. This brought to mind his savings account in Riga, untouched in four years. He still had his passbook, the sum wasn't enormous, and withdrawing it shouldn't attract undue attention from the tellers at the bank.

Nobody but Doctor Strong knew the reason for his self-imposed exile and imminent return. He had told his skipper that he was needed at home to sort out a family matter. Nevertheless he felt, before travelling, that it was his duty to help Cliff find a replacement donkeyman. This entailed several hours spent scouring the dockside taverns for suitable candidates.

"When do you expect to be back, Charley?" Cliff asked as he handed him a pint of ale in the Coronation bar.

"I wish I could tell you. It depends on what happens while I'm over there. If things go well, I might not return at all."

"Well, I hope it works out for you, either way. In the meantime remember this. You'll always find an engineer's berth on one of my boats. I'm thinking of buying a couple of tugs, having them converted to trawlers and registering them at Grimsby. So if you ever find yourself there, be sure and look me up."

"I've seen converted tugboats. It must be a deal cheaper than building new trawlers from scratch. You may find them heavy on fuel though, which might limit how far out you can take them. Think hard before you part with your money, and be sure to consult a qualified engineer.

"As for your kind offer, I thank you very much, Cliff. But whatever happens while I'm in Latvia, I don't see myself ending up in Grimsby."

* * *

It wasn't difficult securing his outward passage. The steam packet ships that bore increasing numbers of eastern

European émigrés westward required ballast for their return journeys. Coal was the cargo of choice, but the captains were glad of any source of income. A berth could always be found for those who were willing to pay, and Carl's money was as good as anyone else's.

The day of sailing saw few other boats put out of South Shields. In fact along the entire length of the Tyne skippers who could afford to lay up for a couple of days chose to do just that, in view of the atrocious weather conditions. Many old timers predicted a bad winter, and fisher wives redoubled their prayers night and morning.

But masters of scheduled services had little choice. Besides, the larger vessels could weather the brewing storms with relative impunity. So the big steamer bravely put to sea, ready to do battle with the elements.

With other passengers and even crew suffering from seasickness all around him, Carl often found himself suppressing a smile and blessing his solid sea legs and stomach, heartily enjoying his food and drink throughout the voyage.

Four days' buffeting journey across the North and Baltic Seas found him at last in the beautiful thirteenth century Prussian port of Konigsberg. He had been looking forward to visiting the city, and promised himself a little time to enjoy its architecture, parks and gardens.

Showing his birth certificate at the Russian Consulate, he was surprised how simple it was, for a small fee, to obtain a Russian Imperial passport in the name of Carl Ewertsohn. He would try to avoid contact with the authorities in Latvia but, in the unlikely event that any official should ask to see his papers, and notice a resemblance to the name of the wanted man Kahrl Evardson, he could explain it away as a coincidence.

But when the Consul's clerk handed him the new document, and he read it through, he was forced to query one glaring error.

"Excuse me, sir, but you haven't completed the section listing distinguishing features."

The clerk's face coloured when the omission was pointed out. But he waved away the complaint saying, "I hope you don't expect me to bother the Consul to countersign a minor correction. After all, it's not as if the document is permanent!"

Carl frowned. "Not permanent? What do you mean, not permanent?"

"If you look, you'll see it's only valid until the tenth of January."

Incredulous, Carl checked the passport and saw that that was indeed the case.

"But, why should that be?"

The clerk sighed, and rolled his eyes towards the ceiling. "It's normal procedure. For a full replacement, you'll need to apply to the authority that issued the lost passport. In your case, that would be the office of the Governor of Kurland in Latvia. That shouldn't be a problem, should it?"

Carl took the paper and turned away, mumbling, "No, it's not a problem."

It would be though, because the Governor's office would have no record of an original document issued to Carl Ewertsohn – only to Kahrl Evardson, now a wanted man. After this replacement passport expired, leaving Latvia again could be a risky business. The implication was clear. If he hadn't cleared his name within twelve days, he must exile himself from his country of birth for good.

So much for his planned tour of Konigsberg. Fate had decreed that the city's charms were not for his eyes.

Time now being more important than money, he gave up the notion of travelling by coastal grain barge to Ventspils. In any case, owing to the current foul weather, the coastal traffic was unreliable. So instead he spent several roubles on rail and road transport, which brought him to the Latvian port within two days, leaving ten days remaining to complete his business.

He arrived at the main railway station in Ventspils late in the evening, tired and dishevelled from his journey, and soon found simple but clean overnight lodgings in the vicinity. Early the following morning he returned to the station and went straight to the ticket office, where he studied the list of fares before addressing the ticket clerk.

"A single to Riga, please." He looked in his purse. "Better make it second class."

Then he added, "How much for an open ticket?"

The clerk smiled. "An open ticket, sir?"

"Yes," he confirmed. "I want to make a couple of stops along the way."

* * *

As the pleasant vista of small towns and intervening woodland sped by, he began to feel almost at home once more, and when two hours later he stepped down onto the platform at Tukums, it was almost as if he had never been away.

He had forgotten how many years had passed since he had last visited his family. He had resumed exchanging letters following the year of his breakdown, so they were aware of his recovery and improved station in life. But because of uncertainty about his likely progress before setting out on this trip, he hadn't written ahead to announce his hurriedly planned visit. He hoped the surprise wouldn't inconvenience them.

He walked up the main street and into the town square, but he didn't encounter anyone he knew. Nowhere, it seemed, was immune from the exodus to find a better life in the Americas and beyond. And yet he noticed some growth here, with more shop frontages than he recalled from his previous visit, as well as some areas of new housing. It was as if the world were a giant cauldron, washing humanity back and forth either to expand the old, or to start afresh in virgin lands.

He spent a few kopecks on hiring a tub cart to take him to Kaive, leaving him as much as possible of the day to spend with his family, for tomorrow he would have to move on again.

There was a flurry of snow as he approached the village, and the horse lost its footing momentarily. At once a large youth ran out of the nearby woods and grabbed the bridle, steadying the rig and bringing it safely to a halt.

Though there had been no immediate danger, Carl jumped out to express his appreciation. Warmly shaking the lad by the hand he said, "Thank you for your intervention, young man. You were very alert."

The youth smiled. "But I always was faster than you, brother! Don't you know me?"

"Fritz!" Carl yelled, hugging the lad close to him, and then stepping away. "But you must be an impostor. Look at you. You're a giant!"

His younger brother shuffled from one foot to the other, turning his cap over in his hands.

"Sorry, Fritz," Carl said. "I didn't mean to embarrass you. Let me pay off the driver and we'll walk home together."

As they proceeded, he asked his brother to update him with the latest news about their parents' health, the smallholding and timber business.

"Mum and Dad are fine. We manage, thanks to Father's pension. Without it we'd be struggling though."

"But in her last letter, Mother said you were doing very well."

"She wouldn't want you to feel bad. Nor should you. You've had your own troubles …"

"And I've risen above them. I'm in a position to help now, if only our parents aren't too proud."

"You've helped us. You've sent money."

They approached the cabin.

"But I want to do more. We'll talk about it later."

The reunion proved as joyful an occasion as Carl could have hoped for. His mother produced a meal fit for Emperor Alexander himself, after which the men drank some strong beer and smoked their pipes. His father spoke sagely, offering advice with the voice of experience, and Carl nodded in all the right places to humour the old fellow. His mother fussed and lectured him about wearing long underwear against the cold weather, and making certain he kept to a wholesome diet.

The conversation soon worked around to the reason for his return to Latvia.

"You all know of my trouble with the police. It's the reason I've stayed away for so long. But I've received word about a new witness, who may be able to prove my innocence. I couldn't pass over this chance to clear my name, but I must be careful. Also because my passport is temporary, time isn't on my side. I must leave for Riga in the morning."

* * *

Later that night on the cabin porch, as they smoked a last pipe of tobacco before retiring, Carl and Fritz chatted and admired the starry sky.

"You know, big brother? I often come out here and look at the Heavens, and wonder if you're looking at the same sky from your front porch in England."

Carl tried to think of the last time he took the trouble to admire the night sky and marvel at the wonders of the

Universe. "It looks pretty much the same over there except that, in the towns where there are street lamps, you can't see it so clearly."

"That's a shame. But what amazes me is that the world is so big, yet when we look up from different parts of it, we see the same constellations. So how big must the universe be? Don't you ever think about such things? Don't you find it a mystery?"

"The only mystery I can see just now, *little* brother, is why you and I share the same father and mother, yet you've grown into such a giant while I've been away!"

Fritz whispered, for fear of waking their parents, "I asked Mother why I'd grown so tall, and she said her father was a big man, whereas Papa's father was a short ... not so tall. She said that, when you're born, there's no telling which of your ancestors you're going to take after."

"It's not fair though. I wish I were a few centimetres taller, and not have to look up to everyone."

"Don't go thinking being tall is so easy to live with. People always expect you to be brave. I'm not brave. And bullies pick on you because they want to prove how tough they are. You're forced to thump them, just to keep them from bothering you. If I were a bit shorter, I'm sure I wouldn't get into so much trouble."

"Well then, little brother, I suppose we are what we are, and all we can do is make the best of it."

"I agree. But tell me ..."

"Yes, Fritz?"

"Are you going to be all right, going back to Riga by yourself? I hate to think of you walking the city's streets alone."

"I know my way around, and the places and people I need to avoid. But it's funny. I was going to ask you …"

"To come with you? I was hoping you would! I'd like to think I could be useful."

"You'll be an asset if anyone bothers us, that's for sure. But can you be spared? Here, I mean."

"There's not much to do this time of year. There's plenty of wood cut for the winter. Mum and Dad will be all right for a week or so."

"Thanks, Fritz. We'll break the news first thing in the morning."

Carl couldn't deny that he would feel safer with his brother by his side. But he had more than one reason for inviting him along.

* * *

They caught the slow train from Tukums and headed towards the capital. After an hour or so they approached the string of coastal towns and villages known collectively as Jurmala. These pretty resorts lay nestled between the snaking Lielupe river and the coast, giving the impression of an extended island retreat. Carl said, "I want to make a brief call here, Fritz. It'll only take an hour and we can catch the next local train to the city."

They alighted at the station of Majori. He knew exactly where to go. He should, because he had made this journey several times with Juhla when they were visiting her mother. This time he intended to ask the old lady about Juhla's whereabouts and well-being. If he was really lucky, he might even find his darling there too.

But as they approached the mansion, he sensed that something wasn't right. The garden was overgrown and the external woodwork showed signs of neglect, its paintwork peeling in many places.

"This looks a bit of a dump," Fritz observed. "I'll bet it's not been tended to in years. Who lives here?"

"My … an old friend and her mother."

His brother smiled. "A lady friend, you mean? Come on, let's hear all about it."

"When I was forced to take the position of welder four years ago, I was pretty low as you know. But I struck up a friendship with one of the cabin maids. Her name was Juhla Matilda Otilya Rachoan. Have you ever heard such a beautiful name?"

Fritz shook his head. "What did she look like?"

"As beautiful as her name sounded. She had the kindest face. We fell in love. We used to come here each time the boat docked in Riga."

"But you lost her, didn't you?"

"How did you know?"

"Because you never mentioned her in your letters. What happened?"

Carl looked at the ground. "I was a prisoner on that ship. I realised I could never afford to marry her. I had to let her have her life back."

"And after this, you became a bum in the English dockyard."

"Yes. I know. I should have talked to her. If she loved me, she would have understood. She would have helped me. But I felt unworthy, Fritz. My mind was in a turmoil. As I told you, Doctor Strong told me later that he believed I'd suffered a complete mental breakdown."

His brother put a hand on his arm. "That must have been a terrible time for you. If only I could have been there to help."

Carl smiled. "You're a good brother, Fritz. But the only person able to pull me through it all was myself."

"And you did."

"Yes, with Doctor Strong's guidance. I owe him a great debt."

"You've come here to look for your lost love, haven't you?" Tilting his head, he stared at the dilapidated building. "This must once have been a marvellous house. Her family must have been loaded."

Carl shook his head. "They were just servants – that is, her mother was. They had permission to live in the annexe. Let's see if anybody's home."

They walked around the back and Carl rapped on the door, but there was no response. He tried again, but still with no success.

"What's this over here?"

Poking around the unkempt garden, Fritz held up a couple of bits of wood that he'd found. There was some faded writing on one of them.

Carl said glumly, "It's a 'for sale' notice. It must have been here for so long that it's blown down. My God! They must have moved out. Is there an agent's name on that sign, Fritz?"

"Yes, it looks like 'Keller'. But the address is illegible. I think the mice have got to it."

"All right," Carl sighed. "We can make enquiries in the city."

Fritz turned to leave, but Carl had to take one last look at the house. He called to mind how magnificent it had been the last time he had seen it, and wondered what calamity could have occurred to bring it to such a sorry state.

Grim faced, he turned to join his brother, and they retraced their steps back towards the road and the station.

* * *

The slow train stopped at every suburban station, but Carl didn't mind. It would be too early to present themselves at Rudolf's house. For the time being he was glad to enjoy the view and savour the colour of the smart holiday chalets and bright vegetation. Fritz, so seldom given the chance of a trip to Riga, had his nose up against the carriage window for most of the journey.

The brothers took the opportunity to attack the packed lunches provided by their mother. Carl was doubly grateful for her thoughtfulness, because finding places he could take meals away from prying eyes was a problem that had been exercising his brain for most of the morning.

His biggest fear, once he stepped onto the platform as the train pulled in at Riga, was the risk of being recognised. He drew some consolation from recalling how he had made those clandestine trips to Frau Rachoan's home several times without being challenged. Since his recovery he had kept his hair trimmed and nurtured his stylish moustache. Also his recent years battling the elements with his shipmates had weathered him, browning his complexion and hardening his skin. Regular good food and English ale had combined to thicken out his form and settle his centre of gravity, so that he could hug a slippery deck like any old-time hand. Surely he could never be mistaken now for the skinny, pale, longhaired youth he had been five years earlier.

"There's not a lot we can do today, Fritz. I won't be able to contact my friend until later on."

His brother looked around him. "I'll never get used to all these people, all this activity."

"You would if you spent long enough here. But don't worry, we'll have you back home in a week or so."

"Where will we stay?"

"That won't be a problem. My friend Rudolf will accommodate us."

"If we have some time on our hands, why don't we look for that agent? You know, about the house for sale?"

"I suppose we could. The name was 'Keller', wasn't it?"

"Do you know where their office is?"

"No, but there used to be a block of property agents close to my bank. If Keller's office isn't there, one of them should know its whereabouts."

They set off to find the agent.

"Do you know you're stooping?" Fritz said after they'd taken a few strides. "You wouldn't draw attention to yourself if you tried to be more natural."

"Sorry," Carl said. "It's automatic when you don't want to be seen. I'll try to straighten up."

His brother risked a harmless jibe. "Nobody will notice you, even if you do." And he laughed.

"I'll get you back for that," Carl promised.

Within ten minutes they stood at the front of Keller's agency. Carl opened the door and they walked straight in to the front office, where a smartly dressed man sat behind a desk in the corner.

He stood up and smiled. "Good afternoon, gentlemen. I'm Keller. How may I help you?"

Fritz seemed happy to let Carl do the talking. "Our name is Schmidt," he lied. "My brother and I are travelling in Latvia and couldn't help noticing the charming villas along the coast to the west of the city."

"Ah, the Jurmala district, you mean? Yes, there are some lovely properties there. Had you any particular one in mind?"

"Yes, at Majori, the blue and white one with peeling paint and unkempt garden. Your sale notice has fallen down, I'm afraid."

The agent blushed at Carl's observation. "The owners have let it go a bit. Unfortunately they left the country without advising me. I don't even have a contact address for them. I can only wait until they're able to get in touch. They're Russian Jews, you see."

Carl nodded. "Yes, apparently things are bad for the them over there. I've never understood why. We Latvians have always made room for Jewish settlers. What a pity they couldn't have just come and lived in their villa permanently."

"I don't know the circumstances, I'm sorry to say. Perhaps they thought it best to head for America."

Carl wasn't sure how to probe for information about Juhla and her mother.

"We took the liberty of peeping in at the windows of the annexe. It looked as if there had been people living there more recently."

"That would be the servants' quarters," the agent said. "An old lady and her daughter – long-term retainers. But it appears the arrangement for them to stay was informal. There was nothing in writing. So when the place went up for sale, they were obliged to leave. I was able to allow them a little time to prepare, and after a few weeks' grace they departed without any fuss. They seemed nice people. I didn't like doing it, but I was under instructions, you see."

Again Carl framed his words carefully.

"That's a shame. I wonder where people like that would go?"

"Again, not knowing much of their affairs, it's hard to say. There are apartments to rent in town, though nothing of quality comes cheap these days."

"Do you mind my asking how long the villa has been up for sale?"

"Not at all. It went on the market a little over three years ago."

* * *

'Tap, tap, tap, tap.'

Carl gave the pre-arranged signal that he hoped Rudolf's servants would recognise. The night air was starting to chill the bones, the hour being around eleven o'clock. Thank goodness he and Fritz had supped at the market stalls a few hours earlier. And he didn't know about his brother, but he was feeling dog tired after spending the afternoon pretending to be tourists among the attractions of the old city.

'Tap, tap, tap, tap.'

The door opened a crack.

"Who is there?" a voice enquired.

"It's Carl Ewertsohn and his brother Fritz. Please tell Herr Krutzberg that we seek his indulgence."

The door opened further.

"It's me, Carl," the voice whispered. "Rudolf. Come in."

The brothers slipped in and Rudolf closed the door. He turned to Carl and put a finger up to his lip.

"Everyone's asleep," he whispered. Then he put out his arms and hugged his old friend.

"So this is your little brother." He offered Fritz his hand, which he accepted heartily.

"Not quite so little though," Carl said.

"There's a lot to discuss," said Rudolf. "But I imagine you're both weary from your journey, so the maid will show you to your room, and we can talk in the morning. I hope you don't mind sharing. It's a big bed."

"It's almost as if you were expecting us tonight, Rudolf."

"Since Muller handed me your letter, I've been expecting you *every* night. I somehow knew that you wouldn't drag your feet. I'll say 'goodnight' now. We can get down to business in the morning."

"Goodnight, Rudolf – and thank you!"

* * *

"Well now, what have we here?"

The three children stood at the end of the dining room table after breakfast, obediently waiting to be introduced to their parents' house guests.

"Children," Rudolf said, "These two gentlemen are your uncles, Carl and Fritz. They'll be staying with us for a while. But it's a game, a secret. So I don't want you talking about them to anybody outside, do you understand?"

Serious faced, each child nodded and joined the collective chorus of "Yes, Father."

"Now I want you to introduce yourselves in turn and to state your ages. Eldest first."

The tallest child curtseyed and said, "Good morning, Uncle Carl. Good morning, Uncle Fritz. I'm Anna and I'm eight. I can speak three languages – well, a bit. And I know all my multiplication tables. I …"

"Thank you, that's enough, Anna," said their mother, who had already been introduced as Teresa. Carl's only memory of her was when he had attended their wedding, and if he had considered her beautiful then, she now appeared to be at the peak of womanhood.

The middle child, a quiet little boy, introduced himself as Wolfgang, and seriously extended a hand to Carl and Fritz in turn, telling them that he was seven and very pleased to make their acquaintance.

Finally the youngest boy stepped forward and declared, "I'm Johann and I'm three! I'm going to be a sailor!"

"Good children," said Teresa. "Anna and Wolfgang, go and prepare for your lessons. Johann, Nanny can take you to the park. Hurry along, now."

"What obedient children you have," Fritz observed.

"If they weren't obedient they would be tyrants," Teresa replied. "But let us waste no time, gentlemen. Let me tell you about the mysterious witness."

Carl looked in Rudolf's direction and frowned. His friend reacted with a shrug.

"It's no use looking at me. It's my wife who has made contact with this woman, so she might as well give you the first hand version. By the way, did I tell you the witness was a woman?"

"I don't think you did," Carl replied, and addressed Rudolf's wife.

"Please continue then, Frau Krutzberg."

"Not so formal, Carl. It's Teresa. Well now, where to begin?

"As a member of the idle rich, I fill some of my spare time with charitable works, to salve my conscience, you see. Part of this work takes me among the shanties. I think you will be familiar with that term, Carl?"

"Yes, Teresa, but for Fritz' sake let me explain that it's an area to the south-east of the city where the poorest people live in makeshift hovels in the meanest conditions."

Teresa continued, "I should stress that I do not go there alone. We are a team of women with some basic medical training, first and foremost dispensing simple advice on sanitation and cleanliness to the destitute women and children. We are always accompanied by at least two armed militiamen. We answer to the city's Public Health Authority, who provide us with simple medicines and dressings out of limited public funds."

"Generously supplemented with post-approved donations from their husbands' bank accounts," Rudolf interjected.

His wife fluttered her eyelids at him.

"Sometimes it is necessary to tend to people with serious illnesses – typhoid, cholera and dysentery. Oh, don't worry. We take all possible precautions. Well, it would be about three weeks ago that my friend and I were called to look after a woman of about thirty with a high fever. She was delirious and said some shocking things, some of which I had reason to believe were connected with your case."

Carl sat forward. "If you can bring yourself to repeat them …?"

"The words she used didn't all make sense. But I keep a notebook with me, so I wrote them down. She spoke in Latvian and her grammar wasn't perfect. But I recorded her actual words, errors and all."

She took a small pad from a pocket in her dress and quoted from its pages.

"He didn't do it. I did it. If he'd told, I would have tortured my babies. I should have gone to the block, not him. I lied another time too. It wasn't the dog man. He was only trying to help. But I said not to tell. The dog man must die for killing the policeman. But I did it."

Teresa looked up. "She didn't say all that at once, you understand. It came out over a couple of hours until her fever passed. And many of the phrases were repeated, in no particular order. But in summary form, those are the ones that she used over and over. I'm afraid they don't make much sense."

Then she added, almost as an afterthought, "And I don't know if it's important, but whenever she used the word 'I' it was with a definite emphasis."

"It's odd," Rudolf said, "that she seems to be accusing herself of what sounds like two separate crimes. And what sort of mother talks about torturing her own babies? It's a riddle. But I'm sure that when she talks about the dog man, she's referring to you, Carl."

Carl nodded. "It would appear so, especially alongside her reference to the policeman. I'm also intrigued by her mention of someone 'going to the block'. What do we know about that?"

Teresa said, "I understand from her neighbours that her man – she wears no ring, so we can't call him her husband, though we assume he was the father of her children – was executed for murder more than ten years ago."

"Really?" Carl drawled, as if the revelation sparked a distant memory. "I thank you, Teresa, for bringing all of this to my attention. But as it stands, it doesn't quite amount to exoneration. There's only one thing for it.

"When can I speak to this woman?"

CHAPTER SIXTEEN
1889 : II – SO LITTLE TIME

Her name was Frieda Bauer. She and her three children lived in a shed about a kilometre inside the shanties district. Carl and Herr Muller were set down close to the slum dwelling just after eleven that morning by a nervous cab driver.

Holding a kerchief over his nose and mouth against the stench of the open sewers, Carl tipped the man and asked him to wait for them.

The driver shook his head. "I'm sorry, sir, but I wouldn't hang around here for any money."

Seeing no point in arguing, Carl asked the fellow to return in an hour. He agreed and drove off, leaving them standing on the highway.

Rudolf had retained Herr Muller's services, not just because he knew him to be a thorough but discreet investigator, but also because he carried a hand gun. Teresa had wanted to go with them, but Carl had tactfully rejected her offer. She had been good enough to tell him of her recent encounter here when under civil protection, but he wasn't prepared to risk exposing her to any potential danger as a private citizen. Nor, Carl believed, would Rudolf have allowed such a reckless gesture. Fritz had offered to come too, but too many visitors might intimidate the poor woman. So his brother had happily gone off to explore old Riga instead.

Muller looked around and shuddered. "Occasionally I am forced to conduct some of my business in places like this, but I can't say that endears me to them to any degree. It's as well that you heeded my message to dress as plainly as possible, otherwise we should have stuck out like sore thumbs."

"You're right, sir. I feel conspicuous enough as it is. Come on, let's find this place and get off the street."

From the directions that Teresa had given, Carl knew they were in the right vicinity, and a couple of discreet enquiries and expenditure of a few kopecks soon brought them to the place they were seeking.

He knocked at the door.

"Who's there?"

"Frieda Bauer?" Herr Muller enquired. "We mean you know harm. I can assure you that we are gentlemen. We believe you may be able to help us with some information, and we are willing to pay for it."

"Just a minute."

After a short pause, the door was opened a crack and a grimy, pock-marked face appeared. The eyes took them in at a glance, as if to assess the truth in their claim to gentility. While their clothes were basic, they were at least clean, and they appeared to pass the first test.

"What information could I have that's worth paying for?" the woman demanded.

Muller asked, "May we come in, madam? It wouldn't do for your neighbours to hear your business, would it?"

She opened the door wider, shrugged and turned her back on them, which they took to imply an invitation. So they followed her inside.

The rickety cabin was dark and dingy, as Carl had expected, and it was only when he became accustomed to the poor light that he noticed three pairs of eyes staring out from one corner.

"Lovely children, ma'am," he offered, in an attempt to break the ice. Then he handed her fifty kopecks. "They look hungry. Buy them something nice to eat."

She snatched the money, as though she feared it might be taken back, and stuffed it into the pocket of the tattered cardigan that hung from her scrawny shoulders.

"This won't buy you much more than the state of the weather," she said, "And you could have had that for free by looking at the sky."

"All right," Carl said, hiding his amusement at her dark humour. "There's more if you'll just answer a few questions."

She made no comment, forcing him to break the awkward silence.

"I am told that you may have been a witness to the killing of a policeman just over four years ago. It took place in the market warehouses in the city. Do you recall the incident?"

She leaned forward suddenly. "Who told you that? I know, it was one of them posh women that come to see how we survive here in the shanties. Dacha, my eldest, said I was delirious when the fever took me. Curse my rotten mouth!"

"Well, madam?" Herr Muller asked her. "Were you there?"

"If I said 'yes', what would you give me?"

"Nothing if it isn't true," Carl replied.

She looked across at his purse. "Well, there's no harm in telling the truth. Yes, I was there."

He handed her a further fifty kopecks.

"I believe you," he said. "Now, I want you to have a good look at me. Imagine me with long hair, in the peasant style, and without my moustache, also not quite so ... well proportioned."

"Turn your head towards the doorway then," she said, and seemed to be taking the trouble to study his features.

"All right. I've seen you. What of it?"

Carl hesitated, so Muller spoke. "Consider this well, madam. There are some who say this young man did the deed that night. What do you say to that?"

While she gazed again at his purse, Carl said, "Your honest answer is worth a rouble."

"Two."

"Very well. Two roubles. What do you say?"

"I saw you leaning across the body with the knife in your hand." The pause that followed seemed interminable, until at last she added, "But it was someone else that stuck him with it."

The two men exchanged encouraging glances.

Then, handing her the promised money, Carl asked, "And would you be willing to say as much to the police?"

Her bottom lip curled. "I might, but before I did, there's another matter needs clearing up. And I reckon the telling of it's worth five roubles of anyone's money."

* * *

"Sounds like a costly day's work, gentlemen," Rudolf observed as he poured some dinner wine for his guests, who tonight included Herr Muller.

"Eight roubles all told," Carl sighed. "But it's a small price to pay for the truth."

Teresa said, "Are you sure she'll testify, Carl? These women are not known for their reliability, you know. Oh, they can't be blamed for taking money whenever it's offered. They're often left by feckless men to bring up their babies on their own in the worst of circumstances. But that doesn't make them any more trustworthy."

Herr Muller said, "She did seem determined to expose the true villain of the piece, of whom she appears to be mortally afraid. And no wonder, if the other part of what she told us is true."

Carl savoured the wine and addressed Teresa. "I understand what you say about women like Frieda Bauer. But she claims the father of her children wasn't such a bad man."

Rudolf scowled. "By all accounts he was a thief who lacked the commitment to make an honest woman of her."

"That's true," Carl conceded. "But according to Frieda, he did provide for her and the children – until he was executed for murder."

"Which she claims he didn't commit," Muller added. "In fact, she insists he wasn't capable of the act."

"But if she knew that," Teresa asked, "why didn't she speak up at the time and save his life?"

Carl explained, "She told us she visited him in prison while he awaited trial, and he begged her not to name his accomplice – his own brother, the real killer – because of what this man had threatened to do to her and their children if either of them should speak out."

"That's right," Muller said. "The devil had sworn to torture and kill them all if he thought there was a chance of his being arrested. And they must have known him well enough to believe he'd carry out such a threat."

"Well, whatever the facts of that case," Carl continued, "Frieda insists on the accomplice being brought to justice before she'll testify in my favour in the affair of the murdered policeman. But she won't divulge the identity of the real killer unless we can persuade the police to guarantee protection for her and her children."

Rudolf sighed. "That's understandable, but it might be a problem. We'd have to have all our facts straight before making any approach to the law."

"But we don't have all the facts," Carl said. "She wouldn't even disclose the name of her common law husband – the man who was executed."

Muller sat up. "Leave that to me. I have contacts in the justice department. Such information is on public record, in any case. I'll go there tomorrow morning and confirm what I – and, I believe, young Carl here too – already suspect."

* * *

"That settles it, I think, my friends."

It was just before lunchtime the following morning when Herr Muller called at the house to deliver the result of his enquiry. Teresa, Carl and Fritz were seated in the drawing room to hear his report, Rudolf being needed at his office.

"Let me guess," Carl said. "The executed man's name was Karpov, wasn't it?"

Muller nodded. "Tomass Karpov."

"How did you know that, Carl?" Teresa gasped.

"Because both Herr Muller and I knew the man's brother, Stefan Karpov. He was foreman at Captain Heuer's graving dock where I served my apprenticeship. I heard that his brother had been executed for murder earlier that year. Herr Muller was Heuer's agent at the time, and can vouch that Stefan was a nasty piece of work, and a terror to work for."

"He certainly made your life hell," Muller conceded. "I had no choice but to sack him. He was an absolute brute of a man. And, it would now appear, a killer as well. Worse, in fact – a killer who would force his own brother to go to the block in his place."

A look of enlightenment came over Teresa's face.

"Stefan Karpov, you say?" She got up. "One moment. Something has just occurred to me." She left the room briefly, and returned holding her notebook.

"Yes, I think I'm right on this. Listen. I'm going to read out again what I recorded of Frieda's ramblings. Only this time, I'm going to replace each 'I' with 'Stefan'."

Carl's face lit up. "I see what you mean, Teresa. The pronoun 'I' translates as 'es' in Latvian, which is also the name of the letter 'S' for Stefan."

Teresa smiled and read her notes aloud.

"He didn't do it. Stefan did it. If he'd told, Stefan would have tortured my babies. Stefan should have gone to the block, not him. Stefan lied another time too. It wasn't the dog man. He was only trying to help. But Stefan said not to tell. The dog man must die for killing the policeman. But Stefan did it."

"Brilliant!" Muller exclaimed. "She must have detested and feared that name so much that in delirium her tormented mind codified it to its initial letter! Well, it would appear that we have the testament we were looking for. But I must ask you this, Carl. In your telling of what happened that night, you don't mention having identified the real murderer. Now think about this very carefully. Could it have been Stefan Karpov, as Frieda insists it was?"

"You're right, Herr Muller. I didn't see the face of the murderer. I saw the policeman grapple with him, and the first flash of the blade – the one that killed my dog. I didn't see the blade enter the policeman's body though, only that he slumped in the killer's clutches. The killer let him down and I went straight to the poor fellow's aid, instinctively grabbing hold of the protruding handle."

Muller pressed him on the crucial question. "In the time it took you to go to help the victim, could the killer have stepped back into the crowd, so as to point the finger at you from the sidelines, just as Karpov did?"

"Yes," Carl affirmed. "Yes, I'm certain of it."

"Good. Then, with your permission, I shall open discussions with the police to have the case reviewed."

Carl still wasn't sure. "Don't forget, Frieda won't testify unless her man Tomass is also cleared of the first murder – and Karpov is indicted. Do you think the police will want to re-open a case they consider solved?"

"I can only put it to them and see."

Carl's mood was still subdued. "At some stage, they're going to want to speak to me. From that point, I'm going to be at risk of arrest. I'd need to be certain the Prosecutor will accept Frieda as a credible witness."

"I'll stipulate that the police obtain the Prosecutor's approval of everything that's agreed between them and me," Muller assured him. "And I won't disclose your whereabouts until I have that assurance."

"All right. But whatever you do, put the case as if Frieda's testament has come out of the blue – which, in reality, it has. Don't even hint that I'm in Riga just now. Otherwise I'll be a stuffed turkey ready for the Christmas table."

* * *

It was agreed that Carl should lie low for a couple of days. Having risked a few outings without being recognised, he had to admit that he had been lucky so far.

The next day was when Teresa was due to join her friends in charitable visits to the shanties, and Fritz expressed a wish to accompany the group.

He explained, "I had a very interesting day yesterday touring the finest of Riga's architectural attractions. It would be educational to see the other side of the city. Apart from that, I'd like to think there's some contribution I can make, if it's only fetching and carrying and talking to people."

"It wouldn't do any harm having an extra man along with us," Teresa said. "We'll feel that much safer."

So Carl was left to his own devices, and enjoyed sampling Rudolf's library, though the two older children, Anna and Wolfgang, soon invited him to assist their tutor in their studies. This involved some reading and help with language translation, in which his knowledge of English proved especially useful. He amused the children with examples of that language as spoken by the natives of Tyneside, where he told them he had lived for the last four years.

"I think," announced Anna after his rendition, "that if we ever visit England, we had better stay in London, or we shall never understand what the people are saying to us!"

The day passed pleasantly, and the impression of benign domesticity touched Carl's heart, throwing into stark relief the aimless futility of the single life to which he feared he was condemned.

But something occurred just after dinner that evening to stir Carl's romantic aspirations. His brother had seemed to be in a hurry to finish his meal. As soon as it was polite to do so, he thanked their hostess and left the table, gesturing to Carl to follow him into the library.

"Is something wrong, Fritz?" Carl asked.

"Far from it. I have some important news that I've been itching to tell you about all through dinner. But I didn't think you'd want to share it with the others just yet."

"Well, we're alone now. For goodness' sake, man, what is it?"

"I think I may have found Juhla's mother."

"Juhla's …? How? Where?"

"In the shanties. We were helping to treat a group of typhoid patients who were being kept in isolation. Each patient's name was written on a card at the foot of their cot. One of them caught my eye because it read 'Rachoan', which I remembered was Juhla's family name."

"How was Frau Rachoan?"

"She was over the worst of the fever, but still quite poorly. I tell you, Carl, you wouldn't believe the conditions down there. The standards of sanitation are atrocious."

He could hardly bring himself to ask his next question.

"Did the nurses express any opinion …?"

"Of her chances? Yes. She should be all right in a few weeks. But the disease will take a heavy toll on her general health."

The agnostic within him could think of no other words. "Thank God," he uttered. "But can you be sure that this woman was Juhla's mother?"

"She was conscious, although very weak. I risked asking her if she had a daughter called Juhla, and she nodded. I must say, she gave me a queer look when I mentioned the name. But when I said, 'I'm Carl's brother', do you know what? Though she had a facial rash and it must have hurt her a lot, she actually smiled and squeezed my hand."

"This is wonderful news!" Carl gasped. Then, with his voice more subdued, he said, "I mean, it's terrible that she's been so ill, but it's good to hear she's recovering. Do you think you could you find your way back to that place?"

"Of course I could."

"Good. If you'll accompany me tomorrow, I must go and see her. I can't forego this opportunity. I have to find out where my Juhla is now."

* * *

Next morning Herr Muller was invited to breakfast, to report his progress for Rudolf's benefit before he left for his work.

"How did the police react to your arguments?" he asked the investigator.

"They know me well enough by now, and that I'm not a time waster. I was granted an audience with the Chief of

Police himself. I spoke at first in very general terms. I told him that medical visitors to the shanties had heard a woman's delirious ranting concerning two crimes of which she had knowledge. His initial reaction was that such a report could only be described as hearsay, and that in any case utterances accompanying fever carried very little legal weight.

"I countered this by telling him that I had personally followed up the report by attending the woman, now in improved health, and succeeded in taking a form of statement from her. It was at that point that I mentioned the accusation made by Stefan Karpov that Carl had killed the policeman, whereas the woman insisted that he was innocent, and it was in fact Karpov who had used the murder weapon."

"What did he say to that?" Rudolf said.

"At first he insisted that it was just one person's word against another's. But I put it to him that there was a third person – you, Carl – whose testimony should carry as much weight, thereby tipping the balance against Karpov. The Chief seemed somewhat swayed by this argument, though in view of Carl's absence, he deemed the matter one of pure conjecture. I then asked him if he believed Carl's voluntary presence would make a difference, to which he simply replied that it might.

"I then referred to the woman's claim that her common law husband had gone wrongly to his death because of threats made by his brother towards his family. The Chief also seemed impressed by this, but argued that the woman might simply hold a grudge against Karpov, and might even have fabricated the story in order to bring about a revenge execution.

"My final argument was that her conscious statement concurred with the recorded ramblings at the height of her fever, and that nobody could possibly invent such damning assertions while in a delirious state.

"I also told him that, should the cases be re-opened, the woman had insisted that she would only testify if she and her children were given police protection. Taking all this into account, he agreed to have two of his officers revisit the evidence, after which he would consult the Prosecutor, and come up with a plan of action within two days."

"Well, Herr Muller," Rudolf said, "I thank you for conducting this matter in such a professional manner. I don't believe we could have hoped for a better result at this stage. Don't you think so, Carl?"

"I must agree that Herr Muller has done his job very well. My only concern is that my passport in the name of Carl Ewertsohn will expire in four days. So having to wait two days for the Chief of Police's answer is cutting things fine if I'm to leave Riga legally.

"Not being a gambling man, I wouldn't venture a guess at the odds but, putting it bluntly, within a week I could be facing the block."

* * *

Later that morning the two brothers took a cab to the shanties, Fritz giving directions to the driver as they drew closer to their destination. The journey was uncomfortable,

311

because the strong breeze made the horse skittish and the driver had to keep apologising.

"This is it," Fritz said eventually. "We shouldn't be long. Will you wait?" Surprisingly this driver agreed.

Then clutching a bag containing fruit and a bottle of fresh water, Carl followed his brother to the door of the makeshift isolation ward.

"You'd best be prepared. It's horribly smelly in there. You might want to hold a kerchief over your mouth and nose."

"No, Fritz, I'd rather she see my face."

They went in and Fritz led his brother to Frau Rachoan's cot.

"Is there no nurse in attendance?" Carl asked.

"Teresa says that even unqualified help is hard to come by. It's usually family members and neighbours who come and wash, feed and tend to the patients' general needs. Here, come and see her. I think she's asleep."

But as they approached her cot, Frau Rachoan opened her eyes and smiled.

"Carl!" she gasped. "Is it really you?" And she tried to raise her head in an attempt to sit up.

"No, don't," Carl said gently. "You must get plenty of rest." He felt foolish and helpless in saying something so obvious, and ashamed for knowing very little about the illness.

Then she said something that almost brought a tear to his eye.

"Why did you leave us, Carl?"

"It's complicated. I'll explain when you're better. You mustn't talk too much," he whispered, thinking what a hypocrite he was, because there were so many things that he wanted to ask her.

But she must have sensed his dilemma, because she volunteered, "Juhla ... cabin maid ... with another line ... sail to ..."

Her voice faded and tailed off. She was clearly exhausted, even from saying so little. Her eyes closed.

He looked at Fritz. "I think we had better let her rest."

But as they turned away she opened her eyes once again and whispered, "Newcastle."

Then she fell into a deep sleep.

* * *

"Do you have any contacts with the line that runs between here and Newcastle?"

Carl was waiting in the hallway to ambush Rudolf as he arrived home from work that evening. His friend scowled as he removed his scarf and hat and handed them to the maid.

"My word, this weather is awful!" he said. "There's talk of heavy gales in the North Sea. One of our boats is a day late. Bit of a worry, actually."

"I do apologise, Rudolf," Carl said. "Here am I, your ungrateful guest, thinking only of my own affairs while you have to cope with all the day-to-day problems of running a shipping line."

Rudolf smiled. "You've no need to apologise, Carl. I've known you long enough to realise you're incapable of frivolous enquiries. Now, why the interest in our firm's rivals?"

"I've learned today that Juhla is working as a cabin maid on one of their boats."

He was now obliged to report his brother's discovery of Frau Rachoan and their brief conversation.

Rudolf led him to the drawing room, where he poured them both an early evening drink. "You must try this Scottish single malt whisky, Carl. One of our captains brought it over on his last trip."

As they savoured the mellow, peaty elixir, he went on, "This woman and her daughter really do mean an awful lot to you, don't they?"

"As much as my own family. I did Juhla a great disservice when I discarded her so cruelly. But I never considered that her mother felt abandoned too. What a heartless brute I've been, Rudolf."

"Don't be so hard on yourself. You were in a tight corner. So let's not dwell on that bad period in your life. It's time to look ahead, and consider what can be done to bring you two together again."

Carl's expression brightened. "Do you really think that's possible? I mean, can I hope that she'll have me back after all this time?"

With a cheeky grin Rudolf said, "Well, from what you've told me, if Juhla won't have you, I'm sure her mother will!"

∗ ∗ ∗

Over dinner, by now having had time to consider the practicalities, Rudolf and Teresa worked out what might be the best course of action in improving the lot of Frau Rachoan and her daughter.

"One thing is for certain," Teresa announced, while the servant topped up her wine glass. "Given their significance to our dearest friend Carl, we cannot allow these two women to continue living in the shanties. We have to find them suitable genteel lodgings as soon as is practical. In the mean time Frau Rachoan must come and stay with us here, so that we may oversee her complete recovery."

Rudolf frowned. "I don't say we shouldn't do something to help them, my dear. But we also have to think of the children. I wouldn't want them to be exposed to that vile disease."

"No, of course," Teresa agreed. "We should have to be certain there could be no contagion. Perhaps then, as an alternative, we could have her removed to a private infirmary, where she would have access to appropriate medical care."

Her husband nodded and addressed Carl. "I'll contact our family physician to arrange it in the morning. Meanwhile you had better compose a note to her daughter this evening, which I can leave for her at the port office when her ship docks. You'll need to tell her to come to us here. She can stay until she finds lodgings ..."

"Which I shall pay for," Carl insisted.

"Always assuming ..." Fritz began.

"Always assuming I'm still alive."

"Carl!" Teresa complained. "Please, don't say such things!"

"I'm sorry. But, whichever way the blade falls, how am I going to get to see Juhla?"

"If all goes well – as I'm sure it will," Rudolf assured him, "I always intended asking you to accept an engine room post on one of our ships – and I don't mean as a welder this time!"

Carl was abashed. "That would be more than I could ever hope for," he said, and took another sip of wine.

Teresa added, "Yes, and couldn't you find a cabin maid's position for Juhla on the same ship, dear?"

"Wait," Carl was forced to protest. "Neither I nor, I'm sure, Juhla would want anybody to be removed from their position for the convenience of either one of us."

"I understand," said Rudolf. "But promotions and transfers take place all the time. It might just be a case of waiting for an appropriate vacancy to come up."

Carl, though by now a trifle shaky from, for him, an unusually high intake of alcohol, stood up and, with his wine glass in one hand and clasping the back of his chair with the other, said, "I should like to propose a toast to our host and hostess."

Since, apart from the two thus mentioned, Fritz was the only other person seated, he also arose and held up his glass.

"To the kindest, most considerate, benevolent, selfless and dearest friends a man could wish to have," Carl continued. "To Teresa and Rudolf!"

"Teresa and Rudolf!" echoed his brother. "True friends indeed!"

* * *

Laipu iela 5, Riga

6th January 1889

My Darling Juhla,

I risk addressing you thus, in the full expectation that you will consider this note an insult to the one I so callously abandoned four years ago with neither excuse nor explanation.

Please believe me, my darling, but I agonised before choosing what I foolishly thought was the least hurtful way to allow you a fruitful and meaningful life. For I could see, because of my circumstances, no way of providing you with that prospect, as befitted such a sweet and deserving creature.

If and when you allow me to see you again, you shall hear the full explanation for my twisted reasoning, and of the terrible period of torment that followed.

I know now that I was wrong, and as retribution our parting has been and remains for me like some punishing illness that pains me night and day.

By a freak accident I was recently reunited with your mother, a dear lady whose own feelings I also cruelly disregarded when I left you in South Shields. I was shocked to find that she had been gravely ill, but rejoiced on learning that she was on her way to a full recovery.

By the time you arrive back in Riga, my very good friends Rudolf and Teresa Krutzberg will have removed your dear mother to a proper hospital for recuperation. In the meantime provision has been made for you to stay with them at the above address, until they can establish you both in more acceptable lodgings following your mother's recovery. So please make your way to their house when you disembark. You may be assured of a friendly and accommodating reception there.

You are not to worry about the cost of these arrangements, as I am earning good money now and wish, in this small way, to compensate you both for the years of misery I put you through. None of this is by any means contingent upon the nature of our relationship from henceforth, as I consider this plan a penance for my past sins. I promise neither to pressurise nor attempt to persuade you to take me back. If you wish to do so, it must be according to your own will. I dare to hope and long for such an outcome, but I am also prepared to spend the rest of my life as a bachelor.

I sincerely wish you a long and happy life. If I have lost you, the fault is my own, and I fully accept the consequences.

Meanwhile I remain,

Your devoted friend and admirer,

Carl

* * *

Because of a slight incapacity the night before, he put off writing his note to Juhla until early the following morning, by which time his vision had improved, though his head was pounding.

He placed the letter in an envelope and over breakfast handed it to Rudolf to leave at the port office for her to collect when next arriving ashore. Later in the day he intended visiting Frau Rachoan in her new surroundings, as soon as the Krutzberg's physician could arrange her removal from that wretched excuse for an isolation ward that she currently occupied. He intended to address her immediate and ongoing needs, for food and other necessities, and ensure she lacked for nothing during her recovery.

Meanwhile this morning he decided that the time was right to take Fritz on the short excursion he had planned while visiting his family in Kaive. This had been, if truth be told, the main reason for inviting his brother along on this trip to the capital.

"Where are we going?" Fritz asked impatiently as Carl hurried along in front of him. "I recognise these streets. Oh, I know. We're going back to speak to that property agent, aren't we?"

"No, we're not. I need to visit my bank and sign a few papers. While we're there I need to withdraw some cash. I'm running a bit low on funds."

"Oh, I see. But – not that I don't look forward to outings with my big brother – why do you need me with you? As a bodyguard?"

"If you like," Carl said over his shoulder. Then he stopped abruptly.

"Look, Fritz. I should have discussed this with you before. I just never got around to it, what with all this business with the police, and the excitement of discovering Juhla's mother. But with all this uncertainty, I feel I should do something to help our parents in their latter years."

Fritz pouted. "You don't need to worry about them .I'll see they don't starve."

Carl sighed. "I feared it would be like this. I know you do everything you can for them. You've proved the more devoted son, I acknowledge that."

"I didn't say ..." Fritz began.

"No, I know you didn't. You're too kind a person to want to hurt my feelings. But don't you think I feel guilty, going off to make my way in the world, and leaving you behind to take care of Mum and Dad? You should at least have the chance to spread your own wings if you want to. Let me do this small thing to make it easier for you when that time comes."

Fritz looked at the pavement. "But I'm happy enough helping with the smallholding, Carl."

"I know you are, at the moment. But I don't want you to feel you're tied to the place. You've had a taste of the world outside, and I think you've enjoyed the experience, haven't you?"

"Well, yes. But ..."

"But nothing. Don't forget, the smallholding tenancy is only guaranteed while our parents are alive. After that, you may have to move on. In that case I want you to be able to take whatever opportunity presents itself."

"What do you have in mind, big brother?"

"Before I was forced into self-exile, I was earning good money as a fitter on the docks here, at least for a single man, and took our father's advice of putting a little money aside each week. Those regular savings grew into quite a sizeable pot, which I was unable to get my hands on during my absence.

"Apart from some cash for the immediate future, I want to transfer the major part of it to you, to supplement the family income, and to give you a decent start in life when you head out on your own."

"But, Carl, why can't you administer this money? It's yours, after all."

Carl hesitated. "From where I stand now, my future is uncertain. One way or another, I may not be around to get my hands on my savings. I'd much rather you took control of them for me now. I realise it's a big responsibility, but it's something I need you to do, as a big favour to me."

"I wish you wouldn't keep saying you might not be around, Carl. Things could so easily turn out well for you."

"Nevertheless, Fritz, it's something I need to do, just as a precaution. So come on, I don't want to hear any more arguments. My mind is made up."

* * *

Herr Muller was again an extra guest at dinner the following evening, and Carl had been on tenterhooks all day wondering about the outcome of his negotiations with the authorities.

As soon as they were seated, Muller addressed them.

"Frau Krutzberg, gentlemen, I am happy to be the bearer of good news!"

What more could the little gathering do but render their talented investigator a round of applause? Each of the men in turn leaned across the table and shook Muller's hand, with utterances of "Well done!" and "Congratulations!"

As seats were resumed and the soup was being served, Muller further informed the gathering, "I received the Chief of Police's report barely an hour ago. It is accompanied by a schedule of proposed actions, which he assures me has the Prosecutor's approval. I believe this document fulfils all of our hopes and expectations."

Carl asked quietly, "Please could we hear the details?"

"Of course, of course, my dear fellow." He produced an envelope from his jacket pocket and withdrew and unfolded its contents. "There's a bit of legal jargon, which I'll skip, but these are the main points."

He coughed.

"First, the police files relating to the murder of Herr Gerald Stein for his gambling winnings in September eighteen seventy-eight, and to the killing of Constable Heinrik Sterz while on duty at the cultural gathering in the central market warehouses in October eighteen eighty-four, are to be re-opened.

"Second, officers will record the testimonies of Frieda Bauer, as party to conversations with Tomass Karpov who was convicted of the first murder, and also as witness to the second murder.

"Third, if the statements given by Frieda Bauer concur with reported statements already given by Klaus Muller, and testimony to be provided by Kahrl Evardson, then a warrant shall be issued for the arrest of the person or persons to whom responsibility for those murders is indicated by those testimonies."

Here Herr Muller paused to take a sip of wine.

During the brief hiatus, Rudolf smiled and said, "This is wonderful, Herr Muller!"

His wife also grinned and said, "Yes, indeed. It's just as we were hoping. Don't you agree, Carl?"

He didn't get the chance to reply, because at that point, Herr Muller put down his glass and said, "There is some more."

All were silent as he picked up the document again.

"Fourth, Frieda Bauer and her three children shall receive police protection from the commencement of these investigations up until the conviction or acquittal of the person or persons, etcetera."

"That sounds fair enough," Teresa said. "But what if Karpov is acquitted?"

"I'm afraid the schedule is silent on that point, Frau Krutzberg."

Fritz said, "For Frieda's sake, we'd better pray for a conviction then, hadn't we?"

"And fifth," the investigator concluded, "all of the above is contingent upon the said Kahrl Evardson surrendering himself to the Riga police at the residence of Herr Rudolf Krutzberg at ten o'clock on the morning of the eighth of January, eighteen hundred and eighty-nine. From that point he would be treated as a witness in custody pending the confirmation of Frieda Bauer's testimony."

* * *

After Herr Muller had left and before retiring, Carl approached Rudolf in the drawing room.

"Can I have a word?"

"Of course. Is something troubling you?"

"I know it shouldn't. Herr Muller has done a wonderful job in acting as go-between, and of course I'm very grateful to him."

"So why do I have the sense that you're still uneasy? Is it because Frieda won't get protection if Karpov walks free?"

"If we get him into court, I don't see how that will happen. No. It's the police. If they take me into custody as agreed at ten in the morning, that will trigger everything the Chief of Police has stipulated in the schedule, and I have no problem with that. I'll be a witness in custody, which I understand to mean I'll be charged only if the case against Karpov fails. I'm prepared to take that risk.

"But – and you'll probably think I'm being neurotic – what if they chose to arrest me beforehand? After all, until ten o'clock in the morning I'm still technically a wanted man. Herr Muller has had to disclose my whereabouts. So what's to prevent them from swooping at any time before then and putting me on trial? This could all be a ruse to force me out of hiding."

Rudolf's expression reflected the serious consideration he was giving to Carl's concerns. "They'd have to be pretty devious to do that, wouldn't they? But if you think it necessary, I suppose there'd be no harm in taking precautionary action. What do you want to do?"

"Ask one of your servants to hail me a cab. I'll get the driver to take me to a reputable hotel where I'll spend the night and return early tomorrow morning. Then if the police should choose to try their luck during the night, you can tell them truthfully that you don't know where I am, and that they'll have to return for my formal surrender at ten o'clock – as agreed by the Chief of Police."

* * *

Next morning at seven Carl returned to the house, where he was admitted by the night butler.

"Herr Krutzberg informed me of your overnight arrangement, sir, and there's something you ought to know."

"Really?"

"Yes, sir. At about three o'clock this morning two policemen called, asking for you. I told them you weren't expected until ten, as arranged with the Chief of Police. I also said I was willing to wake the household so that they might conduct a search, so long as they were prepared for the likely repercussions. Fortunately they chose to leave."

"Well done," Carl said. He felt as if he should give the man a coin, but Rudolf's employees were paid well enough. He thanked him and went upstairs.

A little later, while he was shaving, he heard a commotion downstairs in the hallway.

He picked up his timepiece. It gave the time as seven-thirty. Having already tried one pre-emptive arrest with its attendant embarrassment, surely the police weren't about to make a second attempt to renege on their agreement?

Now he heard shouts, one of the voices, he felt certain, belonging to Rudolf. He mustn't allow his friend to get into trouble on his behalf. He dried his face, slipped on his jacket, picked up his bag and walked briskly downstairs.

But he was surprised to see that it wasn't the police at all. It was Herr Muller. The investigator was leaning forward with his hands on his knees, gasping for air, his ruddy complexion betraying the fact that he must have run at least a full kilometre.

Now that Carl appeared Muller straightened up, and both he and Rudolf looked at him with stern expressions.

"What's up?" Carl asked and, trying to make light of the situation, followed this with an eerily prophetic question.

"Someone hasn't died, have they?"

Rudolf approached him and placed a hand on his arm. "I'm afraid they have, Carl."

Then Herr Muller also stepped forward to announce the name of the deceased.

"It's Frieda Bauer."

Carl's face drained of all colour. "That can't be. The police protection …"

"… was only to begin later this morning, when the two officers were to have visited Frieda to take her statement."

Carl slumped down on the bottom step of the staircase, as he felt the cloud of consequences gathering above him.

"How did she die?"

Herr Muller provided the grizzly facts. "According to my police contacts, her throat was cut. There were also signs that she'd been tortured – wealds and burns to her arms and chest."

"And her children?"

"They're unhurt. Oddly enough, their mother had sent them down the street that evening to stay with an aunt. Perhaps she had a premonition. They returned in the morning to find their mother dead. The eldest raised the alarm. They'll be sent to a municipal orphanage."

Rudolf said, "I'll talk to Teresa about finding somewhere better."

"He must have had a tip-off," Carl muttered. They all knew to whom he was referring.

"Our police force is by no means infallible," Muller conceded. "I'm so sorry this has happened, for everyone's sake."

Carl stood up. "Well, as I'm due to be arrested at ten o'clock, and my key witness has been taken out of the equation, I think I'd better think about shifting."

By now Fritz was also on the move, but was impeded by the little crowd at the foot of the stairs. Carl stood up and quickly explained the situation to him.

"That poor woman. And her children. This isn't good for you either, Carl. What will you do?"

"I won't be assisting the police with their enquiries, for a start, little brother. I need to get clear of here before ten o'clock."

Fritz frowned. "Sooner than that if you can. The police will be expecting you to run now. As you're once again their number one suspect for the warehouse murder, I doubt if they'll wait for an appointment to arrest you."

Carl then gave them a brief account of the early morning police visitation as reported by the night butler.

"My God!" said Rudolf. "In that case your brother could well be right, Carl. Listen. We'll skip breakfast and you'll come with me to the docks straight away. We'll conceal you somewhere until the Dama Katrina makes port. Then we'll fit you out as before with a makeshift position until a more suitable vacancy comes up. Once you're back in England you'll have more options."

"I rather favoured your idea of shuffling vacancies around so that Juhla and I might serve on the same run, until we could afford to marry. But that's all hypothetical now, I suppose."

"We'll have to see how things turn out," said his friend.

"But you'll still help Juhla and her mother find more suitable lodgings?" Carl pleaded. "I'll cover the costs."

"Of course. Don't worry. Our ultimate aim is for you both to enjoy the happiness you deserve."

"Fritz," he said, taking his brother's hand. "I didn't expect this to be such a sudden parting. Will you be all right getting home?"

"I think I can find my way back to the railway station," his brother joked half-heartedly. Carl smiled back at him.

"We must get going," Rudolf said. "I'll send a servant to hail a cab."

Carl said his final 'goodbyes'. "I'm forever obliged to all of you. Please explain to Teresa what's happened and express my sincere thanks for her help and hospitality."

Muller said, "I'm only sorry we didn't pull it off. Nevertheless I wish you the best for the future, and I hope very much that you find what you're looking for."

Then, grim faced, Carl followed Rudolf to board the cab and they sped off towards the docks.

CHAPTER SEVENTEEN
1889 : III – A CHANGE OF PLAN

After a few uncomfortable days and restless nights sleeping on a couch in a back room of Krutzberg's shipping offices, Carl was awoken in the early hours of a cold and dark January morning.

"Carl, it's me, Rudolf. Get dressed and grab your things. The Dama Katrina's just docked. Best to smuggle you aboard before dawn."

The situation echoed that terrible occasion just over four years past, when he had clandestinely boarded that same ship under similar circumstances. This time Rudolf led him straight to the all too familiar stokers' cabin, which he would again be sharing for the foreseeable future.

"I'm sorry this is the best we can do," Rudolf said. "I've confided in the Chief Engineer, since he already knows you, that you have a good reason to lie low. He'll explain your duties. The pay's not great, so for the time being don't worry about Juhla and her mother. Teresa and I will see they're not wanting. As soon as we can find you a real job, you can start contributing."

Soft hearted as ever, Carl fought to control the familiar stinging behind his eyes. "I don't know what I'd have done without you both. You married a woman in a million, you know."

Rudolf cracked a smile. "I make a point of choosing my friends and wives very carefully." Then he added, more seriously, "Of course, if you'd rather resume your career in England …"

"I've thought about it. But staying with the Katrina gives me my best chance of meeting Juhla again. You did say you might consider a transfer when a vacancy arises?"

Rudolf hesitated. "I'll do what I can, though of course I can't force the girl. We do pay the best rates though, so that's one point in your favour. Only …"

"What?"

"Well, do I tell her you're here? If I do, and she's …"

"I know what you're going to say. What if she's taken it into her head to avoid me, and turns down your offer?"

"It's a possibility. Sometimes pride can get in the way."

"On reflection, I think it would be better not to take any chances. If you can persuade her to come back to the Katrina – should a vacancy arise – let it be for the money."

Rudolf nodded. "I understand. But after she's accepted and formally signed on?"

"It wouldn't do any harm to tell her then, I suppose."

Then Rudolf handed him a bag. "Teresa asked me to give you this. There's food and a few bottles of beer in here to see you through until sailing day. After that you can pig out in the galley. Report to the engine room when you're ready."

* * *

By the morning of the third day Carl had finished the last of the food and drink and wondered if the galley might be open yet.

Out of the cabin's single porthole he had watched the increasing activity on the dockside, with the stevedores checking the stowed timber and crew members making their way up the gangplank in increasing numbers. Most appeared to be equipped for rough weather, and he was glad of the sou' wester and woollen jumper that Teresa had thoughtfully packed in his kit bag with the rest of his clothing. He had a feeling he was going to need them this trip.

He heard a sound behind him, and the cabin door swung open to reveal the heart-warming sight of two grinning faces from the past.

"My God!" said Andris, slinging his bag on his bunk and grasping Carl around the midriff in a bear hug. "Look what the storm's blown in! The little peasant from Kaive!"

When he put him down, Ingus approached him with outstretched arms, but fortunately only took Carl's hands and shook them until his arms ached.

"Now then, young Carl! We never expected to see you again!" he said. "They say you jumped ship, but I think there was more to it than that. You can tell us all about it later. Or not, if you prefer. Have you had anything to eat yet? We've just half an hour for breakfast before we have to start stoking. I don't know about you, but I could eat a scabby horse!"

* * *

"Well, if it isn't our Third Engineer!"

Carl had been wondering how the Chief would greet him when he walked into the engine room.

"Had a good breakfast?"

"Yes, thank you, Chief."

"I'm only going to say this once, then we'll forget all about it. I don't approve of jumping ship – for any reason. There's a perfect command structure aboard a ship for dealing with any problems a member of crew may have. You should have come to me or the Second if something was troubling you, if for no other reason than a missing seaman can cause expensive delays, and ultimately jeopardize the safety and security of the ship and everyone on it.

"Herr Krutzberg tells me you had a breakdown and were under a lot of pressures not connected with your job here. Because I respect him I'm willing to accept that. And as I know you to be an excellent engineer I'm glad to have you back. But, please. No more shocks like that. All right?"

There was little point in grovelling histrionics.

"Yes, Chief. Do you want me to help with the stoking?"

"No, I'd rather have you in here. I've not enjoyed the best of health lately and, what with the weather being iffy, I've a feeling I might be spending more time than usual in my bunk. We've already sorted your insurance papers. As before, you won't officially be Third Engineer, but if you have to hold the fort for a bit, you'll be paid the going rate.

Meanwhile, I see no harm in your getting a bit of unofficial practice in.

"So, what are you waiting for? Get her fired up."

Carl smiled.

"Yes, Chief. Thank you, Chief."

* * *

The Second Engineer had also stayed with the Katrina all this time, although Carl knew from past conversations that there had been nothing to stop him taking a Chief's position on another vessel.

But it was a common situation where a Second was perfectly happy serving alongside a familiar crew and under a good Chief when he turned down offers of promotion to other ships.

The Second was also briefed, in broad terms, about Carl's current situation and the cause of his aberration four years earlier. But he didn't speak of the matter when he and Carl were together in the engine room during the Chief's long off-watches during the bumpier weather.

While he was doing some oiling and greasing about half way through the outward leg, Carl decided to probe the Second about something the Chief had said on their earlier reunion.

"The Chief mentioned he'd not been well lately, sir. Was that to do with his seasickness?"

"Not directly, though I'm no doctor, of course, and he doesn't talk about it much. But it seems he has stomach ulcers that give him a bit of bother. He's had to lay off alcohol and take to drinking milk, poor sod!"

"Ulcers? That must be painful."

"I know. Mind you, he's not the complaining sort. But if you watch his face, you'll see him grimace a bit sometimes. I reckon that's when it's giving him the screws. But don't mention anything. As I said, he doesn't like to talk about it."

"No, sir. I won't."

Later in his bunk Carl tried to avoid the nagging possibility, even hope, that lurked at the back of his mind. He knew why he was trying to shut it out. It made him feel guilty. And yet, there it was, eager to be let out for an airing, and Carl realised it wasn't going to go away.

He didn't wish the Chief any harm. If he were a religious man, he would have prayed for the old fellow's ulcers to be gone and for him to be free of pain. But there was nothing Carl could do about that.

Back on the family smallholding, when an old horse was suffering, he wasn't expected to soldier on until he dropped dead in harness. He was given a good feed and a shot through the head to send him to equine Heaven. That was the kind thing to do.

Not, of course, that Carl was suggesting a similar fate for the Chief. But he deserved some years enjoying pottering in his garden or, if he had none, whatever pastime pleased him, before his time came, as it must to us all. Not the stress and smoky atmosphere of the engine room to aggravate his symptoms.

In short, for his own comfort and peace of mind, the Chief should think about retiring. From past conversations with Rudolf he knew that the firm made generous pension arrangements for its long service employees, so money shouldn't be an issue.

Such a move would, of course, create a vacancy, the natural candidate being the Second Engineer. And the position of Second, if Rudolf were to hold to his earlier promise, should go to Carl.

So both he and the Second would gain from the Chief's retirement, which was why Carl was ashamed of himself for considering the possibility.

He decided there was nothing he could do with any subtlety to help steer the Chief in that direction. It wasn't any of his business in any case, and he vowed he would never allow his thoughts on the matter to spill out of his mouth.

* * *

The following evening saw the Dama Katrina turn her nose into the North Sea, and this was when all Hell seemed to break loose.

All available hands were called to help secure the deck cargo, some of the lashings having broken free in the buffeting seas and needing securing. The quickest route to his allotted station took him past the cabin maids' quarters. He remembered the last time he had been in this part of the ship, three years earlier in South Shields, when he had established that Juhla had ceased working for the line. He recalled the cabin maid who had appeared to be entertaining a male 'guest', and was now taken aback when that very same girl put her head out to see what was going on. His immediate duty overriding everything else, he ignored her and rushed to join the galley staff, who were already on deck. Between them they were to control the safety lines attached around the waists of the deckhands, whose task was to reclaim the detached lashings and reunite them with the deck securing rings. The gale was howling and Carl had never seen waves of such magnitude as those that now smashed down onto the ship.

He tried not to think about the massive power of those waves and how they could pound a man to a pulp if caught in the wrong position. He tried to concentrate on keeping a tight hold of the lifeline, paying it out enough for the deckhand to reach the flapping cords, and then to secure them to the deck. He knew that, until this was completed, the man was in certain danger of heavy wooden planks spilling down onto him and knocking him unconscious, or even worse.

The deckhand had two lashings to secure, and when he had taken care of the second one, he signalled to Carl that he was ready to return. Carl hauled in the line while the man shifted his grip along the ship's rail, his head lowered against the screaming gale.

The catastrophe only took a second. Just at that moment an enormous wave engulfed that part of the ship, lifting the man like a cork, and taking the poor fellow over the side.

"Man overboard!" Carl yelled. His mind made rapid calculations of the risk attached to the actions he must now perform. Once the odds were estimated, there could only be one course to take. Free will had nothing to do with it. The deck being temporarily clear of water, he yanked on the lifeline, finding it still taught. So hand over hand he pulled himself towards where the man had gone over, thinking he should find a lifebelt to throw in after him. But the visibility was so poor that he could see none to hand, and in any case he daren't let go of the rope.

Next thing he knew, the ship was deluged by another gigantic wave, bringing him to his knees on the deck. But he managed to maintain a grip on the line by wrapping it around his wrist, while clinging to the ship's lower rail with his other hand. Then suddenly something crashed down beside him.

It was the deckhand. The sea had spat him back on deck, though in what condition Carl couldn't tell, except that he appeared to be unconscious. He was glad to see that the lifeline was still tied around his waist, so he grabbed it and pulled the limp, deadweight body back along the deck towards the swinging door of the companionway. Once there, he dragged the sailor inside and secured the door.

By now two other crew members were there to assist him. Someone asked him if he was all right and, though he wasn't certain, he replied, "Yes. See to him."

He watched as they checked the man for vital signs, and noticed them nodding. They then took the sailor away, to the sick bay, Carl assumed.

He lay motionless in the corridor for a few minutes, then managed to sit upright, so that he could take an inventory of his own limbs and appendages. He worked out that he hadn't broken anything, but he hurt like hell from the buffeting, and would no doubt have a few bruises.

Somehow he dragged himself to his feet and staggered to his cabin, where he slumped onto his bunk and closed his eyes.

* * *

Next morning he went to the sick bay to find out how the deckhand was doing, and was pleased to see him sitting up in one of the bunks with his arm in a sling.

"Aren't you the fellow who pulled me back on board?" the man grinned.

Carl shook his head. "I think the sea had more to do with it than I did. I just happened to be the one holding the lifeline."

"And I thank God you were, my friend. Of course, you realise now that I can never drown?"

Carl smiled. "How's that?"

"It's a superstition, though many say it's true. Once the sea has pulled you overboard and tossed you back on deck, it means she doesn't want you. She won't bother to take me again."

"Well, I hope that's true for your sake, anyway." Carl nodded towards the sailor's dressing. "What's your injury?"

"Broken wrist. It'll mend, but I'll have to take a trip off. I'm thankful I sail for Krutzberg's. They pay you for time off due to accidents. Some lines 'll strike you off the payroll as soon as you're injured."

Carl wanted to say something about the social and political ethics of his friend Rudolf, who he knew was responsible for the benefits the sailor referred to. But at sea it didn't do to boast about having friends in high places, so he kept his connections to himself. Instead he voiced another idea that had come to his mind.

"If you're going to be laid up in South Shields, I know a clean and respectable place where you can stay. The landlady's a good woman. The house is near the docks and not expensive. I keep a room there myself."

"It's good of you to mention it. I'll get the address from you before we land. By the way, what's your name?"

He told him.

"I've heard that name somewhere."

Carl blanched. "Really? Where?"

"In Riga. You know the Black Pig tavern, near the station?"

Carl nodded.

"I like the place. I often go there between trips. It's got a bit more class than some of the dockside dives."

At the sailor's mention of his old home, Carl was almost overwhelmed by a wave of nostalgia.

"Is Karolina still landlady there?" he asked.

"Yes. Marvellous woman."

"I lodged there for a while," Carl said. "Maybe she spoke about me, and that's how you heard my name."

"No, it wasn't that. Ah yes, I remember now. Someone came in drunk one night, shouting your name. The landlord had to fetch help to eject the bloke. He looked like a real troublemaker."

"Did you catch his name?"

"No. But he was a huge man, like a giant. He took some shifting, I can tell you. Took four of us in the end. He reminded me of a big Russian bear."

"When was this?"

"Not long ago. A few days before we sailed."

Returning to his cabin Carl thought about what his shipmate had said. He wondered whether his sighting of Stefan Karpov had occurred before or after the brute had murdered poor Frieda Bauer. Whichever, it was now clear that the ogre had been close to eliminating him too. Thank goodness he'd decided to avoid his old haunts. But hearing about this made it clear that what Herr Muller had alluded to was true.

The Riga police force was not only unreliable. It must be as riddled as a sieve. He resolved never, ever to place his trust in them again.

* * *

He requested a day off due to his bruising, and as the Katrina, foul weather permitting, was only a couple of days from docking, the Second Engineer sent word that he needn't report for duty any more on this leg of the trip.

However, when his stoker cabin mate Ingus came off watch that afternoon, it was with a message for Carl.

"Well now, little brave one!" By now the news about his heroic deed was all over the ship. "The Chief wants to see you in his cabin. Probably wants to pin a medal on you, you little show-off!"

By now Carl was well used to the brothers' warped sense of humour. He didn't expect any reward for what he'd done, so as he made his way to the officers' quarters he wondered why the Chief really wanted to see him. He checked his trim, knocked on his door and waited.

"Come in, Carl!" a voice boomed from inside. Clearly the Chief wasn't expecting any other visitors. He opened the door and went in.

He was surprised that the cabin wasn't bigger than it was, but then, crew space on a cargo ship like the Katrina was of secondary importance. There was room for a couple of chairs though, and the Chief occupied one of them.

"Sit down, young man," the Chief said. "From what I hear, you've become some kind of hero."

Carl found the seat uncomfortable. "I only carried out the task assigned to me, which was to keep holding onto that lifeline until the man at the other end was back on deck. What's heroic in that? To my mind, a hero is someone who, through an enormous act of will, risks his life against all odds to save another person. What I did had nothing to do with will. I just acted like an automaton, a machine of muscle and sinew, performing a series of actions that could only produce the required outcome."

The Chief looked at him wryly. "I've always believed you were a bit of a philosopher, Carl. Would I be right in guessing you're a fan of Spinoza?"

Carl was amazed that the Chief had even heard of the seventeenth century thinker.

"I like to read about such things myself, you know. Perhaps we can find time to talk further on the subject, but not just now. However, in the matter of heroism, I'm sure you'll be gracious enough to accept well intentioned pats on the back and compliments with your usual modest good nature."

"Of course, Chief. The last thing I want to do is to appear churlish. It's just that I find it embarrassing, that's all."

"People need heroes, you know," the Chief assured him. "And it's not often we get the chance to recognise someone from our own company as such. So, put up with the adulation while you have to, eh?"

Carl was hoping the lecture was over.

"Yes, Chief."

He was about to ask if that was all, when his mentor changed tack.

"But there's something else I want to say to you. You know I've not enjoyed perfect health lately."

Carl nodded. "Ulcers, Chief?"

"That's right. And on top of my old trouble, well, it doesn't make for comfortable seafaring. I can put up with the sickness, but when there's pain on top of it, well, life can become a bit miserable."

"I can understand that, Chief."

"Not that I can't pull my weight when I'm well, you understand."

"Nobody doubts that, Chief."

"And the Captain's happy with my arrangement with the Second – well, you know all about that. But it's getting so that I'm putting on him too much. We've been lucky you've come back to us now, because you can keep things going if I'm taken badly on my watch."

"I'm more than happy to do that, Chief."

"Tell me about your training and qualifications."

Carl felt excited as he realised this was developing into a job interview. He took a deep breath.

"I'm a time served fitter out of Heuer's shipyard, and for four years I supplemented that with evening classes at the Free Maritime College in Riga."

"Which subjects?"

"Seamanship and engineering. The latter also touched on advanced maths, mechanics and physics." He mentioned the names of some of his tutors.

"Good men, all of them," the Chief conceded. "That would all be theoretical, of course."

"Mostly, Chief. But I took several unpaid pleasure trips, albeit on smaller craft. And for the last two years I've been donkey ... I mean, engineer on board converted smacks out of Tyneside, fishing in the North Sea."

"My God, Carl, I had no idea you'd had that kind of experience! How come you haven't mentioned all of this before?"

"There seemed no reason to, Chief. It would have sounded like bragging."

"Modest as ever, eh? Well, I've seen you at work and I know you can handle this tub's engines. Not that there's much to it – the rules are simple. You do everything that 'upstairs' tells you to – as quick as you can. And you make sure the engines are able to give peak performance at all times. Got it?"

"Got it, Chief."

But where on Earth was this leading?

"Right. Next trip is going to be my last. From then on, you'll be sailing as Second Engineer."

Carl was speechless.

Then he stumbled, "But what … I mean, how … What will you …?"

"I'll be enjoying myself, after a tour of Europe, that is, looking for a doctor who knows what to do about these ruddy ulcers. And then I've ideas to develop my workshop at home and build a model railway. That should keep me busy for a few years."

Carl found his composure, and for a second forgot about his self-imposed exile. "Sounds exciting, Chief. I'd like to see your railway when it's finished."

"I'll let you know when it's ready for inspection," he laughed. "Meanwhile I'll talk to Rudolf when we land and give him my decision. He'll see you about fixing your remuneration. By the way, the Second already knows of my retirement plans. No doubt you'll notice a spring in his step next time you see him."

He extended a hand and Carl shook it vigorously.

"Thank you again, Chief," he said. "I wasn't expecting this."

Before he knew it, he was standing outside the cabin, his mind in a whirl.

Returning to his quarters, he thought about the preparations he must make. He would need to buy some tools. All engineers had their own tool bag with their favourite hammers, chisels and the like. Also some decent overalls and steel-capped boots. But he would have to purchase these in South Shields. He daren't risk a visit to the chandler's shop in Riga.

From these dreamy heights he was brought down to Earth with a crash.

Because of his act of heroism, his name was now known throughout the ship. His new appointment as Second Engineer would only add to his notoriety. How long, he wondered, would it be until someone spoke about him on shore, in the presence of some keen, young policeman?

And how long before the Riga police presented themselves on the quayside with a Prosecutor's warrant to search the ship for the fugitive Kahrl Evardson?

* * *

The Dama Katrina crawled along the Tyne past row upon row of moored fishing smacks and converted tugs, before pulling in at the Corporation wharf. Some of them looked severely bashed about by the weather, despite being moored up. The hour was about eight on a squally evening, during the third week in January. The heavy seas had added two days to the steamer's passage from Riga, being the cause of many a short temper from Captain to galley boy, since all were paid by the trip, and not per day.

After helping clean up in the engine room, ready to hand over to the fitters in the morning, Carl finally disembarked, accompanied by the deckhand he had reputedly rescued, having promised to secure him a room at his own lodgings in Taylor Street. They entered the bar of the Coronation Inn to find it full to overflowing. It was so crowded, in fact, that it was hard for Carl to find a face that he recognised.

"Charley! Over here, matey!"

He turned his head to locate the source of the invitation and saw the waving arm and cheeky grin of his old skipper. "A minute, Cliff – I'm just getting a drink for me and my shipmate!" he shouted back.

Savouring a mouthful of the nutty ale, he drove a passage through to where Cliff was seated, the bandaged seaman following closely behind. He smiled to see that his old skipper was in the process of emptying the pockets of two novices at the deceptively tricky game of fives and threes.

"Clear a couple of spaces, there," Cliff said. "Make way for a true master of the dominoes."

"Don't tell them that," Carl laughed, "or else I won't get a game. You haven't been out in this lot, have you?"

"We went for a trawl yesterday, but didn't stay out long. It's treacherous, but so tempting, what with the price of fish as it is. Sky high, as there's so little being landed. Every day a few smacks have a try, but they keep it short if they've any sense." He sighed. "We can't go on like this though. Everyone's praying for a change in the weather. How about you? Did things go the way you wanted in Riga?"

Carl took another long draught. "Not exactly. I've more or less burned my boats as far as Latvia's concerned." Then he smiled. "But there are good things on the horizon. To begin with, you know the timber carrier I came in on? The one that usually moors up on Corporation wharf? You must have seen her – the Dama Katrina."

"Of course I've seen her. You told me once before you'd worked on her for a while. What of it?"

"What if I told you I'd been offered the post of Second Engineer after three more crossings between here and Riga?"

"I'd say you were pulling my leg, you lying bugger. No, though, you haven't, have you?"

Carl grinned and nodded.

"You jammy devil!" Cliff yelled, slapping him heartily on the back. "Hey, Mary! Let's have another round here, love! Put it on Charley's slate. He's about to come in to some money!"

Only just then he nodded towards the sling on the arm of Carl's shipmate.

"Hey, pal, what happened to you?"

The sailor grinned and said, "Sorry, my English not good."

"English?" Cliff joked. "This is Tyneside, marra! You won't hear much English spoken here!"

Still grinning, the sailor placed his good hand on Carl's shoulder, saying, "Big water knock me over side. Him pull me out of sea."

"I don't believe it!" Cliff shouted. "He was always a lousy fisherman!" Full of ale, everyone evidently found this hilarious, judging by the peal of raucous laughter that rang around the room.

When the guffaws subsided Cliff put a hand to his forehead. "Hang on, though," he said. "I've only just realised – I've lost my best donkeyman!"

As he said this, Carl remembered that the frowning fellow seated to his right was the replacement engineer he'd recommended to his old skipper some three weeks earlier. He decided to make light of Cliff's thoughtless remark.

"Pay him no heed, lads," he said. "He's in his cups again. He knows as much about engines as he does about dominoes. Look here, he's laid a four against a double two! Give 'em their money back, Cliff!"

The round of drinks arrived and that helped lighten the mood.

"Come on," Carl said, shuffling the twenty-eight tiles face-down on the table top. "Just give me one chance to beat you lads, then my friend and I have to go and secure our lodgings."

CHAPTER EIGHTEEN
1889 : IV – ILL WINDS

At the end of the first week in February, after yet another bumpy voyage, the Katrina docked at Riga alongside Krutzberg's timber wharf. Carl felt he ought to say 'goodbye' to the Chief, as this would be his last chance to see him.

Arriving at the officers' quarters he noticed the old fellow's cabin door was propped open with a wooden box, half filled, mainly with books. The Chief was just turning round with a couple of hefty tomes as Carl approached him, with a hand outstretched.

"I wanted to come and say 'farewell', sir. I didn't think I'd get another opportunity."

The Chief put the manuals into the box and took Carl's hand.

"Thank you, son. The skipper offered to hold a proper ceremony with speeches and the like but, what with the sea conditions, and my bloody ulcer, I couldn't face anything formal. A few of the older crew members have been along with their best wishes. But I can't deny I'll be glad to put my feet on terra firma and get home."

"Speaking of your ulcer, Chief, I took the liberty while in South Shields to mention your ailment to a friend, who happens to be a very good physician. He told me of a man who might be able to help you. Apparently he leads the field in stomach surgery."

The chief grimaced. "Surgery? I don't fancy the idea of being cut open."

"Well, my friend says he's had a lot of success with his methods. It couldn't hurt to talk to him. I've written down his name here."

He took out a piece of paper from his pocket and handed it to the Chief, who mouthed the surgeon's name.

"Jan Mikulicz-Radecki. Well, his name's impressive, if nothing else. Whereabouts does he practise?"

"He has a clinic in Konigsberg."

"Konigsberg? Lovely city. Have you ever seen it?"

"I passed through it not long ago," Carl said wistfully. "But I didn't have time for sightseeing."

"Ah, well," the Chief sighed, folding the paper and placing it in his pocket. "I may well take a trip and see this fellow. Thank you, Carl, for being so thoughtful."

"I wish you a long and happy retirement, Chief. And I wish you many happy hours building that model railway of yours. I've always loved locomotive engines."

The Chief smiled. "It's a pity we couldn't have gotten to know each other better, young Carl."

"Not so young any more, sir. I'll be turning thirty very soon."

"Everyone's a youngster when you reach my age, son. By the way, welcome to your new quarters, humble as they are."

"But surely the Second will be moving in here, won't he, Chief?"

"What's the point? His cabin's the same size as mine." He took one last look around his old berth. "You can start moving your gear in whenever you're ready. Be here two hours before sailing. That'll give you time to go through the checklist with the shore fitters. She's a good ship, and if you look after her, she'll look after you."

"I'll certainly do that, Chief."

At that moment Carl heard footsteps behind him.

"Rudolf!" exclaimed the Chief. "How good to see you!" Both he and Carl welcomed young Krutzberg warmly. "Come to see me off?"

"I've come to see both of you, as it happens. It's handy that I've caught you together. Chief, I know you didn't want a formal presentation, but we couldn't let you go without our first thanking you sincerely for your years of service with the Krutzberg line."

"You've been fair to me," the Chief asserted. "Both you and your father before you. I've not seen him for a while. I trust he's well."

"He is, thank you Chief, though he chooses to play a less active part in the business these days. He sends his best wishes to you, of course." He handed over a parcel tied with a ribbon. "We'd like you to have something craftsman-made for you to remember us by. My wife wrapped it up. It's a little bit fussy."

"Your wife must have had some nautical training, Rudolf. I don't know what they call this knot, but I can't undo it. Wait a moment." He turned back into his cabin, opened a drawer and extracted a pen knife. "There. It's a box. Now, let's see what treasures ... Well, upon my word! This looks exquisite!"

He withdrew from the box what appeared to be a scale model of the Dama Katrina, worked in metal.

"Has this been cast? It's so intricate. What's it made of? Some new alloy?"

Rudolf smiled. "It's Sheffield steel, from Britain. We hoped it would prove a fitting memento for you."

"I'm sure it will, Rudolf. I'm very touched. Thank you very much." He bent to place his leaving gift alongside his books. "If one of you could help me with my box ..."

Carl and Rudolf took the two straps on either side of the box and carried it onto the quayside, where a cab driver hopped down to help them secure it to the driving seat alongside him. Then they helped the Chief Engineer step into the cab itself, from where he shouted up his house address, said his final 'farewells' to Carl and Rudolf, and sped away towards the city.

* * *

"Nice old fellow," Carl said.

"None better," Rudolf agreed.

Then Carl turned towards his friend. "I hope I can prove worthy of this promotion, Rudolf. Let's go back aboard – we may still be able to get some tea in the galley."

He didn't want to admit to Rudolf how exposed he felt standing on the quayside. The fear of discovery had been growing with every day that passed, and he almost expected policemen to approach and arrest him at any moment.

"All right, if you like." They retraced their steps. "As to your proving worthy, I'm willing to take the advice of a man like that, and he held you in very high regard."

"Did he? But I believed I had you to thank … I mean, I was very grateful …"

"My dear Carl, one thing you learn in business is to set aside personal feelings when making commercial decisions. You don't think I would have made such an offer to you without first taking expert advice, do you?"

"Well, no, but …"

"You made such an impression on him four years ago that he had no hesitation in giving his recommendation."

Carl gulped. "Even with my jumping ship?"

"I think he spoke to you about that. In any case, his opinion was based purely on your mechanical expertise. In the matter of your personal difficulties, well, that's in the sphere of my responsibilities."

They turned into the empty galley, where Carl was able to rustle up the various necessities for boiling some water and brewing some tea.

"So it's on your head, you're saying? Your credibility is going to take a pounding if I let you down again."

"Carl, let's get this straight. I never thought in terms of you letting me down. You were in an impossible situation. Time and time again I've wondered what I would have done in the same position, and I've never been able to come up with a satisfactory answer."

Then he hesitated and said, "But …"

"But, what?"

"But I think I can assure you that your troubles with the law are over."

"Sorry?" Carl said, spooning sugar into the milk jug.

"I think you heard what I said."

He realised what he was doing, and said, "You can either have it sweet or black."

"Any way it comes."

Carl handed him the mug of steaming black tea and watched as he sipped it slowly.

"Well, are you going to explain what you just said, or not?"

Rudolf rested his cup on the galley counter.

"After we whisked you away from under the noses of the Riga police force, our very good mutual friend Herr Muller took it upon himself to pay another visit to the Chief of Police." He lifted his cup again, and sipped.

"Yes …?"

"They had a long chat. It became clear that the Chief knew nothing about the two men who had come looking for you in the early hours of the morning. So he made some internal enquiries."

"Go on."

"Turns out there was no widespread conspiracy. They were two ambitious young officers hoping to make a name for themselves. As you'd suspected, they assumed you'd be at my house overnight before your planned surrender into custody. But, because you proved more devious than them, they turned out to be wrong. The rest of the plan, though, was to have rolled out exactly as Muller had agreed with the Chief of Police."

"So you're saying, apart from this botched job on the part of two misguided officers, it was never intended to dishonour the agreement and put me on trial?"

"That's right."

Carl downed the remains of his tea, and poured himself another from the pot.

"But Karpov must have got his information from someone in the force."

"Yes, but that's a different issue – and one that the Chief of Police is determined to get to the bottom of. It's only unfortunate that your key witness was murdered."

"So, what happens now?"

"As far as the police are concerned? Nothing. The Chief of Police has to live with an unsolved murder, but he doesn't believe you did it."

"Even though we no longer have poor Frieda's evidence?"

"The fact that she was killed before she could testify only adds weight to your innocence. And the evidence – all circumstantial, of course – points to Stefan Karpov. The Chief of Police would like very much to have a chat with him."

"So are you telling me I'm in the clear? That I can breathe freely again?"

Rudolf hesitated.

"Sort of."

"What do you mean, 'sort of'?"

"It's political. People in high places would be embarrassed if the charges against you were dropped. So the case remains open, as a formality, with you as prime suspect. Technically."

"So nothing's different, then."

"Yes, it is different. Because the Chief of Police has given his assurance that you won't be hounded as long as you agree not to set foot in Latvia."

"Hmm. Well, I'd more or less made my mind up on that score in any case. I've been scared stiff that we'd have police swarming all over the ship."

"Rest assured. That's not going to happen. You're safe on board the Katrina. But are you happy to exile yourself from your country of birth?"

"Happy isn't quite the word. But I can live with it. I have a good home base now in England. At least now I can see my way forward towards a meaningful future."

As he said this, Rudolf took an envelope from his jacket pocket.

"And on that subject, not that I'm party to its contents, I have something here that could have a bearing." Saying this, he handed the envelope to Carl.

* * *

Laipu iela 5, Riga

31st January 1889

Dear Carl,

I hope you will forgive my delay in responding to your recent letter. This is partly due to the fact that I was at sea when our friend and benefactor, Rudolf Krutzberg, deposited the letter at the port office. Because of this I was unable to read it until my ship arrived in Riga, on the twenty-first of January. Since that day I have agonised over an acceptable form of words to accurately express my sentiments.

When you left the Dama Katrina in South Shields four years ago, I was heartbroken – as you knew I would be. If your intention was to minimise the hurt your parting caused me, then I cannot imagine the level of mental anguish I might have suffered, had you not been so kind.

I believe you when you say that you have been punished. Unfortunately I have been punished too, the hurt only slowly receding, or perhaps numbed by the level of poverty to which my mother and I have lately been driven.

I do not know if you are aware, but the family for whom my mother kept house in Majori were forced to emigrate and, intent on selling the villa, gave us notice to quit. With no one to turn to for help, and my wage as a cabin maid being insufficient to rent a more genteel room in the city, we were forced to take up residence among the shanties.

My mother and I are extremely grateful to Rudolf and Teresa Krutzberg, also to your brother and yourself, in offering us shelter and financial assistance, which, for my mother's sake, I am not too proud to accept. Your further *offer to subsidise us in more permanent lodgings is also one that I cannot refuse – again, for the assured continuation of my dear Mama's improved health and comfort.*

Everyone I have met since moving to Rudolf and Teresa's rooms has spoken very highly of you. They have explained the trouble you were having concerning the false accusation of murder, and how you felt trapped and unable to see any viable future for us. But Carl, why couldn't you have talked to me about these things? I am certain that, together, we would have found a way, if not of overcoming these difficulties, then at least of accommodating them.

My first priority is, and always has been, the well-being and comfort of my dear mother (who, by the way, still holds you in the highest regard). While she lives, I will accept any assistance that is offered.

I return your wishes for longevity and happiness. Whether either, or both of us, achieve as much, together or apart, we must leave to Providence.

I hope we shall always be friends. More than that I cannot promise.

Juhla

* * *

It was just before lunchtime on a quieter day towards the middle of February when the Dama Katrina docked again at South Shields. Carl made one last inspection of the engine room, grabbed his sea bag from his cabin and walked across the Mill Dam timber yard and straight into the bar room of the Coronation Inn.

"A pint of best, please, Mary. Where is everyone? The place is nearly empty."

"Up at St Hilda's, most of 'em, Charley," the barmaid replied morosely. "You're a bit of a stranger here. Where've you been?" She handed him his drink.

"I'm on the Latvian freighter these days, Mary, so you'll only see me every couple of weeks from now on. Plus, this outward leg we lost a day steaming slow, on account of the heavy seas."

He took a long draught. "By ... that's welcome!" He smacked his lips. "I never believed I'd take to English ale, but now I'm used to it, it takes some beating. But why St Hilda's? It's not Sunday."

"Funerals. Or memorials, I should say. None of the seven bodies were recovered, poor souls. There's a collection jar on the bar for the bereaved families."

He dug into the pocket where he kept his English money, and dropped a coin into the jar.

The barmaid's eyes widened. "Was that a crown? Must be a good job you've landed."

"Second Engineer. And a crown's a small price for cheating Death on the high seas, Mary."

She reached down to a low shelf behind her. "You might as well have one of these," she said, handing him a printed sheet.

"What's this? A broadside? I thought these had gone out of fashion."

"A man came round all the pubs who reckoned he'd composed it himself the day after the big gales on the night of the ninth. All the money he collects is to be distributed to bereaved families all along the east coast. It was terrible to see, even here. We lost seven, but Grimsby lost ten times that. Even those crews whose boats weren't smashed up looked like the walking dead. Here, I think some of the lads are coming back from the church."

Cliff was among the first few through the door, and he was quick to notice Carl at the bar.

"Hey up, matey," he said, though his eyes lacked their usual sparkle. "Bad business here – have you heard?"

"Mary was telling me. Were you out that night?"

"No, fear. I decided to lay my tubs up. Though I could barely afford it. We've been earning next to nothing lately. Thank God things are picking up a bit now. But some of the poor sods had no choice but to go out, especially those with nothing to fall back on. What have you got there?"

"It's some verses that someone wrote in aid of the affected families."

"Ah, yes. 'Three score and ten boys and men were lost from Grimsby town'. Very moving. We all bought a copy, fishers and miners alike. It'll ease their families' burdens a bit. It won't bring 'em back, though."

"Sadly, no. It's a strange game, sea fishing, Cliff."

"Perhaps, Charley. But call us brave, daft or just plain greedy – some will always go out in the worst of the weather, because they know whatever they can catch and bring to market will fetch a bundle. It's easy fishing in calm seas, when every bugger and his dog's out there, which means too much fish gets landed, and the price plummets. It's simple economics."

"What if the industry was better organised, limiting catches and fixing a minimum price? It would help conserve fish stocks too."

"Conservation? What for? There's plenty of fish out there. They've nothing to do except feed and breed. Anyway, what you're describing sounds like socialist talk. Take my advice. Don't get yourself a reputation as a radical. Ask some of the miners what happens when they try to organise – the gaffers lock 'em out for a few weeks, until their families are nearly starving, and their wives force 'em back on reduced wages. Believe me, Charley, socialism's nothing but a mug's game. Anyway, what are you worried about? You've landed a salaried job with a good firm. This was your first trip as Second, wasn't it?"

"That's right. I can't deny it feels good to have some security at last."

Cliff gave him a sideways look. "We didn't make a bad team, though, did we?"

"No, my friend. And I'm grateful to you for giving me the chance to prove myself. But I love working with the big engines. The power of them makes you feel invincible."

"I'll believe you, Charley, but don't expect me to understand you. By the way, apart from the cushy job, how did your other business work out?"

"Not entirely as I'd hoped. I'll still be using South Shields as my home base for the foreseeable future. But that's all right. I like it here. And you probably realised there was a girl. But that didn't work out either."

"Never mind, matey. There's plenty of pretty women on this side of the water, especially for someone of your standing."

Carl shook his head. "There was only ever one for me, Cliff."

"Oh, for God's sake. Well, if we're going to cry into our beer, we'd better have some beer to cry into. Mary! Fill us up here, pet. We're gasping!"

* * *

"So, Carl. How does it feel to have achieved one of your main ambitions in life?"

Carl had walked to Doctor Strong's house that morning on the off chance that he might not be too busy for a chat. Even if he was unlucky, the walk helped clear his head after yesterday's longer than usual session in the pub. Though he'd tried to pace his drinking, he had finished up meandering back to his lodgings in Taylor Street like a sailing smack tacking against a headwind. He hadn't been ill, but it had been close. He had been genuinely tired though, and thankfully sleep had rescued him from a repetition of 'the whirling pit'.

Although still blustery, the wind had subsided, and it was hard to imagine the heavy storm force conditions that had prevailed over the last few weeks, buffeting the fleet of tiny boats, and bringing so much misery to the east coast fishing communities. He had been thankful to enjoy a pleasant walk along the familiar streets of this town that had, by now, earned a special place in his heart.

He answered the physician directly. "Being offered this job has been an important achievement, so naturally it brings me an enormous sense of fulfilment. It's what I set out to do when I left Kaive, eleven years ago."

The Doctor smiled. "Would I be right in thinking there might be a 'but' coming?"

"Isn't there always a 'but', sir?"

"Not necessarily. Some people would look at your present situation and consider that your cup was half full, which presumes the filling will continue. You, on the other hand, see your cup as half empty, reflecting with regret on the failures and lost opportunities you've suffered along the way."

After a pause, Carl said, "I accept your interpretation. I suppose it's in my nature, though I always saw myself as someone not driven by ambition, but happy to accept whatever titbits life might throw my way."

"That may have been the case in your early years, before you gained some experience of life. But, whether you like it or not, Carl, you are ambitious. You set yourself goals and you do your best to achieve them. Most self-made people do. But be aware, most of them never achieve all of their ambitions."

"Why should that be?" Carl queried.

"Because successful people are forever setting themselves new targets, fresh objectives. I suspect you will do the same, unless Fate decides to place unexpected hurdles in your way. It does tend to do that, by the way.

But, even then, ambitious people strive to overcome such challenges, and that becomes their new objective."

"So, what you're saying is, that, regardless of our achievements, human beings seldom achieve true contentment?"

"Ah, contentment! Nirvana. The only way to achieve that is to renounce the competitive life, as far as possible suppress all physical wants and desires, concentrate on the spiritual aspects of existence, and seek fulfilment from within. Such thinking occurs in both eastern and western philosophies and religions. I can lend you some books on the subject if you like."

"Hmm," Carl sighed. "It doesn't sound much fun."

The Doctor smiled. "I tend to agree with you. Now, let's talk about your other objectives. Correct me if I'm wrong, but the next most important thing on the list is the girl. Am I right?"

"Aren't you always right? Yes. I can't get her out of my head. I know what you're going to say. This is to do with biological needs whose only function is the procreation of the race."

"Something like that. I must have given you this lecture before."

Carl scowled. "Yes, that's all very well, but how do I …?"

"Get the girl? First, you have to accept the possibility that you won't. But realise that, if she plainly doesn't want you, you won't die, or even necessarily end up an old bachelor like me – which, by the way, is my own choice.

But in your case, nature has provided millions of alternative mates, and I would be very surprised if you couldn't find one who took a fancy to you. Just a minute."

He got up and went into the next room, returning in a moment, accompanied by his maid.

"I'm sure you've seen Hattie before. Hattie, this is Carl, a patient and dear friend of mine. You're taking part in a simple experiment, and I want you to be completely honest. And don't worry about his feelings."

Carl was rigid in his chair.

"Yes, Doctor Strong," she said.

The physician continued, "I want you to imagine this young man is your suitor. In that regard, tell us what you think of him."

Her manner suggested she'd taken part in Doctor Strong's impromptu experiments before, for she didn't seem to find his request at all unusual.

"Stand up, please, Carl," she said.

Awkwardly he rose to his feet.

"Hmm," she said. "He's not very tall, is he? But he's taller than me, so that's all right. He looks smart – I like his clothes, they're stylish but not too foppish. Also his hair is neat and he has a nice face. Honest looking. And that moustache! Very elegant. Could he say a few words?"

Carl coughed and said, "How do you do, young lady? I'm very pleased to meet you."

"Ooh, a slight foreign accent. It makes him sound mysterious. Can you dance at all?"

"I'm afraid not – I don't get time for …"

"It doesn't matter. Neither can my young man."

The Doctor stopped her there. "Thank you, Hattie. And overall, do you find him – superficially, of course – a suitable candidate for your hand in marriage?"

She giggled. "If I wasn't already spoken for …"

"Of course."

"Well, yes. He's the sort of young man any girl would consider as a potential husband."

"Thank you, Hattie. You may go."

Awkwardly Carl said, "Yes, thank you very much, Hattie."

"You see what I mean, Carl? Just because one girl rejects you doesn't mean you can't find marital happiness."

"You make it all sound so very clinical, sir. What about the emotional aspect?"

"As you said before, probably driven by chemistry. You've got to try and see through the fog of your emotions and consider the matter coldly and intellectually. Moping about and getting overly sensitive will do you no good whatsoever. Think of it as a battle, in which you are a general. You have to select your best warriors, armaments, stratagems and tactics in order to win. And you have to remain calm and collected at all times."

"I see."

"Maybe you do. Let's examine your war chest. If we knew her state of mind, that would be a big advantage. How exactly did she reject you?"

"By letter, sir."

"And do you have this letter?"

Carl reached inside his jacket and handed him Juhla's note, which, after putting on a pair of eyeglasses, he duly read.

"Hmm. Interesting. Did you notice how the degree of antagonism tails off towards the end?"

"Does it?"

"How many times have you read it?"

"Once was enough."

The Doctor looked exasperated. "Don't you realise that something like this requires at least three readings before you can fully understand its meaning? Never mind. Tell me, in one word, how you would describe this letter."

"One word?"

"Yes."

"A rebuttal – and I know that's two words."

The Doctor shook his head. "Wrong!"

"Well," Carl huffed. "If it's not a rebuttal, what is it?"

"It's a deferment." He handed the letter back to Carl. "Do me the favour of reading the final three lines."

Carl coughed and then mumbled, "I return your wishes for longevity and happiness. Whether either, or both of us achieve as much, together or apart, we must leave to Providence. I hope we shall always be friends. More than that I cannot promise."

The Doctor grinned. "And the three most telling words contained in that distillation of her final thoughts are?"

Carl looked up. "Together or apart?"

"Yes! Yes, indeed! My dear Carl, can't you see? Her mind is not closed to the idea that you will be together!"

Carl wasn't entirely convinced. "But she says she's leaving it to Providence."

"Then let that be the case, my friend. Only, Providence can be a sluggish girl, I find. Sometimes she needs a bit of a nudge in the right direction, don't you think?"

CHAPTER NINETEEN
1889 : IV – A CURE FOR PASSION

That night, on the pretext of checking the engine room before tomorrow's sailing, Carl boarded the Dama Katrina to do some snooping around.

In the matter of giving Fate a nudge, Doctor Strong had reminded him of an episode that Carl had himself related, some three years earlier, when he had discovered Juhla's replacement cabin maid in what could only be described as a compromising situation. When the Doctor asked him if the girl still occupied the position, Carl had replied that he recalled seeing her during the recent cargo emergency. It might be a long shot, but the young lady's conduct might merit further investigation.

By design he found himself near the maids' quarters, where he stepped quietly towards Juhla's old cabin, and put his ear to the door. He was certain he heard whispering voices, but not clearly enough to discern the conversation, though the rise and fall and intermittent giggles suggested its likely nature. And there was no doubt that one of the voices was male.

A dilemma. If this was a simple lovers' tryst, he could forgive it. But if, as he believed, this girl was using her cabin as a 'guest' room to supplement her income, that would be a different matter. And, as a ship's officer, he would be obliged to report such conduct to his superiors.

But he needed proof. As always, the ship employed two cabin maids, the other being Juhla's former colleague Ruta. He knew her to be a decent girl, so he decided there could be no harm in taking her into his confidence now.

He moved down the corridor to her cabin, and tapped quietly on her door.

She opened it a crack. "Carl!" she gasped on seeing his face.

He shouldn't really be surprised that she remembered him. But their paths hadn't so far crossed on this latter tour of duty.

"I would ask you in, but we both know it's against the rules. If you've come to ask about Juhla, she hasn't been in touch since ... I know her mother has been dangerously ill. I fear they were forced to move their lodgings, and Juhla neglected to tell me their new address."

He pitied the girl and searched for some words of comfort. "She's been through a lot of anguish just recently. I expect that's why she hasn't written to you. But I can give you her present address if you'd like to write to her."

Ruta smiled. "That would be nice. I'll just fetch some paper and a pencil."

He wrote down the Krutzbergs' address for her. "This might not be where she's actually living, but it will find her," he said.

"Thank you, Carl. You're the Second Engineer now, aren't you?" she whispered. "I should congratulate you."

"That's right. And as one of the ship's officers I'm conducting an investigation. May I come in?"

She hesitated only briefly. "Very well, if it's official business."

He might as well get straight to the point, and kept his voice low. "What do you think is going on next door?"

At first she seemed reluctant to answer, as if the situation confounded her vocabulary. But then she took a breath and murmured, "I try to ignore it."

"It is what I think it is, then?"

"Yes."

"A regular occurrence?"

"Yes."

"And would you repeat that to the Captain if necessary?"

"I would."

"What's her name?"

"Heidi Lindt."

"Thank you, Ruta. Close the door behind me. And do write to Juhla. I'm certain she would welcome a few lines from you."

He walked back to Miss Lindt's cabin and knocked.

"Who is it?"

"Second Engineer Carl Ewertsohn. Miss Lindt, I have reason to believe you are entertaining a man in your cabin, contrary to company regulations. Please let me in."

The door opened, and his eyes went straight to the cot, which was occupied by a surprised young collier (judging by the grimy black line around his neck).

"You!" Carl ordered him. "Get up, get dressed and get out!"

"But, I … we haven't finished, man!"

"Already paid her? Hard luck. Now, bugger off before I fetch a policeman."

The lad was gone in a flash. Carl turned to face the girl, though it was with some shock that he took in the sight before him.

"Please put something on," he said, turning his head away, and went outside, closing the door behind him.

"What's wrong, dear?" she shouted. "Never seen a woman's bits and pieces before? Come back in and you can look all you want to – and do what you like! No charge for a gentleman like you!"

"Just get dressed, please."

There was silence for a while, and then the door swung open again. He went inside.

She was sitting on her cot, dressed now, with her head in her hands.

"What have I done? What have I done?" she sobbed.

"Stop crying," he said. "I think you and I should have a talk."

* * *

Six days later, after the Katrina had docked in Riga, Carl returned to his cabin to find Rudolf waiting for him.

They shook hands, Carl having first wiped his on his overalls. "Sorry, Rudolf. I've only just handed over to the shore fitters. I haven't had a chance to clean up."

"No matter. I wish I could invite you home to dine with us."

"That's a nice thought," Carl replied. "But I'm used to living on board ship when in Riga. I'm entrusted with a key to the galley. It's only cold food while the engines are idle, but there's a spirit stove for making hot drinks. And remember, I have pleasant lodgings in South Shields, so I'm not exactly short on home comforts."

"You put a brave face on things. But it pains me to think you might never again see Teresa and our children, not to mention your family in Kaive."

"Are you trying to depress me?"

"I'm sorry. No, of course I'm not. In fact, I have a piece of good news, though I never dreamed such a thing would happen so fast."

"Good news?" Carl feigned surprise, but he thought he guessed the nature of Rudolf's impending announcement.

"Yes. It's out of the blue, but the Chief Steward reports that the cabin maid who took over when Juhla left to take care of her mother has suddenly decided to hand in her notice. She wants to leave straight away, which of course creates an immediate vacancy."

"That's … fortuitous," Carl said, still feeling uneasy about having given Fate a kick up the backside.

"Yes, it's almost uncanny, and the timing unbelievable. I'll offer the position to Juhla then, shall I?"

Carl allowed himself a grin. "Do you really need to ask me? Yes, please do. Do you think she'll be able to transfer straight away?"

"We may have to compensate her present employer, but I'll do my best to make that happen."

"Thank you, Rudolf. I couldn't have wished for better tidings."

* * *

Thank goodness for his absorbing job. Without having to stay constantly alert to tend the engines, he believed he might go mad.

The Doctor had insisted that he mustn't rush to welcome Juhla back into her old position on the Katrina.

"Let her wonder for a while whether your affections have strayed," he had advised. "Let her be unsure of your intentions. Remember the adage that 'absence makes the heart grow fonder'."

That was all very well, but the saying applied to *his* heart too. The Katrina was two days into the westward leg of her voyage, and the new Chief had opted to take all of the night watches, leaving Carl the opportunity to resume his courting after his evening meal.

In deference to his infallible analyst, he had spent the first evening alone in his cabin, shunning his old sparking position on the crew's side of the port companionway railing. It had stretched every nerve and strained every sinew to stay away from the place where he imagined her waiting for him.

If, as he hoped, she did await him on the other side of that rail, what would she now be thinking about him? That he was callous, uncaring, even conceited, to imagine he should keep her on tenterhooks until he deigned to pass an evening in her company? Or that his affections had been transferred to some other young lady, who patiently awaited his return to her irresistible charms in South Shields?

And what of Doctor Strong's plan? What experience did he, a confirmed bachelor, possess of relations with the female sex? With his practical, unemotional regard for the attractive forces between men and women, did the good Doctor even care whether Carl found fulfilment with Juhla rather than any alternative pretty female?

No, he decided. He had gone along with Doctor Strong's absence theory for one night. This evening would be different. He would not play these cruel and stupid games any more. Tonight he would visit their former meeting place and tell her how he really felt about her. Never mind if she didn't appear. He would stand by that railing tonight and every night until she showed up.

* * *

Four nights later found him in that precise location, and there had been no sign of her. Next evening they were to land at Tyneside, where they would look rather foolish keeping their rendezvous in full view of the jeering dockworkers.

By nine-thirty he had decided to give her fifteen minutes. Then, if she didn't appear, he would return to his cabin. As to resuming the arrangement when the ship sailed back to Riga in two days time, well, he would just have to see. The quarter hour passed, and she failed to show up.

But later, lying in his bunk, trying to get to sleep, he was thwarted by her image, some dimly recalled mannerism, the shape of her lips, the sheen of her hair in the sunlight. It was no use. His need for her was too great to ignore. He must see her again soon.

Therefore after docking next day, early in the evening, he finished off in the engine room and returned to his cabin. There he discarded his overalls and washed, changed into smart but casual daywear, and made straight for the maids' quarters, where he tapped at her cabin door.

"Who is it?" she asked.

"Juhla, it's me, Carl. May I speak to you."

There was a pause.

"Just a minute." Her voice was subdued.

The door opened and she stood before him, still in her uniform. But he sensed there was something wrong.

"Juhla, dear," he said softly, "you've been crying. What is it? Is it because of me?"

"No. Yes. I don't know. I don't know what to believe any more!" And she sobbed outright, while he comforted her, holding her in his arms and stroking her hair.

"What is it?" he said. "Please tell me. I want to help."

She felt inside the pocket of her blouse and handed him a crumpled note.

"I've thrown it the bin three times," she said. "But I have to keep reading it over and over again. Oh, Carl. It's horrible. Tell me what it says isn't true!"

He smoothed out the paper on her cabin table. It was addressed to her by name. The first few lines appalled him so much that he had to put it down for a moment.

"Where did this come from?"

"I found it tucked under my pillow while I was unpacking my things on the first day. It's been driving me to distraction ever since."

He forced himself to read the rest of it. Its tenor was straightforward and simple. It described graphically an implied sexual relationship between the former cabin maid and himself, in terms that he would never have considered part of the vocabulary of any decent woman.

"But, my love, you surely don't believe one word of this ... this filthy slander!"

"Of course I don't want to believe it, Carl. But, when you failed to make contact on that very first evening at sea, when we could have been reunited after all this time, what was I supposed to think?"

Carl hesitated. "You mean, you waited for me by the railing on that first night?"

"Of course I did," she insisted. "How else was I to meet you without breaking the company's rules of decency? I could hardly come to your cabin."

"And after that ..."

"I put two and two together and feared that the horrible letter might contain an element of truth – that you no longer cared for me, having immersed yourself in depravity with nothing less than a common prostitute!"

"My darling," he pleaded, "I promise you with all my heart that I did nothing of the sort. My thoughts ever since our last parting have been only for you."

She looked him in the eye. "Is that true, Carl? Has there never been anyone else?"

"Never, my sweet. And I hold with what I said in my last letter to you. If you decide, justifiably in view of my desertion, to have nothing more to do with me, then I swear I shall live the rest of my life as a celibate."

Drying her eyes now, she pursed her lips.

"Actually, in your letter you said 'bachelor'."

"Sorry?"

"You didn't say 'celibate'. You said 'bachelor'."

He shuffled his feet.

"It's the same thing."

"No, it isn't, Carl. I'm no longer the innocent young girl that I used to be. Bachelorhood is a rejection of marriage, but not necessarily of the … associated pleasures."

"But I didn't mean …"

"It's what you said though. It's what I believed you meant."

His mind raced.

"Then I made a mistake. But my error was born out of grief, I assure you."

"I believe you, Carl. But only because you are here now talking to me. With me. Letters are inanimate – they can't express our true feelings. But now you're here, it seems just like before, before …"

"Before I abandoned you?"

"Yes. We had something intangible then that held us together, as a single entity. That's why the parting was so painful, for both of us, if I can believe you. Call it empathy. Or call it unity."

Carl took her hand and said, "Call it love."

Her other hand went up behind his neck and pulled him gently towards her. His arm curved around her waist, as their lips met in a slow explosion of passion. It was a long kiss, urgent and uniting, that released the tightly coiled tension from four years of solitary longing.

They stood holding one another for a while. He felt no shame that his manhood pressed against her, and sensed that she felt guiltless too. But soon the world they had briefly glimpsed receded, and they returned to the one that they must occupy for the foreseeable future.

"Juhla, we mustn't …"

"That's right, Carl. It would be wrong …"

He sighed. "I shouldn't be in your cabin. From now on, we must both observe the rules of the ship, until we can be married."

She smiled. "I don't recall your asking me," she said.

"Then consider this a proposal." He kissed her again.

"And this, my acceptance." She returned his embrace.

"But there is a problem," he said.

"There always is."

"I can't live in Riga, as you know. We could rent a nice house here in South Shields, though."

"There would be no point, since we'll be spending most of our time at sea. Paying rent for a whole house would be a waste of money."

"But, if we married, you wouldn't have to work."

She pouted. "I enjoy my work. Besides, if I left the Katrina, I would never see my Mama."

He smiled. "So be it. We don't have to rush things. We have declared our love. We are engaged now – oh, wait!"

He fumbled in his pocket and extracted a small box.

"I'm afraid I couldn't afford an expensive one, and I hope it fits."

She smiled. "Put it on my finger, then. There! It does fit, and I love it."

"It has a little diamond," he pointed out.

She screwed up her eyes teasingly. "I think I can see it. Thank you, darling." And she kissed him on the cheek.

"At least on the ship we can be close to one another, except when we're moored at Riga, and you go to see your mother."

"It won't be such a bad arrangement," she said.

"And we can enjoy our time ashore here. Tomorrow morning I'll take you to meet my good friend, Doctor Strong. Then we can have lunch at a café in town, and walk off our meal in South Marine Park – weather permitting, of course. Then later you can see my lodgings and meet my landlady. She'll cook us an evening meal and, if you prefer it to staying in your cabin, she has a pleasant spare room where you may spend the night."

"It sounds wonderful, Carl. All I've seen of Tyneside are views of boring old dockyards."

Then she picked up the slanderous note.

"What should we do about this?"

"Ignore it. I don't feel any animosity towards that girl. Only pity. Somehow she has lost her way. I only hope she finds someone who will set her on a more positive path. In the meantime …"

He tore the letter into tiny fragments.

"Let's go up to our usual place, where we can avoid temptation. The dockworkers can make of us what they will. On the way we can drop these pieces into the dock."

Closing her cabin door she said, "Tell me, Carl. What was the reason you didn't come to see me on that first evening at sea?"

He scowled. "I did so want to. But stupidly I took advice from a well-intentioned friend who knows a lot about most things, but, as has now become all too clear, next to nothing about affairs of the heart."

＊ ＊ ＊

And so they settled into a routine of meeting at the railings each evening while at sea, sharing a couple of days wandering around South Shields while awaiting turnaround, and parting at Riga for Juhla's regular visit to her mother.

Their after dinner collusions involved chaste embraces, as dictated by the structure of the railings. But after a time, as they became accustomed to the geography of the iron barrier, they discovered ways in which to maximise their bodily contact, until the sexual tension became almost unbearable for both of them.

Carl could stand this no longer. He suspected she felt the same, but was too much of a lady to mention such a thing. It was up to him, as the man, to raise the subject in as delicate a manner as he was able.

After one especially passionate encounter, he pulled away from her and said breathlessly, "Juhla, I really think we should be married soon, or else I believe I shall go mad."

From her expression he suspected she was suppressing a smile.

"I think I can understand the ... difficulty for you, my darling. I believe God requires our union, and we should therefore find a way."

He doubted that God had anything to do with it, but that the Devil probably played the dominant role in the matter. For his part, all he knew was that he must love her completely, and as soon as possible.

"I think," she said, that we should part now, so that we may both become less … excited. Before we meet here again we should consider how to go about it. But I stipulate, I cannot abandon my Mama."

* * *

The following evening saw them once more by the railings, careful to stand a little apart, following a brief platonic kiss.

Carl kept a serious composure as he voiced his ideas on the subject.

"It seems to me, in order to keep up your regular visits to your mother, that you must continue in your present position as cabin maid."

"I agree."

"If we marry, I would explain our situation to my landlady, and I am certain she would respect our marital needs."

He found it hard to expand on what he was trying to say. But she helped him.

"I have seen that your room has a double bed, Carl. It would be suitable for our … requirements."

"Yes," he said. "But as to our arrangements aboard ship, I think I should have to consult the Captain. There may be company regulations about married couples working on the same vessel."

"You will need to talk to him about that, certainly."

Then she asked him, "But where may we be married?"

"That's going to be our biggest problem.. I expect your mother would prefer us to be married in church. And you know I'm banned from leaving the ship when it's in port."

"I should like a church wedding too, my dear. Anything else would make us sinners in the eyes of God."

He knew her well enough by now not to argue with her on this point. And besides, he realised just how important these things were to a woman.

"Perhaps if we could find a church not too far from the port?" He had allowed his religious duties to lapse since leaving home, and had little knowledge of Riga's array of holy buildings, other than through his admiration for their architecture. "Wait. I remember going with Rudolf once to view a pretty little Lutheran church with twin towers, just across the river. It was dedicated to St Martin. I could make most of the journey by small boat."

"That sounds ideal," she said.

He frowned. "I'll have to leave it to you and Rudolf to make the arrangements with the pastor though. I daren't risk being seen making multiple trips."

"I'll speak to him as soon as we arrive back in Riga." Then she hesitated. "There's one more thing."

"What's that?"

"Well, while I'm working, there can't be any babies."

He looked shocked.

"But, doesn't that mean we can't …?"

She was ready with the right words to answer his unfinished question.

"Not necessarily, if we're careful."

"How do we do that?"

"I'm not sure. But when we see your friend Dr Strong tomorrow, perhaps he would allow me five minutes to speak to him on the subject."

* * *

It was right at the end of his first watch after leaving South Shields that Carl quickly washed and changed and made for the Captain's cabin, knowing that he would be off watch. There was no denying that he was nervous about the impending interview. Not that the great man wasn't approachable, but he was held in the crew's regard to a degree that came close to that of a deity. Carl approached his cabin door and knocked firmly.

"Come in!"

Carl removed his cap, screwed it up in his hands and said, "Captain, please forgive the intrusion, but I seek your permission to marry Juhla Rachoan, one of the cabin maids."

The Captain's usual stony expression didn't alter as he walked towards his Second Engineer. Then, suddenly beaming a broad smile, he took Carl's hand and shook it vigorously.

"My dear fellow, I'm delighted for you! Though I'm not sure you require my permission to marry whom you like – as long as the young lady agrees, of course." And he smiled at his own joke.

Carl shuffled his feet. "Well, sir, it's a little more complicated than … I mean, we want to marry in Riga, and continue working until I'm able to provide a home for us both in South Shields."

This was something of a white lie, because the overriding factor keeping them on board was the poor health of Juhla's mother, which sounded too morbid a reason for not settling down straight away.

The Captain brought himself to his full height, as if to draw inspiration from the polished planks that adorned his cabin ceiling.

"It seems to me," he said after a while, "that there are two issues to consider. First, there's the question of the wedding itself. And second, the practicality of employing and accommodating a married couple. I must say, each of these would be a first for me."

Carl realised the Captain had misunderstood him. "The wedding will take place on the shore, sir."

"On the shore? But, I thought …"

"Yes, sir. I realise I'd be taking a chance. But I couldn't deny my fiancée a proper church ceremony. And St Martin's is little more than a boat ride away."

The Captain nodded thoughtfully a few times. "Yes, yes. I know it. An excellent choice."

"And," Carl continued, "as to accommodation, we would be content to limit our marital … relations to our shore leave at my lodgings in South Shields.

"Marital re ... Oh, I see. Yes, quite. Well, I suppose abstinence while at sea would be no different than for any sailor whose wife awaits him at home on shore.

"But first things first. I think, regarding your proposed working arrangement, we would need the owner's agreement. You know, I've always admired the way you've never used your friendship with Rudolf Krutzberg to seek special treatment in your day to day work."

"I wouldn't have wanted it, Captain."

"Have you spoken to him about this?"

"He knows that Juhla and I are in love, but not that we have agreed to marry. We shall be asking him to help make the arrangements with the pastor."

The Captain pursed his lips and nodded. "I'll speak with him when we land in Riga. I'm nearly certain he'll agree to what you're asking. But, being such a joyous occasion, I also intend to seek his permission to hold the reception in the galley. We could clear the tables and chairs to the side. There might even be room for dancing!"

Carl was both amazed and amused to realise that the Captain didn't just approve the prospect of the forthcoming wedding, he actually relished it.

"We weren't expecting anything too elaborate, sir," he mumbled.

"Don't worry, young man. It'll be a relatively simple affair. But this sort of thing can do wonders for morale. Everybody loves a shipboard romance. I'm sure the whole crew will want to attend. You can leave the details to me and Rudolf. We'll start the ball rolling when we dock, with a view to co-ordinating your wedding with the Katrina's docking in a few weeks' time."

Carl gulped, at a loss for words, as he realised that events were taking over, and that he would very soon be a married man.

"Well, you don't want to keep your young lady waiting too long, do you?" said the Captain with a grin. Then he added with a wink, "And I'm sure that goes for you, too."

Carl felt his cheeks glowing.

"Yes, Captain. Thank you, Captain."

* * *

"This must be just about the craziest way of getting a groom to his wedding, Rudolf!"

Dressed in his best suit, and with his back to the Daugava River, Carl gingerly found his footing on the rope ladder that hung from the Dama Katrina's starboard recreation deck, took a deep breath, and then slowly lowered himself towards the steam tug that bobbed in the water some fifteen metres below him. To heighten his apprehension, the freighter stood high in the water, the cargo being unloaded and no ballast yet taken on board, making his descent seem almost interminable.

"Crazy it may be," shouted his friend from the deck. "But it's necessary if we're to keep you from the prying eyes of Riga's police force! You remember your directions?"

How could he forget? He and Rudolf had spent hours mentally drilling so that Carl could recite them backwards if necessary. Being unfamiliar with the street layout on the river's west bank, he had had to trust to Rudolf's logistical skills in deciding the shortest, safest route for him to reach St Martin's church on foot and avoid keeping his bride waiting. She and the other wedding guests would be making their way conventionally in cabs and carriages.

Half way down the ladder, his mind wandering to his lovely Juhla, he lost his footing momentarily and hung in mid-air, and for a second a wave of panic overtook him. He was reminded of that time when, as an apprentice, he had descended into Heuer's dry dock, and the strangely vulnerable sensation he had experienced then. But once more he was able to control his fears, found the next rung with his wavering foot, and continued the climb down to the safety of the tug's deck, where a couple of deckhands took careful hold of him as if he were some greenhorn landlubber.

He told himself that it was the excitement of the day that had turned his legs to jelly, but nevertheless felt ashamed of appearing so terrified in front of these men, not to mention his friend, whose head seemed so tiny as Carl looked up, now waving and forcing an unconvincing grin.

"See you at the church then, Carl!" Rudolf shouted, pulling back from the handrail to disappear from sight. Then Carl heard his cry of "Don't be late!" fade into the crisp morning air as the tug turned its nose into the broad river and raced towards the western bank.

He automatically checked his fob watch and asked one of the deckhands, "How long till we reach Kipsala?"

This was the island that bulged out on the opposite shore, cut off from the mainland only by the short Zunds canal.

"Ten minutes, sir. No more," came the response.

Though Carl had never suffered from seasickness, the confusing concoction of trepidation and anticipation that he now felt made him glad this choppy trip would be over soon enough. Meanwhile he focussed his gaze on a fixed point on the approaching coast, a trick he'd never been forced to use until now, to help calm his churning stomach.

He reminded himself why he had needed to embark on this clandestine journey. He would probably have taken his chances, had it not been for the fact that Juhla had let slip something about the Lutherans' marriage formalities that made his blood run cold. The banns, or announcements that their wedding was to take place, must be read out for three consecutive weeks up to the day of the ceremony. There would be every chance that some devout and attentive policeman might recognise Carl's surname and hatch a plan to pounce as he travelled to the church on the appointed day. So leaving the Katrina by her main gangway had been out of the question.

Of course, it could be that the police would take no such action, as the Chief of Police had already said he believed Carl's version of the events surrounding the murder. But by leaving the ship to marry Juhla, he was breaking his promise to stay on the ship whenever it docked in Latvia. That might anger the Police Chief and land Carl in prison. No, he must go through with this charade and avoid arrest at all costs. Once inside the church they couldn't touch him, and if necessary he could claim sanctuary, but he hoped matters wouldn't come to that.

Very soon the tug was pulling alongside a wooden jetty jutting out from the beach close to the main road from Riga that bridged the Daugava to make landfall on Kipsala. Beyond the beach here, as Rudolf had promised, was a copse of silver birch, and he took advantage of its cover, hesitating only to thank the tug's crew, who wished him well, grinning broadly, before setting off again to the far bank.

Now Carl furrowed his brow as he recalled Rudolf's instructions. He was to go straight through the wood, where he should meet the first occupied road, Azenes Street. He would then be more in the open, so should not exit the wood until he knew his way was clear. As it happened he was forced to take cover behind one of the trees as a man sauntered past walking a dog. The hound even wandered in Carl's direction and he had to *shoo!* it away silently with his foot. Fortunately the owner shouted its name and it followed him around a corner. Carl took the opportunity of dusting himself down before striding out of the wood and heading left along the road.

Now there was less cover, though most of the roads around here were flanked by avenues of trees. It was important that he act normally and not draw attention to himself. The last thing he wanted was for some busybody to report him to the police as a prowler or appearing suspicious.

Next he must cross the little bridge that spanned the Zunds canal, and this he achieved with no trouble at all. There were people about, but he merely tipped his hat as he would usually do, smiled and continued on his way.

So far, so good. The road that ran in both directions along the canal bank was Daugavgrivas Street. Ironically his easiest route now would be to turn right, cross the road, and walk a half kilometre along the footpath until he came to the back entrance of St Martin's church. Unfortunately though, if he did this he would have to pass the district police station along the way, and both he and Rudolf had decided that this wouldn't be a good idea.

Instead he must take the alternative route halfway around the block, by going left along Daugavgrivas Street, then right along Martina Street, at the end of which he must turn right again along Slokas Street, finding St Martin's a few hundred metres along on the right. This route must measure at least a kilometre and a half. He glanced at his timepiece. He would be cutting it fine, even if he encountered no incidents along the way.

He had suggested to Rudolf the notion of having a cab waiting somewhere around here to take him to his destination. But his friend had argued against the idea. "If the police do get wind of the ceremony," he had said, "your arrival in a carriage or cab would be just what they'd be waiting for. No, you must slip in alongside of the church and enter through the back doors. If the pastor or anybody challenges you, just say you lost your way. I shall be waiting near the altar with the ring."

He mustn't run. That would surely attract unwanted attention. But he quickened his pace as he began this final leg of his journey. Eventually the twin towers of the attractive mid-nineteenth century church appeared above the trees, so he checked his steps and casually approached his destination, trying hard to adopt a nonchalant air.

When he reached the grounds, it was clear there was no-one outside, which could only mean that he was now officially late and his bride, friends and family must be waiting for him inside. Nevertheless having no choice but to enter the church grounds by the main gates he avoided the front doors, since they could well conceal a policeman or two waiting for him within the inner lobby. Checking that nobody was watching, he hurried across towards the cover of the high hedge that ran all the way down the left side and towards the rear of the main building. Less than a minute later he surprised the congregation by making his entry from a door beyond the altar, and took his place next to Rudolf, his best man.

He was certain a collective sigh echoed quietly around the high roof space, and he couldn't resist turning his head and smiling for the benefit of all present. Then he turned to address Rudolf in a nervous whisper.

"Where's Juhla?"

Rudolf smiled. "Don't you know it's bad luck for the bride to arrive first? I had her carriage wait up a side lane until the driver saw you arrive. She'll be here very soon."

As he spoke the words the doors swung open and she appeared. All eyes were upon her as she began her walk along the aisle, supported by the Captain (since she possessed no senior male relative).

She was a stunning sight, which literally took Carl's breath away. He felt by far the most fortunate man on Earth and had to remind himself that he hadn't just dropped into the most wonderful dream. Her wedding dress, which she had made herself with her friend Ruta's help, comprised a simple yet beautiful white gown and headdress. There was a general gasp of delight at such a vision of angelic loveliness.

The understanding pastor kept the proceedings as brief as possible, and within the space of ten minutes the happy couple had exchanged vows and rings, and signed the requisite forms, legalising their marriage.

As they walked out of the church, first followed and then surrounded by their families, friends and shipmates, Juhla whispered to her husband, "Did you meet with any trouble, Carl?"

He smiled. "None whatsoever. I don't know why I bothered with all that skulduggery."

But as he spoke these words a tall figure stepped from out of the crowd, demanding, "Mr Carl Evardson?"

Half smiling, Carl nodded.

"I am arresting you for the murder of Constable Heinrik Sterz in the Riga central market warehouses in October eighteen eighty-four. Please come with me."

Carl was speechless and felt the blood drain away from his cheeks. Shocked, Juhla protested on his behalf.

"But he's innocent! The Chief of Police said he believed so!"

Now recovering his voice, Carl added desperately, "And so did the Prosecutor!"

"I know nothing of all that," the policeman insisted. "The Chief of Police is on holiday. All I know is that the record states that you were seen with the murder weapon in your hand. We have a duty to clear up unresolved cases as old as this one. If you are innocent as you claim, you should not fear facing your accusers and bringing your witnesses at a fair trial. I ask you again, please come with me."

Then a very strange thing happened. The closer family members (whom Carl had not yet had time to greet) moved away and were replaced by dark-suited male crew members from the Dama Katrina – there must have been a dozen of them, or more. In an almost choreographed movement this imposing group of young men formed an impenetrable blockade around the now bewildered policeman, while the newlyweds were ushered away towards their waiting carriage. Rudolf and the Captain climbed up alongside them.

As the vehicle moved off Carl said, "What was that all about, Rudolf?"

"It's what we feared. Whenever the Police Chief is absent for any reason, it seems some ambitious young law officer is going to have a go at what they see as a clean kill. Sorry for the brutal terminology."

"No, Rudolf. It's appropriate, I'm sure. And I must say that this close call has taught me a very serious lesson."

Juhla looked at him. "What lesson, my dear?"

"Today was a special case and justified the risk. But no more can I afford to test the Police Chief's promise. From henceforth I must never again set foot on Latvian soil."

* * *

The galley furniture was arranged as the Captain had directed, but the full complement of chairs accommodated only half of those in attendance at the couple's simple wedding reception. This was of little consequence though, as most of the guests preferred to stand and socialise.

Carl and Juhla's return carriage ride from St Martin's church had been an anxious one, with Carl expecting policemen to dart out from every street corner. Rudolf assured him that the attempted arrest had been an isolated incident. Nevertheless Carl was relieved to arrive alongside the Dama Katrina and hurry his bride up the walk-ashore to meet their guests.

Rudolf's wife Teresa and their children were present, of course. But the guests of honour were Frau Rachoan and Carl's father, mother and brother Fritz. Their presence had been cleverly engineered, Rudolf having despatched a courier to ensure they were provided with tickets for the train journey from Tukums. They would spend that night as the Krutzberg's guests before returning to Kaive the next day.

Though corresponding regularly, Carl had resigned himself to the prospect of never seeing his family again, and had had little chance to properly re-unite with them among the commotion at the church. Now though they all become visibly emotional. Once the tears subsided, however, his parents bombarded Carl with questions about his life, work, lodgings and plans for the future.

Herr Muller, his old mentors, fitters Gustav and Klaus, Karolina and her husband from the Black Pig, along with Carl's two stoker cabin mates, were all thrilled to see them married, and now crowded round them to express their congratulations. Even his old Chief Engineer had been prised out of retirement to come and pay his respects. And he was quick to thank Carl for suggesting the physician who had performed successful surgery on his ulcers.

Carl wished his friend Doctor Strong could have travelled from South Shields too but, understandably, his many patients were in greater need of his attention. The physician had already wished the pair a happy and fruitful marriage, and had a private talk with Juhla about natural methods of avoiding unwanted pregnancies.

Apart from these and the ship's officers, any space left in the galley was occupied by most of the other members of the Dama Katrina's crew, all happy to join in the celebrations, and many re-living their bravado outside the church when they had literally herded that policeman to a safe place until the couple's carriage was well on its way back to the ship. No physical harm had come to him, but his official pride had taken something of a beating.

Now some of the chairs were cleared away, a couple of tables were brought out and loaded with eatables and liquid refreshments from the galley kitchen. Then a trio of musicians, university students known to Rudolf, took up their instruments and set the scene for dancing, singing and general merriment.

* * *

Later in the evening, the food and drink having taken a plundering, and their guests and musicians having departed, Carl and his bride changed their clothes and went up to their old courting place on the port side recreation deck.

"We promised ourselves," Juhla whispered, "that we wouldn't consummate our marriage on board, didn't we?"

"Well, yes. I did suggest to the Captain that we'd abstain while at sea. And as we must avoid any ... unwanted consequences, that would seem to be the best plan."

She was quiet for a while. Then she said softly, "But it is our wedding night, Carl, and it will be nearly a week before we arrive home to our rooms in South Shields. And, according to Dr Strong's plan, I am at a safe point in my cycle."

He hesitated. "But what if somebody should come knocking on my door?"

She pouted. "Why would anyone want to do that?"

"I don't know. Perhaps to sort out a problem with the engines."

"But, surely, the Chief Engineer could take care of that!"

He ruminated, apparently turning things over in his mind.

"Well," he observed, "since it is our wedding night, I think the Captain would forgive us one small aberration from our intended routine. I'll just go and ask him."

Instantly shocked, she placed a hand on his arm and gasped, "You'll do no such thing! How could you even ...?

But his face had already cracked into a smile. With pursed lips she made a fist and pretended to beat his chest.

"You're a wicked man, Carl Evardson," she said. "I'm beginning to wonder if I've made a terrible mistake in agreeing to be your wife."

He stopped her voice with a kiss, and said, "Sorry my sweet. I couldn't resist teasing you. But there is still just one thing that concerns me."

She looked up at him. "What's that, my love?"

"Do you think we'll manage it in a single bunk?"

BENDING THE TRUTH
THE EVARDSON STORY

Below is a summary of the few documented facts around which this part of Carl's and Juhla's story is woven.

c1830   Johann Evardson born in Latvia, career soldier.

c1850   Johann marries Luiza Mosevitch.

c1858   Kahrl Johann Evardson born in Kaive, Tukums district, province of Kurland, Latvia.

1860s   Further sons Fricis Ernsts and Janis Karlis born
decade   in Kaive. Possibly other children too.

1869   Juhla Otilya Matilda Rachoan born in Latvia.

1878   Opening of railway line from Tukums to Riga.

1884   October, Kahrl Johann sets sail on a steamer as a welder.

1888/9   29th December to 10th January, visa issued for Kahrl Johann's 'return to Russia', recording his age as 30.

1889   February, heavy gales cause great loss of life among North Sea fishing smacks and crews, including 70 men and boys from Grimsby.

         Carl and Matilda's wedding at St Martin's church, Riga..

ADDITIONAL NOTES

Collective family memory suggests that Carl was involved in the killing of a policeman in Latvia, and that he and Juhla worked on a timber freighter operating between Riga and Tyneside, he as an engineer and she as a cabin maid.

As more and more items of British and Latvian archival data are digitalised, and it becomes easier to access further information about our ancestors, it is highly likely that facts will emerge to contradict at least some of the suppositions I have made in the foregoing history. If so, I apologise in advance for any significant discrepancies.

A DONKEYMAN'S JOURNEY – PART TWO

THE LOYAL ENGLISHMAN

The second part of Carl and Juhla's story finds them settling and raising a family in the then booming fishing port of Grimsby. Against a backdrop of industrial turmoil, family tragedy and the horrors of war, the family finds strength in unity and the reliance on community in ways that elude us in these present times.

Printed in Poland
by Amazon Fulfillment
Poland Sp. z o.o., Wrocław